The Compact

CHARLIE RAVEN

DISCLAIMER

The roles played by Aleister Crowley and Jerome Pollitt in this narrative are entirely fictional, although their imagined actions do harmonize with known biographical facts within the timeframe of 1898. I have sometimes quoted from Crowley's works and letters, passim, as well as Aubrey Beardsley's letters to Pollitt. For those interested, further biographical information and a short bibliography is available at the end of the book. Otherwise, all resemblance to real people living or dead is the result of the mishmash of my unconscious mind. Sorry.

Visit www.theravensbunker.com or email info4charlieraven@gmail.com

DEDICATION

Max, Marcus and Darya,
Morgana and Pip,
Pandora and Loki:
you amazing people.

ACKNOWLEDGMENTS

Thanks to Rohase Piercy for her encouragement and example.

CHAPTER ONE

Minerva Atwell surveyed herself in the full-length mirror. The colour was satisfactory: deep burgundy velvet; the soft nap of the fabric so intriguingly sensuous; a high linen collar contrasting in white. Waist, tight; bodice, smooth; sleeves, extremely puffed, tight at the wrists and all the way up the forearms. Rows of ebony buttons running up the slender cuffs, each one with a crystal dot in the middle to flash when they caught the light. Yes, satisfactory, yes, flattering. Minerva leaned in to the mirror, patting under her eyes, smoothing eyebrows. A heart-shaped face looked back at her. Goodness, she thought, catching sight of her own concentrating frown. She rearranged the features: the hint of a smile, brow properly clear of lines, eyes warm, not too sharp-looking. Good, good. A turn, yes, from the back view, perfect lines. It's a good cut.

She walked fast along the street, although usually she would have taken a cab, but today, with a bloom in the sky and such a clarity in the light, today was a day to walk. She felt these winter days like an electric thrill through the blood - frost, ice - she loved the cold. Minerva breathed deep. Elation made her want to run, but not here because of the people who would watch. They would see a beautiful, lithe woman, dressed beautifully in burgundy velvet, racing beautifully down the street. She wanted to laugh when she thought of what they would see. She quickened her pace a little, still dignified, but hurrying now, feeling the air sharp in her nostrils, hitting her lungs. She felt the blue snow shadows, the bald cold pressing on her cheeks, the soaring hot air from her own mouth, felt so much.

In the boardroom inside the marble temple of finance, the great mahogany table stretched like glass towards the windows. Three arched and royally draped windows, frozen and textured with frost flowers at the corners, blank mist in the centres, flooded cold light into the room. A longcase clock slowly tocked in the corner like a dislocated joint. Minerva sat composedly at one end of the glacial table, and around its other sides sat the gentlemen, quietly dignified. When she didn't look directly at them individually, they seemed to blend together in their black suits, high white collars, even the moustaches, neatly brushed. She wanted to laugh at the ridiculous image of them brushing those moustaches with such care, but kept the urge well under control. They were waiting for her to speak but she made them wait a little longer, inspecting, serious and innocent, the sheaf of papers they had presented to her. Eventually, she placed them softly on the table and raised her eyes. She looked into the distance, through the opaque middle window, as though she could see snowy peaks far away. Finally, she nodded.

'Yes,' she sighed at last. 'That will do. I am satisfied that moving the manufacture to the Midlands will perfectly meet my needs. However, I must be reassured,' she continued, her voice slipping deliberately into the subtly querulous register she used when dealing with powerful males, 'that the one essential ingredient is to be provided only by me, you know, delivered only under my instruction, guarded against all disclosure at all times.' She looked round the table and added gently, 'I cannot sufficiently stress this to all present. Should any part of this agreement be deviated from, as I have stipulated before, I will regrettably be compelled to withdraw my services.'

'Mrs Atwell,' said Mr Grover, the senior partner, patting his heart, 'you have apprised us of the great difficulty of obtaining the ingredient; and I believe I may speak for all those present when I say that we have no desire either to interfere in or to impede the supply, coming as it does from the remotest parts of the mountains... '

'Yes,' she interrupted. She looked at him searchingly. 'My late husband's very personal and deeply spiritual link with the hidden people of Daylam is the only thing which allows this ancient secret to reach our shores.' The men round the table all nodded sympathetically in unison.

'Yes indeed, Mrs Atwell, we sincerely understand the importance of this to you,' said Mr Grover, sincerely understanding the importance of preserving supply at maximum profit. 'That it is a deeply personal connection you have made very plain. And of course you have explained before about the tribesmen and so on. And, um, I believe it is all quite clearly set forth in the contract before you. We have concurred with all of your previous suggestions, as you will have noted, and particularly that we, the majority shareholders, will not press you to divulge any secrets. All that remains is your honoured signature.'

Minerva allowed herself to be persuaded to sign, exulting secretly at the enormous sum of money specified as an advance in the body of the contract. What a simple thing it was, after all, and her signature was a simple thing. A flourish: and Minerva Atwell was confirmed as a rich, rich woman.

Later on, she was dreaming. She was thirsty. A woman was approaching her, hobbling on bandaged feet. The floor was rocky, there was a tremor running through the stone and through the air, the distance to cross seemed immense. She heard her own voice crooning, 'There, there. Take comfort.'

Minerva woke up with a start, the fold of her neck running with sweat. She kicked back the sheets and blankets and lay spread out, letting the cold night calm her, ridding her of the unease the dream inspired. After a little while, she reached across to the side table, taking from it a notebook and silver pencil and wrote, 'Bandaged feet, next one.'

*

'It's happened again, just as before,' said Mrs Skipton. 'In my opinion, Mrs Day, the mice have got behind the skirting board, and then, you see, the cat has ripped the wallpaper off the walls with her bare claws to get at them.'

Harriet inspected the long strips of wallpaper hanging from the wall. It seemed to her that they showed no signs of having been scratched haphazardly by a cat.

She rose from her kneeling position and glanced round the gloomy room. Everything else looked normal in the cold light seeping under the half-drawn blind: the mattress stripped of bedding and airing, the plain maple wardrobe and dresser polished to a shine, the glint of the shell collection on the windowsill; and the little troop of lead soldiers still marching two by two across the mantelpiece. She noticed two or three were knocked over. The cat again, she supposed.

'I don't know what to think,' she said. 'We seem to be having a lot of trouble with the cat. It will have to be dealt with – in some way, at some point. For now, please keep the door shut firmly, Mrs Skipton. In fact, we'll lock it and you can keep the key. Make sure Daisy doesn't come in and leave it open. That cat must have preternatural powers to be able to creep in here and cause havoc so frequently.'

'It just shows she's a keen mouser,' said the housekeeper, preparing to leave the room. 'She's the best we've had, and it was never my intention to make you think ill of the cat, ma'am. I just thought I'd best bring the damage to your attention.'

'Very good, Mrs Skipton. Thank you,' said Harriet.

She lingered a minute in the frigid room, going to the mantelpiece above the empty grate and picking up the little soldiers to place them back in marching order. Their blurred faces, coated in paint, were set and determined. She went out and locked the door behind her.

'I have to go to Mrs Smythe's this afternoon,' she said, catching up with Mrs Skipton who had been very slowly descending the stairs because of her swollen ankles. 'So I think I'll be out rather later than usual. Don't trouble to prepare tea. I plan to call on Mrs Roberts afterwards – it's conveniently near.'

'Very well, ma'am,' said Mrs Skipton. 'If you plan to return at a late hour ...'

'Yes, yes, of course, dear, just go to bed. Don't wait up for me,' said Harriet. Margaret Skipton had been part of the household since Harriet herself was a girl and there was no point pretending to uphold conventional employer-employee relations. 'Here's the key to Peter's room.'

'Thank you,' said Mrs Skipton, putting it into the serge pocket hanging from her apron strings. 'I was in fact not speaking of going to bed so much as going out to the prayer meeting.'

'Perfectly acceptable to me,' said Harriet. 'Take Daisy with you.'

'No, I think I'll leave her to do the brasses,' said the old lady with satisfaction.

Harriet thought about the empty bedroom and wondered how the cat could possibly keep getting in. There had been odd sounds from that room, audible downstairs, even when the cat was fast asleep by the hearth. It was not the cat.

Three nights ago in the darkness of her bedroom, she had been awakened from a deep dream by a book sliding down from her shoulder onto her ear. She had been sleeping on her side, cheek pressed into the pillow; and somehow the book must have got itself positioned, open and face down, nestled upon the peak of her shoulder. As she moved, it had been dislodged. She thought little of it, being half-asleep, and simply put the book down on the floor beside the bed.

It was not until the morning, about to step out of bed in the grey light, that she saw it there and remembered. Picking it up, she identified it as a poetry book from her bookshelf on the other side of the room. The page at which it was still open – she had placed it face down on the floor – revealed a long-forgotten poem by a minor poet. She sat on the edge of her bed, trying to remember how it came to be there. In the end, she had put the incident aside, as one of those events which would eventually explain itself. Everything else she also put down to mere fancy: the sense of being watched when in the spare room and the brewing tension which seemed to make itself felt throughout the entire house on certain days. The odd little wisp of black which often seemed to flick at incredible speed past the tail of her eye. The cat *was* black; this aspect of it must therefore be the cat.

Nonetheless, she had to half-admit that she had begun feeling increasingly uncomfortable when alone in the house, and was reluctant to enter the little empty room. She stood at the bottom of the stairs and looked upwards towards the quiet upper floors, imagining the lead soldiers marching about all by themselves.

It was cold with a dash of sleet peppering the wind. The streets were brisk, rattling with drays and omnibuses and cabs. Fragments of straw and little pills of ice rolled along the pavements. She crossed the road, picking her way over the metal rails of the horse-tram. The man selling hot sarsparilla nodded to her as she walked past and said something about the weather. A big dapple-grey horse came out of the archway leading to the mews and she stopped to let it go past. Hammer strokes rang out where the blacksmith was at work away down the end there: a smell of fire and hot iron and burnt horsehair.

She should have found a tea room because now she had time to kill and it was cold. She walked on, pausing at the window of a shop called the *Salon de Coiffures* with its swan-necked mannequins and improbable wigs. She glimpsed the young assistant's face in the interior beyond the window, a girl with flat ginger hair, coughing silently, one small white hand pressed against her chest; and then caught sight of her own reflected dumpy figure with its dark-green hat and coat. Between her reflected self and the ginger girl was a wax head modelling an auburn wig, adorned with fake roses and fake white gypsophila and little bits of fake foliage.

The best route to take to get to Mrs Smythe's was through the park; but the pathways were treacherous, powdered white with pellets of sleet at the edges and glassy in places where foot traffic had polished the surface. She walked carefully. The fences were fuzzed with frost. Beyond them were iron banks of earth and brutally-pruned rose bushes. A robin suddenly fluttered to within arms' reach on the fence. It looked at her intelligently. She thought, why didn't I bring a crust? Exactly as she thought this, the bird gracefully cast itself down to the pathway several yards beyond her, where it began to pick at some crumbs. A number of sparrows joined it and a dapper pied wagtail was suddenly there, smartly tapping its tail.

Turning her head to find the source of the food, she could see a slight figure in an over-large black greatcoat some distance away, throwing crumbled bread to the birds from a brown paper bag. There was a crowd of anxious pigeons at his feet, treading on each other to get to the food. The man had thrown some further out, beyond the heaving grey melée, to feed the smaller wild birds.

When she came to the pond it was icy at the edges. She paused to watch some excited red-faced boys, bristling and shrill, fighting among themselves and adventuring onto the crackling surface to throw ice fragments at the ducks. The ducks were all floating together on the inky pool in the unfrozen middle of the pond.

Three o'clock and the afternoon was already darkening. She quickened her pace, feeling the ground-freeze seeping through the soles of her shoes, anxious now to get on to Mrs Smythe's.

It was a mutually-enjoyable piano and voice lesson. Ada would be performing one of her pieces at her mother's musical reception later and the girl was rattling with nerves and excitement at the prospect. Her thin pink fingers shook on the keys, at first barely brushing a sound from the instrument. Harriet spent as much of the lesson reassuring her as teaching; and left the house feeling exhausted but pleased with a banker's cheque for the month's lessons in her pocketbook, looking forward to strolling along to visit Alexandra Roberts and drinking tea.

Widowhood had been suiting both Harriet and her friend Alexandra very well for some years now, in everything except the relative poverty resulting from the complicated state of their respective late husbands' affairs. The necessity had arisen of finding ways to supplement their incomes; and there was little that a respectable woman could do. For Harriet, teaching piano and voice was a satisfactory enough profession, having been thwarted from doing exactly that in youth. Now it was an unfading pleasure to be independent and run her own household as she chose, frugally and without fuss.

Dusk was falling and the lamps in the park were already being lit. She walked briskly past the park gate, not intending to walk through now that it was beginning to get dark. As she glanced over towards the pond, she was surprised to see that young man again, the one who had fed the birds. She recognised his face instantly, lit by the lamplight as he sat on the iron bench near the water. To Harriet's eyes he seemed almost to be perching there, like the robin. And in a little half-circle facing him was a group of boys. They seemed to be singing.

She stopped, trying to hear their voices. As she listened, it struck her that what they were singing sounded like a sinister little chant. Then to her surprise and horror, she saw the group begin pelting the poor fellow with lumps of ice. He protested, protecting his head with crossed arms. Harriet walked straight into the park through the gate, which creaked loudly, determined without quite knowing how, to put a stop to this at once. There were eight or nine boys and they were quite sturdy enough to appear menacing. Harriet had heard about — and witnessed - gangs of beggar-children intimidating the weak and scared, stealing purses and handbags, running wildly through street markets. On her own behalf, she would not have felt so brave, but on this occasion she did not think twice. She swept towards them.

'Stop that at once!' she roared, surprising herself. 'How dare you!'

The children turned to see what the noise was: just a doughy, motherly-looking woman stomping towards them. Without hesitation and with one accord, they turned their fire upon her. Several lumps of ice shattered on the ground around her. She felt one heavy piece thump against her shoulder.

In her bag, Harriet knew she had a hairbrush, a pair of nail scissors, needle and thread, *sal volatile,* a handkerchief and a police whistle. In her hand she held a stout umbrella with a strong wooden handle. Brandishing the umbrella, she charged the gang and yelled something to do with 'police' and 'police whistle'. She wasn't entirely sure what she yelled, but it was satisfyingly loud, coming from a place deep within her chest.

The original object of the attack now attempted to put himself between the volleys of ice and his rescuer, but was reluctant to use physical force upon the children. Harriet noticed that his build was so very slight that he could never have beaten off a determined attack. On realising this, she decided that physical force was exactly what was needed here and she herself would not be afraid to use it: any other kind of persuasion would simply be ridiculed. To a chorus of jeers, she flung herself into the fray and walloped the tallest boy with her umbrella.

'Ow! Missus, you bloody well 'urt me!' yelped the boy, rubbing his elbow.

His gang closed in on her, shouting threats and insults.

'You fat ugly old bag!'

'Get 'er!'

'Bloody old cow!'

'Get 'er 'andbag!'

'Fro 'er in the pond!'

'Fro 'em bofe in the pond!'

The young man now appeared behind the gang as they pressed forward, and began pulling individuals backwards out of the mob by grabbing their clothing. They turned on him now and with small experienced fists and boots went for the attack. It became a seething mass of dark bodies and shouting, and Harriet predicted that they would all end up in the freezing water; and that the ink would run on her recently acquired cheque and she would have to go back and get another one; and somehow was aware, in a distanced part of herself, of just how unseemly the whole incident must look. The other floating thought that bothered her was how heavy her skirts would become if they soaked up water and then froze.

As all that passed through one part of her mind, she was madly searching in her bag for the police whistle and keeping up a loud string of threats: 'I'll call a policeman on you! What will your mother say! Stop that! Don't you dare kick him!'

Just then, penetrating the juvenile voices, she heard a loud voice barking across from the park gate. She caught a glimpse of a bulky man in a long dark overcoat and bowler hat creaking the gate open and walking briskly towards them. 'Hoi! What the devil is going on?' he shouted. He spread both his arms wide and suddenly began running full pelt towards the group, roaring like a lion, and the children seeing him, decided to give up the attack. Light-footed, they scattered into the darkness, shouting insults as they ran.

CHAPTER TWO

Everyone was out of breath and shaken. Harriet sat down on the bench, the young man sat down on the floor and the newcomer leaned against the lamp post. It took a few moments to gather herself enough to focus on their rescuer, who took off his hat to rub his forehead with his scarf. She realised the man was talking to her and it was in fact someone she knew.

'Well, it *is* you, Mrs Day!' she found he was saying.

'Mr Cabot?' she said, still breathless. 'How fortunate that you were passing! That gang of brats was attacking this poor young man – and I saw it all and came to intervene!'

'I thought I recognised you from away over there,' said Cabot. 'What on earth are you doing here? Have you been heroically defending my friend here? That was a miniature battle royal, my dear, and I congratulate you on your courage. Did he start it?' He looked at the young man, shaking his head. 'George, you impetuous boy, did you cause this drama? You have imperilled a lady, you do realise that, don't you?'

The young man listened silently, looking shocked, apparently unable to say anything.

'There, look, dear, do sniff some of this *sal volatile*,' Harriet said, fishing it out of her bag. 'You look quite bewildered. And don't sit there on the freezing ground!'

'It's only George, Mrs Day: my little actor-friend George,' said Mr Cabot to Harriet, helping to raise him off the floor and put him on the bench which, being iron, was not much warmer than the ground. 'I'm taking him home in a minute anyway. He was just waiting for me right there, on that very park bench where the tragedy unfolded. I told him to, you know.'

George took the smelling salts reluctantly. Harriet, who had sat herself back down, also took a shuddering sniff and handed them to

Mr Cabot, but he took out a packet of cigarettes, shaking his head. 'You don't mind my smoking, Mrs Harriet? I know you won't mind. It's like smelling salts for me. And to think, I was just seeing to some business, some theatre business, and all the while poor George was being tormented by Lillliputian *hoi poloi!* What did you do to annoy them, you silly thing?' he asked.

'Nothing. Nothing at all. I was sitting on the bench, nothing more.' George's accent, while not a London voice, was unplaceable in its careful perfection. 'This brave lady came to help me.'

'Well, you must have done something. People don't get pelted with lumps of ice without a reason,' Mr Cabot said. His shoulders shook with laughter as he said, 'You must have annoyed and provoked them and made them think you *deserved* it.'

'It's not really funny,' said George. 'And I don't know what happened.'

Harriet interrupted, 'Mr Cabot, we can't sit about chatting here. I'm worried that the cold will make us all ill, after the shock. He needs to get into the warm and have a hot drink. And so do I.'

'Yes,' said Cabot. 'We have all been shaken and need to be looked after. And preferably by brandy. But first allow me to introduce you to each other. Mrs Harriet Day, may I present my friend and protégé, Mr George Arden? Mr George Arden, meet your saviour, the heroine Mrs Harriet Day.'

'Mrs Day,' repeated George Arden as if committing the name to memory. He darted to pick up his hat, which had rolled to the brink of the water and now placed it on his head in order to take it off again, saying formally, 'Mrs Harriet Day, I am eternally in your debt. All the days of my life I will remember this!' Mr Cabot sniggered a little but Harriet was charmed.

She said, 'Mr Arden, delighted to make your acquaintance, though I could wish it had been under more peaceful circumstances.' Then she added to Cabot pointedly, 'London is a perilous place for a stranger. If Mr Arden is your protégé, you should really keep a better eye on him, Mr Cabot.'

'Oh, he's not really a stranger, Mrs Harriet. He's been all over. And he's staying at Mrs Alexandra's with me, has been for a little while now; and he's working for me too. Marvellous things are happening! And I will tell you all about them as we escort you home, because it is both dark and dreadfully cold.'

Harriet mentioned that she had in any case been planning to walk over to visit Mrs Roberts. Being a regular visitor, she had met Valentine Cabot many times in the two years he had been lodging there but had not encountered George Arden before. Alex's gentlemen boarders came and went and were not really Harriet's business.

A heaviness was sweeping over her as the excitement receded and she had a strange desire almost to sleep right there on the bench. Realising that this was the after-effect of a shock to the nervous system, she briskly gathered up her umbrella and bag and rose from the bench.

The stranger, George Arden, stood quietly by. She could well imagine how unpleasant it must be to be attacked in a foreign country – if he was from abroad, as she suspected from his looks if not his voice - and not only that, to be jeered at and humiliated by children. She remembered that he had also been kicked and punched. 'Are you much hurt, Mr Arden?' she asked before they started out. 'Your attackers were young but very determined!'

'No, thank you for asking, no,' said Mr Arden vaguely. 'There is no special harm done.'

'Perhaps you could tell us how you came to be attacked?' she said.

'I don't know,' answered Arden. 'I was walking about in the park. I was feeding birds. The boys were trying to hurt the ducks. I told them not to. Then I went to sit down, waiting for Valentine, and when I looked up, they were there facing me, like a chorus from a Greek tragedy.

'Amusing, isn't he?' said Cabot. 'You may not think it to look at him, but he is quite a find. He has the devil of a name to him, and you won't remember it. I never do. So I named him George when I met him – and then I thought up a last name to go with it: Arden, after the forest in *As You Like It*. George Arden. It makes it all a good deal easier to have a nice patriotic British name if you look like he does. As I found with Nicolo, an English face should be combined with an exotic name; and vice-versa.'

He slipped an arm through George's, took a last drag on his cigarette and, passing that over to him to dispose of, offered his other arm to Harriet. His spirits were completely restored – but in Harriet's experience, it took a lot to submerge Mr Valentine Cabot. He had insuperable self-confidence. As they walked, Valentine continued his discussion of George Arden's name, talking as usual like a man who enjoys the sound of his own voice. 'It sounds manly and will look good on a play bill. You see, this is all quite subtle. Do listen, you'll like this. Firstly, the name Arden will remind them of the word *ardent*. And you have ardent lovers and ardent patriots and ardent other things; and the first name, ah! the first sounds like a patriotic fairytale hero – *George* and the Dragon, *George* the Fourth, *George* and the blessed what-you-may-call-it Beanstalk. Something for everyone, you see.'

'My name,' said George softly across Valentine when he could get a word heard, 'is not really George Arden.'

'May one enquire what your name really is – and how you yourself would prefer to be addressed?' asked Harriet, amused.

'Well,' he answered apologetically, 'George will do, thank you.'

'Polite too, you see,' interrupted Valentine. 'Not too bright though. You must not expect too much of him conversation-wise. I believe he was knocked on the head at some point and lost some facts out of his brains but it doesn't seem to affect his acting. I plan to build my next production around him, exclusively. Do listen, my dear Mrs Day, because you'll like this: a tragic youth undergoes all kinds of tribulations ...'

Harriet said, "H'mm?' and 'Fascinating!' at various points in an interested way as Valentine spoke and they walked along. After he had given his outline of the plot and nobody said anything else, he went on, 'And it will be sumptuous. There will be bewitching maidens with radiant locks – wigs, my dear, I know a fellow who hires out some very good ones...' He described the imagined production in great detail, ending with, '... and music, music, my dear Mrs Harriet, you must write and arrange the music – a Gypsy Song, for instance – and Mrs Roberts can design the set - '

'How *is* Mrs Roberts?' asked Harriet, whose thoughts had long ago wandered elsewhere. The finished performance would neither resemble the current description nor produce the least financial return; but Valentine talked, it was like a great river in flow and it took almost a muscular effort to divert him. His rolling, deliberately-affected style mesmerised listeners almost against their will.

'Well, when last observed, at breakfast this morning, the divine Mrs Alexandra appeared well-turned-out in a grey shawl adorned with a border of glittering beads, and Mrs Jenkins's kidneys were exquisite,' answered Valentine.

'And so Mr – Arden is staying with you there?' She wondered after she had said it why she had not addressed Mr Arden directly.

'It was such a wonderful chance, Mrs Harriet,' Valentine said confidentially, almost in her ear. 'Because the top front was occupied by that old gentleman, the irritable one who threw things down the stairs from time to time and nobody could ever tell what was the cause of it - well, you'll probably remember that he very regrettably passed away in November. And so of course, Mrs A. had a room going free and I happened to run into young George here one evening - and do you know, the very same thought occurred to me as occurred to you. Which was,' he dropped George's arm to gesticulate towards him, 'this entirely innocent creature needs protection - you know, I swear the entire speech on the Heath flashed instantly through my mind - *Is man no more than this? No more but a poor, bare, forked creature?* - I said it to you at the time, didn't I, George? Because it was drizzling like *blazes*. So I brought him home and stowed him away in that spare room and Mrs A. was so surprised and *more* than happy to take him as our new boarder. Except I think she would quite like some rent – which will happen at some point very soon as we are definitely on the road to success.' Valentine paused to adjust his scarf. 'It's just a matter of time, because I have already got him a slot at the Revue Parnassus in Wardour Street.'

Before he could begin again, Harriet asked sympathetically, 'Mr Arden, have you recently come to town?' If Valentine had found him adrift on the streets of London only a month or two ago, it was more than likely that the poor thing was far from home and family. But George just looked at her warily, as if choosing from a variety of possible responses. She went on after a short pause, 'Is your mother not worried for you? In what country does she reside? I do hope that you have been able to write your whereabouts?'

'Write? No, I don't write things very often,' he pondered. 'I'm not very good with them, you know, letters, thank you for asking. But my mother is long dead.'

'Oh, I am sorry to hear of your sad loss,' she replied. He speaks so curiously, she thought, as if internally frozen - but that could be the result of the recent nasty shock. Nevertheless, I don't think he can really make a good actor for Valentine's purposes, although those looks might carry all before them. He might only need to stand in a certain attitude, lit in a certain way, to suggest all kinds of tragic things. *The Tempest,* Ariel: it's that kind of face, really. A little too fine-boned, though, for much else.

Alexandra welcomed them warmly, especially when she heard the story of the mishap in the park. A supply of hot tea and cake accompanied an account of their shocking experiences (which on re-telling occasioned a great deal of laughter) followed by a pressing invitation to Harriet to stay for dinner and the night too, if required.

Harriet had always liked this house, which had been her friend Alexandra's family home. It still had the forest-green walls she remembered from years before, but the dim brown hunting scenes of the past had been replaced. Now they were more fashionably decorated with Japanese fans and peacock feathers, although above the mirror on the mantelpiece hung a bit of Harriet's own juvenile handiwork: a small, slightly lopsided, woolwork unicorn.

Harriet sipped the tea. George Arden was sitting not far away and on his other side was Valentine Cabot. Beyond him sat Albert Burroughs, whose chair was turned slightly away and who was doing his best to ignore Valentine's almost continuous stream of conversation by burying his nose in a newspaper. Mr Burroughs was a court reporter and Valentine Cabot often referred privately to his 'judge's brow' and 'freezing manner' which he ascribed to the insights into human nature forced upon him by his profession.

Opposite him was Alexandra's other boarder, a young drawing master named Dafydd Williams, who was sitting folded up in his chair. A shy pink fellow, he rarely took his eyes off his landlady. Harriet suspected that Mr Williams was a little bit in love with her: which, Harriet thought, was only right, as Alexandra was tall and graceful with thick looped-up hair and dark intelligent eyes. It was true that that hair was beginning to be threaded with grey, just as Harriet's was. The difference in the two women's ages was negligible but whereas time was inexorably sliding Harriet's body downwards and outwards, Alexandra's was shrinking into angularity. She still wears her clothes so well, thought Harriet with a pang. Turning her attention to the young man whom Valentine had named George Arden, she looked at him sidelong and by chance their eyes met. He gave her a quizzical half-smile. He was listening to Mr Cabot, who was in full flow, saying nothing in particular at great volume.

'This is the most excellent cake ever made,' Valentine was declaring. 'Indeed, take this as your next subject, Mrs A.: the cake, half gone, upon an earthenware platter; a Greekish kind of table; a flagon of wine and in the background, myself cast upon a bench, dressed as - oh, I don't know, Socrates, about to expire very spiritually.'

'Do you sincerely think they had cake of this sort in Athens?' asked Mr Williams timidly.

'Fig cake then. Olive cake. Hemlock cake,' Valentine amended. 'The detail is irrelevant.'

'And your purpose is to imply Socrates was poisoned by cake?' asked Alexandra.

Valentine thought for a moment and said, 'Anyway, now I think of it, Socrates is too old and horribly ugly. Alexander who died young and glorious, that's better. Youth and death, such a delightful combination, like eggs and bacon. The Greeks knew all about that sort of thing. Never just snuffed it. Torn apart by Bacchae or undergoing metamorphoses into a blessed what-you-may-call-it, daffodil.' Valentine kissed his fingers at the air with a sigh.

'Narcissus,' said Harriet. 'And I'm not sure I agree with you. None of us wishes to lose youth and beauty - if we were ever fortunate to possess the latter - but the loss of them, my dear Mr Cabot, is the result of not actually having died. Wrinkles are the mark of a kind of victory, don't you think? Perhaps you're saying that they are more terrifying than death?'

'Death or Wrinkles?' cried Valentine. 'Well, Alexander certainly *cannot* have wrinkles! And I'm quite prepared to admit it: I don't want to die either and so the more my own face sags and creases, the more I shall adore the vision of golden youth.'

At that, Mr Burroughs scowled, cleared his throat, shook out his paper, glared at Valentine and rose to his feet. 'I shall retire to my room for a period of peace and quiet reflection before dinner,' he said in his clipped tones to the group round the fire. As Burroughs left the room, Valentine mimed taking a drink from a bottle and whispered, 'Peace and quiet reflection.'

With a little preparatory whirr, the clock struck six.

'Speaking of dinner,' said Alexandra, 'I must pop down to the kitchen. The duck will be roasted for seven. And you will stay with us and dine, my dear Harriet, and when I come back, we'll freshen up together. And afterwards, we can easily send a message home to let Mrs Skipton know if you choose to stay with me tonight. You did after all have rather a shock, and it is so cold.'

Harriet would have liked to stay but remembered that she had a pupil arriving early for a lesson so decided to make her way home after dinner.

Dafydd Williams trailed upstairs. Alexandra went to talk about the preparation of the accompaniments for tonight's meat with Elizabeth Jenkins, her cook and housekeeper; and Harriet stayed put until she came back. Valentine and George withdrew to their rooms to adjust their apparel or to smoke or lie down. After a while, young Janet walked wearily into the parlour, carrying a tray to gather up the tea things.

Harriet took up the newspaper which Mr Burroughs had tossed onto a table. It was the same she had read that morning and so she idly glanced through the advertisements. They seemed to chime with the theme of their conversation, the desire to remain young: Magnolia Lotion (*Makes a lady of thirty appear but twenty!*), Reducing Garments (*Getting Stout?*), MacTavish's Corsetry (*Uplift the Beauty of your Form!*) and Atwell's Beauty Balm Compact (*Restores the Beauty of Youth to Every Lady's Skin*).

She sighed and cast the paper down. Her throat was beginning to feel scratchy and, shutting her eyes she laid her head back, listening to the restful tick-tick of the clock.

CHAPTER THREE

D inner had come and gone. The gentlemen of Mrs Roberts's house had either retired to their rooms or were lingering at the dining table over port while Alexandra and Harriet were sitting together with coffee in the parlour. Harriet, who was growing rather long-sighted, was peering at a pamphlet advertising an exhibition of work at a small gallery recently opened by some friends of theirs. The pamphlet had the word *Incendiary!* in large orange letters across the front, and beneath it, *New Women Artists: The Amazons*. Behind it all, a star was outlined in evening blue. At the bottom was the address of the venue and the printers, Penthesilea Press.

'"Penthesilea Press" is actually just Ethel and Mabel all on their own, isn't it?' said Harriet.

'Yes, just the two of them in their kitchen. They've got a little old-fashioned thing that does it but it's hard manual labour. The whole place smells of ink now and there's indelible sunburst-orange all over the floor; and all over Mabel, too. I was there yesterday, that's when I got the pamphlet.'

'It's a remarkably good effort. I do so hope it all works out for them. But I fear they'll go bust before the next rent day.'

'Yes, probably,' agreed Alexandra. 'But I promised some of my stuff to go in there. It will have to be "incendiary" enough though and I'm not sure any of it is. Let's go together. It isn't too far from Oxford Street. Let's arrange it now, let's look at the new work by the Amazons and then lunch at the Sybil Club and then – well, we could make a day of it, go somewhere for the afternoon.'

'I think I might be tired out after a whole morning of Ethel and Mabel and Frances and the others. And the weather, Alex. We don't want to be wandering wearily about in the hail and rain.'

'But we won't be weary, we'll be inspired. Unless Ethel smokes those cigars again. That will make us weary.'

'Don't talk about it. It makes my throat sorer just to think of it,' said Harriet. 'Do you remember going to the Dorothy Restaurant and seeing Mrs Wilde there? That was the first place I saw ladies smoking in public. And people gawping through the windows at us.'

'I tried it, of course. It made me feel sick and I never persisted.'

'Yes, you did go rather green. Happier thought, then: I'm very excited to hear about your new project. You could hardly get a word in edgewise with Mr Cabot in full flow at dinner, so now, tell me again, what are the details and what is it about?'

'It's very lucrative, that is mainly what it is about,' said Alexandra. 'The subject is a lady of immense wealth and beauty. The commission is to present her as such. Easy. And I think I have a good chance. My ideas are under consideration, apparently – even though the usual crowd are elbowing their way in.'

Harriet added, 'A good portrait can make a society hostess.'

'Yes, not to mention an artist. But this is interesting because it's not just a beauty, you know – she's a successful, lone businesswoman. So my idea is to represent her struggle in mythical terms. It will make such a delightful change from charming brides on the verge of womanhood.'

'Don't forget the pretty babies and spaniels,' said Harriet.

'They are a millstone round my neck. As is my popular sideline in still-lifes of fruit and flowers. Needs must when the devil drives. I'm not ashamed of it either. At least we keep our heads above water, you and I. Not a small feat.'

'That's true. So, will your rich businesswoman be armed with something? An umbrella?'

'Oh no. She'll be holding up the dripping head of my own bank manager, in the style of Beardsley.'

'You're not serious. I know it will be a respectably-draped figure of Juno or some such, looking superior and infinitely well-bred, whatever you might really want to paint. '

'That's a coincidence, your saying Juno. Her name is Minerva. I was actually envisaging a reference to the name. With a spear or something and a little owl.'

The clock struck ten and reluctantly, Harriet decided she should leave. Alexandra tried to persuade her not to go, particularly as she seemed to be coming down with a cold, but she asked for a cab to be procured. When Alexandra rang the bell, Janet Fairlight the maid arrived looking rather ill too. She was pale and her eyes were glittering with fever. 'You're not well, Janet,' said Alexandra immediately. 'Are you hot? Sore throat? Right. To bed with you. Where is everyone else?'

'Mrs Jenkins is in the kitchen, ma'am, but Amy and Lily have gone to bed. They're worse than me, all feverish.'

'Oh dear!' cried Alexandra. 'That won't do. You must go to bed too and stay in bed. We'll manage – I'll get some agency staff in tomorrow to cover your work. All I want now is to get Mrs Day a cab so that she can go home.'

'Well, I'll do that, ma'am,' said Janet stoutly.

'No, no, you shan't,' said Harriet. 'I can manage perfectly well on my own. The cab rank is just down the street at the junction by the Three Feathers. I can very well walk there.'

'No, not alone,' said Alexandra. 'I'll send someone to get the thing to pick you up here.'

'The Feathers is not far, it's a respectable hotel,' said Harriet, 'and I am an extremely respectable woman.'

'I know you can fight off gangs of cut-throats armed only with an umbrella,' said Alexandra (Janet boggled), 'but I insist some creature accompany you. After all, it is, in the main, males that one must guard against, so let one of them atone for the offences of the rest. Who shall we have? Valentine? He makes an impressively stout silhouette.'

'Very well,' said Harriet, rising to put on her hat. 'Let a sacrificial Valentine be prepared and brought hither to guide me through the underworld.'

'Please ask Mr Cabot if he would be so kind as to come to the parlour, Janet. And then, you go to bed,' said Alexandra. 'And ask Mrs Jenkins for honey and lemon to drink, and for the other girls too.'

Five minutes later, the door opened and George Arden appeared, looking apologetic. 'I am sorry to intrude,' he said, 'but Valentine seems to have fallen asleep. I think the port had something to do with it. I wonder if I could be of service? Janet said you need a guard to the Underground, but she didn't know what you meant by that, as the nearest station is half an hour's walk, and she said it might be that you need someone to accompany you to the cab rank.'

'I merely intend to walk to the Three Feathers Hotel to get a cab, Mr Arden,' said Harriet. 'Mrs Roberts feels that I need a guard of honour, that's all.'

'Would I do?' asked George.

Alexandra looked doubtfully at him. He was taller than Harriet, but about half her weight, and had already shown this evening that he could hardly defend himself against a gang of boys. Nevertheless, Harriet was already giving her assent. He would have to suffice although Alex was on the alert because the servants had noticed a ragged fellow hanging about in the Square from time to time and generally there seemed to be an increased number of loiterers on the streets. She suggested that George accompany Harriet in the cab all the way to her door and then take the cab back here. That way he too would be safe from assault and battery, although she did not express this last thought aloud.

The two of them set out. There was a slight sense of awkwardness on Harriet's part as she walked beside Mr Arden. She was determined not to allude to their adventure in the park, having come to the conclusion that he must be embarrassed by it. Valentine Cabot had made a lot of comic remarks on the subject throughout dinner. As Mr Arden had said nothing in his own defence, she had begun to concur with the opinion that he was a little 'slow'. She was almost surprised therefore when he began to talk coherently to her.

'Mrs Day, I've been thinking a great deal about the events in the park. I am very happy that it was you who helped me. It could have worked out very differently.'

'Yes, we could both have ended ankle-deep in the pond,' agreed Harriet.

'What made you come to my rescue then?' he asked.

'Well, if you want to know the exact truth, it was because I had seen you earlier. You were feeding the birds. I like birds, especially the little ones. So I suppose it's the birds you must thank. And besides, it was the arrival of Mr Cabot which made them run. The boys, not the birds, I mean.'

They walked on in silence. Then he said, 'The birds were hungry.'

'Quite so,' said Harriet. As she said it, she noticed again that her throat hurt. As she sat in the foyer of the hotel, she tried to decide if she were feeling shivery or not; but ten minutes later, they were in the hansom cab and half way through the short journey back to Harriet's house. She watched Arden silently as he commented on the things they could see out of the window. Like a child, she thought. In the darkness of the interior, his face, as the light from the street struck it, looked very young. He exclaimed at anything he noticed: 'Look, outside that pub, there's a dancing man with a little dog!' or 'That lady has a very fine hat!' or 'How tired that old man looks!' Then she heard him say, 'How tired *you* look, Mrs Day!' and she knew she should pull herself together and answer.

'I am a little unwell, I think, Mr Arden.'

'Yes. But I hope you'll be better tomorrow when Isabelle Daniels comes for her lesson.'

Harriet sat up very straight. 'Did you say Isabelle Daniels? Do you know her? She is one of my pupils.'

'You posted me a picture,' said Arden, still looking out of the window. 'She is pretty and she wears a lot of pink. You think it clashes with her red hair.'

'I posted you a picture? But, Mr Arden, how could I ever have posted a picture to you of one of my pupils? I never met you before this afternoon!'

'That's true,' agreed Arden peaceably.

Harriet tried to pin him down on his strange statement but he seemed either to be completely unwilling to discuss it or to have forgotten that he ever said it, for he just looked mildly regretful at being unable to help her when she pressed him on the subject.

When they arrived at Harriet's address, Arden insisted on seeing her to the door. She was fumbling for her keys and thanking him for his company when he suddenly moved back down the steps and looked up at the first floor of the house.

'Oh, you have someone in your window waving down,' he said.

Harriet joined him and also looked up. She thought she saw a movement for a moment at the window of the empty bedroom, but then realised it was the flash of moonlight on the pane. 'It's a trick of the light, Mr Arden,' she said. 'There's no one there. That room is always empty.'

'He's still waving,' said Arden, glancing at Harriet calmly and then back up at the window. 'He is there at this moment.'

Harriet squinted up again. The big moon's reflection hung in the glass. It was possible to imagine that a slight ripple in the pane was a movement, especially if one moved one's head. She said firmly, 'No, I don't think so.'

'I could tell you what he has to say, if you like,' said Arden diffidently.

'But ...' Harriet stopped herself. Perhaps George Arden was genuinely a little soft in the head but, if so, that was not his fault. Was it wise to insist that he was mistaken? Harriet had nursed her own mother in the last stages of her illness, when she had been inclined to insist upon all kinds of impossible things. Arguing with a disordered imagination had never got her anywhere before. 'Perhaps you are right, Mr Arden,' she said, finding her key at last and realising she had left her umbrella at Alex's. 'But your cab is waiting to take you home.'

'May I come again?' asked Arden. 'To see you, I mean, and to make sure that you are well?'

'Well, yes, I suppose so,' said Harriet, slightly wary. 'Thank you again for your company. Now go in the warm, go home!'

Arden said, 'I hope you feel better soon.'

'What in the world?' Harriet murmured aloud to herself, thinking about the strange young man and his strange behaviour as she got herself into the hall. It was comforting to find Mrs Skipton had left the gas bracket lit and turned low. The black cat, who was sitting neatly on the bottom step, came forward to meet her, enquiring, 'Prrp?'

The next day, Harriet found herself with a sore throat and a headache but otherwise more than equal to undertaking her teaching duties. She was glad though that she had only two pupils that day. Young Isabelle Daniels came and went, followed in the early afternoon by the other; and Harriet completely forgot about Mr Arden's curious foreknowledge. She had in any event dismissed his talk of people waving at the window almost as soon as she heard it; and now it seemed dream-like, just a still image of herself looking up at the moon reflected in the glass.

About four-thirty, as the early evening was creeping closer to the house, there was a ring at her door and Mr Arden was shown into the room holding his hat in one hand and Harriet's umbrella in the other. 'Good afternoon, Mrs Day. I thought I recognised the way the last house has a kind of turret on the top, and I thought I might see if this was your street. And when I saw the steps and the upstairs window, I was sure.'

'Well, you are welcome, Mr Arden,' said Harriet. It was a strange way to explain his visit.

'And I've forgotten to mention why I'm here,' he continued with a little laugh. 'I apologise. Your umbrella! And also I want to make sure that you are well. Are you well?'

'Yes, thank you. Very well. And thank you for bringing the umbrella. It's very kind of you to call and I am glad you recognised the street. It's Cairncross Street.'

'I remember it began with a C from when you told the cab driver last night. But there are several C.s between Mrs Roberts's house and here.'

'Have you been walking about in the cold, looking for my house, Mr Arden?'

Arden looked a little embarrassed.

Harriet, thinking it was endearing but also rather pathetic, said, 'Perhaps you could have checked with Mrs Roberts about the address before you left the house. Or Mrs Jenkins, she knows.'

'Oh, I wouldn't disturb them,' said Arden as if that might be a little dangerous.

'Well, now that you've been so kind as to return my umbrella, please do come and sit down by the fire. Though it's not quite as cold as yesterday, I think. The frost on the windows had gone by mid-morning.'

'Yes, it's warmer but very damp,' agreed Arden.

Harriet cast about for something to say. 'So. How is Mr Cabot's venture coming along, Mr Arden?' She picked up some crochet work, expecting a cosy flood of confidential information.

'I didn't come to talk about that, Mrs Day,' said Arden politely. 'It was the ghost business, that was why I came. He is malignant and I can discern a real intention.'

Harriet left the crochet untouched in her lap. 'Could you explain a little more, Mr Arden?'

'It's very straightforward. Oh, listen!'

There was a clang from the room above.

'That's the bootjack,' said Harriet, frowning at George as if he were responsible.

'He chooses that room because it already works like a door. It changes, it's a turn-about room, sometimes good and sunny, sometimes sad and dark. You need to stabilise it. Because when he's here, he'll keep annoying you by throwing things about.'

Harriet waited for further explanation. When none came, she said again, 'Could you explain a little more, Mr Arden?'

'Oh,' said Arden, as if surprised. 'I'll try if you like. You have a person, a personality really, who obviously isn't in a body but thinks perhaps that he is, and he comes into the room above this one. He's glaring down at me. I can tell you that he has thick whiskers.'

'Good lord,' said Harriet.

'I can tell him to go, if you want,' said Arden. 'Or you can let him stay. But he moves things and wants your attention and enjoys scaring you. His name is … Ostrich? He's showing me a big bird. Oh, it's Ozzie.'

'Good lord,' said Harriet again.

'If you let me go into the room, I can sort it all out for you,' said Arden, as if he were talking about the plumbing.

'Well, then, I suppose you'd better,' said Harriet. She really did not know what to think. 'Mrs Skipton has the key. I'll ring for Daisy.'

While they waited for the key to be brought, Harriet sat mutely and George chatted merrily about the Revue Parnassus where he was due to appear this evening. He told Harriet that Valentine was very particular about punctuality so he would unfortunately have to leave shortly or he risked making him angry.

The key arrived and Harriet showed him up to the room. The stairs and landing were dim and she carried an oil lamp, apologising about the shadows and for some reason gabbling about the electricity which was being laid on in the next street. They stopped outside the door of the empty room. Behind them at the top of the stairs, the carved Swiss clock on the landing wall ticked heavily.

'Would you like me to light the gas in the room? Or would you prefer to take the lamp with you, Mr Arden?' she asked, wondering if she was expected to watch or assist. Her skin prickled uncomfortably at the thought of entering the room and seeing the little soldiers inexplicably moving about on the mantelpiece.

'I don't mind really,' said Arden cheerfully. 'It's not a physical eye-thing, if you see what I mean. I don't know how to describe it, quite honestly, and it's not worth trying. People often get quite cross about it if I do. It's just that I remembered how you helped me at the pond yesterday and I wanted to do something to help you. That's fair, isn't it?'

There was a creaking noise from just beyond the door, as if someone were standing there. She imagined a person with an ear pressed to the wood, listening to their conversation.

'Can I just ask you, Mr Arden, are we talking about a ghost? Because I don't believe in ghosts or any such nonsense,' Harriet said, her voice coming out rather shriller than usual. 'I can't imagine what it is, and I know it can move things so it has a physical force at its disposal, and I also understand it isn't the cat; but it isn't a ghost either. Because there is no such thing.'

Arden nodded admiringly. 'I am not in the least offended if you don't call it a ghost. You can call it anything you like. It can be something to do with magnets or the underground railways they've been digging, or interference from all that electricity pouring into your neighbours in the next street. Would that do?'

Harriet looked at him doubtfully, not sure if he were mocking her. She decided that he was not. 'Very well,' she said. 'I think it's best if you do what you want to do, with the proviso that I don't have to believe what you believe about what you want to do.'

'There, perfect! Anyway, it'll probably be quicker if I do it alone. Don't worry. You just make yourself comfortable and I'll come down when it's finished.' Before she could say another word, he opened the door and slipped through into the dark room beyond.

Harriet sat motionless by the parlour fire, wondering if Mr Arden were bonkers. There were undoubted sounds from above. A scraping across the floor. The sound of something immensely heavy shuffling forward, one creak at a time. She decided it was the wardrobe. Then there was a scatter of little heavy objects dropping – the soldiers, she supposed. George Arden was upstairs wrecking her spare bedroom and she was sitting downstairs allowing it to happen.

A thought struck her and she went to the desk drawer. She pulled it open – it stuck a little on the right-hand side because she rarely looked within – and brought out a red cloth folder with a cord binding it shut. It was crammed with papers: handwritten letters, legal documents and in an envelope on top, a fat gold locket and chain. She poured the chain out and the locket plopped after it into her palm like a tiny egg. She opened its front. On one side it was inscribed with her Christian name and a date, 1868. On the other was a miniature portrait on ivory, in rather garish colours, of a gentleman with generous mutton-chop whiskers. She looked at it briefly and put it away in the folder, along with all the other papers, and pushed the drawer shut. At that moment, George reappeared, tapping on the door. She motioned to him to enter and he immediately came to pick up his hat from where he had left it on the piano stool. She faced him with a question on her lips.

'Yes. All finished,' he said in a rush, before she could speak. 'But you need to keep the room open and moving. I suggest putting a goldfish in there or a little bird. I know it's a sad room for you but you could put some growing things on the windowsill, not dead things. Some plants.'

'What's happened?' asked Harriet. 'Is the room a terrible mess?'

'No, no, just the wardrobe needs pushing back a little bit and some toys need to be rearranged. I would do it for you but I have to dash. I'm sure I can remember the way back, if I just go to the end of the street and cross, take a left and then a right, or no, a left. But I'll remember when I see it. Please excuse me, Mrs Day. Valentine will absolutely murder me if I'm late. We're still only half-done on the *The Grenadier's Farewell* and its first performance is tonight. But it was fun and I'm so glad you're better.'

And with that, Mr Arden departed. Harriet saw him to the door and then stood wondering in the hall. She had to admit to herself that her expectations about him had been wrong. And his manner was far more relaxed, less 'frozen', than on their previous meeting. Perhaps the absence of Valentine was the explanation.

She decided she really ought to go up and look at the room, although she had a strong inclination to leave it till daylight. But then she pictured herself, lying in bed wondering about the dark objects standing in its emptiness and waiting to hear odd noises across the landing. No, the best thing to do was go in with a stout heart and have a thorough look and poke about in all the corners. She went warily upstairs, once again carrying the lamp. Opening the door, she walked straight across and lit the gas lights. There were the soldiers, scattered as she predicted all over the mat. She picked them up and placed them on the mantel in a little heap. As for the rest of the room, all looked as before, except for the wardrobe, which was pushed away from the wall by four or five inches. A good opportunity to dust behind it, she thought.

She was about to re-order the soldiers in their usual ranks when a thought struck her. She went to the bookcase and took down a painted wooden box jammed above the volumes on the shelf. It contained a few dried, age-darkened conkers, dropped from a tree and gathered up one autumn day twenty years before. She put the toys away. The little soldiers fitted snugly among them, like troops hiding between boulders. Before she closed the lid, she thought, 'These are seeds. There have been trees inside this box all these years.' Then she replaced it on the shelf. Remembering to leave the door open as she left, she thought that the room felt warmer. But then, the weather was warmer and all the frost had thawed.

She walked downstairs thinking that she could not account for what Mr Arden had done – it was irrational. But neither could she account for his familiarity with her husband's appearance; and his inexplicable knowledge of the pet-name she had called him on their honeymoon, thirty years before.

CHAPTER FOUR

D r Watson's cough seemed to recur with the regularity of the ticking of the clock. It was particularly annoying and left him exhausted with each fresh attack.

'Watson, please take some medicine,' said Holmes in a voice of iron calm. He was in the midst of packing a valise in his bedroom, dividing his attention between that and darting back and forth to scribble notes on a sheet of paper at his overburdened desk.

'I won't say,' said Watson weakly, holding a handkerchief over his mouth, 'that this bronchial condition may not have been partially exacerbated by your experiments with gases the other day.'

'You won't say it but you will think it,' said Holmes drily without turning round from his writing.

'And I also won't say that it is very vexing to be unable to accompany you to St Petersburg.'

'Yes, it is vexing for me too. And please put the whole matter of where I am to be found out of your mind. Forget to remember it, my dear fellow. This case will not be suitable for publication.'

'How can you be so sure? I have very discreetly –' he broke off to cough – 'managed it in the past. *The Second Stain*, that was a diplomatic affair ...'

'I doubt that this will be so easy to transform into a story for your readers. Now, listen,' said Holmes, coming and sitting down opposite his friend with the air of one who still has pressing errands and a deadline. 'My train leaves in half an hour and you are *not* to accompany me to the station. No, I insist you stay at the fireside. There, you see, you try to object and you break out coughing again.

Do not expect to hear from me, my dear fellow, for a few weeks. I shall probably be far from a post office.' He laughed a little grimly.

'I know,' said Watson gloomily. 'But I trust that from time to time you will remember to send me word – even a postcard from Eastbourne!'

'I shan't *be* in Eastbourne, Watson,' said Mr Holmes patiently.

'I know very well you shan't be in Eastbourne, Holmes,' Watson said. 'And you know very well what I mean. Send me word, that's all. My health suffers when I become unduly anxious. Particularly my chest.'

'Tut. You sound like an elderly spinster.'

'Well, *you* are prone to the darkest of depressions when forced into inactivity –'

'I know. But you won't be inactive. Look, there're all the files on my desk – you could beguile the time away by organising some of that monstrosity. And you could write your stories.'

'I am definitely not well enough to touch your desk. I may consider some cases to write up, of course, but it is immensely vexing and I –' The cough returned at that point and precluded any possibility of finishing his speech.

Holmes regarded him for a minute. 'I am so sorry, old boy, but there simply isn't time. I must get on.' He rose to finish his packing with a little sympathetic grimace; and in ten minutes, he was ready to depart. They said a reticent goodbye and Watson listened as his friend's footsteps descended the stairs to the front door. Then he was gone.

Left to himself, Dr Watson sat feebly by the fire, feeling both restless and exhausted. He had got to the point when each cough made his sides hurt so much he feared he had cracked a rib. The absence of Holmes and his current state of health made him feel so low that it brought to mind a desperate time some years before when he had been led to believe his friend was lost. I must keep myself occupied, he told himself sternly. And as soon as I'm fit, I must be sure to get out and about, meet people, see off this loneliness. I'm damned if I'll let myself sink into melancholy again.

*

'Yes, I am pleased with it,' agreed Alexandra, standing back to assess her handiwork. On the easel was a large preliminary sketch in oils, designed to flatter and persuade her potential patron to go ahead with the commission. 'I thought mystical or mythological with some unique touches to capture her personality.'

Valentine Cabot raised an eyebrow. 'It's her personality that attracts you, is it?'

'Don't laugh. It's an important commission for me, Val. People will see this and want it for themselves. And she's rich, rich, rich. Look. There'll be a sense of movement, you see, as if she's just turning round to look at you, startled. But in her eyes, you'll see a challenge – and the dress I think will have a feather motif, textures so rich you'd think you could unpick the embroidery, unless this is too silly? With sage-greens and purples and coppers. You know the kind of feel I want to get?' While Alexandra spoke, she continued to work, and her sentences coincided with little jabs and strokes. 'It is rather Poynter-ish, I know, but I think that may be what the Bank wants. I met her just once and dashed off twenty pencil sketches. I think she might like me. I told her a little about myself, where I live, where I work, that sort of thing, hoping she'd be sympathetic, you see, to a lorn businesswoman and, do you know, it must have worked. I must find more common ground today, things to talk about. Am I talking too much? Oh lord.'

'Oh, you'll persuade her, Alex, as long as you don't talk her to death. Just speak concisely to her and at certain important moments, fall silent. Intrigue her. Quote poetry. Drop hints. Never explain,' said Valentine, who was sitting on the arm of a chair and talking between bites of an apple, feeling rather out of sorts. The mention of somebody else's good fortune and the prospect of somebody else earning a lot of money was always a trial for his good nature. He munched for a moment and said critically, while Alexandra bent to a detail in her work, 'And you may not have realised this, but you can't have a high priestess or whatever she is, on a perfectly ordinary London window seat. It's a careless anachronism. People will notice'

'How observant you are,' said Alexandra. 'I wasn't planning to paint a hansom cab passing by, you know. Maybe a chariot.' She dabbed at the canvas. 'And when, pray, have you ever spoken concisely about anything – or fallen into silence, for that matter?'

'And have you ever thought that a photograph would do the trick just as well?' He glanced down at Mr Arden who was seated in the chair upon the arm of which he was perched. 'H'm. George appears to have dozed off.'

'People don't just want photographs, Mr Cabot,' said Alexandra without looking away from the canvas. 'Big portraits are all about status. Money doesn't want the commonplace: it wants the unique.' She took a step back to test the effect of an ochre strand of light.. 'The trick of adding depth like this,' she murmured to herself, 'is to ... please don't stand in the light, Mr Cabot!'

Valentine had got up and was wandering about the room, apparently cogitating on a new thought. He was chewing his lip. He stopped and faced Alexandra. 'You're absolutely right, Mrs A., it is time to face the truth. I have been looking in the wrong places. Always the low, you see: the common and the commonplace, the revues and music halls, the fleshpots with their tawdry dancers and vulgar comedians. And your example has suggested to me that since I have something of an asset, I should aim high and with nobler ambition. I shall revive my previous creations, my little box of scripts, my higher aspirations. Yes, the unique, refined, high status. No more snake dancers for us.'

'By which you mean ...? No, let me guess,' Alexandra said, beginning to clean a brush absently on her smock. 'Poor Mr Arden is your asset. You're going to force him to learn yet another dreary monologue and then, inflict him upon some particularly rich individual. Am I correct?'

'Well, I certainly would not put it like that,' said Valentine with a snubbed air. 'It so happens that I heard just yesterday that a real, genuine patron of the Arts is visiting town. Freddie told me. Your words have inspired me, my dear Mrs Roberts. You make me see that I have been lax and unfocused. I have permitted myself to become discouraged. To drift. To lower myself and my genius. And now my intention is *carpere diem.*'

'Indeed. And so you should,' said Alexandra, absently pushing her hair back from her forehead and smudging a streak of ochre on her face as she turned again to the canvas. She glanced down at Mr Arden. 'But is he a bit ... insubstantial?'

'Well, I must say, I don't think you appreciate the talent of our young Hamlet. And I do wonder sometimes whether for a lady-artist, your eyes work quite so well as they should.'

Alexandra laughed. 'Well, I beg your pardon, I'm sure. Don't be offended! You wish to convert me, I know, to your viewpoint. The thing is, my friend,' she said, standing back from the sketch, 'for me, this is beauty, Val. Here. Look at those eyes!'

Valentine glanced at the painting again. 'Yes, yes, she's very "tolerable", as Mr Darcy might say. Womanly curves and all that. And by the way, you have a smear of paint on your face.'

Alexandra turned to the mirror above the mantel and began rubbing at the mark hurriedly with a turpentine-smelling rag. 'Oh, good lord, what a disaster! I must go and get ready. Go on, Mr Cabot, take your Hamlet with you. Put him to bed, for goodness' sake, I don't like sleeping bodies lying around. She'll arrive in an hour and I want Amy and Janet to be able to clear up properly before she does. They can't work with bodies lolling about ... oh, here is Mrs Jenkins. Bless you! How did you know I was about to ring? You should have sent one of the girls up.'

Elizabeth Jenkins the Cook and Housekeeper, who had entered the room with sedate and deliberate tread, inclined her head to Alexandra. 'You said to come up at ten sharp, ma'am, and I just heard the clock striking.'

'So, Mrs Jenkins, I have a sitting in one hour. But it's not an ordinary client. I want to make sure we are at our very best. So by that time, I want this room tidied and freshened, hearth swept, fire mended. Tea - or perhaps coffee would be better? And - oh, some other refreshments - for a quarter past eleven. Use the china with the pink petals and be sure to find the good sugar tongs this time…'

As Mrs Jenkins listened to Mrs Roberts's instructions, out of the corner of her eye she watched Mr Cabot prodding Mr Arden into wakefulness. He had been very deeply asleep with his face half-buried in a beadwork cushion. There was an indented pattern across his right cheek and an uncharacteristic flush on his face. She heard Mr Cabot say very quietly to Mr Arden, 'Wake up, lazy.' They were a rum pair, in her opinion. And that Mr Cabot was a bit of a bully to the younger one too. Her disdainful attention came back to the Missus.

'So don't use the Indian silver, it's so light and the pot has such a dent in it; use the new one, the Boyton set, looks so modern; oh and you'd better set up over here, on this little table,' Alexandra went on. 'We can sit and chat nicely, looking across the Square, and then I have the light too. And is there cream for the coffee? If not, send out for some. Though perhaps she does not care for coffee? But we must have it prepared, you know. Thank you, dear Mrs Jenkins.' She turned away, unknotting the ties of her smock at her back. 'What would I do without you?'

Mrs Jenkins thought Mrs Roberts looked pink and was a little overexcited. She didn't normally make a fuss over sitters; there were so many of them and they stayed for an hour or two and then wandered off. Mrs Jenkins considered a simple cup of tea more than enough for them; after all, all they were doing was sitting down. Not to mention the inconvenience with so much else to do in the house. It just showed how rich this here customer was and how the portrait was costed - did she charge by the square foot or the hour?

A rushed hour later, everything was prepared. Mrs Jenkins had the water heating in the kettle but she was lecturing them about coffee and tea and how to serve both at perfect heat and perfectly brewed.

'But Mrs Roberts won't get in a temper if they in't right, will she?' whispered Janet to Amy, round-eyed. She had only been in Mrs Roberts's employ for a relatively short while, rarely went into the parlour when guests were present and still lived in real dread of doing wrong.

'No, not her, she's one as crossed the desert on a donkey or some such. Mrs Jenkins told me about it. She did it when Mr Roberts was alive. She won't never fuss about nothing like that. And she wouldn't fuss, anyhow, in front of a guest,' said Amy, shining the flank of the slow-dripping coffee biggin with a corner of her apron.

'It's a funny house, don't you think?' ventured Janet. 'My mum thought it was funny. Her being a painter, and all her books, and having travelled in heathen places, and them funny boarding gentlemen and all them visitors coming through the front door. Theatricals they are, that's what mum said.'

'Don't you worry yourself about 'em,' said the more experienced Amy, with a sniff. 'The best thing about *them* is that you don't need to stand in dread of them. Gentlemen are trouble for us in our line of work. Theatricals are better.'

The brass bell labelled Front Door which hung in the row above the kitchen door jangled suddenly. Janet jumped guiltily.

'Tch! Don't jump so, you silly thing! I'll get the door this time, but you know it's going to be your job one day soon and you need to know what to do. You've got to start stepping up to the mark, you have.' With practised speed, Amy threw off her work apron and threw on the white lace-trim, smoothed her hair and flew up the stairs. Janet dithered near the kettle. She would have to assist in bringing up the things and she hated carrying heavy trays up the stairs: she was small and thin, at fourteen not yet fully grown. She was accustomed now to the Gentlemen, who mainly minded their own business and only appeared to enquire about shirts coming back from Mrs Lehmann's laundry or shoes that needed blacking; and to eat meals. She was still a little fussed about the 'Theatricals', mainly because she often caught surprising glimpses of them arriving or departing at odd hours of the day. And them in such fancy dress too. She wondered how Mrs Roberts allowed it.

*

George Arden was not feeling very well. Naturally, he had not intended falling asleep. He had intended sitting quietly and listening. This was his favourite thing to do. The wispy connections between words and thoughts often seemed unreliable, often misleading. It took a great deal to hold the pieces together, to make sense of everyone's cross-currents; and sometimes the effort was too much and he grew tired. He had been sitting in the armchair because that was where Valentine told him to sit, listening to Valentine, listening to Mrs Roberts, looking at the early morning sunlight filtering through the lace which cast a jumble of disconnected shadow-shapes on the walls and table in such a way that sliding pictures came and went. He had sat up straighter, tried harder to listen, to understand. The sketch kept attracting his attention: the lady looking back at you as you come towards her out of the dark interior of a cool temple and you find her there on the threshold, sharpening a knife - except Mrs Roberts had not painted a knife because she did not yet see it. The woman had commanding eyes, and the white light grazed the very edge of her cheek. And he could see it as it would become, how Alexandra Roberts would caress the flesh of the throat and the rich hair, the sheen and pile of it, ready to tumble down, so that the head was like a heavy peony, chestnut-red heavy peony - and he had fallen asleep. And in the dream, a woman with bandaged feet hobbled towards him across a vast cavern.

When they got upstairs to his bedroom, Valentine pushed him down onto the hard chair at the writing desk. It was festooned with clothes but he paid no attention to that. 'Look here, my dear boy. I have had the most superb idea. I am going to make a push for us, a real effort, because we cannot go on as we are. Our expenses are simply dreadful. Our debts are worse. Cigars and clothes and wine – well, very well, those are not necessarily your expenses personally, but you do benefit from them, you know. So. You and I will go to the club soon, as soon as I can arrange something, and you will be dressed in that lovely coat I purchased for a full ten shillings from the last production of *The Riven Heart* - the measurements are exactly yours and the shoes - those patents there – they're only half a size too small ...'

'But, why such a hurry?' asked Arden.

'Because we simply cannot go on as we are. Why do I have to repeat myself? Mrs A. has had some good fortune and it is high time that I got my share. Seize the day, seize the attention of the rich hungry moneybags who'll want to meet you!'

'Not again, please, Valentine.'

'Oh, tsk! Theatre people, theatre people, dear boy! I must assemble them in one place and then I can present you and make my pitch, like a barker at the fair, only far, far more genteel and calm but with a frisson of anticipation. And let me see, what do we need to provide?' he went on, rapidly searching through a drawer for black silk socks and knee-garters, and wondering if he had a set of cuffs and a decent collar, and spare studs. 'Yes, there are a good many purchases to be made before we can be said to be quite ready. Stage clothes, on reflection, will not do. It is all so obvious when seen up close, the fraying bits and the bits round the back which are tacked together. We must have decent attire or the entire idea is sunk. You see, Freddie Shortland tells me that Pollitt is in town. He is absolutely the ideal person.' He stopped and tutted. 'Why do you always look so blank when I talk to you?'

'Sorry,' murmured George.

'It is time to rise up, rise up, out of the gutter. When they see you, they will see the most promising young actor in London.'

'I'm not sure that it's absolutely truthful, Valentine. Because last night, the audience became quite restless and chatted amongst themselves and ...'

'That was not because of you, you silly boy. That was the snake dancer coming in and disturbing the tables at the back with her serpent creature festooned about her neck, the hussy, trying to get Lord Fettenden to pay attention to her full-blown and indeed blowsy charms. At the front, among those who were in range, my dear, they were mesmerised. Their eyes were welling with tears. Indeed, I saw several drops fall down in full view. Let me be the judge of quality. Why, my entire being is attuned to the theatre.'

George sighed quietly and Valentine drifted into his usual monologue. He was just wondering what it was that he was meant to be doing, when he heard a carriage drive up. There was a chime from the doorbell, followed shortly afterwards by the sound of feet trampling rapidly up the back kitchen stairs to the hall, then the front door being opened; the maid's voice and then her footsteps passing into the room below to announce a name.

He felt curious and wanted to look at the visitor, who would be waiting in the hall at this moment; and simultaneously troubled. He experienced the beginnings of a smothering sensation and a compelling need to escape the confines of the house. 'Do you know, I absolutely need to get some fresh air, Valentine,' he said suddenly, trying to loosen his collar. 'I am so sorry. I promise I will listen to you when I get back, but there is something not quite right with me. It all feels suffocating.' He stood up, catching his breath, hand on chest. 'A half-hour's walk will set me right.'

'Oh, well, I shall come with you then,' said Valentine, now sliding a comb through his thinning ginger hair and inspecting his portly image in the dusty tilt-mirror. 'I need a little constitutional and we can discuss our budget.'

'No, please, I beg you do not trouble yourself,' answered Arden as he escaped, descending the stairs as quickly as he could before Valentine could catch him. Suffocation. He pattered down to the hall, saw the door to the parlour was slightly ajar, did not like the fragrance from the visitor who had just this moment disappeared within. He drew back, pausing like a cat sensing a dog nearby and, turning his head to see what was there, was taken aback to see Albert Burroughs lurking by the hatstand in the hall. George froze and their eyes met for a long moment.

George could have passed by him to leave by the front door but he turned aside for the back stairs, his heart pumping. At the bottom of the steps, he found himself facing the back door, between the kitchen and the scullery, stupidly confused by the locks. There was a large bolt at the top, a heavy black chain and a rim latch in the middle. He reached up to draw back the bolt but it was not well oiled and gave a squeal of protest.

'Who is it? What are you doing?' a reedy scared voice said. He turned and saw one of the servants peeping out of the kitchen. Only Janet.

'Oh it's you, Mr Arden. Mrs Jenkins'll be down in a minute, if you want something. She's just gone up to do something.'

'Thank you,' he said. 'I don't want anything, I am so sorry to trouble you. And frighten you. I just wanted to go out of this door.'

'Well, that door is for tradesmen, Mr Arden. You ain't a tradesman, you are a gentleman. So you should use the front.'

'I don't think it matters, does it?' Arden asked. 'The door doesn't mind if I am a gentleman or not,' he added with a sudden little smile because she looked so comical standing there with her cap falling to one side.

'Ooh.' The girl considered this perspective for a moment, staring at him with her mouth slightly open. She had liked Mr George from the day he arrived in the house, not long after she herself took up her post. They had been sort of new together.

Mrs Jenkins appeared at the top of the stairs, peered at them from on high and bustled down at great speed. 'Oh. It's you, Mr Arden,' she said warily, as jealous of the red peony beadwork cushion as of Janet's virtue. 'Can I assist you, sir? It's just that we have a job of work to do here and Janet is under my instruction ...'

'I don't wish to impede your work, Mrs Jenkins,' said Arden, feeling that things were going off at a tangent. 'Could I please make an exit through this door? I -' He could not think of a reason to avoid the front door, but unexpectedly Mrs Jenkins said, 'Oh, you want to go out the back, sir? Nothing easier. Mr Cabot is always going out the back way.' And she shot the bolt, disengaged the chain and turned up the latch. George slipped through the door with a quiet word of thanks.

'Avoiding creditors,' said Mrs Jenkins wisely. 'Theatricals. Don't you mind 'em, Janet., they come and go as they need.'

CHAPTER FIVE

In the room upstairs, Alexandra had greeted her guest and ushered her towards the portrait. Minerva Atwell peeled off her kid gloves and stood before the large sketch on the easel as Alexandra nervously explained how it would express certain concepts about power and courage and beauty.

'Yes, I see how it will be done. I very much like your sketch, as a matter of fact. I like the ideas. It will take how many sittings to complete?' asked Minerva, scrutinising the canvas. 'Because the unfortunate thing is that just now, I fear, I can't spare a good solid run of time, even for such an interesting portrait.'

'A portrait like this will take between ten and twelve two hour sessions to complete the face and figure,' said Alexandra. 'There is no point pretending it will be a quick matter. I sense that no average effort can do the subject justice. Yours should not be a standard portrait, Mrs Atwell. But it should be undertaken in one particular room at one particular time of day.'

'H'mm. Yes. As it happens, this house would in fact be quite convenient for me to attend. It is on my way, you know. Very usefully situated. So, a considerable investment of time,' said Mrs Atwell thoughtfully. She sat down, regarding the sketch with head on one side. 'But I do like what you've done – it compares favourably with what I saw of your work on Mrs Flamborough's portrait, which first brought you to my attention. And is superior to the sketches of the other artists I viewed yesterday. The concept is even bolder – which is what I wanted. Something suggestive of power. Yes. I am decided. I have the final say, you understand, although it is the Bank's idea to have the thing done. The commission shall be yours.'

Alexandra almost laughed in surprise but managed to rein in her exultation and bowed her head. 'I am honoured, Mrs Atwell. I would above all like to paint you.'

41

'And I long to make a beginning,' said Minerva, 'but, as I said, I am a woman of business, and I seem not to be able to escape the pressures of my affairs. But there, that is the price of success. And I enjoy the combat of business, unusual though some may think it.'

'Well, it may be unusual in some people's eyes, Mrs Atwell, but my business, although messier than yours,' she said, indicating the pots of brushes and paints on the oilclothed table, 'has taught me that it takes courage to run one's own affairs in a man's world. It's that sense of determination that I want to convey in your portrait.'

Minerva smiled too, her eyes brightening, and inclined her head at the compliment. 'Oh, my business is quite messy too sometimes. I like to keep an eye on it though which means that I am obliged to travel regularly to oversee certain procedures in person to keep all as it should be. Should we postpone our beginning? Or could we make a start today?'

'Perhaps we should simply begin by discussing matters today and while we do, I would like to take the opportunity to make further studies of your face. And then let us make a firm agreement that eleven o'clock will be our rendezvous for several further meetings, as soon as you can spare the time.'

Minerva inclined her head again. 'That sounds admirable. I would love you to sketch me a little today. Should we have this hat off? I like the idea of a wild tumble of hair, as you've hinted in the sketch, both piled up and falling down.'

'Oh, let us first have some refreshment.' Alexandra walked over to the bell rope, saying, 'Tea, coffee, cake and so on, something like that?'

'Actually,' Minerva answered softly, 'My physician advises drinking only water, iced water - or very weak lemonade. My constitution is peculiar and sometimes excessively warming or stimulating food or drink disagree with it. I'll trouble you therefore only for a glass of water.'

Before Alexandra could return to sit down again, Amy had already appeared at the door bearing a tray, followed by Janet, whose cap had by now been adjusted and pinned satisfactorily. They made their way across the room and mutely began to arrange the things on the low table by the window seat in the bay. As she turned to leave with a burning face and a curtsey, Janet threw a shy but piercing glance at the guest, like pinning a butterfly into a collection. But she made her exit calmly enough and overheard Mrs Roberts saying, as she passed out of the room, 'Please bring some iced water and lemonade, Amy'.

Janet surged down the stairs, wanting to giggle, feeling her face and ears so red. 'My ears are that burning,' she exclaimed to Amy as she also arrived in the kitchen. 'They must be talking about me! Lord, whatever could they be saying?'

'Nothing good, you can be sure. Typical, ain't it, Mrs Jenkins? She don't want tea or la-de-da coffee, she wants la-de-da lemonade and iced water,' Amy said.

'Well, she's just fortunate that we've got some left-over bottles,' Mrs Jenkins said. 'Amy, look in the pantry for a bottle. And you, Janet, you put your coat on and run out and find old Stokey, he passed by not five minutes ago on his way back up the market, he'll be finishing the rounds. Ice!'

'She is so beautiful and genteel, that lady,' said Janet as she pulled on her coat. 'With an alabaster brow.'

'Genteel is not making a nuisance, and she is making a nuisance, in my opinion,' said Mrs Jenkins. 'And as for alabaster brow, you get them when you are rich, miss, and never have nothing to make you frown.'

'All it means,' called Amy from the pantry, 'is she don't go out in the sun and lolls about in a carriage all day.'

Mrs Jenkins snorted. 'Run and get the ice, quick!

Meanwhile, Alexandra was sipping coffee, listening to her guest. They had agreed on the delicate matter of a retaining fee and Mrs Atwell said she would send round a generous cheque that afternoon, which was all good news for Alexandra; but she was getting restless to begin work. As she watched her speaking, quite involuntarily, she began to see her in terms of planes and angles and light and shade and she became distracted even though Mrs Atwell had begun talking about her married life, and it was immensely discourteous to look inattentive when a widow discussed her late husband. Alexandra's own husband, Edward, had been buried these nine years. The subject was no longer painful to her, but she imagined that Mrs Atwell's bereavement must be far nearer. The woman looked scarcely above five-and-twenty.

She spoke with the formality of polite conversation but when she met Alexandra's gaze, an eager appraising intelligence was suddenly there. Alex felt as if her fingertips, reaching to the back of a dark cupboard, had brushed the tips of other fingers reaching out to hers. Like the ping of electricity, she thought in surprise. Then she became aware that there was a pause as if Mrs Atwell was expecting her to make a remark. Something made her ask clumsily, 'Were you not very young to be moving in high diplomatic circles?' She was fishing - she did not quite know why - for some hint of discontent within the marriage, a struggle remembered. Or something like that.

'The disparity in our ages, as you say, was interesting, but ours was a true love match. My first husband was a man of great personal charm and ability,' answered Minerva Atwell. 'When Joseph fell asleep in the Lord, I was naturally stricken. Utterly wretched. Our happiness had been so complete and was so abruptly cut off.'

'And it must have taken a great deal of determination to personally take on your late husband's business enterprise at such a young age,' Alexandra said, reflecting firstly that Mrs Atwell had implied that she had managed to squeeze two husbands into a very short space of time and secondly, that she had at last heard someone use the phrase 'fell asleep in the Lord' in general conversation, and that she would be sure to amuse Valentine with an anecdote later.

'Oh, there was no business enterprise at the time, dear Mrs Roberts. My Joseph was a diplomat and I was like a butterfly, accompanying him to Embassy balls. Although he was not a natural traveller, being rather physically delicate, he was ever eager to explore as best he could the lands in which we found ourselves - indeed it was he who introduced me to the pleasures of mule-riding in the mountains. Do not laugh, Mrs Roberts!' she declared, although Alex had shown no sign of doing so. 'I can assure you that I enjoy it immensely. Indeed, it was whilst exploring mountainous regions that we discovered what later became the inspiration for my enterprise. It was after I had been widowed, and only as the result of many years of study and experimentation that I took my first tentative steps into the business world.'

Alexandra was confused, but not able to ask how Mrs Atwell's youth could logically allow this to be. 'How inspiring,' was all she said.

'Ah, Mrs Roberts, I read thoughts, you know. You are thinking that I am too young to be in control of a business empire and to have had two marriages. Well, I will say this: that although my second husband is a subject I do not choose to discuss, he did have something to do with my success. And I reverted to the name of my first in order to conduct my business – and as for my youth, do you not know the nature of my business?'

'No, Mrs Atwell. I try to paint each subject directly, unfiltered by preconceptions,' she answered, not quite truthfully, 'so I never make enquiry about their personal history. Artists, you know, have to cultivate an impartial eye.'

'Well, my business is also centred upon the nature of beauty, Mrs Roberts, and how best to present and preserve it. And I believe I am my own best advertisement: for the product of my manufacture is Atwell's Beauty Balm.' She sat back, smiling.

'If you wish,' said Alexandra solemnly, 'I can inscribe the words Atwell's Beauty Balm above your head in the portrait.'

Minerva laughed. 'I was not looking to advertise my discoveries, although I think you'd find them interesting. It is such a pity that I have less time than I would like to enjoy our conversation. Please, Mrs Roberts, help me remove my hat. I am dying to try some sketches.'

Alexandra stood up and began tentatively to pull out the long pearl-topped hat pins holding Minerva's delicate hat in place. It was a neat straw affair, one side a shapely fold, the other all artificial crocus and pleated purple ribbon. It looked like a hat that was willing Spring to come early. When she removed it, a perfume rose up from the sleek chestnut-red hair beneath.

She walked over to the table and took up her notebook, penknife and several pencils and sat down again. She kept herself busy sharpening the pencils. 'It is the structure of the face that I need to study, the relation between the features. Please, just turn your head a little that way – yes, like that, just look towards the curtain trim, that puts your profile in exactly the right position.' She sketched in silent concentration.

Minerva stayed perfectly still for a while. 'Am I permitted to speak?' she asked.

'By all means, but please hold your head as still as may be.'

'Well, I'll amuse myself by telling you what is going through this head while it remains so very still. I am minded of the carpets of the Rudbar region. Your charming Turkish cushions over there, those are the culprits distracting me. I know you told me to look at the curtain trim but I do have a roving eye and it can't be helped. It's that motif there, if you can recall it, of the *mina-khani*, the linked daisy design. I remember shopping with Mr Atwell among the bazaars, so intriguing, and loading our servants with impossibly intricate rugs. Afterwards we sought out the villages where they were made. Extraordinary places, Mrs Roberts. Are you much travelled yourself?'

'Well, to a certain extent. I was very fortunate in my marriage, Mrs Atwell, as were you. Mr Roberts had business which took him frequently to Cairo,' said Alexandra, as she sketched. 'He had emancipated views, and I benefited from them. Without his protection and encouragement, I might rarely have strayed beyond the confines of British society whilst I was there. But he took me to see many wonders in Egypt. I was lucky. I too became quite a seasoned mule rider. But it was many years ago. Alas, I have never set foot out of England since Mr Roberts died. I'm not tempted to mix with the society of middle-aged ladies trotting about the globe looking for another husband. And I dislike the behaviour of our countrymen abroad. They are stultifying. It is all money-making, money-making, and contracts for building railways and laws and snobbery. I apologise if I offend you, diplomatic wife as you were.'

'Oh, you can't offend me by saying things like that, Mrs Roberts!' said Minerva in a lively tone, but still keeping her face turned correctly. 'In our defence, I imagine that much the same may have been said by any Italian lady of the days of the Roman Empire. In fact, I can hear a voice from the past now: let's call her Claudia Livilla who lived in the wretched damp provincial town of Londinium nineteen centuries ago, the bored wife of some governor or other. And she's saying "The Romans abroad are stultifying. It is all money-making, money-making, contracts for building roads and laws and circuses and orgies ...".'

Both women laughed.

'The life of a Roman lady was rather interesting, then,' said Alexandra, finding herself refreshed by Minerva's departure from good taste. 'But where was your husband stationed?'

'Cairo at first,' said Minerva. 'I loved it just as you did. In those days, I could bear the heat. Things are different now. But I shall never forget my first sight of the Great Sphinx, coming upon it at sunset, half buried in the desert sand, that ruined face, veiled in the mystery of the ages – '

Alexandra paused and looked up. 'You know the Fellahin call it Abu al Hul, the Terrifying One? Because there is something terrifying about great age, is there not, Mrs Atwell?'

Minerva turned her face and met her eyes. 'Oh, yes. Age is terrifying. But let me resume my pose!' She positioned her head and eyes as before.

'I regret that the process of sitting can be so tiring and boring,' said Alexandra. 'Please do talk about anything you want. I cannot offend you, you say, and I assure you, you can't offend me.'

Minerva made a little sound of amusement. She said, 'If you say you can't be offended, I am awfully tempted to test you.' She waited a moment for Alexandra to respond but when she saw that Alexandra merely smiled and sketched, Mrs Atwell went on more soberly, 'But to return to ancient wonders, can you imagine, I was lucky enough to see Priam's Treasure before it was smuggled out of Anatolia! It was pure good fortune, of course, but such a sight! I travelled through all those lands, you know, but best of all was old Persia. Ah, the evenings, Mrs Roberts, the warm evenings when the very sky turns purple! And the slim black cypress trees with a golden moon peeping between them.' Minerva closed her eyes in luxurious memory, which may not all have been theatrical.

'How wonderful to have visited the country of Khayyám!'

'But you should go!' said Minerva, clearly pleased with the reference. 'Go now, before the Russians take it all over and turn the people into Cossacks.'

'Perhaps, one day, if ever I find a travelling companion,' said Alexandra.

They fell silent and the ticking of the clock was loud. Various distant domestic sounds from within the quiet house drifted into the room. It was nearly lunch time. Alexandra decided the sketches had gone fairly well, though they were not as accurate yet as she wished. Still missing was the vitality in the woman's eyes, the drama in her manner. She laid them aside when Mrs Atwell announced that time had run out for today. She rose to admire the work with exclamations of delight. Then she began to replace her hat, standing at the mirror.

Suddenly she said, 'Do you know, the most wonderful idea has come to me! As I told you, I am to be away in a few weeks. Part of that commitment is to visit a concern of mine in the West Country. How would it be, Mrs Roberts, if you were to accompany me? I have no travelling companion, you know. We could talk about archaeology and history and poetry. You could do some wonderful work there. And if you keep me company, you could make as many studies of my face as you fancy; and take full advantage of this deliciously exacting winter light.'

Alexandra found herself answering, 'That would be delightful, Mrs Atwell'; and felt her face suddenly too hot, like a schoolgirl's. 'But like you, I have work, commissions to undertake. It would probably be difficult to re-arrange everything – unless you felt it was essential for your portrait.'

Mrs Atwell turned away from her own reflection to face her. 'You are merciful, Mrs Roberts, because you've left me with some hope. You can't imagine how boring it is for me, travelling all alone, and never having any intelligent conversation whatsoever. You can't imagine how tiresome, always to be chit-chatting with invalids at the Adsullata. Do permit me to persuade you … because I believe you want me to persuade you. So let's continue my persuasion in a more comfortable manner over lunch. I sense that we have a great deal in common.' She smiled and at that moment the sun came out. She was lit like an angel.

CHAPTER SIX

George was surprised to catch sight of Janet racing down the pavement on the other side of the street. She was ahead of him and could not see him; but when he waved at her departing back, she slowed for a moment and looked up at the sky. Then she trotted on. He carried on in the same direction, finding that walking in the cool day was helpful. He was not quite sure what had come over him just now. There had been an urgent sense of smothering, associated with the visitor to the house. The shadow of Albert Burroughs, standing silently in the hall, had upset him too. Sometimes he felt the man's attention like a cold blowfly crawling across his skin.

He concentrated on watching things, like the pavement or the cold-tin reflection of sunlight in the wet gutters. Walking more and more slowly along the quiet street, he drifted towards the noise of a little market up ahead, paying attention to more things outside of himself: the houses with red roofs and porches and odd little windows amidst the cream brickwork and the whistle of starlings. Bluetits whisked among naked twigs and red buds, and the sun ignited the yellow lichen on tree bark. A contented tabby cat was munching up a scrap of food under a hedge.

Suddenly, he found himself almost bumping into Janet Fairlight. She was standing in the middle of the pavement, holding a canvas bag in both hands which she was swinging gently to and fro as she stood talking to an elderly lady in a little old-fashioned bonnet with a bunch of dark cherries pinned to the ribbon above the left ear. Both of them turned in surprise when George came to a sudden stop, inches from barging into them, looking alarmed. 'I do beg your pardon!' he said, holding up both hands.

'Mr Arden,' exclaimed Janet, looking pleased to be interrupted. 'You gave me a shock.'

'I really do beg your pardon,' said George again.

'I was just running back to Mrs Jenkins,' said Janet. 'I just got the ice from Mr Stokes. Look!' She held up the bag with its newspaper-wrapped load.

'Ice, is it?' asked the lady, peering into the bag. 'Then get along straight away. What are you doing chatting here in the street? Mrs Jenkins will scold if it melts. You should have brought a cork box. And in this weather, I wonder who on the Good Lord's earth would be needing ice?'

'Mrs Roberts's visitor wants it, Mrs Skipton. Oh, she is like a fair lady in a story! She's like a queen. And she wants iced water or lemonade. Not tea or coffee at all even though we are using the most heavenly pink tea service and coffee cups. It is always so refined at Mrs Roberts's. And, Mr Arden, I have to inform you that we are going to have to use up the last of your lemonade.'

'Well, never mind about it,' said George.

'Bless me, hurry up!' said the old woman sharply. 'I'll tell your mother I saw you dawdling in the market place. Girls today!'

Janet flushed and began trotting back to Mrs Jenkins.

'Came out without her hat, you see,' said Mrs Skipton. 'Elizabeth Jenkins needs to keep an eye on those girls there, three of 'em, a handful of trouble at their age, just as I do with Daisy Etherington at Mrs Day's establishment.'

'Mrs Harriet Day?' asked George with an air of remembering something. 'I am acquainted with Mrs Day.'

'Indeed, sir? Well, I am the housekeeper for Mrs Day, as I was of her mother's before her. Fifty years with the family,' said Mrs Skipton, beginning to gather up the handles of the two bags she had put down on the ground.

'Ah,' said George. 'Can I help you with those bags?'

Mrs Skipton let him pick up the bags, and as he did so, he noticed that Janet had dropped her handkerchief. He picked it up and put it in his pocket, meaning to give it back to her later.

'I appreciate your carrying those bags, young man. Now. This way. We can avoid the market if we take this side street. And I must mention that the costermonger is selling the most wormy apples ever seen.'

George supposed this to mean that he should bring the bags all the way to Harriet Day's house, so he meekly walked beside her. He was not sure if he was meant to speak or wait until spoken to (he had the same difficulty with Mrs Jenkins: cooks and housekeepers were ladies of immense power and status in his eyes). Nevertheless, he accompanied her all the way home; where he spent an hour with Mrs Day drinking tea and enjoying an unfamiliar sense of freedom.

*

Meanwhile, Valentine Cabot was fidgetting quietly while Madame Baranovsky read her Tarot cards. Her room, heavily curtained, admitted no ray of sunlight. Three wax candles in a silver candelabrum were reflected in the polished wood of the table, which was partially spread with a plain silk square of dark blue.

Madame Baranovsky had been something of a disappointment to Valentine. The name had sounded interestingly exotic to his London ears and he'd expected to be ushered into the presence of a tall, wildly handsome dowager, perhaps attired in white furs or something. In fact, she had wiry greying hair, dressed in solid uneventful black and spoke with a distinct West Country burr. Although she worked with a chilly, competent air, Valentine could not see how any of the pictures on the cards made sense, except the kind of sense you get in a fever-dream, when a dog can turn into a daffodil. His witty comments on the matter had been received with a stony face by the lady herself, while the other gentleman present, Mr Pollitt, had gone so far as to shush him. At this, he tried to breathe more quietly as the guidance was given; although he suspected it would not be in his favour.

Mr Jerome Pollitt also sat very still, further up the table and nearer the lady, regarding Madame Baranovsky with great seriousness and a certain cat-like primness. Valentine stole glances at his face from time to time. In repose, it looked very solemn indeed, even rather anxious, despite its frame of golden hair and the large blue eyes; but he could not honestly tell whether Pollitt was acting or not. He wondered how much longer this might all take and hoped it would be worth it. He was still a little surprised at finding himself in this situation at all, entailing as it did an uncharacteristic deviation from his original Plan. And Valentine, once set on a course, was usually capable of swamping smaller vessels in his wake.

The Plan had all come about after George Arden had disappeared that morning, saying he felt suffocated. It had been most vexing and partly in a spirit of vengeance, Valentine - in stockinged feet - had crept into George's room and looked through all of his belongings, including under the mattress and behind the curtain pelmet, to see if the dear boy had stowed away any unwanted excess money.

'It is for the greater good,' he reasoned to himself as he searched. 'Quantities of future money will come from spending – no, investing – a little present money. Nobody will be impressed if I, Valentine Cabot, am found to be walking about London with nothing in my pocket to pay for a bottle or two. It just won't do. A gamble needs a stake.'

To his relief, he found George did indeed have a small store of money in a sock rolled up and shoved into a boot. Valentine took it out and counted it. It was by no means sufficient; but somehow, he willed himself to believe more would come if this were invested wisely today. And he needed to invest it in a person of influence, a person who understood the theatre, who appreciated Art, who was prepared to take a risk. Mr Pollitt would be that person.

'But when you think it through,' he often told people, 'a West End hit amounts to very little. It's all actors and lighting – as for the plot and the dialogue, why, I could write any number of pieces if I chose. The financial backing is the thing that counts.' He had said this to George just last week too, sitting on the edge of the stage at the Parnassus with a glass of gin in his hand, in between bellowing directions about how to position his arms and when to turn his face to show his profile. And as he knelt on the circular rag-rug by the bed, an empty sock in one hand and the money in the other, he knew he must begin softening up his first choice of target this very day.

A little later Valentine sauntered along the street, planning to walk towards the lodgings of Freddie Shortland. Freddie's work for a publishing house had previously brought him into contact with Mr Pollitt; and it was Shortland who had procured Valentine an introduction to this influential patron. Pollitt, who was not normally resident in London (and therefore beyond Valentine's reach on a daily basis), was currently residing somewhere tantalisingly close by and Freddie might know where to find him. At the very least, Freddie would be good for a hand of cards and a civilised glass or two.

As it happened, by extraordinary luck, an elegant figure was actually coming down the steps of Shortland's lodgings just as Valentine rounded the corner of the street. Valentine saw him before he saw Valentine, or things would have gone differently. So it was that his victim had no opportunity either to delay leaving the house or rush off in another direction. Mr Cabot fell upon him, scooped him up and, insinuating an arm through his, began chatting effusively. And it was beyond Valentine Cabot's limited powers of perception to notice the resentful sigh his hostage exhaled.

'My dear Pollitt, what a surprise! I had no idea you were visiting the swamp of corruption! Not that I mean Shortland is a swamp of corruption, of course. He's a very decent chap, as a matter of fact. London, I mean London, the *capital* of corruption. How gorgeous to see you. You look stunning!'

'Thank you, thank you. One does one's best.' Jerome sighed again and shook his head. 'I came hoping to sort out something on behalf of our poor Aubrey with his engravers. It's quite beyond his power to oversee matters and I have been waiting for my *Bathylle* for some time now.'

'Oh? Where is Mr Beardsley at present?'

'Menton, for the agreeable climate. God help him.'

'Shocking,' agreed Valentine, shaking his head too. 'We are losing the best of us. Our very best talent plucked away. Not that Mr Beardsley has yet been plucked away.' He cleared his throat and, noticing Pollitt's expression, added hurriedly, 'And let us hope that he is not plucked away at all. But it concerns me deeply, the very thought.'

'Aubrey is a very dear friend of mine. I would be visiting him now, if circumstances only permitted – but everyone's in France these days. Except Oscar,' he added languidly as he lit a cigarette.

'Oh?' said Valentine, dropping his voice discreetly. 'And have you information about where he is now – after he was released from the, after the, you know?'

'He was in Dieppe last August but I think he's in Naples now,' said Pollitt. 'I would go abroad myself, but for the fact that something keeps me in Cambridge for the time being.'

'A business engagement? Because, as it happens I was on my way to talk to, um, Edwardes, you know, of the Gaiety Theatre, about a business opportunity, something very exciting – but since we have so fortuitously come across one another, it would far suit my personal preference to offer the opportunity to you. You being a person of taste and ...'

'No, not business,' said Pollitt firmly, ignoring the rest of Valentine's speech. 'He's staying with me here in London, picking up supplies of woollen underwear or whatever it is. He likes climbing mountains. So you see, I'm actually rather busy these days.'

'Climbing mountains? You?'

'Not I. My friend. He likes it.'

'Oh, I see. Then let me tell you about the quite extraordinary opportunity that's come up, so tempting for gentlemen with a sense of adventure who are – er - ready to scale the heights of success and reach the very peak ...'

Pollitt was ambushed. He was made to hear all about the unrepeatable opportunity that was now presenting itself to people like himself, not to mention his mountain-climbing friend (should he prove to be equally discerning and wealthy).

As it had gradually become apparent that Cabot had no intention of relinquishing his grip ('Like a blessed bulldog,' thought Jerome), the gentle Pollitt had to extemporise a plan of escape. It was not in his nature to offend and when, quite by chance, they found themselves walking along a certain street that he recognised, an innocent scheme occurred to him. He stopped and held up an imperious hand. 'Say no more, my dear Cabot. It is as if the voice of an Angel had just spoken in my ear or heart, or somewhere internal. This very house, this house you see before you, contains someone who can give very sound advice on matters of business. I beg you to enter now with me and let us consult her about your plan, She of the Third Eye.'

Valentine looked doubtful. 'But, pray, my dear Pollitt, to what purpose?'

'Oh, I never make decisions about investments without consulting the Unseen Powers. As a matter of fact, my friend is very hot on that sort of thing and has spoken endlessly, absolutely endlessly, about the importance of it all. If she says go ahead, then, go ahead we shall.'

Valentine had waited for a good five minutes in the vestibule, sitting on a tapestry-backed chair and staring at an ebony hat stand, while Jerome talked privately with Madame Baranovsky in order, he said, to persuade her to allow a less illumined individual into her presence. 'It's complicated, old chap. These mystic types live on a higher plane, most of the time, and people like you and me, well we bring them down to earth with a bump. One of us is bad enough but two, well, imagine!'

After only a brief discussion, however, Mr Pollitt had persuaded the lady and she had permitted Valentine to enter the sanctum. Thus he was now wondering how he could possibly influence the fall of the cards to favour his investment plan. He had more than a sneaking suspicion that he'd been set up. That hurried consultation when they first arrived, it was nothing to do with some rot about higher planes. Pollitt had done what Valentine would have done in his place: he'd slipped the old girl half-a-crown to make sure her reading gave him a let-out from the business proposal.

'It is unclear to me, Mr Pollitt,' said Madame Baranovsky after due consideration of the cards. She shook her head. 'Your spread is full of the Greater Arcana, which speaks of matters of the Soul. It deigns not to show me matters of mundane finance. Someone you care about is destined for high things.'

'High things?' said Jerome, blinking. 'That'll be the Alps.'

'Higher, higher, dear Mr Pollitt,' said Madame Baranovsky patiently. 'Of a higher nature, a higher vibrational plane entirely. Your questions are always to be resolved on the subtle planes.'

Valentine cleared his throat politely. 'And may I ask, Madame, whether there's anything pertinent to the question of the Theatre?'

'These cards speak not of the mundane, as I have already told you, sir,' said the lady. 'In order to get a clearer answer, it will be necessary to undertake another spread. But there is a great spiritual influence in your life, Mr Pollitt.'

'Well, if it's a spiritual influence, it certainly isn't Valentine's,' murmured Pollitt. 'My friend goes on a good deal about the Higher Planes and Veiled Things, Madame Baranovsky, so quite probably it's him.'

As Madame Baranovsky gathered up the cards for another go, Valentine saw his chance. 'Oh,' he groaned, suddenly clutching his head. He shuddered slightly, rolling his eyes upwards. 'Oh! I feel a strong vibratorial force affecting me. Oh, the ectoplasm! Help me, Madame Baranovsky!'

Madame Baranovsky looked up with the air of a governess and said, 'You are suffering the effects of the presence of my Guides.

They are particularly highly evolved and can affect those whose subtle bodies have not been trained to handle the force of their auras. Breathe deeply, sir, breathe deeply. Think of the colour violet. Your chakras are unused to this kind of thing.'

'No, no,' moaned Valentine, still clutching his head. 'I've been getting these fits, getting these fits since I met him.'

'Met whom?' asked Madame Baranovsky.

'Arden, George Arden. He ... he is particularly highly evolved too.'

Jerome Pollitt looked annoyed. 'No, it can't be, Cabot. It's her guides, not your blessed George Arden.'

'Yes, her Guides are here and they're telling me about him. Right now, it's Arden ... I just have this vision, a vision of light coming into my Third Eye. Bright as anything,' breathed Valentine.

'Speak, sir. Let the vision express itself through your means,' advised Madame Baronovsky.

'I see a golden flow of wealth, and a wonderful building lit up with hundreds and hundreds of stars, and a crowd of finely dressed people streaming into the building. Happiness, great happiness, and laughter... ah, the vision fades ... but here are three figures approaching ... Lo! It is I, and it is Mr Pollitt here - we appear to be crowned with gold - and well, here's George Arden. His name seems to be in golden letters in the sky ... no, the vision, the vision, it is gone.' Valentine covered his eyes with his hand and bowed his head.

'Ah, the sense of exaltation leaves him, you see, Mr Pollitt,' said Madame Baranovsky sympathetically.

Pollitt sighed heavily.

'And how is one to interpret this vision?' asked Valentine, raising his head wide-eyed as if awaking from sleep. 'What can it all mean?'

'I think I know exactly what it means,' said Pollitt bitterly to himself. More loudly he said, 'Please, Madame Baranovsky, time is short. I'm sure Mr Cabot could come back here again on his own and have a reading for himself and get into communion with your Guides any time he wants to. He does, after all, live in London and not too far away either. Could you please give me the guidance *I asked you for when I first arrived?*' He spoke the last words with an emphasis that was not lost on Valentine.

Madame Baranovsky looked long and hard at him while she shuffled the cards solemnly. Valentine thought she was none too pleased with Jerome. She got him to cut them three times. She laid them out and looked at them, frowning. 'There is clearly such a great deal happening on the Astral Plane. You know, do you not, that Mercury is retrograde? Therefore I am not to be held responsible for muddles in your thinking or planning. You should return to me for a reading every day in order to get a better insight into your best path. I will go so far as to say this, however: do not make rash choices, Mr Pollitt. Here is the Fool, the greatest of the Trumps. You see he is Nought, he has no number? Who can say where he shall go? But be sure not to walk blindly over the edge of the cliff.'

'I've no intention of jumping off a cliff, Madame Baranovsky,' said Jerome sulkily after he had waited a while in vain for further elucidation. She had fallen silent with her eyes closed, as if to announce that she was now undertaking a profound inner journey and wouldn't be at home again until tomorrow.

'Well, if that's all you have to say, I expect we should be getting along. At least you've warned me against playing the fool – or a fool with a play.'

As the pair walked away down the street, there was such antipathy emanating from Mr Pollitt that even Valentine was able to apprehend it. He refrained from commenting upon the Tarot consultation for a good five minutes. After that time had elapsed, it became impossible to restrain himself.

'So,' he whispered confidentially, 'the lady was very clear, wasn't she?'

'Extremely,' agreed Pollitt loudly, looking directly ahead.

'She was warning you, wasn't she?'

'She certainly was,' agreed Pollitt, still looking directly ahead of him.

'She was warning you not to make a fool of yourself … by missing an enormously important opportunity.'

'She was warning me not to make a fool of myself by running headlong off a cliff, pursued by a little annoying ... creature. Or ending up with all my belongings in a bundle over my shoulder due to losing all my money.' He stopped suddenly on the corner of the pavement, shaking off Valentine's limpet grip. 'All these blessed peregrinations and I've lost my way. Damn it, Cabot. I'm meeting my friend at the Army and Navy. How in the devil's name do I get there from here?'

'Victoria Street. It's not far. Look, down over the other side of the square, behind that church, there's Cambridge Street. You know that, don't you?' said Valentine encouragingly in soothing tones, intent on blandishing his victim into compliance. 'That's where Beardsley used to have those salons. That's where we first met. All we have to do is walk up here, look, twenty minutes toddle, I'll take you, and while we walk, let me tell you about a wonderful dining club I know ...'

Pollitt had no choice. He had been contemplating a bid for freedom for a long time, planning to stalk away in solitary splendour; but since he discovered he was lost amidst the squares and streets of Pimlico, he must needs depend on Valentine Cabot for his guidance. Jerome had begun to loathe Valentine. The man was a blunt instrument. He began to pity George Arden, whoever he was.

'Oh, very well,' he sighed. 'Lead on. But let go of my arm, for Pete's sake, you're pulling me off balance.'

Valentine made the decision to continue sticking to Pollitt like a limpet, however long it took, until he could persuade him to meet George Arden at the Dame Fortune's Club.

Much later, after Pollitt had finally shaken Valentine off by jumping into a cab with his friend outside the Army and Navy Store, he said, taking off his hat and smoothing his thick fair hair, 'You know, that damned fellow is going to be a nuisance. I just know it. He'll follow us everywhere. He's determined to take us into some awful, third-rate, smelly club and meet his awful, third-rate, smelly little tart of an actor. I won't do it. We must escape. Let's go back to Cambridge.'

'You know I have business to attend to here,' said his friend.

'Then I hold you responsible. You must warn me if you see him approaching and we'll sneak away.'

'It would be unlike you to sneak anywhere, Jerome,' said his companion, concentrating on a catalogue of Alpine equipment. 'Just don't encourage him. You encourage everyone. Stop doing it.'

'It is very difficult for me to turn off my personal charm. It bubbles out naturally and gets sprinkled all over the place. I can't be responsible for how people react when they get sprinkled. You should know that.'

His friend laughed, without looking up.

CHAPTER SEVEN

Later that afternoon, Janet was catching up on the brasses. She was sitting alone in the scullery and very slowly, with tiny circular movements, applying paste of rape oil and rottenstone to 'them blimmin great candlesticks' which usually stood on the marble-topped sideboard in the hall. She had a lot left to do but was devoting a disproportionate amount of time to staring at the green glaze tiling and singing all the way through *Alice, Where Art Thou?* to enjoy the echoes bouncing off the walls. It was a favourite of her mother's. She had just reached the pathetic climax, 'Oh there, 'mid the starshine, Alice, I know art thou', (after the narrator had looked 'he'enward' a fair few times in the course of the verses) when she heard a little tap at the back door.

She got up, rubbed her hands on the sacking apron worn for brasses, and crept to the back door, putting first her eye to the crack and then saying, 'Who is it?'

'It's me, it's - it's Mr Arden. Please can I come in this way?'

Janet reached up and slid the bolt back, unhooked the chain and unlatched the door. That Mr Arden was standing out there in the cold, looking slightly brighter than when she saw him in the market place. 'You feeling all better now, sir?' she asked politely as he stepped inside.

Arden darted a look upwards. 'That depends,' he said. 'Is the lady gone?'

'What, Mrs Roberts?'

'No, not Mrs Roberts, the other one, the one who arrived this morning, just before I left.'

'Oh, you should have said. Yes, she has gone and Mrs Roberts with her.' Janet had been thinking about the morning's visitor all the while she sang about Alice being in the starshine, and was garrulous.

59

'Mrs Jenkins is having a lie-down, because when I got back here, lunch was cancelled and all her work was ruined, she said, because of that chicken pie. They went out together to somewhere a lot swankier than Mrs Jenkins's poor pie, she said. She was cross and went off upstairs. Not that she said that to Mrs Roberts but it struck her to the heart like a knife blade, she said. So the lady went, sir.'

'Thank you,' said Arden, who had listened carefully but without quite comprehending everything Janet said. He turned to go upstairs. He went very quietly. He walks as silent, Janet thought, as one of them theatrical visitors.

When he got upstairs to his room, George found that Valentine was lying on his back fully clothed on George's own bed with his eyes closed and his mouth open, emitting an occasional gurgle. He had at least kicked his shoes off: a small hole in a sock revealed a pink, grimy toe. He paused in the doorway, seeing that he was dozing and, smelling the breath of alcohol in the room, not wanting to wake him. But he felt so very tired he needed a doze himself. He supposed the only thing to do would be to lie down on Valentine's bed instead of his own.

His gaze fell on the toe of a boot protruding from the darkness beneath the bed. He knew instantly that it was not where he'd left it. Valentine must have been raiding his room again. That money he had been putting aside for rent day would no doubt now be in Valentine's pocket. The boots had been left under the bed because they were not only too small to be comfortable to walk in for any distance, they also happened to be adorned with oversized tin spurs. They were part of the costume for *The Grenadier's Farewell, A Poem of Waterloo*. Valentine had got him a regular slot performing such pieces - in between the suggestive shadow diorama and the snake dancer - at the Revue Parnassus, Soho.

George could learn lines by ear with facility. He could not remember where or when he had mastered the trick. He tried to explain it by saying that poetry seemed to reside in a different area of his head and he could produce it as needed. But it was always Valentine who handled the money and gave George an appropriate (in Valentine's opinion) portion of the fee – and as the act was getting rebooked, they were able to survive. However, the snake dancer at the Parnassus had once taken him aside and, whilst trying unsuccessfully to seduce him, warned him that Valentine would steal him blind. George had thanked her politely for her interest and for her point of view, and thought about her advice quite a lot afterwards. It was this counsel which had prompted him to begin saving a little money in a sock under his bed. With a sinking sense of disappointment, he turned away and walked across the landing into Valentine's room.

He sat down on the hard chair, still festooned with clothes, which stood near the desk. Resting his elbow on a knee, George put his cheek in his palm and looked vacantly at the carpet. Motes of dust settled slowly, disturbed by his passage. There was a burn in the middle of a stylised woven flower where Cabot had accidentally stubbed out a cigarette, and another unidentifiable dark stain over here where a scroll of foliage escaped into abstraction. Amy Matthews had apparently not been into the room to sweep it today. Scattered across the broad surface like the details of a landscape were ginger hairs, flakes of ash from the 'Wills Woodbines' that Valentine smoked and a crumpled card from the cigarette packet depicting a ship in full sail. An old newspaper lay discarded beside the bed where Cabot had been reading the horse racing results; and, just glimpsed further into the darkness, three rolled up socks, a brown farthing and the corner of a letter. All little fragments of Valentine. George yawned, lifted his head and stretched. As he did so, he glimpsed a gentleman in a powdered wig walking silently past the doorway. He ignored him and walking over to Valentine's bed, cast himself down for an hour's sleep.

Later that evening, Alexandra arrived home with half an hour to spare before dinner. She went straight upstairs to her dressing room, taking off her hat and throwing her bag onto the floor. Then she sat down heavily in the padded swivel chair in front of the desk, feeling exhaustion pulling at her like an additional force of gravity. Physically tired, unlacing and levering off her boots with a weary hand, her mind was still running like an ant hill.

It had been so stimulating to wander through the Antiquities with such a vibrant companion. Minerva Atwell was so alive to what was ranged so dully in glass cases. Indeed, she declared that the British Museum was a kind of second home for her and that her favourite pastime was seeking out these poor fragments made by the hands of long-dead humanity. To her mind, she told Alexandra, they were so full of pathos, speaking of the inexorable passage of Time; and yet so uplifting, speaking also of the persistence of Art.

Alexandra felt inspired. She was determined to take a sketch pad to the museum and work on her own interpretation of some of the glories there. Not the large stuff, she told herself, patting at the sole of one of her damp stockings and half wondering whether to change them; no, the little things, the things which Minerva had made her see. A child's crude toy horse; a broken chip of painted stone on which was preserved a single lustrous eye; a woven sandal yet betraying the impression of a narrow foot: these were glories, large with the dimension of emotion. Minerva had brought them alive for her as they walked and talked and compared impressions. The luncheon had extended to fill the afternoon, the afternoon could have extended to fill the evening, but that Minerva had remembered an engagement; and so Alexandra had found herself alone, rattling home in a cab through the busy streets.

On descending for dinner, she found that Mr Cabot and Mr Arden were sitting opposite each other, both looking rather glum and inclined to silence. From time to time, Valentine complained of a headache. Mr Burroughs was as inflexibly taciturn as usual and kept himself at the far end, apparently concentrating on his soup and steak; but something about him gave her the impression that he was listening to the conversation as she began to talk to Dafydd Williams, who made a more sympathetic audience.

As Alexandra spoke about the fascinations of the Egyptian and Assyrian Galleries, she was surprised to discover that Mr Williams was himself an occasional visitor. He spoke diffidently, in his pleasant Welsh accent, of his emotions when contemplating the Mummies, the Rosetta Stone or the mighty fist of Ramses II (out of the corner of her eye, she noticed a certain restlessness on the part of Valentine in the course of his rhapsody). Alexandra refused to be put off and joined in as he speculated what further splendours might be uncovered in Mesopotamia or Egypt and how these intriguing clues brought alive the mysteries of remote antiquity.

'I was so fortunate today, Mr Williams,' said Alexandra. 'I was in company with one who has herself visited some of these archaeological digs and seen treasures in situ. I can hardly imagine how gripping it must be to unearth such things after twenty centuries or more lost in darkness! But Mrs Atwell had the good luck to see Priam's Treasure when it was dug up – few had that privilege, I understand.'

'Indeed?' said Mr Williams, his eyes lighting up with recognition. 'Priam's Treasure, the Jewels of Helen! Why, it was only the other week I was looking at a photograph, I'm sure of it, in a magazine with a picture. I think it was the Illustrated London Omnibus. I left it over there on the shelf. With your permission, Mrs Roberts, I'll bring it here to the table and we can look ourselves upon this wonderful stuff.'

Mr Williams went to the bookshelves and found the magazine. He riffled through until he came to the piece he wanted, opened it wide, folding the page back as he returned to his seat. Valentine tried to hide the fact that he was dying to see the picture by loudly addressing Mr Arden on the subject of some theatrical business or other. Alexandra directed her attention steadily to the magazine.

She saw a portrait photograph of a lady with striking dark eyes and arched eyebrows, gazing thoughtfully down to her left. Her hair was adorned with a thick shining band, apparently made of hundreds of flat golden beads hanging like a curtain over the forehead. Strings of gold fell either side, framing the face, while a rich necklace of threaded beads lay on her breast.

'What a discovery that must have been!' said Dafydd, shaking his head. 'Was it found in a box or an urn, do you think, Mrs Roberts? And why would they have strung the beads just so? For the silken thread or whatnot would have rotted, now, would it not? Unless they are joined on the finest gold wire. Who can say what the original construction would have been?'

'How interesting!' said Alexandra.

'Oh, how very gaudy,' sighed Valentine, finally allowing himself a glance towards the magazine and then at George, who was looking downcast. He had barely touched his food. This kind of behaviour always annoyed Valentine. He was just sulking about the money, silly boy. There would be much, much more money in the future if he could get Pollitt and his friend interested. He kicked him under the table. 'Eat something!' George obediently speared a potato and began to nibble at it.

As Alexandra was speculating with Mr Williams on how else the beads could have been configured, she looked more closely at the photograph. 'But this must be a mistake,' she said. 'It says the photograph was taken in 1874. Why, that's nearly twenty-five years ago. Mrs Atwell saw them quite recently, I believe. Within the last five years.'

'Perhaps your friend saw the treasure elsewhere? I believe the jewels are in Berlin now?' said Mr Williams, helping himself to cheese.

'No, I don't think so. She was very certain that she'd seen them in Anatolia before they were removed – she specifically mentioned them having to be smuggled out. Something about her husband, but I can't remember the details. He was a diplomat and had a passion for ancient history.' She scanned the body of text. 'You're correct though, Mr Williams, they are in Berlin now. Well, I must be mistaken. I obviously misheard her. That teaches me not to repeat stories without fully acquainting myself with the facts!'

'You could always ask her,' offered Mr Williams helpfully. 'If that wouldn't be ... but, it would be rather, wouldn't it?'

'Rather what, Mr Williams?' asked Alexandra, raising her eyes from the magazine to look at him.

Dafydd found himself blushing and wished he wouldn't. 'It would sound as though you weren't believing her, is all I thought.'

Valentine made a little snorting noise. Dafydd's coyness amused him. 'Perhaps your friend is being delicate about her age,' he said with a wink.

Alexandra frowned at Valentine and, noticing Mr Burroughs also looking affronted by this vulgarity, said, 'You're being unkind, Mr Cabot. Mrs Atwell has no need to be delicate. The mistake is entirely mine. I shan't ask her anything about it.'

She looked down and continued reading, privately vexed with herself for the muddle. Minerva had told her the story twice: once whilst sitting for the sketches this morning and once in more detail in the tea shop at the museum. There had been absolute clarity in the account. After a minute, she concluded firmly that Mrs Atwell must have meant to name a different treasure altogether and had made a perfectly excusable slip of the tongue. There were so many 'treasures' being dug up these days. The Ottoman authorities were always disputing with archaeologists and items were continuously being smuggled out. And she would have visited a multitude of different sites. That was the explanation, then.

CHAPTER EIGHT

A day or two later, at half-past seven in the morning, Alexandra was surprised to receive a note.

My dear Alexandra (I may call you Alexandra?) -
Our little excursion on Tuesday was so thrilling for me. I have
hardly stopped thinking about the pleasure of your conversation
and company. I am glad you received the notes I sent you – but
your answers were so short! So I am sending my carriage for you
at Ten Sharp. I have such a treat planned and I know you will
not let me down. We ladies of business must stick together!
Minerva – or, if you prefer, Claudia Livilla.

'Well, that is unexpected, to say the least,' said Alexandra aloud. She put the note down thoughtfully. It was the fourth note from Mrs Atwell since they had met for that first consultation and visited the museum together. Each time she had replied cordially but with brevity, not wishing to overstep polite boundaries. She would certainly enjoy seeing Mrs Atwell again, but the inconvenient thing was that she had a full morning of work planned – the small portrait to be finished for Miss Annabella Frampton's fiancé – and then she was going to meet Harriet at the club for lunch and walk on to visit their friends at the 'Amazons' gallery afterwards. This note now, this put her in an awkward position. Should she risk offending Mrs Atwell or should she fail an existing customer and upset her old friend? It would not have been a difficult decision before Tuesday, because before Tuesday, Minerva Atwell was no more than a customer. Since then, however, she too should perhaps be viewed as a friend.

She was alone in her dressing room, sipping a hot chocolate quietly before changing her clothes. It was the place she liked best for thinking and planning: a small, comfortably messy room with a scarlet leather-topped desk in the window, writing materials and a pile of art books and magazines. The walls were hung with half-finished sketches and portraits in pencil or charcoal. Some of them were of her daughters, some of Harriet and other friends; and there was one of Valentine, looking rather comical in a top hat. There was a nice little one of George Arden too, in three-quarter profile, which she had dashed off on a scrap of paper one evening. She had done several that time but the others had got lost, probably thrown out with the newspapers. This remaining one perfectly caught a characteristic expression of his, like someone trying to identify a piece of music being played a long way off.

Alexandra weighed her feelings and then set them against the demands of prior commitment and proceeded to write a little note of apology. She began by thanking Minerva for her kind invitation and went on to explain that she very much regretted that it was impossible to abandon her engagements today, but perhaps another day they would be able to enjoy each others' company again. She sealed the envelope, rang for Amy and asked her to take it to the post. With the efficient postal service, it should reach Mrs Atwell within the hour. She thought little more of it and continued with her preparations.

When the clock down in the hall below struck nine-thirty, she had already been up in her attic studio for an hour and a half. She had got to the point of painting shades of juniper green into the corners of Miss Frampton's betrothal portrait. She had just decided to add a foam of white gypsophila to the bouquet of flowers the subject was holding. The composition was wanting something to enliven the whole effect of the foreground and perhaps echo the shine in the girl's eyes. It was coming along very prettily.

There was a knock at the studio door and Amy was there, holding another note. Wiping her hands, Alexandra took it and unfolded it. It was not in an envelope.

But my dear Alexandra, this is impossible! I am feeling so ill today. I did not like to speak of it before. You really must cancel

everything else. I do require your urgent attention and advice on
something too. My carriage will come at Ten as I suggested. M.

Alexandra stood holding the note for some time, wondering what
to do. Was it too late to reply? And Mrs Atwell was ill. That was a
pity; but what would she want Alexandra to do about it?

After a long moment, she sighed and began cleaning her
paintbrushes and palette. Then she went back down to her dressing
room, aware that she smelt of linseed oil. After washing, she changed
into her best grey dress, and remembered with a pang that she would
have to write a note to Harriet. She sat straight down at the desk and
began. In it she apologised profusely for letting her down, explained
that Mrs Atwell was urgently sending her carriage because she was ill
and ended by hoping that they would be able to meet very soon to
rearrange their engagement .

At ten, a shiny carriage arrived as promised; but instead of taking
Alexandra to Mrs Atwell's residence, where she expected to find her
lying on a couch or something, on opening the carriage door, she
found the woman herself waiting inside. She gave Alexandra a
brilliant smile.

'There!' she exclaimed. 'Isn't this better? You and I have so much
to talk about, so much to see!'

Alexandra found it difficult to hide her astonishment. 'But I
thought you were indisposed, Mrs Atwell?' she said.

Minerva was dressed in a deep-rose outfit which warmed the
interior of the carriage like a summer afternoon. She waved
Alexandra to come inside. 'Minerva, please. You may call me that, if
you wish. And I was very indisposed. Very, very indisposed – to be
left alone all day. So now you're here, let's spend the entire day
together. Let's lunch at the Café Royal and watch all the artists. That
should amuse you. I can summon a convenient and very tame escort
for us easily. We shall be perfectly respectable, never fear! Sit down,
sit down here next to me, facing forward. I am sure you dislike
travelling backwards as much as I do.'

'No, I am perfectly able to …'

'I won't hear of it, dear Mrs Roberts. Settle in here, next to me,
that's right - and how prettily that shade of grey-blue, slate-blue I
suppose one could call it, goes with my deep-blush – so fortunate
you are not wearing a clash - and as we ride along, we can look out at

the streets together.'

Politeness and prudence forced Alexandra to swallow her objections although she felt a slight prickle of guilt at the thought of Harriet, who would undoubtedly have cancelled paying students in order to keep their engagement. Soon though she discovered that she was not after all displeased at the thought of visiting the Café Royal. She began to allow herself to feel a little flattered. Leaning back into the bottle-green leather of the upholstered seat, she reflected that Mrs Atwell surely meant well. Her actions were perhaps typical of an imperious, spoilt kind of person, but perhaps typical also of a lonely person; and they were intended to give pleasure. She should not show ingratitude. She decided - with a wry glint at herself - to make the best of it.

'Drive on!' called Minerva merrily. Then she turned to Alexandra and took her hand. 'This is exciting, is it not? But what is this? Dear me, these gloves are not quite — well, they are not quite new, are they?'

Alexandra laughed, puzzled. Her gloves were by no means old either. To her eyes they were perfectly acceptable grey kid. 'I'm sure they are not altogether new, Mrs Atwell. But neither are they altogether ancient. Rather like myself. We old things are still serviceable, you know.'

'But you are not an old thing, and I will thank you to keep a civil tongue in your head when speaking of my friend Alexandra. In any case, however you try to insult her, I should like to make her a present,' said Minerva decidedly. She tapped at the roof and a face appeared at the hatch. 'Take us to Barrington's, Alfred.'

'I really cannot accept …'

'Oh, stuff and nonsense or whatever it is the novelists imagine people say! Of course you can accept something. It will be a gift to your real self, to my artist-friend Alex, not to conventional Mrs Roberts! Don't be bourgeoise, Mrs Roberts, you know Alex is not. Hadn't you realised that Minerva is her muse? And muses always buy their musees a present. What is someone who is inspired by a muse called? Obviously not a musee, but it should be.'

Alexandra was disarmed and could not help but laugh. 'Muses are known to inspire madness at times, I am afraid, Mrs Atwell. And I trust you are not intent on splitting me in two? Alexandra and Mrs Roberts are not separate people. We are one, and quite sane at the moment, with our feet on the ground.'

'Call me Minerva. Or you can embarrass me and call me Minni, which is what dear Mr Atwell would call me in private. And your sentence structure implies that you may be two – or more perhaps.'

'I don't know that I would quite dare to call you what your ... but, thank you, Mrs Atwell. And I assure you, I am quite undivided.' Alexandra felt as if she were answering two or three strands of thought a the same time.

'Oh, I see. You want to think about doing it. I can read your thoughts, you know, Mrs Undivided. You are thinking, what is this rich woman doing treating an employee like this? What is the hidden trap? Well, there isn't one. I am a very impetuous creature, and when I decide I like a thing or a person, I simply take a run at it and make it happen, if that is not a mixed metaphor. Minerva really does not care what the rest of the world thinks about her. Not a jot! And that, believe me, is why – let me whisper it - my business is an international success.'

Alexandra raised her eyebrows with a smile, but said, 'Very impressive. Well then, if you are to be a muse, you have to promise not to cause madness or blindness or any other of those unfortunate side-effects of inspiration. It is a very demanding job, you know, and I really can't have a muse who threatens my sanity or eyesight.'

Minerva went into a peal of laughter. 'And that is precisely why I wanted to spend the day with you, dear Alex. You make me laugh. And you're not afraid of me. People often are, you may be surprised to hear. Or you may not be at all surprised to hear. Do tell me which is correct. Oh, but not now, because look! There is Mrs Langtry, do look, going into the shop there, looking absolutely elegant. And that is Hugo de Bathe following her in. Now there is a case of a woman making her name entirely based upon a pretty face – a face which happened to be painted by a society artist. You people have such power, you see. And may I tell you, she is one of my best customers. Lillie, now, she is – let me see – forty-five years of age, and about to marry a rich young fellow of twenty-something. And how do you suppose she does it? Aha, that is my little secret. But if you said it had something to do with Atwell's Beauty Balm, I would not tell you that you were mistaken.'

So they drove on; and Alexandra very quickly forgot about her objections at being prevented from completing her work and meeting

Harriet. Even the half-acknowledged misgivings she entertained - that Mrs Atwell had lied fluently to get her way - retreated. For her companion's commentary as they rode along was daring, humorous, ironic and flattering by turns. Alexandra gradually allowed herself to be drawn in by a scintillating line in gossip, fascinating even for someone as uninterested in the froth of high society as Alexandra was.

'Yes,' Minerva continued as they drove, 'and Lillie is but one of the many. If I were to say the names The Honourable Violetta Lindsay, Camille d'Aurore, Lady Henrietta Worcester and her sister the Duchess of Wilmington - and I could add two dozen more without even looking at my accounts book — you might gather that the P.B.s are my lambs.'

'Your lambs?' queried Alexandra.

'My lambs to the slaughter. The Professional Beauties, my dear Alexandra, are simply desperate to maintain every porcelain dimple of their temporary divinity. This fear is very good for me and I exploit it quite mercilessly. They are cooing doves to my hawk or perhaps mice to my hunting owl. I like to hint to them, whilst discussing the formation of crow's feet, of how my future business plans include an effective remedy for their situation. How they beg me for reassurance! It is quite moving. But they do seem to want to come to me for advice. "Violetta, my sweet," I said, "if H.R.H.'s attention is allowed to stray, he will see plenty of fresher flowers in further meadows. You must be distant and beautiful and adorably warm and promising, all at the same time, like an orchard seen from afar." They seem to think I know something of that. But I prefer my anonymity and to work behind the scenes.'

'Of course,' said Alexandra, as if she had ever thought about these things before. 'It would be an empty kind of fame, that, to have one's face and figure judged and critiqued throughout the land in cheap magazines. And the fame of the society beauty is in any case dangerously fragile, depending upon the impossibility of stopping the sun in the sky. I am afraid we must all languish in Time's slow-chapp'd power.'

'Perhaps,' said Minerva. 'But I would agree with the poet, *Thus, though we cannot make our sun stand still, yet we will make him run.* And all my P.B.s have every intention of giving their sun a run for his money. And that poem, by the way, is one of my favourites, although it is a very casuistical and manipulative way of relieving a lady of her honour, it is also very true. *But at my back I always hear Time's wingéd chariot hurrying near.'*

'Yes, how apt for women who depend upon their youth!' said Alexandra. 'And yet, I prefer "The Garden", which speaks of the power of Nature to bring us peace of mind.'

'Oh, time enough for that when the game is over and won,' said Minerva. 'I seem to remember that in the very same poem, Marvell says something like, *When we have run our passion's heat, Love hither makes his best retreat.* That's "when" not "instead of". He spent plenty of time in passion's heat, you may be sure. No doubt one day all my P.B.s will retire to country estates and wander about in straw hats with baskets of lavender and so on. And, you know, Alexandra, they would surely be right to. I am just like you. I adore the peace of Nature, particularly the wilderness. I think you do too. I think this urban life is tiring for you, as it must be for every sensitive mortal. How you would love to see my secret valley! The hills are delectable in the spring and summer, of course, but in winter there is a bleakness which appeals to the ascetic in me. Do you not love a wild wind, Alexandra? Or a thunderstorm?'

Alexandra hardly noticed that at every turn of the conversation, Minerva matched her thoughts, mirrored her attitudes and changed her opinions. By the time the morning had been spent in purchasing a beautiful pair of gloves for Alexandra, visiting shops, buying books and lunching at the Café Royal, she was under the impression that they effortlessly shared one outlook upon life. Alexandra once again returned home feeling exhausted but strangely elated.

*

The scene in the Café Royal was as busy and opulent as usual. Dr Watson was not particularly fond of the décor, with its gilding and vast mirrors. The place was worth visiting mainly because he enjoyed watching the patrons. Over here were famous faces from the art world in deep discussion; in a corner to the right was a noisy group of exquisite young men, somewhat the worse for wear; to the left a decorous, well-dressed pair of ladies with their escorts; and nearby a couple of intense poetic-looking characters, sipping pale, wicked drinks and conversing almost in whispers. But Watson was alone. He had not intended to come into such an expensive place at all but, finding himself so much better today and having taken himself out for a restorative walk, he found that he needed somewhere to rest. A small coffee with brandy seemed to have helped his general sense of well-being, but it was time to make a move. He made his way to the door and was bumped into by a portly chap who was just coming in. The next moment, he was being gripped by the elbow and steered to one side. It was Valentine Cabot. Watson sighed internally and began to make an excuse about needing to leave immediately. Cabot was impervious.

'How gorgeous to see you, my dear Dr Watson! You look stunning! Such a long time since we coincided – but I must say this place is horribly expensive and full of gawpers and hangers-on. And are you still writing up accounts of criminal cases for the magazines?'

'From time to time,' said Watson, trying to edge towards the door.

'Does very well for you, I hear? Yes, very well indeed, so far as short stories can go; but, you know, your readership would increase vastly, my dear Doctor, if you were to take some part of your work to the stage. An adaptation of one of your detective stories would be most appealing.'

'I'll think about it, Mr Cabot,' said Watson. 'If ever I wanted to, I'd certainly take your advice on the matter. And now, I'm afraid I'm rather late for an appointment ...'

'Well, I would be delighted to help you adapt something. You would be amazed at how mere prose springs to life when presented by really good actors. I am lucky to have such a client now – a good actor, I mean. A promising young fellow, name of Arden. You might have heard of him? I count myself fortunate to be his manager, I can tell you!'

'Oh? That is excellent. And now, I must ...'

'So you may even consider working with me, depending on my next production? I have a most intriguing idea for a play and, do listen because you'll like this, a musical tragi-comedy, based upon Hamlet. Intriguing, is it not?'

'Alas,' said Watson carefully, 'I am not in a position to consider such an opportunity just now. But I congratulate you on your actor. It must be fortunate to manage a great talent. Well, it's been pleasant to chat, but now ...'

Cabot sighed and glanced towards the group in the far corner. 'I am, if you insist upon knowing, in the process of arranging a meeting. My friend's over there – somewhere in the middle of that noisy huddle – and he's definitely interested in the scheme I mentioned. Perfectly ecstatic about it. I've just come in to find him – casual arrangement, and all that, so need to wander over. Unfortunately, I seem to have left my wallet at the bank – I couldn't ask you to …?'

'Not really, Cabot,' said Watson hastily. 'Crime doesn't pay, you know, not nearly as well as it should. Certainly not the writing about it anyway.'

'Oh. Well, I hope we'll bump into each other soon. Will you be going to Dame Fortune's?'

Watson hesitated. 'Ye-es,' he said, 'I expect I will, at some point.'

A burst of laughter from the group in the corner attracted Valentine's attention. 'Ah, mirth, wit, flowing champagne! There they are, divine youth and all that. I shall go to them. Mr Pollitt and his circle of admirers await.'

Watson escaped.

*

Two days later, Valentine looked peevish when, at about four o'clock, Alex came to sit in the parlour with a quiet cup of tea. He was reading a tattered copy of *The Stage*, occasionally making dangerous snorting noises into its pages. 'Why, Valentine, how goes the world this afternoon?' she asked pacifically.

'The world? The world thwarts me at every turn, that is what the world does, Mrs A. and I am tired to the bone of feeling it. I feel things very deeply, as you know. Very.'

'Who has thwarted you today?'

'I could say the entire human race. But I will not, I will refrain from tarring the whole species with the same pitch-black brush.'

Alexandra guessed that the problem was money – it usually was with Valentine. He would eventually, if pressed, mention the real cause of his aggravation, but would blame others along the way for his misfortune. It was often poor George – or whichever young actor Cabot had in tow - who was held culpable. She herself was feeling buoyant as a consequence of another amusing day in Minerva's company. Today there had been lunch and riding in the beautiful carriage and a concert. These glimpses into the life of a wealthy, autonomous woman had a tendency to release Alexandra from financial care by proxy. Without bothering to question Valentine further about his situation, she found herself saying casually, 'Listen, Val, I can lend you some money. Let's not beat about the bush. You need an advance and at this moment, I happen to be in a position to help you out.'

There was an immediate change in Cabot's face, as if the sun had blazed suddenly forth. After thanking her and finding out exactly how much might be available, in what form and how soon, he went on to explain his woes in a more good natured fashion.

'It is the blessed what-you-may-call-it wandering to and fro, and the wear on shoe leather, not to mention waiting about for people who don't turn up, which causes a depression in one's spirits. One must wait about in certain establishments and when one is there, one cannot not be seen to eat and drink; and one's dress must live up to the establishments in which one finds oneself. Luckily it is only myself. Heaven knows what I would do if I had to pay for George too. But he is flighty, Mrs Roberts, terribly flighty. It is best he does not accompany me. I leave him to work on his own at the Parnassus. He has been permitted to help out with the moving of scenery and so forth. It will put a few more pennies in our pockets. And then, tonight, when he takes to the boards himself, he will know exactly where everything is, because he put it there himself. I call it a distinct advantage. When I told him he could put in extra hours every day he was so pathetically grateful to me, there were tears in eyes, I swear. He does well by me but I too am grateful for the opportunity to do him good.'

'Very laudable,' said Alexandra, doubtfully picturing the slight George Arden hefting stage scenery.

'But the gentlemen whose patronage I am trying to attract have not yet heard me out. I follow them, I lie in wait for them, they evade me. This is what cast a shadow over my countenance when you came in – a shadow which, thankfully, you have lifted for me. I'm prepared to swear on my own mother's grave that when I came into Pagani's today, they saw me and departed through another door. Can you believe it?'

'Oh, is it not a mistake to assume you know what other people's motives are, Mr Cabot?' said Alexandra, drinking her tea. 'And is this still the famous collector or actor you told me about?'

'Yes, it is. Did I mention Mr Pollitt to you before, then?'

'Nearly incessantly. He's rich, knows everyone, interested in the theatre, that sort of thing. And was it something about skirt dancing dressed as Loie Fuller? Or am I getting mixed up?'

'No, you are correct. You'll find his portrait in The Sketch, my dear Mrs A. He sings and dances divinely, most exquisite in every way. But in an amateur capacity, you know, nothing vulgar. He is seen in all the very best places. Which means I have to be seen in the very best places too.'

'Perhaps I have seen him then, Val? Does he visit the Café Royal?'

'Yes, yes, of course.'

'What does he look like? I've been there practically every day this week,' said Alexandra carelessly.

'Oh, you wouldn't be able to get near him. There is always a knot of hangers-on around him, almost as if he'd told them to keep me at a distance, and they are horribly rude to me, but I'll break through.'

'But if you're tending to haunt their steps, may they not be feeling under siege? Would it not be better to let them come to you? Establish *yourself* at a table at the Café Royal, surrounded by fascinating beauty and talent, and they'll be seeking you out and begging to invest in your plays. Why, just today as I mentioned, Minerva said - '

'Oho! Minerva is it? This is the lady with the extravagant bundles of auburn hair and the glorious shape? So that's what you have been getting up to!'

'Mr Cabot,' said Alexandra, who was not in the least offended, 'I have not and never would "get up to" something, as you so vulgarly put it. Mrs Atwell has kindly condescended to -'

'Condescended? Now, come, Mrs A., you must admit that's new. Unusual too. I seem to recall many long and weary conversations about equality and the sturdy independence of the artist from the corrupting influence of Capital and Miss Eleanor Marx's ideas and her father's too, and lord knows what it all was. And now we witness not so much a revolution as a convolution.'

Alexandra laughed. 'Don't judge me so harshly, Val. It is no different to you and your gentlemen investors. I have had a most delightful day with my patroness – who, may I add, seems to have become rather a friend too.'

Valentine sniffed. 'I don't like to say anything but - '

'But you will!'

'But I must. Your lovely patroness is a rich, young, socially-advantaged lady, is she not? And you, my dear Alexandra, are in many ways quite the opposite.'

'And?'

'What possible advantage is there for her to be seen with you? You said yourself that she's a business woman. Rich, rich, rich, were the words you used, I recall. Is she likely to want to spend time with a lady of, well, a lady approaching maturity?'

'That is possibly one of the cruellest of many cruel things that you've said to me, Mr Cabot,' said Alexandra with a little laugh, feeling nonetheless genuinely discomforted by his words.

'The way of the world, my dear lady, is that the young and beautiful require the old and wealthy only when they are poor. Why is George Arden doing my bidding? Is it perhaps that he likes the look of a forty-year-old fellow with a pot belly and ginger hair? Or is it that I find him work? That I can sell him? Sell his acting talents, I mean, of course? I operate by being ruthlessly, poignantly, catastrophically honest with myself.' He extended his hand in a slow sad gesture as he went on, 'I am ugly, I am getting old, I am also poor. I smoke and drink too much. I probably smell. George stays with me because he has nothing else. The superb Mr Pollitt and his wealthy young friend avoid me because I am not pretty and not rich. When they see George, perhaps he will be pretty enough to make them listen to my ideas. Ruthless, you see.'

'You are very dismal, Valentine. I believe there is such a thing as friendship, too. It isn't so ruthless and poignant and catastrophic as you would like to imagine. There is such a thing as mutual compatibility and liking.'

'Yes, between equals, between you and Mrs Day, for example. Between you and your artist friends, yes. As long as you can co-exist without one feeding off the other. But when there is inequality of wealth, what then?'

'I believe that we have things in common: a love of ancient things, history, art, theatre, conversation. And she is isolated by the very wealth which you say precludes our friendship. She needs a friend and we can be friends - without feeding off one another. We can simply be two souls meeting, quite apart from our relative wealth. Don't you think?'

Valentine shook his head. 'Sadly, no, I don't think. I don't believe it and I have never seen it. I do beg you to forgive me, I can see that I have mortally offended you. Come, dear Mrs Roberts, Pax! I don't say that you have no charms. I simply compare the charms of a Mrs Atwell to those of the average mortal.'

'I don't see the point of making me feel low and weak, Mr Cabot,' said Alexandra with another, less convincing, laugh.

'The point is – well, no there is no point. I would just prefer you to be careful and not get yourself broken under the chariot wheels. There is a fortune telling card like that. Did I tell you about my fascinating trip to the fortune teller a few days ago? Well, I will, in a minute. But there is a card which shows that very thing, a chariot driving forward, coming out of the picture, with a wicked-looking armoured gent riding along in it, and a pair of stomping cart horses ready to run straight over one. And that, strangely enough, is what I thought of just now.'

'The chariot would have to be a brougham then, with gentle dapple-greys. No, I don't concede your point, Mr Cabot. Old friend as you are, experienced in the ways of the world as you are, horribly bitter and twisted as you are, I cling to my belief that true friendship is capable of existing despite inequality. There. And now I must go and talk to Mrs Jenkins. Later, over dinner, I would like to hear all about your fortune teller too. So prepare your monologue.'

Alexandra left the room with a smile to hide her annoyance with Valentine. Like a cast of oil spreading over clear water, his doubts began to taint the day. With a momentary prickle of wariness about her new friend, she thought of the oil sketch for the portrait against the wall in her studio. Before the short winter daylight was gone, she decided to go up and look at it to judge the work against her now more-accurate knowledge of the face.

As she approached the darkening stairs leading up to the attic, she was almost bumped into by Lily Jones, one of the maidservants, who was coming out of the linen cupboard. 'I'm sorry, Mrs Roberts,' she said. 'I wasn't looking where I was going.'

'No, no, Lily, it was I who wasn't looking. Don't worry. Just carry on.'

'Thank you, Mrs Roberts. I just shut the studio up again for you.'

'Shut it up again, Lily?'

'Yes, after Mr Burroughs was in there. Or I think he was in there, at least he was coming down the stairs an hour or so ago. He might have gone up for something else – the other little cupboard with the coat hangers and so on is up there, but I'm of the opinion he must have been in there because of the door being ajar. I went and shut it up again to keep the cat out. I haven't forgot what happened when Tiger got the turpentine on his fur! Me and Mrs Jenkins soaping him down and him yowling! So I locked the door but left the key in the lock, as usual. That's all, ma'am. Just thought you should know.'

'What would Mr Burroughs be doing up there I wonder?' murmured Alexandra almost to herself, adding more loudly, 'Thank you, Lily. I'll be down shortly.'

She went up and opened the door. The light was fading fast in the cold room, although there was still a bloody look to the clouds through the skylight. In the wintery stain, Alexandra looked round the studio. The portrait she was currently finishing was just as she had left it; and everything else in the room was still and familiar. She looked at the paints and pigments, the bottles of linseed and oily rags, the jars of brushes and pencils and the aprons and smocks hanging behind the door.

Then she saw that the oil sketch of Mrs Atwell had been turned to face the light. She had left it facing the wall, as was her practice, finding it best not to have work-in-progress constantly in view for fear of dulling her judgement. But there it was, fully exposed. She was disconcerted at the thought that someone – perhaps Albert Burroughs – had indeed been poking about in her studio. Her mind supplied an image of him, alone, staring at the picture. The studio was almost dark by the time she shut and locked the door behind her. She decided to take the key and keep it safely in her study.

CHAPTER NINE

A few days later, George Arden had a free morning and decided to call on his friend Harriet Day. He found her sorting out letters and photographs. A drawer from her desk had been removed and the contents had been divided up and piled on the floor. She seemed pleased to see him and stopped her work immediately.

'You see, Mr Arden, I am taking your advice a step further. Not just the spare bedroom but all the nooks and crannies of the house. I'm going to go through each one and discard any old sad unnecessary remnants. It's all going. I've sent Peter's old clothes to the poor and his toys to the hospital. I have to confess I rid myself of Mr Day's clothes long ago. And I shall have more plants and flowers growing absolutely everywhere, as long as I can remember to water them. A jungle of them!'

'How interesting,' said George. 'I would never have thought of doing that.'

'But this is a direct result of your intervention,' said Harriet with a quizzical look at him.

'Ah, good,' George nodded. 'This is so nice, though, isn't it? Sitting here like this. I like your house now. It's a lot more peaceful.' He looked round the room as they talked. The pale-blue papered walls were hung with a variety of pictures, large and small. In quite a few he thought he recognised the fluid, confident brushwork of Harriet's friend. 'Surely some of these are by Mrs Roberts?' he asked, peering intently at a little picture not far from where he sat.

It was of a young lady in a bonnet and white dress, looking back over her shoulder. She was standing at the end of a jetty; and there was an opal sea-light behind her. Wind was tugging at a deep-blue ribbon and the painter had made the shine on the silk the same colour as the young lady's eyes.

'And this is you yourself, isn't it?' he said, glancing across at Harriet to check her eyes.

'Yes, it is,' said Harriet shortly. 'By the sea at Ramsgate. Mrs Roberts was a keen artist, then as now. Not Roberts then, of course. She was a Silver.'

George stood up to look more closely at the picture. Then he reached out a finger and, touching the silver of the frame, said, 'Your life is full of secret signs. Clever of you.'

Harriet made no comment and turned the conversation to how his work was going.

'It's going well, thank you,' he answered slowly, pushing the dark hair back from his forehead. 'Quite hard, currently. I am helping almost every day from twelve o'clock at the Parnassus, moving things and running to and fro; and then performing, afternoon and evening; and getting home at one or two in the morning. Valentine says this is a good thing for us. The moving things behind the scenes is dusty and cobwebby.' He sighed. 'But today I'm free, no work at all. Valentine has something much better planned. He keeps saying there is a great opportunity coming for us, a play which will be famous in the West End. We're having a meeting tonight at Dame Fortune's with some rich gentlemen.'

'That is simply wonderful!' exclaimed Harriet with real enthusiasm. 'What is the play?'

'He's very secretive about it,' said George. 'Between you and me, Mrs Day, I think he hasn't really written it yet. He's got his shoebox of scripts out and he's shuffling the papers to and fro and combining them in different sequences, but mostly he just goes out lunching and dining. He says this is because there is a particular set of people who will pay good money to help us put on the play and he has to make them interested. It costs a lot of money to make them invest, so that's what has to happen.'

'Oh, I see. So the idea is still only an idea? Well, mighty oaks, you know, Mr Arden!'

'Oaks?'

'From little acorns grow. Big things come from small beginnings.'

'Yes, yes, I see.' George nodded seriously again. 'And you are well, and Mrs Skipton?'

"Mrs Skipton is very well indeed. She speaks of you often, as a matter of fact. You must have been especially kind to her because she seems to think you are rather a paragon of Christian virtue. As for myself, well, as you see, keeping busy. I have my students.'

'I rather hoped I would see you at Mrs Roberts's one day,' said George.

'Oh, yes. I'll be coming over soon, you'll see. Mrs Roberts is a busy person, a busy woman of business.'

'I'm sorry,' said George.

'Why sorry, Mr Arden? All is well, all is as it should be. Rather like your Valentine Cabot, she too has to pursue her patrons. Commissions don't fall from trees.'

'Not even oak trees,' added George. There was a long silence and he continued to regard her sympathetically.

'Well, there's no point pretending to you, I can see that,' said Harriet. 'I think you and I are friends, aren't we? Even though you're so young and I'm so old, and you're male and I'm female? And I don't know, there are so many other reasons why we should not be allowed to be friends, in the normal course of events.'

'I can't think of any reasons,' said George. 'And you're not old and I'm not young.'

'Very well,' went on Harriet, 'I'm going to tell you something which I hope you will keep to yourself. Can you do that?'

'Like the Sphinx,' said George.

Harriet, looking at his face with its pale olive skin and luminous dark eyes, said, 'The Sphinx, yes, perfect. As silent as the Sphinx then. Well, Mrs Roberts seems to be very much taken up with a certain patroness of hers, a certain very rich, very beautiful, but rather young woman. And it is making me feel – not happy. I'm worried about her, truth be told. I can't say a word about it, of course, any more than you can object to your Valentine pursuing all his rich patrons.'

'He's not my Valentine,' put in George very calmly. 'He's tiring. It's tiring being with him. But point taken.'

Harriet paused at these words, but being in full flow on the subject of Alexandra, she continued, 'And she has changed remarkably over these past two weeks. I think she gets anxious about what this woman will think of her, or say to her, or suggest next. The first warning sign was a sudden illness which made her cancel an engagement between us – not Mrs Roberts being ill, you understand,

Mr Arden, but a fake illness the woman had concocted to steal Alexandra's day from her. Alex told me of it when we met afterwards and the thing which struck me as odd, and very unlike herself, was that she thought it was *funny*. An endearing, funny little trick like a kitten tangling one's wool. And then she seems to have engrossed her attention every day, day after day.

'Then there was an afternoon last week when she, Mrs Roberts, turned up here out of the blue and was in distress because this woman had taken something she said amiss. It had turned into a most terrible argument, apparently, and the woman had stormed off and threatened to – well, this really has to be a secret, Mr Arden – she threatened to harm herself in some unspecified way. Of course, she did no such thing. But the upshot was that Alexandra Roberts, an independent, dignified and experienced woman, was hammering on this other woman's door in a panic.

'Well, that is such girlish nonsense for one thing, and for another, it is most upsetting. And then there was some kind of exchange of expensive gifts to make up for all the boiling panic. I don't know. How can she have the money to spend on expensive gifts? I know she has not! And I'm sure I don't know the half of it because when I made some very slight disapproving noises – really the very slightest and most discreet – Alex flew into a rage with me. We haven't spoken since. And I do know this: some people are accustomed to causing chaos and drama wherever they go and it's a way of controlling everybody around them. Best avoided, best avoided if possible.'

George listened silently to this uncharacteristically vehement speech, nodding from time to time. 'And what will you do?' he asked when she had fallen silent.

'What can I do? If I say something to criticise this woman, it will simply harden Alexandra's resolve to stick with her. She has got it into her head that she has a tragic history and this is why she is so lonely and desperate, and she needs a mentor; and that she herself is to be that mentor. I think this is how she makes herself feel equal to her, because the lady is wealthy and so on and so forth, as I have said. It's a tiresome muddle. And they'll travel together and see mountains and deserts and treasures and I don't know what else. And it will look as if I'm jealous and unkind if I say a word of criticism. Do you see?'

'It's very painful,' said George.

'Yes, it is. That is exactly the word. And I told you before all about our long, long friendship. I would have thought that counted for something, but it seems not.'

They both sat staring into the fire. Finally George said, questioningly, 'I think it might be the lady with the knife?'

'Lady with the knife? No, no. It's a lady with face cream and powder puffs, that's all. It's very good, the powder puff. I know because Mrs Roberts was so very kind as to bestow a Beauty Balm Compact upon me, gratis. Very thoughtful of her. Wasn't it.'

George regarded her with his head tilted very slightly to one side and she immediately added, 'Yes, I know. Bitter. I won't be bitter, not for long. I'll throw it all out. That's what I was doing. All her letters. I'm putting them in the kitchen fire.' Harriet felt her eyes prickle with tears. She stood up hastily. 'And so I must get on, dear Mr Arden. I have a student coming in – oh – twenty minutes, it seems. Come and see me again soon, won't you? And good luck with your meeting tonight. I do hope your rich gentlemen help you and Valentine.'

George looked thoughtfully at her for a moment and said, 'I think the next time I see you – it will be very dark.'

'How very mysterious,' Harriet said with a smile. Silly thing, she thought fondly as she watched him through the window, walking away down the street.

*

At the club later that evening, Dr Watson settled himself into one of the high-backed chairs near the fire. He was very glad to find that the place was not yet full. A quick scan of the dimly lit room with its red-shaded electric lights showed that nobody he knew had yet arrived. The area near the fire was furnished with deep armchairs while the further part of the cavernous room was a maze of lamp-lit tables and gilt chairs. The clink of cutlery and the hush of distant conversation drifted over from the few diners already seated there.

This place, The Dame Fortune's Dining Club for Actors and Managers, commonly known as Dame Fortune's or even just The Dame's, sprawled throughout the entire top floor of Carvel's Hotel. It was not the kind of place where you would find the Prince of Wales dining tête-à-tête with his latest mistress. Its clientele tended to foresake it, shaking its dust from their feet and gravitating towards the West End, once they had tasted success. Yet there was something energising about it, thought Watson, precisely because its patrons had not yet made their names. If something new were stirring, it was here that you'd hear about it first. He had felt well enough to venture into the night air and the process of dressing for the evening had cheered him up considerably. He'd chosen this club because, in his own quiet way, he was a great appreciator of the Arts generally and particularly of the Theatre. From time to time, he would sink a small sum into a production and once or twice had made a tidy penny in profits. D'Oyly Carte, for example: *The Gondoliers* had been a great success. Mind you, *The Grand Duke* hadn't done so well. Still it was a form of speculation which Watson enjoyed and which brought pleasure to many. Holmes, of course, sneered at his fondness for Messrs. Gilbert and Sullivan.

Stretching out his legs in the warmth of the fire, he contemplated the tarnished gilding on the ceiling and the knot of thuggish-looking putti who were crowning the Goddess Fortuna. She looked vaguely disreputable too, having from this distance the appearance of a knowing smirk. Her robes, which should have been an aerial blush of white and dawn pink, had turned gradually to tobacco brown.

Time wore on and more diners arrived, while acquaintances drifted over to sink into the armchairs and smoke and settle down for an amiable discussion of theatrical matters in general. The group round the fire was well into a slightly alcohol-influenced appraisal of how important their financial contributions were to the state of culture in England, when the figure of Mr Valentine Cabot slid into view.

'Don't look now,' said one. 'It's Cabot.'

'Who's with him?'

'Some fifth-rate actor fellow,' said another.

Cabot was accompanied by a thin young man in black. Dr Watson immediately guessed that this was the promising young actor he had heard about before. He focused his attention firmly within his group, for although Cabot was no more shady or pushy than the average manager, he had poorer than usual taste and a louder than usual voice. Watson, listening to the discussion of a recent flop, *Sweet Nancy*, half-expected to be tapped on the elbow at any moment. It was with relief therefore that he saw, when he dared to glance up surreptitiously, that he and his companion had walked past the group round the fire and on towards the back of the room, threading their way among the dining tables.

The club gradually became a submarine fug of tobacco smoke and Watson noticed a growing tightness in his chest. He excused himself, saying he needed a breath of fresh air, with his eye on the further windows where the sashes were raised. He made his way over and was taken aback to find Cabot's young actor in black standing partially hidden by the heavy red curtains. He seemed to be watching the reflections of the room rather than the dark street below. His eyes briefly met Watson's in the glass as he quietly sat himself down at an empty table nearby.

Watson shook out a medicated 'Cigare de Joy' and gingerly lit it. As he smoked and coughed, out of the corner of his eye he noticed Valentine Cabot was stationed dangerously nearby. He was in deep conversation and Watson could hear his rolling voice above the din of the diners around him. There were two men at the table with him, listening with a captive air. One had his chin resting on a hand, the other was sitting back with hands behind his head. The starched linen of the table had been cleared of the remains of a meal and supplied with ashtrays, coffee and cognac. The red lamp in the midst cast an intense circular glow onto the white cloth like a fireball speeding straight up from hell.

Even from this distance, Watson could see that Cabot was in the throes of salesmanship. He gestured towards the window where the youth stood hidden and as he did so, his eye fell upon the doctor; and Watson cursed himself. Now it would be impossible to beat a casual retreat for Cabot's face had instantly lit up in recognition. His own good manners forced him to stand and walk over to the group at the table.

'My dear, dear Dr Watson!' called Valentine loudly above the clink of cutlery and buzz of conversation. 'This is exceptionally good luck! Please join us!' He turned back to his companions, explaining loudly so that Watson could hear him, 'This is such a lucky night. Fortuna smiles upon us indeed! Here is a man, a leader in the Literary Arts – let me introduce you!' He paused to flap his hands at a passing waiter to supply another chair, gabbling to his companions (much to Watson's embarrassment): 'This is *the* Dr Watson. You do know of him. A friend of mine, a very good friend. We go back years, absolutely years. Always running into each other. A writer of crime stories, very successful stories, sensational, you must have read them?'

With that, Valentine came forward, swept his arm through Watson's and holding onto him rather too tightly, gestured with a little obsequious bow towards a serious-eyed gentleman at the table. 'Mr Jerome Pollitt, may I have the honour to introduce Dr John Watson? Dr Watson, Mr Pollitt. Mr Pollitt is not only an adornment to the stage but also a patron of the Arts - a friend of many of our major modern artists, you know, those at the very forefront of innovation.'

Watson gently disengaged himself from Valentine's grip and leaned over to shake hands. Pollitt half-rose gracefully and murmured something about 'charmed'.

'And this is Mr Pollitt's companion,' went on Valentine with noticeably less enthusiasm, indicating a pale young man with an impassive stare. 'A promising student, you know, destined to be a gifted poet, I believe - is that right?' he asked Pollitt, with a wary eye on Pollitt's friend. 'And chess master, and - er – mountaineer, Mr Alexander Cr-'

'Oh, please,' said the friend of Pollitt with an impatient flick of ash from his cigarette.

'Forgive me, my dear fellow,' said Valentine hastily, 'it's just that Jerome did tell me and odd little facts like that will inconveniently stick in my mind. So, allow me to introduce Mr - um - Aleister Crowley. Who dislikes being called Alexander, apparently.'

Aleister Crowley stared at Valentine. 'I despise the name just as vehemently as Jerome hates to be called Herbert. Please do not use it again. Particularly the shortening to 'Alick'. Has anyone ever heard a more absurd sound?' Despite his annoyance, Mr Crowley also stood up and extended a hand to the doctor, saying he was pleased to make his acquaintance.

'Did I hear Cabot say that you are a poet, Mr Crowley?' asked Watson pleasantly, instinctively soothing ruffled feelings. He sat down opposite him. The red light, glinting in the glasses and coffee cups, shone in Mr Crowley's rings. Watson noticed he was wearing several, silver, of curious design. His hands looked unexpectedly strong.

Crowley took his time to answer, drawing on his cigarette. 'A poet? Yes. I am a poet. I write and after I have written, sometimes I find that it is poetry, if I'm lucky.'

There was something gripping about his gaze. It was difficult for Watson to look away. 'You only discover afterwards whether it is poetry or not? How interesting! So, do you write in a dream-like state, as Coleridge is said to have done occasionally?' asked Watson affably. 'Do you find your vision, when fully formed, has become a Xanadu or an Inferno?'

'Are you asking about my poetic method or the results of it, doctor?' asked Crowley seriously.

'Oh, both, I suppose. Doesn't the method lead to the result? Or am I old-fashioned? I hardly know the latest theories on Art, I'm sorry to say. I do think that the Muse is readier to visit when one simply sits at one's desk and gets on with it. Don't you agree, Mr Crowley?'

'There are other preparations I prefer to make,' said Crowley. 'But pen and ink are certainly also necessary.' He thought for a moment and said slowly, 'But tell me, doctor, since you are a doctor, can you answer this question: where does it all come from? I mean, whence comes the Muse? What power compels us to listen to her? And what is the penalty for heeding her?'

Watson raised an eyebrow but saw that Mr Crowley was serious. He said, 'Do you truly feel that poets must pay a penalty for bringing beauty into the world? Why should there be a punishment for being a poet? Is it a criminal offence?'

'It depends, doesn't it?' said Crowley with a very slight twist of a smile. 'It depends what the poet chooses as his subject. If one writes holy claptrap, there is unlikely to be any kind of opprobrium. Personally, I wish to sweep the old order to aside.'

Dr Watson decided he was not equipped at this moment, what with the increasing noise and laughter in the room around them, to argue about the social obligations of the poet. 'Well, that is a discussion for perhaps another time. Have your own works been published, Mr Crowley?'

'They will be shortly: *Aceldama: a place to bury strangers in*. That will be the title.'

'A place to bury strangers in? Unusual title,' said Watson, feeling a little disquieted.

Crowley nodded. 'The Field of Blood, bought with Judas's money. Or, some accounts say, where he hanged himself.' He fixed his eyes on the circle of red light beneath the lamp and slowly went on, 'What troubles and amazes me is the weight of strange treasure we bring up from this Underworld, this unconscious self within.'

Jerome Pollitt leant over at this point, placing his hand almost warningly on Crowley's forearm, and said to Watson, 'He's looking to get a fellow who does things for Aubrey to handle it: Smithers. Do you know him? It has to be done privately, in a very limited edition - but Aubrey half-promised me a drawing for it too. Of course, it's not suitable for ladies, you know.'

'Indeed?' said Dr Watson, thinking that Smithers's notorious association with Wilde and Beardsley was unlikely to secure him an audience of ladies in any case. Watson strongly suspected that he himself would be subjected to a forced read-through of erotic juvenilia unless he quickly changed the subject. He busied himself with inspecting his cigarette.

Pollitt continued, 'Dr Watson, you yourself have connections in the world of publishing, or so Cabot mentioned. Smithers has been most unsatisfactory recently – I've been chasing up some of Aubrey's sketches for him, kept in a dreadful state in his print shop, you know. It isn't acceptable. You could perhaps advise us of a more reliable publisher?'

'No, no, Mr Pollitt,' said Watson. 'My abilities are very modest and my published works are nothing more than magazine stuff. All that side of it is handled by my agent, Dr Conan Doyle - and I don't aspire to poetry. Any little public interest there has been in my writings is entirely due to the extraordinary abilities of the friend whose adventures it is my privilege to describe.'

'Yes?' asked Mr Pollitt.

'My friend - you might have heard of him - is remarkably clever at investigations, detective work. Dark crimes, you know, devilishly complicated mysteries and such like. I write them up.'

'Ah. Police work. How perfectly sweet,' said Pollitt with a vague smile. His eyes wandered away following Valentine, who had taken himself off towards the windows.

But Crowley looked with renewed interest at Watson. In fact, he locked eyes with him in his disconcerting way. 'Mysteries and devilish crimes, you say?' he said. 'Your friend is drawn to these? And your friend is right. It is part of my own discovery, which I try to express within the poem, that we must explore this darkness…'

Dr Watson cleared his throat apologetically. 'That sounds remarkable, Mr Crowley, but before you go on, I should put the record straight, I fear. I think you would find my friend Mr Holmes is not so much intent on exploring the darkness in a poetic sense as bringing criminals to justice. Protecting the weak, you know.'

'But of course,' said Crowley. He sat back, looking a little annoyed or crestfallen.

Watson half regretted cutting across his talk. The strange fellow was after all very young. He went on cheerfully, 'But you would probably be interested in some of our cases. They do indeed deal with the darkest of human instincts. I thoroughly recommend reading them, Mr Crowley, inadequate as they are. For example, *The Adventure of the Speckled Band* is one that might appeal in its atmosphere and strangeness. It was perfectly horrible at the time, but it wrote up pretty well. Sherlock Holmes is my friend's name.'

Before Crowley could respond, Cabot returned. He had been standing for some time near the curtains to address the hidden actor at the window. After a short colloquy, he had been observed to reach in and draw him into the light and lead him over to the table. 'This is he, my friends,' he announced solemnly, gripping the other's arm and giving it a little shake. 'Mr George Arden. A rising star of the theatre! A lightning bolt falling to earth!'

As Valentine indulged in his hyperbole, the actor's face expressed nothing but glum reluctance. After the introductions were done and Mr Arden had been sat down at the corner nearest to Aleister Crowley, Valentine Cabot began to sketch out the proposals for his absurd play concerning pirates and stolen princes. He described it as a comedy with musical interludes and a tragic undertone. Pollitt and Crowley had obviously heard most of this before because they looked increasingly vexed, but Cabot persisted in his speech without any regard for their restlessness. Dr Watson too shifted in his seat. This was exactly what he had hoped to avoid.

Valentine explained his idea that Hamlet – a dashing if despondent figure – could be used to examine the theme of amnesia 'for Hamlet has had a mighty blow on the head, you see,' he explained. 'And as a result, he forgets who he is.' Apart from the addition of Doris the sea nymph, who reveals her identity whilst rescuing Hamlet from a watery grave, the whole thing could be performed as an interlude within the play while the serious actors took a little rest. He kept telling everyone that 'this young actor here' had the exact talent to portray the complexities of a Pirate-Hamlet; whilst George, apparently primed to sit in a certain attitude throughout, looked wistfully into an empty coffee cup.

As he spoke, Watson sighed and a forlorn weariness descended upon him. He listened politely, hoping that something would rescue him before his natural warm-heartedness tricked him into a worthless investment. Luckily, Jerome Pollitt, who was bored almost to distraction by now, began drawing Cabot out on plot details in order to expose the weakness of the thing. Cabot took his best efforts at mockery for genuine interest and answered at length.

Watson looked away, wondering if he could escape; and turned his attention to the two others at the table. A curious sight met his eyes. George Arden was watching Aleister Crowley warily and Crowley had turned his chair towards his. He seemed to be staring fixedly into his eyes and talking in a low voice. Despite the surrounding noise - and almost against his will - Watson found himself bending towards them to listen in. 'George Arden is not your name, is it?' he overheard Crowley saying. 'George Arden is not your name, but you can tell me your secret. I know you have a secret. I feel it. I keep secrets. Your name can be our secret.'

Watson did not feel entirely happy with what he could hear. His experiences abroad had brought him into contact with many a strange thing, from Sufi dancers to Fakirs charming snakes, and it struck him that Crowley was employing a subtle oriental method of influencing the mind. He wanted to break up the conversation immediately, but before he could speak, was surprised to hear Arden's reply.

'George Arden is not all of my name,' he answered softly. 'But all of your name is not Aleister Crowley. I see further into you than you see into me. You walked in Thebes long ago. I know your name. The dead man Ankh-af-na-khonsu hath made his passage into the night. But take care. Fear the beast.'

It was as though Crowley had been stung. He drew back suddenly but his face was not angry. It was delighted. Dr Watson, observing the exchange, hastily concluded that they were as misguided as each other. If that wasn't some Spiritualist Blavatsky nonsense, he didn't know what was. But, at the same time, his curiosity was piqued. He watched Crowley draw closer to Arden again - but this time the whisper was so quiet that he couldn't hear what was said. He saw Arden shake his head and Crowley sit back, perhaps rebuffed but nonetheless smiling slightly, as if he had planted a seed. The two soon began talking again. It was disquieting and Watson began to feel that he really did not like it much and it was time to be leaving. He rose casually, hoping not to attract too much of Mr Cabot's attention, but in vain. Valentine rose too, but being torn between his wealthy victims sitting at the table and his less-wealthy victim making a bid for freedom, he chose to concentrate on the richer prizes and sat down again. Watson apologised for having to leave and promised that he would think deeply about Valentine's proposal.

He was detained quite a while saying goodbye to his various acquaintances – may even have had another small whiskey in the process – and noticed vaguely that the talk at Cabot's table in the far corner had become general and perhaps rather loud. He then wandered slowly out to the cloakroom to collect his things. He had shrugged himself into his greatcoat and was just about to walk out of the door when he found that Cabot's young actor was at his side. 'Why, my dear fellow,' he said, surprised. 'I did not know you were leaving at the same time or I would have waited for you.'

'Yes,' said Mr Arden, 'I've decided I don't really like this place. Let me please walk out with you, sir.' He glanced back at the crowded smoke-filled room.

'With pleasure,' said Dr Watson kindly. He paused just beyond the door. 'Have you no greatcoat, lad?'

Arden shook his head and immediately began pattering down the marble staircases towards the ground floor. Watson followed at a slower pace, wondering what was going on. The club premises were on the top floor of an hotel and as they descended, they began to encounter guests and staff using the stairs. As he reached the bottom, he thought he heard a voice from above calling down the name 'George', but he chose to ignore it. Anyway, Arden was already disappearing out of the front entrance.

It was not late in the evening, being but ten o'clock or so. Dr Watson would normally have spent a considerably longer time at his club and perhaps returned rather the worse for wear in a hansom, and that had been his plan tonight - had it not been for Valentine

Cabot. But now he would have to wend his way back to Baker Street early: and the empty parlour. There wouldn't even be a cryptic note to tell him what was happening. Watson sighed deeply and started coughing as the cold night air hit his lungs. He had to stop, leaning against a lamp post. Once again he was surprised to find George Arden appearing at his side.

'You're not well, sir,' he said. 'Can I help you?'

'H'mm,' said Watson, when he had regained control of his cough. 'I have a touch of bronchitis, my lad. It's a combination of this cold air, the damp and the soot. Nature's way of clearing the paths. Perfectly normal.'

'Perhaps you should get out of the night air, sir.'

'Yes, I should. Let's look for a cab. Can I drop you somewhere?'

The young man paused. 'I should like to visit Mrs Day,' he said. 'But I can't remember the name of her street except it begins with a C and has a laurel bush in the garden. Perhaps I should return to Mrs Roberts?'

Watson waited patiently. 'Don't you know where you live, my boy?'

Arden looked back towards the hotel. 'I'll find my way on foot better, I think.'

Dr Watson also looked over at the hotel. He could discern a knot of gentlemen just reaching the bottom of the stairs and beginning to traverse the vestibule. He could not see if they were Cabot and the rest, but they might be. He turned to look at Arden. 'You could come with me,' he said. 'We'll walk a bit together until I find my cab.'

The streets were busy and it was easy to use the crowd as cover. Watson wasn't sure why he had such an ominous sense of being pursued or how it had turned out that he was hurrying arm in arm through the cold night with a young man in a black velvet jacket. It was not at all what he had planned for the evening. He wondered what Holmes would say – if he'd been at home - if he arrived at Baker Street like this. 'May I ask,' he said to Arden as they walked along, 'why you were so anxious to avoid the gentlemen in the club? Was that not your own manager working hard to get backers for a play? A play in which you would be the lead? Don't you think he needed your presence and support?'

'Yes, yes,' he answered. 'And he'll be very angry with me later. Very angry. But he wasn't the problem. It was that other one. He was talking to me about - secrets, mysteries, and I saw, how can I put it? I was reminded of something ...' he broke off and they walked on for several minutes. Watson remained silent as his companion seemed to be trying to formulate his thoughts. 'But, doctor,' he began again, 'You are a doctor, a medical doctor, aren't you? Do you know what it is when someone can't remember things? Because that happens to me. I keep worrying about it and I think something might be wrong with my brain.'

'How do you mean?' asked Watson.

'Every day I know that yesterday happened,' said Mr Arden hesitantly, 'and last week and last year, but they seem to get out of order. I know they existed but I can't ...' Arden grasped at the air before him. 'The connections between things are muddled up. I'm worried that sometimes I act strangely and people look at me and see something I don't know is there.'

Dr Watson glanced at him in sympathy. 'There are many reasons why the effect you've described might occur,' he said. 'A blow on the head, for example. But the mind and body are mysteriously linked. My training, you see, is in surgery and my experience is of the field of battle. Stitching up the body, that's what I do – but I've noticed that odd things also happen to the mind in war and in situations of strain. But I'd recommend looking first for organic explanations. I'd advise you to get a check up with a good general medical man, and take it from there. I'll think if I know anyone who might be suitable. And above all, don't worry! That is the very best advice I can give you.'

Arden thanked him and they walked thoughtfully on, Watson trying to remember the name of a doctor he had once met who would be interested in a case like this. Perhaps he could arrange a consultation? He chatted about this and that as they walked, feeling a natural inclination to offer reassurance to the fellow, who seemed distracted or deep in thought and kept returning to the subject of the strange conversation with Crowley. His talk was confusing, peppered with names that Watson did not recognise and which, as he said them, seemed equally confusing to Arden himself. They came at last to a cab stand and Watson found one to take him back to Baker Street. Arden would not get in, saying he needed to walk.

'Are you not cold, Mr Arden?' asked Watson, looking out from the cab window. 'Surely I can drop you nearer your lodgings?'

'I don't feel the cold much,' answered the actor. 'I don't know why but I feel I need to walk about more anyway, get this odd feeling straightened up. But thank you, thank you for helping me.'

'Listen,' said Watson, again moved to sympathy. 'Take my card. That's my address. Call round if you need advice. I'll think about your case and if I come up with a name, I'd be happy to pass you on to him. Do come and see me, if you want to look into it. And that fellow, the one who upset you, if he comes troubling you, come and talk to my friend Holmes. If anyone can clear up a mystery, it's he.'

CHAPTER TEN

Inevitably, the discussion round the table at Dame Fortune's became intense when Crowley joined in. He had previously been observed to be in such close conversation with George that Mr Pollitt had been obliged to call across the table in a voice with the slightest of edges, 'Aleister dear, what are you doing? What do you think of the treatment of Hamlet's madness? Could our insight be improved by the introduction of a mermaid – I beg your pardon, Mr Cabot, a sea nymph?'

Crowley turned his chair round with an exasperated air and Valentine thought he was going to make juvenile and unworthy comments; but he obviously liked an audience and he had very firm ideas about Shakespeare and madness, it seemed, not to mention poetry. In fact, Valentine was rather shaken by the firmness of them. He began to dislike and admire the young man in approximately equal measure. Meanwhile, sweet Mr Pollitt listened with a remote air of regret that the play was being torn to pieces, as if he were watching someone else's attack dog eat a butterfly. Valentine became flustered under the onslaught of unkind judgements. He did not notice when George rose and discreetly disappeared: he was too busy arguing that Doris would bring a much-needed dimension of unselfishness to the play.

When he did realise that George's chair was empty, he rose suddenly, quite glad to change the subject. 'But this is disastrous,' he exclaimed to their surprised faces. 'Where is my actor? He is to recite for you, he must recite! I have primed him to make the speech *Oh, that this too, too sullied flesh would melt* at an appropriate moment. He always does it so nicely. When he comes to the words, *That it should come to this! But two months dead*, listeners weep quite spontaneously. Truly. Three times I have seen it happen at afternoon performances at the Parnassus. I call it the George à la Gin effect.'

'A terrible loss,' said Pollitt sympathetically.

Crowley looked towards the entrance. 'He's gone out.'

'Did you see him go?'

'No. But he has left the room. He's going downstairs.'

'How, may I ask, do you know that?' said Pollitt to Crowley. Valentine caught the words.

'Our minds are attuned,' said Crowley.

'Oh, really? How interesting. No doubt you have much more to say to each other.'

'Yes, actually. We have,' Crowley said coolly. 'It's a spiritual connection. You wouldn't understand.'

Cabot knew when to exploit an opportunity and did not bother to pretend that he had not heard the exchange. 'Well that is delightful, Mr Crowley. You appreciate talent. He has many, many talents. Let me arrange for you to meet...'

At that, without a word, Jerome Pollitt, very gracefully and neatly, rose from his seat and stalked beautifully towards the door. Cabot hurried to follow, his sparse gingery hair sticking out at a precise right-angle above his left ear. Crowley sat sullenly for a moment, then finished his cognac in a gulp and followed too.

It was extremely cold in the street. They stood rather foolishly in a knot on the pavement because there was no sign of George Arden anywhere. Jerome was vexed. His plan had been to sweep grandly out of the club and make his way home to Chancery Lane, where he and Crowley were staying. Things had gone astray when he found that the annoying Cabot was sticking to him again like glue – was even trying his bulldog trick of catching him by the arm. Aleister had followed too and they now had to decide how to face down each other's annoyance.

Pollitt adopted a freezing dignity. 'I shall go to Chancery Lane tonight, Aleister. After that, I intend to return to Cambridge and thence, perhaps, to Kendal. You may, if you are lucky, catch me before I leave for the early train. Good night, Mr Cabot. I regret to tell you that your leading man is an unreliable amateur and your play is absolute rubbish.' Valentine gasped. With that, Pollitt turned briskly on his heel and departed.

'Oh don't worry about him,' growled his friend as he watched the vanishing figure. 'Tell me more, Cabot, about this actor of yours. I need to know. There's a use for him.'

'Ah,' said Valentine, a look of smooth discretion washing over his features. 'As his manager, I receive eighty percent.'

'What?'

'As his manager, I – um, I am always anxious to place him in productions around the capital. Around the globe itself.'

'Not an acting gig,' said Crowley, regarding Cabot with a look of disgust. 'You wouldn't understand. You're a slimey little thing, aren't you, Cabot? Don't be. You can't debase it, you know.'

'Slimey? Me, slimey? What do you take me for?'

'What you're on your way to becoming. It shows. And I can see it. Listen, you odd little man, I want to talk to your client for my own purposes. He has talents you can't dream of.'

'There! I told him, I told your friend Mr Polllitt, over and over. I told Madame Baranovsky too. Didn't believe me –'

'And I told you, it's not an acting gig. I have a society, a – well, a club, shall we say, which would be very interested in meeting Mr Arden.'

Valentine cogitated. He was getting cold and there was little to be salvaged from the wreckage of the evening but this. Although he was burning under the insults he had just received, he said soothingly, 'Then we can negotiate a fee for his services, Mr Crowley. Which would be -?'

'Merely his time, his conversation, his presence, at a kind of church.'

'You want him to do some readings at a service? He does a most beautiful speech at funerals. *Break, break, break At the foot of thy crags, O Sea!* Something like that perhaps? We did a recital at old Mr Ellison's wake. Attired in deepest black, very pale face, bit of greasepaint. A most mournful effect.'

Crowley looked at Valentine. 'Yes,' he said slowly. 'That's exactly the kind of thing I had in mind.'

'And the play we were discussing, Mr Crowley? I can make any number of adjustments to suit your tastes. You and I are privileged to be in a position to invest some of our wealth in the young man. Might I interest you in owning a portion of his future success?'

Crowley shrugged. 'Give me time to think it over.'

'Excellent! Then, this is my business card. Here is my residence – my offices are in the same building so you can call for me here – and we can discuss it all in more detail. Do come and see me. Think it over, of course, but pop by soon. Monday, Monday would be best, now I think of it, as we have a packed series of performances until then, part of our very successful and much talked-about run at the Parnassus.'

Crowley took the card and held it out under the lamplight to read the address. 'Monday, then.' He nodded briefly to Cabot and walked away. Glancing back, the manager's portly figure looked strangely lost, solitary among the crowds. He saw him hesitate and then go in the opposite direction.

When Crowley got back to their flat, he found Jerome was lying on the sofa asleep. The gaslight, turned very low, puttered quietly. He intended to creep past him to his bedroom but accidentally made a noise by kicking something made of glass which had been smashed on the floor. Pollitt woke up, looking tousled.

'So. You've come back,' he said with icy calm. 'I'm surprised you didn't stay out chasing that little freak.'

Crowley folded his arms and stood looking down at him with a sardonic smile on his face. 'You know I'm not interested in the average man. I cultivate the freak.'

'Obviously. Anyway, I've decided I don't much care. Do what you want. But I know very well that you're just as anxious about your reputation as any of us. You should be more careful.'

'I thought you were angry about my conversation with him?'

'I have come to the conclusion it doesn't matter as much as I thought it did. You've made no secret of the fact that you like abnormal people. You've actually said it to me before tonight. I suppose I should just let you get on with it. Go off and find as many abnormal people as you like. Just be more discreet; and give me a cigarette first.'

Crowley lit and passed one to his friend. 'I simply maintain the scientific attitude that it is from the abnormal that we learn.'

'And I suppose you'll say next that you've learned a lot from me.'

'And your implication is?'

'But it's true, isn't it? Am I one of your freaks?'

Crowley shrugged and sat down on the end of the sofa. 'That's for you to say. I'm pleased to find you more reasonable now anyway. And you have nothing to fear. This fellow happens to be an extraordinary find. Never mind about his being an actor or whatever. He saw into me, into my *past*, just like that. He is undoubtedly a step on the way. There aren't any accidental meetings on the Path. This is what I've been waiting for. He may be the guide I've been seeking, the one who will lead to the Hidden Church. He named – well, at least, he gave me some clues to a past incarnation. Or I think he did.'

'I'll bet he gave you some clues,' Pollitt said coldly, staring at the ceiling while a white tape of smoke unwound from his neglected cigarette. 'I hardly care any more; but I happened to notice that you were practically sitting in his lap. And he spouted some rot - and it could have been any rot really, because it's quite unfalsifiable - and you *wanted* to believe it because you *want* to find evidence in support of your rotten old magic.'

'He is simply a psychic, a natural medium.' Crowley said calmly. He gazed into the darkness of an alcove by the fireplace, across which a black velvet curtain was drawn. 'Where's he from, though? He has a face like one of those extraordinary portraits from that necropolis, those images painted on wood. What's the name of that place? Damn it, it was in a magazine I saw.' He got up suddenly, going to the magazine rack to spill newspapers all over the floor.

'What's his face got to do with what he had to say?' asked Pollitt softly. 'Unless you have a passion for the anaemic look of one long dead. I suppose that kind of face ought to interest you. I had no idea mine would become so boring for you so very quickly. Less than two months of perfect bliss and you already want to throw it away.'

'Do stop it. His face has nothing to do with it and neither has yours. You're interrupting my train of thought,' answered Crowley from where he knelt. 'I am only now, at this moment, beginning to get a glimpse of the importance of this discovery.'

'Are you quite lost to human feeling, Aleister?' asked Jerome in a small, frozen voice.

Crowley looked startled. He rose and sat on the end of the sofa again. After a moment, he said, 'Very well, you're jealous. And if you're jealous, it means you're feeling possessive. Perhaps you have allowed yourself to cultivate a sense of ownership.'

'Shouldn't I? Isn't there anything between us but the physical? Or am I *too* much of a freak for you?'

Crowley got up and started walking slowly about the room. He paused by the mantelpiece and picked up a stone from a little heap of pebbles arranged there. 'Don't ask questions like that,' he said restlessly. 'Don't force things. You know how it is, you know how things are. You understand me enough to know that I regard any attempt to control my actions as an impertinent intrusion.'

Pollitt enunciated a particularly forceful profanity in answer to that. Crowley ignored him and went on, 'Anyway, it's not only for me. His talents will be of particular interest to my fellow students. My one and only innocent purpose in obtaining Cabot's address is to persuade his client to accompany me to a meeting for examination..'

'Wait a minute,' said Pollitt, looking up sharply. 'Wait a minute. You obtained Cabot's address? You failed to mention *that* before, didn't you?'

'It's not what you think it is,' said Crowley a little dangerously. 'Please don't allow this taint of emotion to confuse the discussion.'

'Taint of emotion? Is that what emotion is to you? A taint?'

'Stop it, stop. Now. I want you to completely separate in your mind this matter of the actor tonight and this confusion about – about us, about what we can be to each other – and imagine something new. Imagine how it would be to invoke a great Power and to harness the clarity of vision of a person – a person such as this actor - actually within that invocation. Do you not see, he's simply a sensitive technical instrument? And he might be a battery too, a voltaic coil, a *source* of power ...'

'Rubbish and piffle,' Pollitt answered, flinging his cigarette end into the fireplace. 'I went with Cabot to see Madame bloody Baranovsky a few days ago and all she did was take my money. I even paid her to prophesy what I wanted but she got completely taken in by Cabot's fake vision. You're being taken in too, Aleister. Why would he sit there simpering mysteriously into a coffee cup, showing his profile, and then disappear except to make us all go chasing after him as if he was ... I don't know, something worth chasing? It's to intrigue us, to pique our interest. And he certainly piqued your interest, didn't he? All I can say is if you think that any associate of Valentine Cabot's isn't fake, then, well, you're an idiot.'

There was a great deal more like that. Jerome had never taken seriously Aleister's principal preoccupation, to obtain first-hand sensory evidence of spiritual beings. Every explanation he offered was subsumed within an emotional morass – or so it seemed to Crowley – and however much he tried to steer the conversation towards his passion for scientific research of the paranormal, Pollitt brought it back to a kind of possessiveness that Crowley was not prepared to understand. Eventually, he had to accept Jerome's intention of going back to Cambridge for a while – although Pollitt conceded that he might not go on to Westmorland; but, he said, if Pollitt was going away, he would be taking himself off too, in quite another geographical direction. He kept saying (pompously, in Jerome's opinion) that it was time to make serious preparations for 'the Alps expedition' and that he needed to talk things through with his climbing mentor, Eckenstein. (Talk things through with that little tart, more like, thought Pollitt). Tight-lipped as they said good-bye, they agreed to meet at Chancery Lane next Monday, to be together for a while longer and see how things turned out. It felt on the verge of being final.

*

In the early hours of that same morning, Valentine Cabot came home with one clear purpose: to get as drunk as possible before George came back. As soon as he got upstairs, he retrieved a heavy bottle of brandy from the back of his wardrobe, which he had liberated from Alexandra Roberts's Christmas wine cabinet, and went into George's room. As predicted, it was empty. He lit the oil lamp and plumped himself down on the side of the bed. His feet were cold and wet and as he took his shoes off, he flung them one after the other at the opposite wall. They made a kind of wet flapping noise like mackerels. Then he punched the pillow into a dome and deliberately sat on it, his back to the iron rods of the headboard and the wet from his socks blotting into the eiderdown.

He was already a little bit drunk when he left Dame Fortune's but now he decided to finish all of this bottle and see what happened. He would sit right here and drink and wait for him to come home. Because after Crowley had left him, Valentine had wandered the streets for well nigh three hours, asking for George everywhere he could think of, anywhere he might have gone. He had got frozen to the bone and laughed at and pitied. He'd gone into the Parnassus and asked the manager there. In passing, he had also asked the snake dancer and she had jeered at him publicly. People had laughed. And before that, it had all been going so beautifully.

After Dr Watson had left, that was when everything fell to bits.

He tried to recall all the details – it was so confusing now, a memory of glinting glasses on the table and the cacophany of background laughter and noise, and Jerome Pollitt's soft blue eyes and cigar smoke and a little too much champagne. He had been so intent on trying to reel them in, he had hardly paid attention to much else. And after all that, Pollitt had asserted that he was an unreliable amateur. 'And,' he had said in that misleadingly languid way he had, 'your play is absolute rubbish.' The words stung even now, particularly as he had believed that he and Pollitt were in sympathy on some level – he was always putting his arm through Valentine's, for example.

He balanced the bottle carefully on the surface of the pillow between his crossed legs and scrabbled out his notebook from his breast pocket. With the small attached pencil, under the heading 'Ingrate', he began to make a list of all the things that had gone wrong this evening because of George. All their slender finances had been sunk in this night's endeavour: George's sock money, his own rent money, Alexandra's loan, advances from the Revue Parnassus, his cigar money, every kind of money. He owed enormous sums to his tailor and bootmaker (though it was a long time since his last pair of boots) and had a stupendous tab at every club and restaurant in town. And the best that could be expected from this evening's supreme effort was a performance at a church service.

By the time Valentine began to see the dimpled bottom of the bottle when he tilted it up, he was entertaining cruel suspicions about Dr Watson, who had vanished shortly before George did. Watson, Watson. Had he mentioned Arden when he bumped into the fellow before? Had it been mere chance that he was hanging about at Dame Fortune's? He'd been sitting with his cronies by the fire, so why had he come and sat himself at that empty table so very near the curtains? Had he been signalling to George? For that matter, who had George been talking to this very morning?

Valentine tried to reconstruct the scene from memory and felt sure, now he really thought about it, that Watson had looked guilty when he had been spotted over there: quite as if he did not want to be noticed. It was a premeditated act of blatant theft. He would not allow it: if another manager wanted George's business, then he would have to pay. There was a contract somewhere, for one thing, and it was all legal and binding – even if it was written on a napkin. If Watson dared to entice Arden away, he would have to offer sufficient compensation. After all, the actor's income was Cabot's livelihood. *Money first,* he scribbled; and then added a fair number of choice words in his notebook to express his outrage at the plot, although by this time the letters tied themselves in knots with tails at unintended angles. At the thought of his betrayal, he sincerely wanted to shake George by the lapels like a rabbit.

Later, when George Arden did finally creep into his bedroom, it came as an unpleasant shock to him to see Valentine once again on his bed. He was awake this time, and sitting in his holey socks, crosslegged on the pillow, with his back to the ironwork and a bottle between his legs. He stared at George with bloodshot eyes which had difficulty in focusing. The wick from the oil lamp on the desk was sooty and the tall flame flickered constantly, shadows distorting his face and pulsing over the walls.

'George, why?' Valentine said in a slurred but pathetic whisper. 'Why, George?'

'Why, what?' he whispered back, seeing the warning signs and not creeping further into the room but lingering warily by the door he had just shut behind him.

'You know I would have done everything for you, don't you? You and I, we would have been rich and famous. Beautiful clothes, lovely socks, everything.' Valentine shook his head sadly. 'Yet I shouldn't complain. It is the way. I sow, others harvest. I expect you're surprised to see me drunk like this. So uncharacteristic. All caused by you. And keep your bloody voice down when you answer.'

'But all I did was go out for a walk,' said George in a low, wheedling tone. 'I went for some fresh air, it was stuffy. That man made me scared. Like the lady with the knife. And Dr Watson helped. I just walked, just thinking about the things he said. I forgot to come back, that's all. Nothing else. Don't be angry.'

'What?' Valentine massaged his forehead. 'As God is my witness, every farthing was spent tonight. And if you'd just said your little speech, but two months - or is it three months? – dead – we could have been in with a chance.' He began to align the bottle elaborately for another careful sip. 'One magnificent chance. Pollitt likes me. He knows what I've done for you, you ingrate. You ingrate. The things I've done for you...'

George decided it would be better to leave. He could see that

Valentine was never going to go back to his own room and his best hope was to get himself out of his way. Tomorrow, he would have calmed down and become bitter and depressed, but reasonable. He began stealthily to turn the handle of the door behind his back. 'I'm sorry, Valentine,' he whispered. 'I'm truly sorry. It's not my fault, the way my brain works, it's just the strain and stress, Dr Watson said it was.'

In a sudden flash of rage, possibly set off by the name Watson, Valentine surged off the bed and came towards him. George thought he must be more than usually drunk because walking in a straight line was almost beyond his powers. Nevertheless, he zig-zagged surprisingly fast. George started to pull the door open but he had only got it a few inches wide when he found himself whirled away from it. The room flashed past him and he was suddenly on his hands and knees. He looked up to see Valentine slide the bolt with a gesture of finality, and lean his back against the door. He had a satisfied look on his face, as if George had done the thing he hoped he would do. Surprisingly, he had managed to retain the bottle in his hand.

'Yours is a mean, acquisitive character, George, but you're mistaken in him. He's just a petty magazine writer, you know. Not an original playwright like me. No point in going off with him.'

'But I didn't go off with anyone. Or yes, I did, I did go off with that doctor but only for a little while because he was leaving the club at the same time, I remember it clearly, and it was mere chance!' His own voice sounded unconvincing. 'Please, Valentine, put down the bottle, go to bed ...'

'So you admit it. That is actually very helpful.' Valentine looked up at the ceiling and beginning to speak more loudly, raised his hand in oath. 'As God is my witness, I just can't trust you anymore. Nothing you say can prove your innocence. What is the point of living when every farthing is gone? It's just as if you'd murdered me in cold blood.'

'Sshh! Everyone will hear us! And how can I prove my innocence? And trust me about what? And why is it my fault if you spent all the money? I didn't do anything!'

'But you did do something. You ran away! You betrayed me!' Valentine continued in a louder voice still. 'You left me floundering and you ruined everything.'

It was rare for George to assert himself but kneeling there on the carpet, he frowned and said angrily, 'You have to stop stealing from me. You stole Mrs Roberts's money for the rent.'

Valentine propelled himself away from the door by pushing himself off from it like a swimmer. He did indeed feel as if he were swimming quite slowly through the air as he advanced on George where he crouched on the floor. He was still gripping the bottle, and for a moment, George must have thought he was going to hit him with it because he cowered down, raising his arm. The gesture annoyed Valentine and he caught him by the front of his shirt. He twisted the fabric in his fist and shook him just as he had hoped he would be able to, like a little rabbit, hissing, 'Prove it then. Prove it was me who took the rent money! Prove it wasn't you who stole it!'

George was light and the brandy made Valentine powerful. A stud pinged off as the shirt ripped and the collar came away in his hand. Valentine laughed suddenly, 'Oopsydaisy!' He swayed back, looked at the collar, dropped it and took another swig, squinting down at George.

'Don't do that!' said George, clutching his throat. 'I'll go, Valentine. You'll never find me again. And how could I steal my own money? It was money I'd saved in a sock under my bed and it was you who stole it. You steal my money and use me and hurt me. And I can go. You are a thief and I'm not your slave.'

'You're going?' breathed Valentine, suddenly afraid that things had gone too far. 'No, no, I'm going to teach you how to respect me and … and not keep running away. Three very important lessons.' He tried to pull George up onto his feet. His intention was genuinely to help him up because he was now sorry he had shaken him about but he was very drunk and his balance was shot. 'Stand up. Geddup, geddup!' The control required to bend down was beyond his power and he capsized, sprawling face down on the carpet. George swiftly rose and unbolted the door.

Valentine tried to work out why the pattern of the carpet was suddenly so close to his face. With a great to-do, he heaved himself upright and began very ineptly to give chase. When he got to the head of the stairs, he saw that there were several phantom Georges down in the dim hallway. He focused and they slid together and he saw that he had paused, looking back up from the front door. Maybe he was thinking he had nowhere to run to this time. Good, thought

Valentine.

Valentine didn't want to shout and wake everyone, so he did the logical thing and threw the bottle at him. It sailed in a perfect silent arc all the way down, all the way down, falling far short of George and smashing on the marble floor just by the bottom step, a big splash in a pattern of golden brandy and broken glass. Then he decided to go roaring down the stairs to catch him. He wanted to smack his dim-witted face, for one thing; and because he'd already smashed the bottle, it wouldn't matter now if he made any more noise. As he began to run down, his stockinged foot slipped. He went rolling painfully over and over, finally hitting his head with a bone-breaking impact on the last step at the bottom. And he lay there completely still. Terrified, George ran across to the body just as various voices were heard throughout the house. Mr Burroughs was the first to stick his head over the banisters.

'Hey! Down there! What's going on?' In the dim light below, Mr Burroughs saw the weird witch-boy, George Arden, kneeling next to that fat idiot Cabot and looking up at Burroughs with his great dark eyes. He saw a black pool spreading on the hall floor under Cabot's head. He could smell brandy even from here. 'You down there, Arden! What have you done to him?'

'What's happening?'

'Who's there?'

Voices of servants floated down from the very top floor, and those of Dafydd Williams and Mrs Roberts were heard as they emerged from their various rooms. Feet were drumming on the stairs.

'It's murder, Mrs Roberts!' shouted Mr Burroughs decidedly. 'Murder in our own house. Valentine Cabot is done for and that little madman has done it. Smashed him over the head! Killed him outright! Look, down there! I told you he was a bad lot. I told you.'

Mrs Roberts, Elizabeth Jenkins, Janet Fairlight, Amy Matthews, Dafydd Williams, Albert Burroughs, all were running downstairs towards the body in the hall, shrieking or shouting in horror.

George ran away.

CHAPTER ELEVEN

George moved like lightning. He ran out into the street, escaping the clamour behind him, the feet rushing down the stairs and the sight of Valentine. His hands were covered in blood where he had tried to raise his friend's head from the ground and call him back. There was no time anyway. The words shouted by Mr Burroughs soared out like a thrown noose. George had no defence against such things, had never had a defence: just to disappear, lie low, fly away. So he did.

Outside there was a tall street lamp ten yards from the house and he glimpsed a figure beyond it walking away into the night. He dared not go that way. Across the street were the railings round the little Square and beyond them earthy flowerbeds and grass and winter shrubbery and bare trees. George ran across the road and climbed the fence. He threw himself into the shadows of the thick evergreen hedge. Under his hands, he felt the prickle of twigs, broken flints, crumbles of soil. He was acutely aware of the fact that the dirt would stick to the blood and that it was Valentine's blood. Valentine's blood.

He sat there, trying to hear above the pulse in his ears what was happening over at the house. After a little while, he vomited, as silently as he could. Then he just continued to sit there, shivering, damp, laying his head on his knees. The skin on his hands began to tighten as the blood dried. He knew it would be under his nails, rusty brown, and he needed a nailbrush to scrub it clean. This distressed him disproportionately and he kept thinking about it. And he kept seeing the pure, serene glide of the bottle through the air before it hit the floor and Valentines lopsided red face peering down at him from the top of the stairs. As if by resting the bottle in memory there in the air, nothing further would happen. As if the smash of the bottle had been the cause of Valentine's death.

As the hours slouched by, George tried to account for everything leading up to the crash but he failed to make sense of it at all. He knew that Valentine had been suffering in some way and he knew it was a kind of despair, angry disappointment. 'But I didn't cause that, did I?' he thought. 'Did I make that happen?'

He heard people arrive and make noises over at the house. They would be doing something to Valentine's body, but he was already gone. There was no point doing anything to it, except taking it away and putting it in the earth. He knew a little bit about the police. He had encountered that kind of authority and he knew it was always best to keep away from them. And he knew that Albert Burroughs didn't like him and would lie and try to hurt him. George was so sorry. He began to weep. He thought how Valentine had cared about him and for him. He knew that he had been exploited and used by him, that was also true; but it had nonetheless been a kind of protection, even a kind of love. Valentine had found George work and made sure that he could earn money for them both; and George had accepted and tolerated it because that was what his life was like. He had to barter what he had in order to survive. It was his long-standing method of existing, as rudderless as a leaf on a river, swept from one eddy to another. Valentine was an eddy which had ceased. Now he would drift until another one took him somewhere else. On and on, never reaching the sea.

Without anywhere to go and aware that he should not be seen abroad looking as he did, George stayed under the hedge for the duration of that night and all through the next freezing misty day, listening to the police and the servants coming and going at the house. At one point, a ragged-looking man came and sat next to him and talked nonsense about dead heads in shopping bags and George was not sure if the man was really there or if he was a ghost. He slunk away as soon as he could.

He wanted to find water very badly. He needed to wash and he needed to drink. He was hungry too, although the gnawing mess of feelings in his stomach made it oddly irrelevant that part of that complexity was a simple need for food. He waited until darkness had fallen again and began to wander. At about midnight, he crept up to a horse trough and broke the ice on the water to wash himself. He felt the cold but it did not trouble him much. George sometimes even wondered if he himself were a ghost. Or half a ghost. Could there be such a thing as half a ghost?

He weaved his way through the streets towards the Thames and along its banks, thinking that he could perhaps find a boat to take him away. Dawn found him sitting on a crate by the Pool, smelling the river and staring at the masts going up like white pencils into the mist. Hundreds of ships were moored there, along the wooden quays and to each other, reaching out into the Thames, rafts and forests of them. They were living things, vibrating with every breath of air, the ropes singing strangely, the clop of dark water against their sides a stealthy indecipherable language.

Noises of humanity on board: people were stirring. Men were arriving to work on the dockside, calling to each other cheerfully through the fog. On the water, small deft lightermen were knocking against the hulls as cargo was unloaded or loaded onto them; ropes were pulled, shouting and snatches of song filled the air. It was overwhelming: sacks and barrels and crates of produce being brought to shore, spices, sugar, fruit, cloth, tea, coffee, coal, iron, everything under the sun. He watched entranced, almost forgetting his troubles.

Nobody looked at him much. Eventually he saw the distant figure of an officer from the River Police, whose job it was to oversee the Pool of London, take notice of him sitting there and begin to stroll towards him. At that point, George drifted away. He must look so out of place, as fragile as glass, still dressed for the evening. He tried to think how to get other clothes but his internal map of London had shattered into fragments. Where was the Parnassus? Where was Mrs Day's? All he found in his pockets were seven pennies, a little clasp knife and Janet Fairlight's handkerchief. He had kept it, with the intention of giving it back, ever since that day he retrieved it from the cobbles in the market. Painful homesickness flared at the sight – as if Mrs Roberts's house had been anything other than a temporary refuge.

It was over thirty-six hours since he had last eaten and by mid-morning he was faint and sick, so he used a penny to buy some bread. He next became aware of himself on his way along Shoreditch High Street. Then he was resting under an awning because the rain had started coming down. Liverpool Street Station – people, too much noise, more luggage, more bundles and bags being transported to and fro. And then on and out again, down behind a market, along a little alley as night fell and there was a deserted house in front of him in the gloom. He slid in through a crazily-boarded window and crouched down on a smelly pile of ancient and mouldy material that could once have been clothes. Half-way through the night, he began to be bothered by a ghost who remembered the Plague years and asked him plaintively over and over again what had happened to Nell and little Simon? Nell, Nell? Why did she so? Why comes she not again? I'd be rare good to her now, I swear it.

'Too late,' said George at the ghost as he stumbled out of the place.

*

'And you say you saw this as it happened, sir? Actually saw him take the bottle in his hand and attack the deceased with it?' The lined face of Inspector Miller creased a little more as he tried to decipher notes made with a blunt pencil stub by someone else in the early hours of the morning. 'And yet you also say that you "emerged from your room at about five minutes past the hour of two o'clock in the morning due to having heard an almighty crash"?'

'Yes, that is correct, inspector,' said Mr Albert Burroughs. 'I heard the crash, came out of my room, looked over and saw the foreign rascal finishing him off with the bottle over the head, bang. But as mentioned previously, I had already been awakened by raised voices. I was on the alert for something like this, in fact, been expecting it. In his room, Arden's room, there was an argument going on.'

'Foreign rascal, you say, sir?' asked Miller, glancing at the neat gentleman sitting opposite him. His hands were resting in front of him and the nails were particularly white and clean. He had a habit of making little taps upon the table and Miller's eye was drawn to a black ring on his finger.

'Well, he looks like a foreigner. Dark eyes, hair.'

'Very dark skin, sir?'

'Well, sallow. Foreign-looking.'

'Accent foreign too?'

'No, not at all. Perfect English, quality accent.'

'I see. Note that, Browning. And you did not emerge from your room until the sound of the "almighty crash", it says here.'

'No, but I was awake and listening.'

'And you state that you heard the following words or phrases uttered, "You'll murder me in cold blood", "You've betrayed me", "You are a thief". Is that correct, sir?'

'Yes, it certainly is. Much of the conversation was in low tones but those phrases were said in a louder tone and were clearly audible. I have no doubt that the younger was out to rob the older man.'

'Could you be absolutely sure whose voice was speaking, sir?'

'Oh, yes. It was Cabot for the most part who was speaking loudly, probably trying to protect himself. I think he tried to flee from his attacker.'

The Inspector nodded calmly. He looked again at his notes. 'But he didn't cry out for assistance. So the sound that caused you actually to come out and have a look was what, sir?'

'The crash, of course.'

'Might that crash have been the sound of a bottle smashing on the *floor*, sir?' put in young Detective Browning, who was making notes of the interview. He received a sardonic glance from the inspector.

'No! I believe the wretched youth threw or pushed his manager down the stairs, which was the crash I heard, and then picked up the bottle and brought it down hard on his head. It smashed and you saw for yourself the blood, the glass, brandy on the floor.'

'Large chap is he, sir?' asked Inspector Miller.

'Well, not really what you'd call large. But wiry. Hidden muscle, that kind of thing, must have - because I heard them talking about his occupation, shifting scenery at the theatre. And twenty years younger than the deceased.'

'Very well, Mr Burroughs. I think we have enough to be going on with here. Thank you for your time, sir. Should we need to speak to you again, you'll be continuing at this address, sir?'

'Yes, Inspector. I hope I know my duty. I am a court reporter, as I mentioned - and I hear the very worst of what humanity is capable of. As do you, Inspector, of course. And I would like to add this, to be noted, if you please, Detective. Valentine Cabot was in the habit of bringing young actors into the house. He was their manager but, in my opinion, based on impartial observation, he did not maintain a respectable professional relationship with his clients. This George Arden was the only one of the young men to actually reside in the premises. I protested at the time, I protested to Mrs Roberts. She informed me that Cabot deliberately, deviously, introduced the fellow into the household by placing him, under cover of darkness, without prior consultation, in the empty room of a recently deceased boarder.'

'Deliberately and deviously were her own words, sir?'

'No, not as such. But they were implied; and in my opinion, she should not have submitted to this subterfuge. The fellow had not

111

been assessed or interviewed and as far as any of us knew, was little better than the sweeping of the gutter.'

'So you would say that ironically enough, the deceased brought his own nemesis into the house – no, don't write that down, Browning.'

'I would indeed. And I want to add that Arden was a liar. His words are not to be trusted.'

'And have you evidence of his lies?'

'He is a subtle liar. Question him on any matter and he will change his story half a dozen times without turning a hair. Whatever he were to say about the household would be tainted with falsehood. He has a particular dislike of me myself. I am aware of it.'

'I see,' said Miller. 'And did you personally feel threatened by this fellow, Mr Burroughs?'

'Oh, yes. All the time. He was the kind that would carry a stiletto. I avoided him as best I could.'

'Have you got all that, Browning? Very well, thank you, Mr Burroughs. We may need to interview you again of course, but this is enough to be going on with. And I do seem to recall seeing some of your work in the newspapers. I'll look out for it.'

Mr Burroughs was shown out of the dining room where the police had set up a temporary office. They were interviewing all members of the household in depth. There were only four policemen involved by now, two constables who was still poking about upstairs in the suspect's room; and Inspector Miller and a Detective Browning who had come in this morning fresh to the case. The original officers who had arrived last night had taken the first witness statements and had gone off duty. And the body had been taken away by the undertakers. Now it was those initial notes that the Inspector was using as a basis for questioning.

'Right. Elizabeth Jennings, Cook. Show Mrs Jennings in please, Detective.'

'Jenkins, sir. Elizabeth Jenkins, Housekeeper,' said Browning quietly.

It was a dreary business and there was nothing particularly interesting about the case. It was turning out to be a sordid matter; but they were all sordid, really. The household was obviously a morally lax, tainted kind of place: artists, actors, writers, assorted theatricals (who apparently turned up night and day without being challenged, according to the maidservant). Miller was unimpressed by the lady of the house, a Blue Stocking type, who nevertheless was so excessively upset by the recent tragic events that she could hardly speak. That made him suspect an improper relationship between landlady and lodger right away.

'Mark my words,' he said to young Browning, 'there was more between those two than was respectable.'

The relationship between the murder victim and his alleged murderer was also a rum go. The victim had called himself his 'manager'. Exactly what aspects of Arden's talents he managed remained to be seen. Inspector Miller supposed he would have to send someone round to Wardour Street and ask questions at the Revue Parnassus, try and glean some background information and whether the acting job had really been enough to financially support the pair of them. As for their exact relationship, he suspected the worst. Albert Burroughs the court reporter had his damning tale to tell. The man would naturally be on the side of Justice and Impartiality. After all, it was upon the veracity of his accounts that the reputation of his newspaper stood or fell. And as he thought about it, Miller was almost sure that the name of Mr Albert Burroughs was attached to a rather complimentary report of a case that he himself had been associated with. He would check later in the scrapbook where he pasted his newspaper cuttings.

Miller had had his constables make notes of the visible evidence, had gone through the two men's rooms and seized papers and effects to show the relationship of the deceased to the suspect, along with assorted wigs, costumes and bags of stage make-up. He then gave permission to one of the maidservants to mop up and clear away the scene of the crime. She was doing so right now: he could hear her snivelling in the hall. The whole household was in shock.

The inspector said to the detective as they walked away, 'So. Catch the little bastard. Sounds like a wog. We'll have the warrant today. You take care of it, Browning. Open and shut. He'll hang alright.'

'Yes sir. Except, sir, I don't see how he threw that big bloke down the stairs, then ran to the bottom to bang him over the head hard enough to kill him – was the victim standing up or lying down? And those brandy bottles are thick, sir. If that smashed on his head, it would have stove his skull right in. But the wound was a different kind of thing altogether, a gash such as would occur if the head struck the sharp angle of the step at the bottom. And I think the neck might have been broke, not to mention the position of the wound doesn't make sense either, nor the way the ...'

'He did it, Detective. We've got a reliable witness who says he *saw* him do it. Can't argue with that. And he didn't *throw* him. A little push would do it, what with the alcohol involved. Maybe he slid down the banisters after him. Don't make things complicated. I want a nice, neat case sewn up quickly. We've got enough on our plate already and this isn't the bloody Ripper.'

The younger detective very much wished he himself could have conducted the interviews and separated and pinned down each and every thread of the evidence. He didn't like doing things shabbily when they could be done thoroughly and well. His mother had given him an old copy of *The Strand Magazine* and he very much admired the methods of a Mr Holmes he'd been reading about.

*

On the day of the funeral, down below stairs, the girls were all huddled round the kitchen table, listening to Mrs Jenkins reading from the Psalms. She read very slowly, using pince-nez glasses to help her make out the tiny print.

For the Enemy hath persecuted my soul; he hath smitten my life down unto the ground; he hath made me to dwell in darkness as those that have been long dead...

Occasionally she stumbled over a word but she persisted solemnly to the end. Then she shut the book and took off the glasses and looked round with unusual tenderness at the attentive girls.

'So. There it is,' she said. 'We don't none of us know a thing. One minute up and about, the next dead as a doornail.'

'He was always nice to me,' said Amy.

'Yes, he was. He was a gentleman and kindly, however odd he might have behaved from time to time,' said Mrs Jenkins.

'He was a funny gentleman too. He made me laugh. He could sing. He *did* sing quite often,' said Lily.

Amy sighed, 'I don't ever remember thinking that Mr George would go murdering people though.'

'It's a wicked idea,' said Janet suddenly. She was particularly red-eyed; and although she did not like to confess it openly, her tears were not so much for Mr Cabot as for George Arden. 'He would never do nothing to harm nobody,' Janet muttered.

'Mr Burroughs said he did it,' said Lily in a hushed voice.

'Now then,' intervened Mrs Jenkins. 'I don't want to hear you girls talking about Mr Burroughs or what he might or might not have said. It's evidence. That means it's going to be used in a court of law. And if Mr Arden stands trial for murder, then Mr Burroughs will have to take the witness box and say it all aloud to the judge.'

'And if he does say it all aloud, like, that means that Mr George would be hanged dead,' said Janet. 'Because I heard him, I heard him talking to Mr Williams about it.'

'You was eavesdropping again,' said Lily. 'She's done that before, Mrs Jenkins. She was eavesdropping when I took the meat in from the butcher's boy yesterday. I caught her.'

'She don't like anyone to hear because she's sweet on the butcher's boy,' whispered Amy to Janet behind her hand but Janet had more pressing things to think about than the butcher's boy.

'I never did, I never did go eavesdropping anywhere, but as I was cleaning in the parlour, they were talking in the hall. Horrible things he said, such as Mr Cabot being drunk -'

'Well, he was,' said Amy.

'Tch!' said Mrs Jenkins, who had been thinking about preparing the cold cuts and pickles for when Mrs Roberts came back with the others and only half-listening to the girls. 'Speak no ill of the dead, Miss Matthews, or they come back and haunt you.'

'Well, if Mr Cabot *could* come back,' said Janet, interested in the idea, 'he would be able to tell the truth, and he would say straightaway that he slipped on them stairs and landed on that smash at the bottom – and that Mr Burroughs is telling a big fat lie.'

'Janet Fairlight, I am shocked at you. You will remain silent for the rest of the day. The idea! Speaking to me like that about one of our gentlemen! I shall have words with your mother next time I see her. No more of your cheek. Get on and scrub them pans!'

Janet pressed her lips together, but her face was so white and her eyes so red that Mrs Jenkins immediately regretted being so harsh. But discipline was discipline. Later on, perhaps, she would give the girls some liquorice from the jar and sit them down again and tell them about Mary in the garden finding the stone rolled away, so they could go to bed with hope in their hearts.

CHAPTER TWELVE

When Jerome Pollitt got back to Cambridge, he was delighted to run into a whole crowd of acquaintances. It was impossible to resist them: their enthusiasm was so very flattering. Consequently, he found himself quite accidentally agreeing to put in an informal guest appearance on the Friday night. For the two years previously, he had been voted President of the Footlights Dramatic Club; but among the undergraduates, he was most adored and celebrated for his wonderful performances as a female impersonator. There was his Diane de Rougy, for example. 'Diane' was his homage to the fascinating Liane de Pougy, Parisian dancer and Sapphic demi-mondaine; or there was his Loie Fuller persona, the American girl whom Paris was raving about. It was in the wigs and extravagant costumes of Diane and Loie that Pollitt crossed the threshold to another dimension. He soared lighter than air, sometimes a glorious blonde, sometimes a dark beauty, undulating in the shimmering silks of the Serpentine Dance. On this occasion, of course, it was no more than an informal song or two for an appreciative audience of friends but the champagne party afterwards cheered him up considerably. The resultant hangover kept him quiet and sedate until lunchtime on Sunday. He spent the morning flicking through his scrapbook and re-reading some of his notices:

> *The great success of the evening was once more Mr H.C.Pollitt who made a most bewitching 'Diane de Rougy' in a charming costume of light blue trimmed with black. His song and dance, 'Di, Di, Di' from 'Go-Bang' was given with all the grace of an accomplished young lady, and his Serpentine Dance sent the audience into rapturous applause, which was not satisfied until Diane had responded with a couple of recalls.*

As the afternoon brightened up, he found the spare key and strolled down to Crowley's rooms in Trinity Street. The place had been shut up for weeks and smelt fusty. He got the landlord to send someone up to light a fire and make a cup of coffee for him and then, nursing a lingering headache, he loitered about trying to find something amusing to do. He picked up this and that magazine or pamphlet and threw them back down without reading them.

The trouble was everything here was so freighted with Aleister's personality. Over there the shelves were loaded with his books: acres of them. In the corner was his fishing rod; above the door, a worn ice pick. Sitting down next to the card table with its scatter of poker chips, he opened the mahogany box of chessmen and picked up a little lead knight. He always beats everyone at chess, he thought. He held it for a moment and then placed it carefully back.

To be truthful, their divergent interests were becoming more and more apparent as the weeks passed. They shared nothing. Aleister might currently be affecting the floppy bow ties and rings of an Oscar but really, he wasn't ever going to *be* an Oscar. Pollitt wondered frequently what exactly he would be in the end. He was certain it would be something unconventional; but he was also becoming certain that he himself had nothing to contribute to it. It was preposterous anyway, thinking about permanence. He must hold back, keep something in reserve: for there was no such thing as certainty or even safety. Ridiculous to look for it.

To distract himself, he took out and re-read the last letter he had received from Beardsley.

Hôtel Cosmopolitain, Menton
10th January 1898

My dear pretty Pollitt,
I will make you the most adorable Bambino as soon as ever I can say 'finished' of Volpone. Continue to light candles for my safe delivery...

His mind went back to that hotel verandah, looking out at the incessant Dieppe rain last summer. And Aubrey had been forced to change lodgings all because poor disgraced Oscar had turned up. Nobody could be seen to associate with him now, not after the dreadful scandal which had sent them all scurrying for cover and reduced Aubrey practically to penury. England was becoming impossible. How carefully Jerome worked to contrive a life for society at home, a presentable vista to roll down like a painted backdrop – just as fanciful, just as flimsy. How tiring it was always to lie. But no, it was easy. It was only difficult when one kept a foot in both rooms, as it were, and dithered on the threshold. Completely immerse oneself in one or the other and the equal-and-opposite reality simply faded away –

His thoughts were interrupted by a knock at the door. He folded the letter and thrust it into his pocket. A friend of his, Arthur

Radwell, had heard he had arrived back in town and had managed to track him down. Arthur's family were from Bath and he was about to return there for the duration of the Lent term. He explained heatedly at the door, even before being invited to enter, that he had just been rusticated for insulting his tutor but it was all a misunderstanding because the old man was deaf anyway and he had never meant what he said he had meant. Pollitt listened indifferently but nevertheless waved him in for a chat. After describing the events leading up to the unjust rustication in copious detail, Radwell asked Pollitt how things were working out. At this point, Pollitt became quite glad to have an interested, partisan and captive listener.

'The main problem, as I see it, is that Aleister is becoming more and more involved in the whatever-it-is, Search for Ectoplasm, and I find it tedious. I dislike the secrecy and gloom of it. And you simply can't guess what he's got set up in the sitting room, hidden behind a curtain! How can I contend with it all?'

'Oh, don't worry about it, Pollitt. He'll lose interest soon enough. It's an undergrad thing, always wanting to join secret societies and be different from everyone else. We all go through it. You wait. He'll turn into a banker or a brewer or something.'

Pollitt shook his head. 'No, it's gone a lot further than that, Arthur dear. Crowley not only likes to give the impression that he's seeking out the very worst kinds of diabolism, he actually does seek out the very worst kind of diabolism.'

'Then you must get to the root of it all,' said Radwell cheerily, who was very keen on the new theories being developed in Vienna. 'Work out why it is. Confront him with the reason and hey presto! he'll leave it all behind. It'll be something in his childhood. It usually is, they say.'

'Really? How terribly original,' said Pollitt kindly. 'Nobody ever thought of that before.'

'Well, that idea's pretty obvious, obviously,' admitted Radwell. 'The point is that if Crowley can find out what suppressed thing is causing him to behave so irrationally, then he can integrate it, overcome it. Rise above it. You know, get it out in the open. It'll be a repressed desire to kill his father and marry his mother, of course.'

Pollitt laughed as a thought struck him. 'You look so sweet when you're being an amateur alienist – your eyes behind those spectacles go quite fanatical, you know, it's utterly charming – so to encourage you, I'll tell you a secret: the poor fellow's mother thinks hansom cabs are inventions of the devil and any reference to them is considered obscene in his family. How would you incorporate that into your system?'

'Has she been committed to an insane asylum?' asked Radwell.

'Not at all. They're all frightfully respectable. Just very, very afflicted with religion.' Pollitt sighed. 'In fact, I remember the exact words he used when he told me about it. He kicked over the traces, you see, like any self-respecting young fellow would, but in the most extreme way. Tried to drown his tutor or something. Delightfully amusing story. Anyway, he said to me, I swear in these exact words, *I simply went over to Satan's side – and to this hour, I cannot tell why.*'

'But this makes perfect sense, really!' said Radwell enthusiastically. 'The oppressions of his early life were caused by Christianity; therefore, he's flipped the whole thing on its head. The Christian Church is his patriarch, his father, and he needs to kill it off.'

'So is Satan his dear mama, whom he wishes to marry?' asked Pollitt in some confusion. 'I don't think it's as crude as that. For one thing, he is also extremely clever, Radwell. He does half of it to shock and mock people, and I'm not always sure how seriously he means what he says. At the same time, he's brimming with earnestness about these powers and spirits and demons. He actually frightens me sometimes.'

'Well,' said Radwell, 'that *proves* it's a form of rebellion, doesn't it? It's a kind of weapon. And we all have a youthful inclination to revolt. It's Nature's way.'

'Quite,' agreed Pollitt. 'But it could be done far more elegantly, don't you thing? If it *is* a need to shock, which I am not entirely convinced it is, it can be done through collecting Aubrey's pictures and dressing up very beautifully in ladies' clothing. Aleister says that in a wig, I'm a perfect Rossetti come to life.'

'It has to be admitted, Pollitt, you make a beautiful woman.'

'Exactly! And I bring joy to all – and perhaps just a little healthy confusion to the undergrads. I do not feel the need to become endangered, either physically or spiritually. Crowley, on the other hand, has a horrible need to master and break things, master mountains, break rules. And do the most disgusting experiments in the living room. I'm at my wits' end, Radwell, and heaven knows what the domestics think. I tell him all the time to clear up after himself.'

Radwell nodded, not quite grasping the full extent of Pollitt's sufferings under Crowley's growing obsession. Jerome could see this but did not feel well enough to explain further. He ran his hands through his golden hair, rather making it stand on end, and said, 'Arthur, I have such a terrible headache. What I really need is a sandwich or better still, a pie. Just a little one with gravy in it. Is there anywhere at all that you can think of where you could purchase me something nourishing? Look, I am wasting away to a coat hanger. Pity me, dear friend.'

As Jerome was blessed with the kind of charm which almost always got him what he wanted, Arthur Radwell departed, promising to seek out food for the hungry from somewhere or other, even though it was Sunday. When he had gone, Pollitt took to wandering through the digs again, thinking again about the oddness of someone like himself associating with someone like Aleister Crowley. 'Be realistic, my dear,' he said softly as he dawdled into the bedroom and flopped down on the bed. He lay there, looking up at the ceiling, smoking another cigarette. 'It will all go nowhere. There is nowhere for it to go. Perhaps it really is time to pack up the wigs and heels and leave him be.' Feeling a hard object beneath his head, he fished a notebook from under the pillow, carelessly flipping it open to read the pencilled lines:

The red lips of the octopus.
They reek with poison of the sea
Scarlet and hot and languorous
My skin drinks in their slaver warm, my sweats his wrapt embrace excite.

'Why, why, why, Aleister?' he sighed. 'Why don't you think before you write? An octopus has a beak.' Disdainfully he pushed the book back where he had found it.

It already made him sad to think back. It had started in the usual way, their eyes meeting whilst he was performing as 'Diane' on stage, a conversation at a noisy party afterwards. Jerome had given him a book with some code words inscribed inside – enough to make matters clear. And there had been passion and arguments and fascination and tender playfulness. Something like love, then: one might say that. Is he more attached than he realises? Am I? Or am I one of those 'abnormal people' he likes to study? Anyway, whatever we think we feel now, the result will be the same: he'll marry and have children. That's what the future holds for him and, I suppose, for me too: probably. Or improbably.

'But I'm going back tomorrow. I'll see him again.' He rolled over. The letter in his pocket crackled as he moved and he remembered Beardsley, stuck out there in Menton. He thought, I'll write to him today. Perhaps I'll light a candle somewhere too.

A large tear slid annoyingly into his ear. He sat up, drying his face, glad he was alone.

*

Alexandra was sitting, as usual, in her dressing room staring out over the bare trees in the Square. She had been forcing herself to go down for breakfast each day but afterwards preferred to retreat here. She did not feel like drawing and painting, nor anything really. Not eating, not sleeping. The same circular thoughts ran wearily through her head. At first, she was angry. Valentine obviously hadn't understood what he meant to her. If he had understood, he would be here now to laugh about it with her, this strange fact that deserved to be laughed at, that he was so quickly, so ridiculously gone. Everywhere seemed unnaturally quiet since she had given the customary order that all the clocks be stopped. So. The pulse in the house had simply finished.

At three o'clock there was a ring at the front door and someone went to answer. Janet Fairlight came shyly up to her room with two calling cards on the little silver tray to announce that there was a lady and gentleman to see her. Alexandra's heart beat more quickly: Minerva Atwell. Upon the other, she read the name Aleister Crowley, Esquire.

She was immediately aware that her hair and face and clothing were not fit to be seen. That was all right. She had sent a letter to Mrs Atwell on that very first morning after Valentine's death, saying that she was too ill to see her and requesting to postpone their projects for a week. She didn't think much about it (because she didn't have thoughts to spare on anything, what with seeing to the hasty funeral arrangements, interviews with the police, the brief inquest). She half expected Minerva to take offence and cancel everything; or to turn up unexpectedly and be difficult. But all she had received in answer was a slip of creamy paper with the words, *Ego tristis, ne male comparati. Claudia Livilla.*

She asked Janet to see the visitors into the morning room and tried quickly to see to her clothes. As she did so, she wondered whether news of last week's terrible event had reached Mrs Atwell. There was every reason to assume it would have done, if she had been reading the London papers; for although no big splash of crime reporting had appeared (at her express request, Mr Burroughs had used his influence to put a stop to that – on the promise of exclusive interviews after the trial took place), there had certainly been a paragraph about the death and the postponed inquest. An artist's impression (based upon her own sketch) of George Arden had also been printed on the back of various papers, alongside a notice saying he was wanted to help the police with their enquiries; but two addresses were cited besides her own, the Revue Parnassus in Soho and the Dame Fortune club in the West End. Her own name was left out of it.

She smoothed her hair and used a clothes brush to freshen her dress. She put on lace cuffs. She pinned a jet brooch at the throat: that was for Valentine. Then she took out the black Spanish lace shawl and stood up tall in the mirror while she draped it round herself, squaring her lean shoulders ready to brave their enquiries.

The gentleman, whose name on the card was Aleister Crowley Esquire, was sitting with legs crossed, leaning on an elbow, staring at the door when she entered. Minerva Atwell was on the other side of the room furthest from him, insouciantly turning the pages of a little book of poetry (Alexandra always left a selection of such works there for waiting visitors).

They both rose to greet her. They explained, talking over each other somewhat, that quite by chance they had arrived at the house at the same moment. Alexandra apologised that she'd left them alone together, having been under the impression that they knew each other. They both made gracious comments along the lines of 'think nothing of it', et cetera, but Alexandra could immediately see that there was a tension or dislike between them. Minerva Atwell was not wasting any flattering charm upon Crowley, while Crowley's gaze was directed anywhere but towards her.

'Excuse me, madam, but I don't want to take up even a second of your valuable time,' said Mr Crowley as soon as he could. 'I did not wish to intrude upon you at all. Your parlour maid showed me in here before I had a chance to explain myself. I am simply here seeking an acquaintance of mine. I met him in the company of Mr Valentine Cabot, by whom I was given this address. I wish to renew that acquaintance. His name is Mr George Arden. Would it be possible to speak to him or leave a note?'

He spoke ingenuously, not in the least as though he were concealing prior knowledge of the recent tragedy; yet Alexandra doubted very much that word of the death had not reached all of Valentine's large circle of friends. It was a little odd therefore. 'Are you – have you been out of town this last week?' she asked with as steady a voice as she could command.

'Yes. I have been engaged elsewhere, but I returned this morning,' answered Mr Crowley with a hint of surprise at the question.

Alexandra had to break the news. There was no hope of hiding the facts. Minerva Atwell would also have to hear it all. Murder was scandalous and scandal did not improve reputations such as hers, either as an artist or as a friend.

'I am exceedingly sorry. There have been terrible events in this house and I must be frank. Please prepare yourself for bad news, Mr Crowley. Last Wednesday night – or Thursday morning, I suppose - Valentine Cabot was found dead at the bottom of the stairs. It has been alleged by a reliable witness that George Arden killed him.'

Saying it all baldly like that made it far worse. Alexandra found her throat closing up. Minerva said nothing but Crowley raised a slow hand to his mouth. Then he said, 'And Arden, where is he? They haven't got him, have they?'

'We don't know where he is,' said Alexandra.

'If they catch him, he'll swing,' said Crowley. He saw Alexandra's shocked look and added, 'Sorry for my bluntness, but it's true. Anyway I know George Arden is incapable of committing a crime like that.'

'There was a witness, here in this house. He saw – oh, I can't repeat the details. It's too brutal. Valentine Cabot was a very dear friend, Mr Crowley. George Arden was less known to me but nevertheless I – I believe it will be shown to be an accident, an unintentional act, manslaughter...'

'Yes,' agreed Crowley.

'It is extremely painful to talk about this. The police, of course, are investigating. That is all there is to say on the matter really. Except I wish it had never happened.'

'I understand, and I won't intrude upon you any further.'

Alexandra immediately showed him to the front door, leaving Mrs Atwell alone for a moment with an apology. As he was about to walk away, he seemed to be struck by a thought.

'May I just ask one question? What is the name of the witness who saw the deed?'

She saw no reason not to tell him and said, 'Mr Albert Burroughs, who also lives here. He was the first to see – he looked over the banister and saw the dreadful thing actually as it happened. He's a court reporter, a trusted man whose work takes him, I hear, to the Old Bailey and other notable courts of justice. I am afraid his testimony is reliable.'

Crowley thanked her and then took his leave.

Minerva Atwell looked thoughtful when he had gone and spent some time adjusting her stylish fur-trimmed hat before saying anything further to Alexandra. It was as if she wanted to be punish Alexandra or perhaps just needed to recover her composure. Finally, she looked directly at her and smiled.

'Well, well. That's all horribly unpleasant, my dear Alex. For once I am lost for words. I apologise for my silence. I really do not like that man, whoever he is. He would not even look at me, all the while we sat in the same room. He did not so much as beg to introduce himself or wish to learn my name. So shockingly rude. Let us put him out of our thoughts. So, tell me then, this man who died, he was a friend of yours? And it happened here, right here in this very house? Dear me, you poor thing! And was that the illness you mentioned, the shock of it all?'

She came and sat next to Alexandra and took her hand, stroking it gently. She was wearing silk gloves to match the colour of her hat. Alexandra caught the scent of lily-of-the-valley toilet water.

'I have missed you, my friend. I had nobody to laugh with and absolutely nobody to gossip with. I was dining with boring strangers, and boring P.B.s, and talking to bankers and financiers, and I needed you so much. You did let me down, you know, and I was almost a little bit angry with you. But now I understand you had a reason. You didn't want to let me down but you had to. So you're forgiven. Completely. And you have been quite done in by all this, my dear,' she said, looking into Alexandra's eyes. 'You and I need to restore each other's spirits. For you see, I feel just as tired as you. But I'll tell you what, my dear, my plan is to go to my health spa – did I tell you about it? Down in the West Country?'

'I think you mentioned something about it, Minerva. That day we went to Kew – '

'Yes, I remember. We had such a pleasant day, didn't we? And all these days we've been apart, every time I was ready to scream, all tangled up in financial papers and sealing wax and red tape this past week, I remembered us, walking through the conservatory and talking about those ferns. Do you recall it? How interesting it was and how very much in sympathy we were. Because we really are the best of friends. Like twin sisters.'

'Oh, I would be very flattered to be taken as your twin sister,' said Alexandra with a wobbly smile.

'Ah, that reminds me – I have something else for you. But wait a moment, I am jumping ahead of myself. And you know that is one of my faults. So let me first explain my idea. You see, as I mentioned, I have to visit my beautiful restorative health spa to see my customers and make sure everything is as it should be. There is a great deal of building work arranged to begin soon and many other affairs to see to, so I have planned to spend some time there and set all to rights. And my idea is that you should accompany me.'

'Well,' said Alexandra slowly, 'that sounds very inviting. But I am afraid there is so much to be taken care of here. The household, the … the police may need to come and see me.'

'Oh never mind them!' said Minerva firmly. 'What is to be done? That you stay here for an eternity, wasting away, while they bumble about trying to find whomever it is they're looking for? No, no, no. Let them send a telegram if they need you. I can see already that you are thinner; and you know, my dear, there comes a time in a woman's life when she cannot lose plumpness in the face without looking ragged and ravaged. Which reminds me!' She reached into her elegant little handbag and produced a round tin and handed it to Alexandra.

Alexandra took it and inspected it. It was heavy in her hand. There was no lettering to be seen on the face of it, just pretty shades of gold and sky-blue with a picture of a slender woman wearing a moon crown.

'That, you see, is a lovely goddess,' said Minerva. 'This is my

Beauty Balm. Exclusive. Not the Beauty Balm Powder, which can be purchased in many shops. This is the Balm itself, concentrated and very effective. Only available in the very best places. One outlet in Paris, one in Rome, one in London. Ladies advertise it simply by using it. Word of mouth makes them clamour to know more – I make them follow whispered clues to find where to buy it. They love it! Everyone loves a mystery and this tin - well, I won't tell you how much an ordinary customer would need to lay out to purchase it!'

'What does it do?' asked Alexandra, turning the pot upside down and seeing the words 'Atwell's Beauty Balm' written in flowing letters underneath. She didn't want to mention anything so crass as not being able to afford it.

'It is the essence of my most secret research. I obtain an ingredient from a deep valley hidden in the mountains - somewhere. Just a small supply every year. That is what goes into my Balm. The fabled beauties of antiquity, Semiramis of Babylon, Atusa of Persia, Cleopatra of Egypt - and Helen of Troy for all I know - used the secret ingredient to calm the mind and renew the body. Or so they say. You can believe that or not, as you like. Personally, I like to!' Minerva laughed. 'I cannot pretend it's not a useful selling point. Especially to rich women these days who like to imagine themselves empresses. And this is yours, this nice pot. Open it!'

Alexandra opened the lid. Perhaps Minerva's story affected her senses, for an air breathed from it, hints of frankincense and cinnamon and styrax, that seemed to hang in her mind. She shook her head, half laughing. 'This is an ointment for visionaries, I think,' she said.

'Why?' asked Minerva, leaning forward a little. 'What can you see?'

'Oh, nothing. Just my mind's eye gave me an image when I smelled this pot.'

'Oh, please do tell me! I love to hear about such things. Come, we can trust each other with our visions, can't we?'

'Well,' said Alexandra with a little laugh, 'I saw a far off desert place and a temple. I suppose it was a temple, it had pillars and was large. And the sky was a wonderful deep purple. Suggested,' she said, smelling the pot again, 'simply by the ingredients you have put into your Balm. How clever of you. Did you choose the scent yourself?'

'Oh yes, every detail is my own work, even the design of the tin. Of course, the manufacture goes on elsewhere now, but the original development of the Balm was my own labour. Are you not impressed?' She regarded Alexandra humorously. 'And you instantly saw a temple on a hill? Now try it, put some on your hand first. That's it.'

Alexandra could indeed see that the skin on the back of her hand was smoothed simply by the application of a film of emollient. 'That is extraordinary! And the fragrance is so calming. I believe I shall sleep tonight.'

'That's right,' said Minerva. 'You shall sleep beautifully. That first application, you know, the effect from that won't last very long of course, but as the formula penetrates deeper beneath the dermis, you will see a real change. Particularly on the face. But I'll tell you how to make best use of it in a minute. First let's confirm our plans. I feel excited, like a schoolgirl! You will come with me and you'll be doing me a great service. My guests are always old and usually ill. You can be a ray of sunshine for me.'

'I'm not very ... sunshiney at the moment.'

'But you will be! We'll talk about the beauties of nature and we'll read history and we'll write poetry and you'll paint me. You have to say yes, Mrs Roberts.'

'Well, if you put it like that, I suppose I must say yes,' said Alexandra as a feeling of relief swept over her. It was so hard to resist Minerva.

'Good, good, good! Tomorrow! We'll go tomorrow. If it can be managed, and if not, then the day after.'

'That's wonderful,' murmured Alexandra, suddenly feeling remarkably tired. 'How far do we have to go?'

'It's not too far from Bath, you know, but not so busy or so full of the vulgar people,' said Minerva. 'You will find it wonderfully healing for your nerves, wonderfully healing for your body and mind.' Her voice had such a gentle quality and Alexandra felt so tired that she actually closed her eyes for a moment and imagined drifting away into the deep purple sky. Yes, she needed healing and restoring and being away from this house. Every time she looked at the staircase here, she saw Valentine's heavy body crumpled at the bottom. Every time she walked through the hall, she smelt blood and brandy.

'I would love to come,' she said.

CHAPTER THIRTEEN

Detective Browning licked the end of his pencil and regarded the gentleman opposite him with wary interest. He had his notebook ready and he knew what he wanted to find out and, although he wasn't a very experienced interviewer, he intended to do his best. Inspector Miller had more or less dumped all the paperwork concerning the Cabot case on his desk, saying that he, Miller, had better things to do than investigate pansies killing each other and, unless the names of any members of the aristocracy or government came up, talk to him again when they'd caught the suspect.

Browning was therefore at liberty to explore his doubts about the case. He had come looking for any evidence of premeditation in the murder. It had only taken a little research to discover Cabot's and Arden's movements that night because Cabot had conveniently announced to his landlady where he was going. It was equally easy to get an idea of how the pair had spent their evening, once he had established their presence at the club. Valentine Cabot had been a long-standing member of the Dame Fortune Club and his guests that night had been entered in the register as Mr Jerome Pollitt, Mr Aleister Crowley and Mr George Arden. The guest book required an address to be given for each visitor.

By the time Browning had done all the leg-work, he had got round to see Messrs Crowley and Pollitt on the Friday afternoon. He was disappointed to find he'd missed them: they both were out of town. The housekeeper told him they were expected back on Monday late. Early Tuesday morning, therefore, Browning was on the doorstep asking for an interview. This time Dame Fortune smiled upon him.

It was nine o'clock in the morning and both men appeared rumpled and half awake as Constable Browning began the process of jogging their memories about conversations conducted in a noisy club nearly a week before. He asked to interview them separately, and he was allowed to use the sitting room for the purpose. It was a rum kind of room, though, with a chilly atmosphere. Browning could not guess what were the interests of the various gentlemen who resided there.

He started with Mr Jerome Pollitt. Mr Pollitt explained in a tired way that he was a gentleman of leisure, a collector of fine art and something of an actor. Browning made a secret note of Pollitt's appearance (*long-hair, manicure, artsy=Decadent?*). Browning found the gentleman needed very little encouragement to talk about last Wednesday night. The problem was keeping him focused.

Pollitt said he had been informed about Valentine Cabot's murder only yesterday in the late afternoon by his friend Mr Crowley. He said he had spent most of last night tossing and turning in horrified contemplation of the wickedness of George Arden; and apologised for his consequently dreadful appearance. He said he did not normally look so horrid first thing in the morning. He was remarkably vindictive towards George Arden and accused him of being a suspicious opportunist out to exploit Cabot, Crowley and himself.

'Cabot was mesmerised by the fellow,' said Pollitt, 'and there is simply no justification. Those showy Mediterranean looks fade very quickly, you'll find, Constable, sorry, Detective. It's all very well prancing about the stage when you're twenty but just you wait! As for the play, it was utter dross. The man was off his head, Cabot, I mean, head over heels in …' at which point Pollitt stopped short and said warily, 'But you understand, it was merely the noble interest of an older man in a much younger business opportunity, Detective Browning. Nothing Greek about it.'

Browning dubiously noted down the exact words. But although Mr Pollitt was eloquent on the subject of the manipulativeness of George Arden, it was disappointingly difficult to pin him down to any specific word or deed to back up his claims. In the final analysis, it seemed that Arden had said scarcely a word at the meeting and had disappeared without explanation after a mere thirty minutes. Why had Arden disappeared?

'Well, that's the question, isn't it, officer? We simply didn't know. That's what caused all the to-ing and fro-ing and arguments. I thought it was just a way of increasing his mystique; unless it was to do with Watson, because he went off shortly before, you know. But I think that was just coincidental, because Watson began looking sea-sick when Cabot described the plot of *Hamlet, Prince of Pirates*. We all did.'

'Watson? Ah, yes. The other gentleman present. Could you tell me anything about him?'

'Yes, some chance meeting in the club. An occasional backer of theatrical productions, apparently, a patron of the arts. Not much to look at. Was he a Sir or an Honourable or something? No, just a doctor. A Dr Watson. Valentine claimed to know him intimately, but he obviously didn't.'

'Did you notice any undue interest in the suspect on the part of this Dr Watson, sir?'

'I am sure I have no idea, officer,' said Mr Pollitt with an air of discretion.

'You didn't hear talk of contracts and such like?'

'Not in my hearing but who knows? He might have been interested in the actor but he certainly did not appear to be interested in the play itself, stayed just long enough to hear what a flop the thing would be and then he extricated himself from the scene of the crime – I don't mean *crime*, Detective, I am speaking metaphorically of a literary crime.'

Detective Browning noted the words on his pad but kept his thoughts to himself. There was but little further information to be gleaned from his next interview. Mr Crowley was also a young gentleman who could live as he pleased, although he said he was still an undergraduate at Trinity. But it interested Browning very much to discover that he had called at Cabot's address yesterday afternoon immediately upon arriving back in London. 'What was the particular reason that you hurried to see Mr Cabot, sir?' he asked.

'I was not hurrying to see Cabot,' answered the young man, flicking ash from his cigarette towards the fireplace. 'I wanted to talk to Arden.'

'And that would be related to –?'

'Not really relevant to the matter in hand, I'd say,' said Crowley lazily. 'Don't see that it bears, you know, on anything that happened between him and Cabot. But of course I learned of the shocking events from the lady of the house when I went there. Most unfortunate.'

'Excuse me, sir, but it's my job to be the judge of what is relevant or not.' Browning smiled affably and was rebuffed by an unblinking stare. He continued, 'So, I'm obliged to ask you again, what was the reason you hastened to speak to Arden more or less the moment you got back from –' he consulted his notebook – 'Buckinghamshire?

Was this meeting related to a managerial role, sir?'

'Managerial role? No, not in the least. I have no interest in the theatre. Pollitt has, of course.'

Browning noted this. 'And when you spoke to the suspect in the Dame Fortune Club, what did your conversation touch upon?'

'Our conversation? It was entirely upon spiritual matters.'

Browning regarded Crowley with a hint of doubt. 'Religious, is he, sir? Wasn't upset after this conversation, was he?'

'I would not know.'

'Did he look upset to you, disturbed or on edge, as you might say, like he was unusually affected by your words, sir? '

'Not in the least.'

'Didn't behave or say anything confusing or spout foreign words during the course of that discussion?'

'Not in the least,' repeated Crowley.

'Is the suspect also a member of this Alpine Club you mentioned?'

'No, he is not. Not known to me in any way before that night. When I left London, it was to visit my trainer and mentor, Mr Oskar Eckenstein, for advice on matters pertaining to an expedition. Nothing to do with George Arden, nothing to do with Cabot, nothing to do with theatres.'

'An outdoors man yourself then, sir?' said Browning approvingly, crossing out a word in his pad, despite Crowley's rings. 'So Arden was no mountaineer, then? Would you say he was strong, muscular? Could he have managed a fight?'

Crowley snorted. 'Certainly not. His abilities are not of the physical type. He is incapable of violence.'

Browning paused. 'Now, I have to ask this, sir, and I don't mean to offend in any way, you being a devout gentleman, but it seems that there are aspects of the relationship between Arden and the deceased which don't bear close inspection. I am referring to certain suspected activities, abominable crimes, crimes such as put that Oscar Wilde behind bars,' - Browning drew a breath: there, he'd said it - 'and in the light of these suspicions, I need to ask you if you witnessed anything which would lead you to suspect such criminal activity on the part of Arden or the deceased?'

To Browning's surprise, Crowley sat back and laughed. 'Well, now. Why is that material to the case?'

'It's material, sir,' said Browning with a little flush creeping along his ears, 'because it's our suspicion that Valentine Cabot was improperly exploiting George Arden, and in looking for the circumstances leading to the attack on Cabot, we need to look into every possible line of enquiry. It was a shockingly brutal attack, sir. Smashed his skull in, force of the blow broke his neck. We have a witness who saw it happen, a model of respectability, outraged at what he understood to have been going on under his own roof. So I'm not trying to establish whether it happened, I'm trying to understand what motivated it.'

'Oh, the witness is outraged is he?'

'Well, yes, he is, and rightly so. We have to come down hard on this sort of thing, sir. My Inspector wants to make an example of this case, to discourage others, if you get my meaning.'

'I see. How interesting. Perhaps you think that my zealous religious bent made him understand his state of sin? Ah, what an interesting thought! And do you think, Detective Browning, that an awakened conscience would lead him to commit murder?'

Crowley leaned a little closer and Browning found his gaze was suddenly locked. 'Listen,' he said softly, 'Take my word for it: Arden is incapable of violence.' After a second, he sat back again. 'And as for the moral outrage and the unspeakable crimes of Oscar Wilde: well, I suppose there is a sense in which this information might be relevant - but it would neither offend nor even particularly interest me to see evidence of it.'

Detective Browning descended the steps into Chancery Lane, feeling no nearer discovering the meaning of certain cryptic words in the deceased's notebook.

Half an hour later, Pollitt said politely, as he handed Crowley a slice of buttered toast to accompany a plate of kippers, 'I hope you were honest with the nice young police officer about your motives for seeking out the little tart?'

Crowley frowned slightly as he fixed his attention upon the newspaper folded up beside his plate. 'Oh Polly, give it a rest. You'll never understand. Anyway, don't trouble me now. I have to think of a way to nobble a witness.'

*

The Compact

Adsullata Spa Hotel,
Whistanwell, Somerset.

My dear Harriet,

Well, you will see from the note paper where I am. I am sorry not to have communicated with you before. We arrived a few days ago and I would have written sooner but it was all very rushed and time just seems to go so quickly. But before I say anything else, I want to apologise to you for my recent coldness. I don't have to tell you why. I am sorry too about the unpleasant scene after the funeral. I fully understand why you felt you had to question Mr Burroughs like that and I cannot excuse his remarks to you. I think the shock affected him, as it did all of us. Think what he must have seen! Anyway, my harsh words at the time were uncalled for and I beg you to forgive me. Like the good old friends we are, let's put it behind us. Now! Let me tell you about this place.

We took the train to Bath, of course, and then entrusted our luggage and ourselves to a rather alarming but very sturdy equipage that Mrs Atwell had arranged to meet us. It was drawn by two immense muddy drayhorses and I soon understood why they were necessary. The carriage, as black and shiny as a beetle, at least looked in no danger of overturning, which was well - for it had to thread (rather dangerously, I thought) up and down steep foothills and through country lanes in the darkness. Mrs Atwell of course is a seasoned traveller and often comes here. She says the soft airs of the place, even in winter, are particularly conducive to health both of body and mind. There is a pretty village not too far away with a convenient post office too.

Anyway, we are settled now, dear Harriet. Mrs Atwell is a fascinating companion but she is often busy and you and I could chat very comfortably here. I have not had an opportunity to explore everywhere as yet, particularly as part of the hotel is shut up and undergoing repairs. It is being modernised, Mrs Atwell says, in preparation for the much busier seasons she expects in the future as the Spa builds up its reputation.

There are but three residents here at the moment, each of whom receives the very best care. Mrs Atwell tells me the waters of a marvellous local spring provide such benefits to the nervous system as are almost impossible to enumerate. She says the source is the same extraordinarily deep volcanic wells as supply the renowned hot springs at Bath. She herself discovered the forgotten well in the valley here and had it restored, diverting the waters to supply a pump room in this romantic old place. It has taken a great deal of work to get it right, she

133

tells me, and she says the Bank has 'sunk' a lot of money into it, but the modern building is now almost perfect and will rival Bath itself in time.

With her keen interest in history, Mrs Atwell assures me that she has found evidence that the use of the well dates back to pre-Roman times. Her workmen discovered various stones under the water in the course of their work. They are crudely shaped to suggest human heads. Apparently the poor superstitious fellows would have destroyed them but Mrs Atwell intervened and had them set up in the salon, much to local disapproval, as you may well imagine! She had them thoroughly scrubbed and they have come up as white as alabaster. She believes the very name of this valley is inspired by them – perhaps a fanciful idea, but who can say? You would be much interested to see them – I intend to append a sketch of one. You will agree, I think, that they retain a certain power.

I am sitting, my dear Harriet, in the comfortable salon having 'taken the waters' myself these two days running. I have drunk them – tastes like metal and blood, very odd - and also immersed myself in the beautiful pool which Mrs Atwell had built here. You would love to see it (and you would laugh to see me in it attired in a voluminous bathing gown!). It is tiled with blue and gold fishes – the pool, that is, not the gown. Don't laugh – my head is a muddle. One hardly wishes to leave the pool once one is fully immersed. I can truly feel myself relaxing into a better state of health.

I have made a great friend here too, a Mrs Halliwell, who as I write is sitting near me by the fire. She, poor thing, suffers much from gout and rheumatism. By lucky chance, she once also lived in Cairo for a while so I have enjoyed chatting whilst pushing her about in a handsome bathchair (or else she must hobble about on bandaged feet).

Dear Harriet, after the recent terrible tragedy – of which I can barely think or write - I hope that the healing qualities of this place are restoring me to my right mind. Quite soon I plan to begin work on the famous portrait of Minerva Atwell. She particularly wishes to work at it here because she says the atmosphere, light, etc. are very 'artistic'. It made me laugh when she said that.

I feel very blessed to have such a friend – for I think I may increasingly trust that I am her friend – and even more blessed to know that I remain your A.

Alexandra read the letter through, signed it and folded in a small sketch she had made the previous evening. She sealed it into an envelope and walked out to leave it at the reception desk with other letters waiting for the post. She was alone for now. Mrs Halliwell had dozed off in her chair. The other two residents were receiving various treatments from the staff. Minerva was somewhere about the place or busy in her office.

Alexandra looked out of the windows of the solarium towards the head of the valley. At the top, a shoulder blade of brown-gold hillside caught the winter sunlight. Leafless trees marched down the slopes to flank the road leading to the hotel. Above it all, the sky looked as thin and blue as a pane of ice. It would be good to work again, to get the easel and some pastels, perhaps, and begin to sketch some of this. She had forgotten how compressed she habitually felt in London; and although there was still a physical pain inside when she thought of Valentine, here it seemed easier to manage it, to breathe and to think alongside it. Stepping outside, she saw that waxy snowdrops were already nodding in the chilly wind by the wall in the sun.

Half an hour later, sitting on a tree stump with a board on her knee, Alexandra began a pencil sketch of the view back down the slope towards the house. She liked the irregularity of the building and the lie of the pale shadows on its complicated face. It had two distinct sides. One had a plastered façade in a Palladian style; the other was darker and far older. And from up here, she could see that there was more to it than she had originally thought. The more ancient half of it had a kind of prison of ash-pole scaffolding set up at one end but no workmen were in sight.

The wind was cold and her hands quickly reddened. Too cold to stay exposed here for long, after twenty minutes she put the board on the ground, leaving it well-weighted with a lump of limestone. She decided to warm up with a walk and chose to aim for a thicketed little fold down near the bottom of the slope. As she stumbled over the tree roots, glad of her sturdy boots, she was thankful that the descent among the trees was taking her out of the wind. She hesitated, wondering whether to go back and collect up her things and recommence work from here. A few pretty sketches of the house and valley would be an appropriate thanks to Mrs Atwell for her kindness.

She looked around to see if there was a worthwhile view, peering between the ranks of green-grey tree trunks. Nothing was moving. There was no sound at all. Further down, she saw a plume of steam rising from a hidden cleft. Fascinated, she realised she may by chance have found the source of Minerva's original 'White Stone Well' and immediately set off to get closer to it.

This must be the well all right, she thought; but it was a weird place. A little further down the slope, she could see where the water had been diverted and hurried away underground into modern pipes, but here at the source, all was untouched. A few flat green stones led down in a shallow stair, natural or perhaps man-made, for she imagined she could detect the wear of feet. She followed them down to the spring itself and stood suddenly astounded to watch it gush out of the crevice. The strength of it was breathtaking. The copious brown stream rippled strongly up and out, steaming, powerful, pumping from a deep gash. The water-smoothed stones were red in the steam.

She sat down on a rock, staring, silent, and after a long time, dared to stretch down and touch the water. It was so hot. It was almost indelicate – fleeting associations of menstruating, giving birth, passed through her head. A most extraordinary sight, her modern rational self said again and again, as the water forced its way out, staining the rock surfaces, immodest, sinewy, from the deep into daylight. At long last, she turned away, feeling that she owed the wellspring something, a token, because it seemed alive and she had watched it.

Feeling foolish, she pulled one of the silver hat pins from her felt hat and threw it into the spring; and, as she moved to go, saw that she was not alone in this irrational urge. There was a shining edge of a hidden thing poked into a cleft in the rocks. The returning ferns and mosses would be covering it a few short weeks from now. Gingerly, she extracted it. It was crudely drawn, mere scratches on a tiny sheet of copper. She brought it closer to her eyes, eager to find out what it depicted. As far as she could make out, it showed a somewhat bizarre female figure. She rubbed the metal and slanted it to get a sight of the rough engraving. A standing naked woman was flanked by two birds. It's the oddest thing, thought Alexandra, because someone's drawn her with very unusual feet. The cloak drooping from her shoulders looks almost like wings. She replaced it carefully, deciding to discuss her discovery with Mrs Atwell after dinner. 'Because it isn't very old at all,' she said aloud.

CHAPTER FOURTEEN

It was far too late for visitors. When Aleister Crowley stepped through the door, although Dr Watson recognised him immediately, he was not altogether pleased to see him. He had just finished making notes on a project he had decided to revive in his friend's absence – a little story he planned to entitle *The Baskerville Dog*. It was a case he and Holmes had tackled almost ten years before and to write it up would require considerable planning. Perhaps *hound* sounded better? The research was proving a useful distraction for him, but he was more than ready to retire to bed. His lack of enthusiasm for a meeting with this strange young man may have showed on his face. 'Ah, Mr Crowley,' he said, trying to remember if he had given him his calling card. 'How pleasant to see you again.'

'Forgive the late hour, Dr Watson,' said Crowley, taking off his hat and gloves. 'I won't stay long.' He looked cold and somewhat agitated.

'Think nothing of it,' said Watson, deciding to make the best of things. 'Do take a seat. But I am afraid my friend Mr Holmes is not presently in London. If you've come seeking his help, I must serve as a very poor substitute.'

Crowley nodded. 'You are too modest, doctor, although it was indeed your Mr Holmes that I came to talk to. Is he likely to be back soon?' He sat down, looking round the cluttered sitting room with interest.

'I'm afraid not, Mr Crowley. I regret that a case has taken him away and it is always impossible to predict how long these things will take – he is not even in the country.'

'A pity. I think he would be the man for the job. I took your advice, you see – read your *Adventure of the Speckled Band*. I rather liked it. But since the matter concerns you too, doctor, can you spare me ten minutes?'

'In that case, your business can only be the Cabot murder,' said Watson.

'Well, yes, it is. And to be honest, I've been walking about wondering whether to ring your bell. It's not like me to be undecided.

But I thought about it and I like your friend's approach, his emphasis on rationality and scientific detachment.'

'Excellent,' said Watson, not sure where this was leading. 'So how may I help you, Mr Crowley?'

'I'll come straight out with it then. I know that the police have interviewed you in the past week. I've been away and it wasn't until today that they spoke to me. So I went to that shabby club this evening in order to obtain your address, just as Detective Browning did when he looked for you. Or so they told me. I assume it was Browning you saw? I doubt that the police could spare too many other men on this investigation.'

'You are commendably quick to learn the ways of the detective, Mr Crowley,' said Watson. 'Yes, an officer interviewed me last week – not called Browning, another officer - and so I have already heard some of the details of the death of our unfortunate acquaintance.'

'What do you think of it?' Crowley asked, watching his face. The low fire crackled suddenly.

'The death? The crime? It strikes me, as these things often do, as without rhyme or reason.'

'But you don't believe that little actor is capable of killing anybody, do you?'

'Mr Crowley, I've come across a great many terrible crimes committed by the mildest of characters. A sad result of this is that I no longer make assumptions about human nature.'

'Yes. I can believe it. But I can't believe that *this* fellow could have killed a man. Did you detect repressed violence in his character?'

'No, I did not see "repressed violence" there, as you put it,' answered Dr Watson a little testily. 'And I'm not entirely sure how one would detect it if it were repressed. But I only walked about with him for a half-hour after we left Dame Fortune's.'

'Ah? That's interesting. You walked about with him?'

'Yes, but only because he seemed upset by something – or, actually, someone. And since we are talking frankly, he said the cause of his anxiety was you yourself.'

'I? I caused him anxiety?' Crowley said in surprise. He sat back and regarded Watson.

'I won't pretend to understand it, Mr Crowley, but you worried him in some way. And then he asked me about a condition he suffers from, a form of amnesia, I suppose. That was the extent of our conversation really. But, you see, although I told the police that the poor fellow struck me as of a gentle disposition, I also had to say that he was in an anxious or disturbed frame of mind that night.'

'Oh really? I see, Dr Watson. So you think Arden was disturbed?' He frowned into the fire for a moment and went on, 'And you think that the disturbance was because of *me* ...and this actually formed part of your statement to the police? Now I understand something which made little sense before: the questions I was asked. Yes. What did you tell them then? You were listening in on our conversation, I take it. What did you overhear?'

'I beg your pardon?' said Watson with dignity. 'I did not recount any of the details I may have overheard, although it would have been my duty to do so if I thought them material to the investigation. Nor did I go into detail about what Arden told me – it was in any case a hotch-potch of bizarre words and disconnected thoughts.'

'You told them *that* though, didn't you? They asked me about foreign words or some such nonsense. Because of your statement. I understand it all now.'

It was Watson's turn to frown. 'I did say that he had been talking to you and that you might be able to throw light on the matter. And I did say that his speech was in places incomprehensible. I saw no reason to conceal that fact.'

Crowley bit his thumbnail thoughtfully for a few moments and said slowly, 'I apologise. To you, I mean. I didn't mean to imply that you had been deliberately eavesdropping. Perhaps we were speaking loudly. But I am sure I never meant to cause him anxiety. I must have overstepped the mark – he's perhaps not as aware as I thought. But that is interesting. He followed you out, then, and chose to walk about in your company.'

'Yes,' said Watson. 'Although I wouldn't say he followed me out. It is more accurate to say that we coincided at the exit.'

'Coincided,' said Crowley with a kind of private emphasis as though the word meant something different to him.

Watson continued, 'And I have already given a full statement to the police. I think it is a very terrible thing that he tipped over the edge, only hours after I spoke to him; but it was in no way related to his conversation with *me* - as I was at pains to emphasise in my statement.'

'And is *that* what you told the police? That in your professional opinion, George Arden tipped over the edge due to *my* influence?'

'No, no, no!' said Watson, wondering why this conversation kept sliding off at a tangent and getting splattered with unwanted nuances. 'That would have been quite unjustified, Mr Crowley. I simply gave an account of the circumstances I had observed. It's just unfortunate that Cabot made some speculative notes before his death.'

'Notes?'

'Your interviewer did not mention them? Ah. Yes, well, Mr Crowley, you'll be interested to know that Cabot scribbled something to the effect that he thought I had been intending to poach his star actor from him. Seemed to imply I had a professional, managerial interest in the fellow. It is merely a line of enquiry, nothing more.'

Crowley began to smile. He said, with an increasing appearance of amusement, 'So the police entertain the possibility that *you* are the cause of the argument which culminated in Cabot's death?'

'I would hardly put it as strongly as that,' said Watson looking a little flustered. 'I believe Cabot was inebriated – there was certainly alcohol involved as the weapon that killed him was apparently a heavy spirits bottle – and in that confused state, prior to the altercation, he scribbled certain accusations. Which have no basis in fact, absolutely none.'

Crowley said nothing and sat staring at him. 'You'd rather your name had not been in Cabot's death note. But you knew him, Doctor. Tell me, was Cabot the kind of man to hurt Arden if he suspected him of disloyalty?'

'I hardly knew the fellow. And it was not a *death* note. Please stick to the facts uncoloured by emotion. The late Mr Cabot did no more than jot down some thoughts pertaining to finances, or so I was told, and an unfounded suspicion. He was prone to drinking excessively, poor man, as I have observed before. It seems likely that he would confront Arden, even though his ideas were absolute fantasy. What would Arden do under those circumstance? Defend himself? There may be a case for self-defence rather than robbery.'

'Robbery?' snorted Crowley. 'They think Arden robbed Cabot, do they? Presumably after I had disturbed his peace of mind with religious speculation and you had tried to persuade him to work for you! This is ridiculous. A complete muddle. I don't believe he did anything of the sort.'

'I am sorry to say this, Mr Crowley, but loyalty to a friend will inevitably cloud judgement. I agree there is a muddle in the police enquiry but this is surely because the investigation is just beginning. Aspects will be discounted in due course.'

'But even so, I don't believe Arden stands a chance of a fair trial.'

'The trial will depend upon what evidence the police have gathered from the scene, not to mention testimony from those who saw him last – including ourselves, of course. The court will listen and, one hopes, discover the truth from among the conflicting tales.'

'Or the judge and jury will be persuaded by a professional entertainer in the form of Council for the Prosecution, who will turn pirouettes round all these motifs.' Crowley gazed thoughtfully at Watson and continued, 'And there's a witness, you know, name of Burroughs. Says he saw the fatal blow being struck.'

'Yes, I know. An eye witness: what hope can there be then? Very difficult to argue an eye witness down in court, Mr Crowley. The police have a duty to look at all circumstances leading up to the murder, but they are not in doubt that it *was* a murder. I am afraid that the inconvenience of his story contradicting your personal opinion is not sufficient reason to discount his evidence. What possible gain would this person get from lying?'

'I don't know. Perhaps he would kill part of himself,' Crowley said casually. 'You understand that, don't you? You take my meaning.'

Dr Watson took a deep breath. 'I'm not sure if I do take your meaning. Let us stick to the facts. This witness has made other unsavoury accusations. You, no doubt, were questioned about them, just as I was.'

'Oh yes. The witness imagines himself very upset about unnatural crimes, "outraged", I was told. He wouldn't be so very troubled if he hadn't imagined them in the first place.' He laughed.

'These are dangerous times, Mr Crowley, and it would be wise to be less flippant. Perhaps his evidence is well-founded, perhaps there *is* an aspect to this case which might lead Arden to take action to – to free himself from the clutches of Cabot.'

'You mean the thing about Cabot being Arden's pander? I did wonder, you know, but I have no real grounds to suspect it. Perhaps it was just a passing thought in Cabot's mind. I find I catch ideas from time to time and the fellow was desperate for money – anyone could see it. But anyway, who could testify on that matter? Cabot? Arden? Where would they find an unbiased witness?'

'Presumably, among their acquaintance. And be that as it may, witnesses must be left to testify unmolested.'

'We shall see,' said Crowley, beginning to draw on his gloves, 'I came to consult your partner Holmes on how to proceed in clearing the fellow's name; but I see now that you yourself are part of the picture.' He rose to leave. 'I won't keep you from your rest any longer. Thank you for your time and for your candour. But it was not quite fair, you know, to deflect the enquiry from yourself to me. Now, here is my card – you'll need this when you come and see me. I think we'll be consulting further.'

Watson sat for a long time after he had gone, frowning somewhat wrathfully into the fire.

*

Harriet jumped with surprise at a knock at the parlour door. Each time there was a break between students, she found she had unconsciously resumed a particular position, staring dumbly at a little portrait in a silver frame. That girl, apparently hundreds of years ago, had stood on a jetty at Ramsgate with a blue ribbon curling away in the wind. She felt as though someone had told her the picture held a secret but she couldn't remember who. She found she kept returning to look at it in these interludes of quiet. She couldn't have said why.

The knock was Daisy Etherington bringing her a letter from Alexandra. Harriet read it with a sense of relief. They had certainly not parted on the best of terms, so it was reassuring to read the words, 'Like the good old friends we are, let's put it behind us.' She decided to write a long letter this evening and make it a lighthearted one - although she personally did not feel lighthearted at all. The events on the day of Valentine's funeral still rankled.

It had been rushed and quiet, hurriedly arranged. The ground had been frozen. Alexandra had stood clutching at her arm on one side and that of Dafydd Williams on the other. Albert Burroughs had excused himself from attending. Afterwards, in the dark interior of the railway carriage, jolting back from the Metropolitan Necropolis, Harriet remembered saying, 'Dear Alex, I'm so sorry. I know Valentine was a good friend to you but – well, you've done everything that could be expected of you.' At that, Alexandra began to sob and it took a while to calm her. 'It's the shock of it all,' Harriet had said sympathetically.

'In fact, it isn't even that,' said Alex, trying to assert control over herself. 'Or not just that. It's the police and that awful inquest – so soon after the – the death, and everything in a mess and it all spilled out. I feel so – vile, Harry.'

'But it was adjourned, you said, dear. They won't be able to conclude until poor George has explained it all.'

'I know, I know, it's just that I feel as if a mirror had been tilted and everything about myself and my home has been reflected back from the wrong angle. It looks so – immoral. It makes me feel sick.'

'Immoral? What on earth do you mean?'

'Mr Burroughs. What he had to say, right out there in the open, I don't even want to say it to you. He said something so vile about Valentine. He said he believed he was living off George and that was why George killed him.'

'But he was his manager,' said Harriet doubtfully, a number of remembered conversations with George Arden immediately crowding into her mind. 'He just means he was living off his earnings as an actor – which was true. And George would never have hurt him. Try to recall him as he really is: a gentle, small, harmless creature.'

'No, he *didn't* mean living off him as his manager. I wouldn't care if it were that. He meant *living* off him. He said it was like the Wilde case. Like *that.* And from *my house!* And when he said it, I remembered a conversation I had – and Val said, he said, something garbled, something which implied he was prepared to use Mr Arden's looks for financial gain. I took it to mean his theatrical projects, but now I'm afraid ...'

Harriet could still hear the tone of her voice and feel the swoop of shock in her own stomach as she heard it. As it surfaced in her mind now, she sat down at her desk, and swore fluently in words no lady should even know, let alone use. She was unwilling to recall the scene that followed. She had been so incensed by this poisonous and completely unjust accusation (against a dead man too!) that when they returned from the funeral, she herself had approached Albert Burroughs.

They had come in, trailing the emotions of the freezing graveyard and the distraught ride home; and he was there in the parlour, standing by the table of cold meats and pickles and funeral biscuits, waiting for them. He was dressed sombrely but not in mourning, looking dignified and self-contained, with his little square moustache and his hair brushed sleek. At first, Harriet had been so angry she could hardly speak. But after a quarter of an hour sitting silently fuming with a glass of sherry, she had gone up to him and privately demanded to hear every concrete detail to back up his accusations against Valentine. He refused to discuss it. It had been an uncomfortable scene, particularly after she had started to raise her voice. He said he was an important witness, the only witness to murder, and he had a duty not to talk about anything he had surmised and definitely not to allow himself to be swayed by emotional women. He implied that she was hysterical.

Harriet was too furious to trust herself to be civil; and had left the tiny wake as soon as manners permitted. Alexandra had been so ground down between grief and shock and shame that she had apparently capitulated to Burroughs's opinion: she did not support Harriet in her arguments, did not question Burroughs's assertions, sat white and useless in an armchair by the fire. Harriet's last image from that horrible afternoon was of Burroughs standing in front of the fireplace, seeming to dominate the room, whilst poor Dafydd Williams looked as though he were trying to understand what was going on; and Alexandra Roberts drooped under a weight almost of contamination.

The memory of it was unbearable. Harriet stood up and walked to the window, looking out on the street, thinking about poor George. She left the letter. Much later that evening, she wrote: *I am so glad you are feeling better, my dear old friend. We mustn't let tragedy overwhelm our little boat. Remember how we used to want to go travelling? Let us make serious plans to do that, just as soon as you are in good health again.*

As soon as she wrote it, she crumpled the page and tossed it into the fire. Minerva Atwell would be the one taking Alexandra travelling for her health. Harriet decided to leave it for a while and answer the letter in the morning.

*

Janet was carrying the big tray loaded with silver ready for cleaning and she kept looking at the tongs and thinking they were already dented so if she dropped the tray and they got crushed beneath the tea urn, it wouldn't show too bad. The tray got heavier and heavier.

For some reason, she found herself unable to make a sound when she ran into Valentine Cabot, who was sitting at the bottom of the stairs, wearing evening dress and a pair of holey socks, and looking up at her with a smile. He said something to her. At first she couldn't understand but when he repeated it, it gradually became clear. It was, 'Where's George?'

'Nobody knows, sir.'

'It's been most confusing,' said Valentine, and now she found she was walking round the parlour with him arm in arm. 'At first I went down a long tunnel and saw the light and so on and so forth, just as one is led to expect, but shortly after I had begun to settle in comfortably, I realised that I had some blessed what-you-may-call-it unfinished business. It worried me immensely. Before I knew it, I was hanging about here again. I don't like it at all, Janet. I want a nice cup of tea and a lie down.'

'I'll get you one, sir.'

'No, no need, Janet. I haven't got your attention for long. Ask me a question.'

'What's your unfinished business, sir?' asked Janet.

'It's George, isn't it, of course, you silly little thing? Aren't they saying he hit me over the head with a bottle or some such rot? Anyone who looks at him can see that he couldn't. Anyone who could be bothered to see, that is. You need to talk to someone about it, you know. They don't care, Janet, but the fact is George could never hurt a kitten.'

The parlour was suddenly filled with kittens. Janet picked up a little grey and white one and began to brush its fur. 'Why are there kittens, sir?' asked Janet.

'Oh, you put *those* there,' said Valentine. 'Very pretty but something of a distraction.' He touched the kitten lightly on the nose with a finger.

It exploded in a clap of thunder as Amy Matthews knocked at the door to tell her to wake up.

CHAPTER FIFTEEN

After dinner, it was Minerva's habit to spend time in the salon with her spa guests, sometimes playing cards but more often in conversation. Only three were currently installed, staying on after the busier Christmas season. Minerva had privately told Alexandra that she was very bored by them, but she still managed to keep up a stream of anecdotes to amuse them at dinner. Alexandra was in no doubt that Minerva was one of the attractions of the Adsullata and hoped that she herself could be a kind of added bonus. For, as an unpaying guest, employee and slightly insecure friend, she felt herself to be in an uncomfortable position: rather like being the court favourite of a capricious monarch. As a contribution and as a subtle way of asserting her independence, she had begun sketching a series of little informal portraits of each guest. She was aware that Minerva was watching her now, sketching Mrs Halliwell – and flattering her with an appearance of youth.

Mrs Atwell was different now, far from London and her P.B.s. No less beautifully dressed and perfectly capable of performing a kind of witty folly when it suited her, she had a more thoughtful air. Sometimes Alexandra noticed a brooding look on her face. She wondered if it was the result of boredom – and yet, she had announced that she planned to stay for at least a month; and that Alexandra would stay too, as her confidential companion and resident artist.

Later, after the guests had been helped back to their bedrooms by the staff and the salon was empty, Alexandra was standing inspecting the stone heads set upon alcoves in the wall. These alcoves, she had been informed, had each originally held a marble bust: a young Queen Victoria, a Prince Albert and a small Pallas Athena. Minerva told her how amusing it had been to see the reactions of the staff here at the hotel when she had installed her finds from the well. Her employees, she explained, were local people and, being countryfolk, retained their superstitions. Even the dignified housekeeper had come to Mrs Atwell, apologetically requesting on behalf of the parlour maids that they need not touch or dust or otherwise interact with the nasty heathen things in the course of cleaning.

But the water-smoothed boulders do look out of place, Alexandra thought. She herself did not feel comfortable with them; but it was not her house and not her choice to display them. One stone had no more than two dark holes for eyes and a scoop where a mouth would be. The imagination had to work to complete the face. Another had a sad look with a trace of rudimentary drooping moustache. The third had blind-looking almond eyes and a short slotted mouth.

'I wanted to ask you about something I discovered today,' said Alexandra coming and sitting down near Minerva. 'I was exploring the valley and I believe I came across your original "white stone well".'

'Extraordinary, isn't it?'

'Yes. It certainly inspires a strange contradictory set of feelings. And one of those feelings – don't laugh - was an urge to leave a gift in the water.'

'How droll,' smiled Minerva, patting her hair into place.

Alexandra nodded. 'Isn't it? To find that one is not at all free from the impulses of our ancient forebears. Believe it or not, your display of those curiosities from the well over there fills me with a kind of dread. I can't even put a name to it. It reminds me of the old trees bedecked with ribbons and cloths one sometimes sees in the countryside. We don't really get civilised, do we, Minerva? We have the same set of emotional equipment in common with humanity everywhere and at every time, I believe. Don't you think the people who decorate the trees and leave little gifts at wells are expressing the very same religious urges as those who built the sun temple at Stonehenge?'

'Or one assumes so,' Minerva nodded. 'Because we do not know and cannot really guess. It takes study and detective work, my dear Alexandra, to deduce the motives of the long dead.'

'And that is our favourite subject, you'll say next. And as a matter of fact, I discovered a funny little thing at your well which bears out these observations. A little metal plaque depicting a kind of goddess. Owl-footed and winged, flanked by owls too. What do you make of that? And this is the interesting thing: it didn't look old at all, rather the contrary. Can there be a local cult for such a figure?'

'What? A cult?' whispered Minerva with a dimple. 'Should we inform the emergency vicar?'

Alexandra laughed. 'Imagine what that would be like. Do you suppose there is such a thing? Speeding across the land at the first hint of heresy?'

'Read your Reformation history, my dear Alex.'

Alexandra nodded. 'Yes, of course. But surely this is worthy of study? Anthropologically speaking, a modern local cult in a corner of Somerset for a hitherto unknown goddess would be extremely interesting.'

'No,' said Minerva. 'It wouldn't. It would just get them into trouble with their parish church. Did you leave it where it was?'

'Yes, of course. I didn't want to stir up the powers of the Owl Lady by taking her little plaque away.'

'Perhaps it is my guests who are responsible? What do you say? Which one is it most likely to be the culprit – Mrs Halliwell, Major Farnsworth or Lady Helena?'

'Now you're being facetious,' said Alexandra. 'None of them could get down there. Lady Helena would lose her way among all the crossing pathways in the woods; Major Farnsworth would get distracted and want to go and shoot some harmless wild creature and then eat it; and Mrs Halliwell's poor feet would never let her get near.'

'Well, perhaps you're right and it is one of the cooks or the porters or the bed-makers or the nurses – there is a large staff here, unfortunately, and each and every person in my employ eats too much and drinks too much and requires too much in wages. Perhaps I could weed out the pagan ones and save myself some money.'

'Very well. You're being facetious, Minerva. If this was in Mesopotamia, in a remote tribe encamped round a Tell, you would be all fascination and serious study. Because it's merely Somerset, you are making fun of me.'

Minerva picked up a magazine and began flipping through the pages. 'And when you start your portrait again, do you want my facetious look or would you prefer a studious frown?'

'The frown, oh definitely the frown,' said Alexandra.

'No, no, my portrait is my advertisement, remember, dear Alex. I need to look young and beautiful at all times. Every minute of every day!' She held up the magazine to show a full page advertisement for Atwell's Beauty Balm Compact. 'This is myself, the lady in the illustration, did you know? I asked the engraver to change the features slightly but I personally sat as the model. Amusing, isn't it?'

'Beautiful,' said Alexandra. 'And I must say again that since I began using your Beauty Balm, I find that my skin is remarkably improved. And you made the Compact as a more generally available form of the Balm itself?'

'Yes, it is more inexpensive. The active ingredient is present but in far smaller amounts. I was unsure whether pressed powder would convey the benefits, being so drying, you know, but my customers seem to be pleased with the results – but I must stop talking shop, as they say. It is so boring of me and not what I want to do - when I'm with you.'

'But the balm and the powder are marvellous. You should be proud of what you've achieved.'

'Oh, I am. I can never bother to be modest, dear Alex. It is one of those social postures that evades me, although I have tried. But the Balm, yes, it is wonderful, is it not? You look very well, my dear Alex. Your face is looking younger and fresher and plumper already – and since we're talking about it, this is a good opportunity to tell you about the next step. *Mais pas devant les domestiques.*'

Servants had come in while they were talking to set out a light supper on the sideboard. One of them was lingering by the decanters in the corner and Minerva said sweetly, 'Thank you, Tamworth. You may go now.' After the man had left and they were alone, she continued in a lower voice, 'You are responding so well to the Beauty Balm, we can now introduce the Balm Supplement. It's a more concentrated form of the product, suitable for ingestion. I use it myself.' There was a long pause and she looked seriously into Alexandra's eyes. 'But it is a great secret. It is, as I tell my impatient financiers at the bank, still in the final stages of development. But it isn't. It's been finished for years. It is simply that I was not yet ready to share it – there is no other woman in the country who knows anything about it. No one else has yet had the benefit of this formula. You will be the first.'

Alexandra was astonished and flattered. 'I hardly know how to thank you, Minerva,' she said.

Minerva waved away her appreciation. 'This is special but you are special too. Very special because you understand me. But it is also rather in the nature of an experiment and you must accept that to be the case. I need you to agree wholeheartedly to join me in this venture. After you have begun it, you won't want to stop. It gives many advantages apart from a youthful complexion. And once your course of supplements begins to take effect, you and I will truly be of one mind.'

Alexandra was surprised and even disquieted. 'An experiment? Then you cannot be entirely sure of the results?'

'Oh, I am sure. At least so far as I myself am concerned. It has its side-effects but I believe you will find them to be more than acceptable.'

Alexandra sat in thoughtful silence. 'And this is to be a secret between us?' she asked.

'Yes. And of course, as a business woman, you'll understand the necessity for a contractual obligation on your part not to disclose any detail of the Supplement: anything you should learn of its composition, anything of its effects. You see, after a while, Alex, I will launch a version of this into society.'

'Fascinating! I wish you would tell me more.'

'Oh, everyone will want to know *more*. People will want to steal the formula. They will come to you to bribe you for information and offer you heaps of jewels and chests of gold. Wars will break out to possess it.' She went into a peal of laughter at Alexandra's grave face so that Alexandra laughed too, not sure if she were joking. 'Helen of Troy in a little pill! Believe me, people - especially women - really will sign their souls over to the devil to get at it. If there were really a devil willing to receive something so flimsy as their little souls. Personally, I have always thought it rather a paltry thing to lust after.

'But listen, only if and when you begin a course of treatment will I feel able to trust you fully, Alexandra. At the moment, I trust you as far as I can trust another human being – which may not be very far. No, don't be offended. There is no advantage in pretending that I would give away the secret I worked so long and sacrificed so much to find, without some cast-iron assurance that you would not betray it. The assurance will be that you are *using* it yourself. You will need it so you will guard it; and the advantage to me is that I gain something I have missed ever since dear Joseph died: an intimate companion and a loyal advisor and a fellow explorer, sharing bonds of secrecy. Do I sound harsh? No, not at all. Never think me unkind, my dear. I am simply a woman of business.'

Alexandra nodded. 'Of course,' she said. She pondered what

Minerva might be implying. Did she want to make her a partner in the business? Why should she want that? Under what terms? What had she herself to invest or contribute? There was long silence.

Minerva observed her and said, 'I see you need time to think this over. I can only take you with me – on this metaphorical journey, I mean - if am absolutely certain that you agree to my conditions. Let us put it aside for a few days. We'll discuss it again in due course.'

They lapsed into silence and Minerva returned to her magazine. After a while, she said impishly, 'But I believe it is not just my wonderful Balm that makes you look so rejuvenated, but the pure pleasure of being here with me. I suit you. I am your spa.' Alexandra laughed. 'Don't laugh! I'll find you a rich husband.'

'No thank you. I have spent quite enough years exploring that aspect of a woman's life. It holds no attractions for me, nor has done for many years. I wonder sometimes if it ever did.'

'Really? How intriguing. But I see it more as a blood sport, you know,' said Minerva. 'Something to combine with my other interests.'

*

Events always seemed to come at George unexpectedly, looming up like ships on a misty night and then inexplicably disappearing. Now, without any idea of what he should do, he spent days doing nothing but trudging from one place to another. One of the complicating factors was the way his surroundings would sometimes get unpleasantly mixed up. His world comprised many layers. One was the usual one that he presumed everyone could see, the places that were recorded on maps and which had all the solid people still in their flesh walking about in it. Then there were others underlying it in an indescribable way, the more recent, the clearer, he supposed; while the older stuff seemed thin, as fragile as a soap bubble about to pop. He explained it to himself, when he thought about it (if he thought about it at all) as like imprints, like smeared whorls of fingerprints on sheet upon sheet of glass, overlaying each other, almost impossible to tell where each lay. Sometimes he was not entirely sure which layer he was in and he had to invent things, confabulate, so that the joins were smoothed over. It was then, he suspected, people thought he was an imbecile or a lunatic from Bedlam. He hated this and worked hard to concentrate, to fix himself where he should be and hide it. When he thought about hiding it, he faced a great sea wall, enormously high, stretching on either side as far as the eye could see. Or perhaps it was a dam, restraining a heavy body of water or a weight of sand. He could not understand this wall, what it was or indeed how it had got there. But it was useful.

It was no surprise to discover that the best places in London to shelter (if you were scared of the police) were already ferociously defended by other people, most of whom wanted to rob you. As for the knotted slums where he might have hidden himself, every inch was the territory of family-gangs. Courtyard connected courtyard via passages so narrow they never saw a sunbeam. Easy to get lost in. George sensed the pull from them, like water circling a drain. He found himself floating perilously near once or twice. His air of abstraction invited exploitation and to protect himself, he was gradually driven to seek safety further out of the city, following the sliding green line of a broad canal.

One evening, as he sat on a wall by a busy little marketplace, a woman talked to him. He was preoccupied with keeping his eye out for dropped food, but he dimly gathered that she was associated with a gang discreetly haunting the cobbled square. While he had sat there almost unnoticed, occasionally foraying out to pick up a scrap from the ground and then slipping back to his perch and re-wrapping himself in an old blanket, they had been preying equally upon shepherds driving their flocks to the city butchers and upon coal backers and other traffic from the barges on the canal. These were stopping to take refreshment at a large inn on the square which served the nearby lock and moorings. The gang, consisting of an assortment of ages and sexes, were all intent in various ingenious ways on relieving drunken men of their cash and valuables.

She eyed George for some time from the other side of the square before sidling into his vicinity. She had been adjusting her position to get a clear view of him, piercing a line of sight between poles and awnings and backs of vendors; and she watched him for a long time before she came over, trying to work out what his game was. He spoke to nobody, did nothing but hunt for food, but he looked promising. So she came and stood nearby for a while, and then a little nearer, until she was ready to sit herself down on the same wall as he. After five minutes, she gave her name as Sukey and said she was but one-and-twenty. George looked at her warily. She was of indeterminate middle age. She wore a bonnet adorned with a little stubble of broken feathers and her nose too had once been broken. Her mouth smiled but her eyes were tired. After a while she said confidentially that she knew a place where there were rich pickings to be had, and she would introduce him if he gave her a cut of his take.

'No, thank you,' said George politely.

He had the blanket wrapped tightly round him with the thick edges folded round his hands. It had been getting colder and colder all day. His main thought was that he would like to stand near the brazier over there where they were selling hot things, chestnuts and potatoes and fat bursting sausages. The smell was glorious. He had been rehearsing a speech about needing to eat something hot but he knew it would sound wrong. People kept noticing his foreign looks and then remarking on his accent and calling him a toff when he spoke. Opening his mouth attracted more attention so he tried not to do it.

The woman said suddenly in a matter-of-fact tone, 'This is our pitch, right. Lardy Kate's coming down in an hour and you'd better not be about the place when *she* walks through. She'll cut you proper, without a cut.' She laughed as if she found it amusing. 'Wordplay. Got a name?'

George thought for a second and said, 'Valentine.'

'Valentine. Excellent name. *Miss* Valentine, I take it?'

George said nothing. She shuffled her bottom along the low wall nearer to him and then spat over the other side of it in an almost dainty manner, shielded behind her hand. The wall they sat on topped a steep grassy slope running up from the canal. George, glancing beyond her, saw mist rising from the slab of twilit water and lamps in barge windows and horses tethered on the grass. There was the clinking sound of a metal bucket being carried and somewhere down there a man and a woman were arguing in a friendly joshing way.

'Got any baccy?' she said suddenly. She was within six inches of him now.

'No.'

'No, course not. You don't smoke. Got money? Want a little cuddle?'

'No.'

'Got the pox then?'

'No.'

'What you here for?'

'Hungry.'

'You're very nice with them Aitches. You English? No, you're not. You a Dago?'

'No.'

'Go on, don't be shy, you can tell me, I don't mind what you are. Nobody minds if you're Miss Valentine round here, so long as you clear it with Lardy Kate.' She nudged him heavily. 'Cheer up! You got your health, in'tcha? No need to go begging.'

'I'm not begging,' he said.

'What then, you thieving? No independent thievery in the market. Someone gets robbed and we get the Blues coming round and everyone loses a night's earnings. Just be agreeable to the people, that's all we ask. That's our motto, just be agreeable.'

'I'm just picking up things, little scraps that people drop. And sometimes ha'pennies and farthings, that's all.'

'Then that's stealing. You should give them to the authorities, them ha'pennies. Pass 'em over and I'll do it for you if you're shy. You look shy to me.'

'I haven't found anything today,' said George. He began to feel it was time to move and he suspected that Sukey was rather drunk.

'Here, Miss Valentine. See here. I'm going over there in a minute to The Lamb and I want to give you some advice, gratis. You got looks like a picture postcard. You need to look out for yourself.'

'I do look out for myself,' said George.

'Got a shiv?'

'No. I had a penknife but I sold it.'

'You're a right pigeon, my nabs.' She laughed quite kindly, whilst casting a professional eye over a small knot of bargemen about to enter The Lamb.

George shook his head, thinking about walking further along the canal. But the further he went into the countryside, the more exotic he seemed to appear. People stared at him anyway, even in the middle of London. Out here – wherever he was – things could only get worse.

'You're in want of assistance, you are,' Sukey remarked, searching for something in a little pouch covered in red silk flowers like a limp anemone. 'No baccy left. No wait, here, in a twist.' She spent a while cleaning and tamping a little pipe and then went off to cadge a light from a man coming out of the public house. George paid no further attention to her or to the bursts of noise from the pub. The market was packing up. There was an exchange of cheerful insults going on among the group near the brazier. A stallholder was singing melodiously into the evening air as he rolled lengths of cotton fabric; and the lamps were being lit. Now was the time to scour the leavings for anything edible, before it got too dark to see. Then Sukey came back, and she was carrying an old and dirty sheet of newspaper.

'Well, well, Miss Valentine. Look what I came upon,' she said, settling herself comfortably next to him like an old friend. 'I said you looked like a picture. And here's the picture. This is you, innit?' She held it out under the newly-bright gas flare and George saw himself in the paper. His heart sank. Mrs Roberts's little drawing had been coarsened by the engraver, but it was recognisably his own face.

'Reckon there's a reward?' asked Sukey, scanning the short paragraph printed underneath. 'I can't read long words but I know me numbers. Read it to me, my love, won't you?'

'I can't read very much either,' said George carefully. He began to get up off the wall he was sitting on, letting the dirty blanket fall from his shoulders to the wet cobblestones.

Sukey gripped his arm and pulled him back down, smiling. 'Now, now. Don't be so quick to leave a lady all alone,' she said. 'A gent like you. I can help you. We can work out a way of getting money out of this here.'

'I've got to go,' he said.

'What you done? How bad is it?' she asked sympathetically.

'Nothing. I honestly did nothing to anyone. Someone is lying about me,' said George.

'You'll be safe with me and Lardy Kate, then' said Sukey. She approached her face close to his ear and adding confidentially, 'Lardy Kate can hide you.'

'Please let go of my arm,' said George, not liking the fumes of alcohol. 'What do you want with me? I don't mean any harm to anyone. I just want to go somewhere safe and quiet.'

'We all want somewhere safe and quiet, sweetheart, with a nice garden and a husband and a pianner. You're not the only one in trouble.'

'I can't help that,' said George.

She slipped her other arm round him and squeezed. 'Yes, you stay with us. We'll get some tea and rum first. Then we can have a lovely time together. Why not? You and me, this one time? Go on. What does it matter? Nobody need know. What do you care?'

George felt her grip; and his mind's eye, like something breaking open, suddenly showed him Albert Burroughs, his lips, thin oilslick lips and hard hands tightening their grip.

'I don't want to,' George said abruptly. He tried to pull away from her, something blaring inside him. Burroughs talking. What was he saying? Sukey was talking over it; but what was the meaning hidden in *Nobody need know. What do you care?* George stood up. Burroughs always stared at me.

He took three steps into the market square, almost empty of traders now; and then, confused, turned and faced the wall where he had been sitting. He thought Sukey's face suddenly looked very strange, the flattened nose in the middle of it and her eyes the colour of haddock skin staring at him; and he could not hear what she was saying. He didn't think again. He jumped over the wall and without a word, scrambled down the steep slope onto the tow path ten yards below. Then he was running into the darkness under the bridge and he heard her shouting something over and over again.

He did not stop running, limping, walking through the damp night until he found himself again nearing the busier parts of London. He left the tow path as soon as he could, slinking along a side street like a trench and up a staircase of lightless steps, finally losing himself among black wet alleys lined with warehouses. He expected to come staring face to face with Sukey at every turn, but gradually he understood that the pursuit was in his imagination. What could she do? Who would listen to her anyway?

When he slid between the flaking rails of a padlocked gateway, he found a dray falling to pieces in the corner of a yard. The floor had rotted and one end had slipped right down to touch the ground, creating a slope-roofed little compartment walled on two sides. Under this shelter he dragged a mouldy sack. Exhausted, he lay down upon it as the dawn came, gazing up through a split in the wood at melting heights of pearl.

It troubled him a great deal to think that he did not know when Burroughs's assault had occurred. The rain had been battering the windows. Yes, that was true. And nobody was home – but there must have been somebody home? No servants, no Valentine? Then he knew it was near Christmas time and perhaps they had gone to church. He was new to the house, that was it, shy of everyone. The abandoned house, and himself sitting in the parlour; the rain inventing a strange silver light in the winter room. He had looked up and Burroughs had been there, staring down at him, very neat, but his speech was clipped, indignant and there were the fumes of alcohol.

So you're another one from the streets - No, I was working somewhere respectable. I was rooming somewhere respectable. I am respectable –

The details of words had evaporated but he remembered the shine on Burroughs's shoes and a formal suit and how he was angry with Valentine for bringing him home. And then he, George, had got up quickly to get to his own room and he remembered the fire irons had clanged on the fender when he knocked into them; and surely there must have been a reason for that? You could lock the door in your own room, that was why he wanted to go there.

It was that dangerous look on his face, repelled fascination, that made George run away up the stairs. He got as far as the door of his room before he was caught. He had not shouted and fought: he did not have that competence. He had pretended, servile, because he could only comply; frozen at the time, filled with disgust and self-loathing now. Of course he had said nothing to Valentine; and then it had all drifted out of reach. He was able to remember how Burroughs became savage afterwards and hated him more, like the shame of stained linen, and yet dogged his steps. He watched the sky for a long time, breathing tight little breaths and not noticing the cold.

After a while, he came back and realised that Sukey had showed him that his picture was in a newspaper. He wondered if there was a hot pursuit on his trail or if anyone really cared very much? A plan began to form of getting on board a ship and sailing away. For this he needed money and clothes. And he was starving, felt as thin as air. He wanted to go and see Mrs Day. He wondered if he would be able to say the right words to convince her that he hadn't killed Valentine. He certainly would not be able to explain about Albert Burroughs.

The thought spread out inside him, very slowly and gradually, that none of this was his fault. He pulled out the card which the kind doctor had given him and once again spelt out the words written upon it. George had looked at it from time to time and each time put it away. He couldn't risk it. But he needed a messenger. Then he took out the little grubby handkerchief belonging to Janet Fairlight and held it in two hands. The dim cave where he nestled became far away for him. Tentatively, slowly, he began to slide between the layers, between the cracks, finding dim and shifting highways to follow.

*

Janet Fairlight had never known herself to do anything quite so courageous or so out of character before. Part of herself was looking on, continuously aghast at her own presumption. Another part of herself felt so confident and calm that she just didn't care. She was sitting in the parlour of Mrs Harriet Day's house, wearing her brown straw hat, the one with yellow-hearted daisies round the rim which had belonged to her big sister, Rose. She was sitting here, and she was about to talk to Mrs Day like a lady.

She amused herself in various ways as she waited for her to come home. She swivelled her feet on the floor, making her boot heels clump together. She would have bitten her nails to pass the time but she had on a pair of silky brown gloves (slightly empty at the very ends of the fingers, as these too had belonged to Rose). It was all she could do to prevent herself from going over to the big shiny piano and lifting the lid and walking those gloved fingers up the keys. Mrs Day was a piano teacher, and it was one of her secret wishes to learn a bit of piano one day, when she'd saved up enough to do so. She planned to play for her mother, actually on her actual mother's real birthday one year. But today, Janet had another kind of errand. It had been extremely kind of Mrs Skipton the housekeeper to let her sit here and wait. Mrs Skipton was a member of Janet's mother's congregation, of course, so that made her sort of family.

Harriet Day came into the room with a look of kindly concern. Janet always liked her face. She stood up and curtsied.

'Why, Janet, little Janet Fairlight, are you quite well? I know your mistress is away for a while. I hope there is nothing amiss at your house? Is Mrs Jenkins in good health?'

'Everybody is enjoying very good health, ma'am, and Mrs Jenkins sends her politest respects and says as she guv me permission to come and see you, and she hopes you don't mind.'

'Certainly I don't mind, Janet. As long as all is in order at Mrs Roberts's house. I am sure your nerves – like mine – have hardly begun to recover from the recent tragic events. Do sit down, my girl. No need to fear. Now, tell me what's the matter?'

'First of all, I have to say that you're not to worry and get upset.'

'Very well, although when the first thing someone says to me is that I shouldn't get upset, it tends to put me on my guard. I won't get upset, then.'

'And I have to say that you won't believe me at first but I have to show you something which will help you to believe what I say,' said Janet, as if reading from a list.

'Have you been instructed by someone to come and speak to me, dear? Could they not come themselves?' asked Harriet, beginning to feel dubious about the motives for the visit.

'Yes,' said Janet, 'I have been instructed. And before I tell you all about it, I have to ask you to promise to hear all of the story right the way through to the end before saying anything. And not to get angry.'

'Well, these are a great many stipulations. I confess I am beginning to feel rather wary. I hope it isn't a prank of some sort?' She looked at the girl's earnest face and decided that whatever came of it all, the child was acting in good faith. Best hear her out and get to the bottom of it.

Janet began to speak. First she told Harriet about Valentine Cabot sitting on the stairs and telling her that Mr George had not killed him. She didn't mention the kittens. Then she told her that George Arden had visited her just before dawn. At this point, Harriet gasped and began to ask something, but Janet held up a small, brown-gloved hand and said, No. He was there but he wasn't there. He was there as his dream self. She said he came to tell her something important. He had asked her to come and see Mrs Harriet Day and tell her that he was innocent. He was scared and he was hiding. She knew where he was hiding because he'd showed her a picture of it.

Harriet listened with her mouth slightly open and did not interrupt. She was just wondering how to tell the poor girl that her brains had been disordered by the death of Mr Cabot and that her dreams were producing a fairytale answer to the shock, when Janet stood up.

'And now I have to show the proof. Mr Arden told me that you wouldn't be able to believe me straight off. He said you have a picture on your wall in a silver frame. He says there is a girl in the picture, who is you when you was young, ma'am, and the colour of the ribbon is the same colour as your eyes. I gotta find that picture and take it off the wall. With your permission, ma'am, I will now do that.'

Janet spoke with such extraordinary self-possession that Harriet simply nodded her head. She did not point the picture out. Janet looked over the walls, full as they were with sketches and paintings of various sizes. Finally, she pointed to the picture. 'There we are. Found it, ma'am. Can I take it down? 'Cos I have to, he says.'

Once again, Harriet nodded. Janet reached out and removed the little picture from its hook. She turned it over. The back of the frame was taped over with brown paper. 'I'm very sorry, ma'am, but this is what I have to do,' she said. She pulled at the brown paper until it tore. A corner of something white showed beneath. Little by little, she tore the paper back until a small folded piece of paper was revealed. 'He says this is yours, ma'am, put in there for you a long time ago when the frame was made. But you never knew and you ain't never seen it nor read it before.'

Harriet took the scrap and held it on her open palm in amazement. Very slowly, she unfolded it. Written in schoolgirl copperplate, she saw the words: *My dearest darling H.! Wherever I go, whatever I do, I will never, never not love you! Your friend forever, A. 7ᵗʰ July, 1867.* After some time, Harriet said, 'And what now, Janet?'

'Well, do you believe me, ma'am? That is the question I have to ask you.'

'I have no choice, Janet. I believe you. I have no rational explanation for any of this, but I have to believe the evidence of my own eyes and ears.'

'Then that's good, ma'am. In that case, if you believe me, you just have to answer the door. If you have any doubts, just don't answer the door, but please not to tell the coppers.'

'Answer the door?' asked Harriet, turning her eyes towards the street as if she expected to see him walking up the front steps. 'Surely he won't risk himself by coming here?'

'Three o'clock in the morning and a knock at the kitchen door.

That's what he showed me: a big clock face in the dark and that knocking sound. And that's all, ma'am. That's all I have to say. So now I'd better be going.'

'Wait, wait, Janet. Tell me, did you inform Mrs Jenkins of all this? Is that why she let you come?'

'Oh no, ma'am, she'd never understand all this kind o' thing. Mr George said she wun't and best to not talk. So she don't know. I said I had my mother's permission to come and ask to have pianner lessons off of you. That's why she let me out. I found out something too. Only me and Mr George can see them theatrical visitors. Do you know, I thought they was real, but it turns out they're just ghosts? And Mr Cabot, he can see them too *now*, I expect. I in't afraid of any of them now.'

There were many different questions Harriet would have liked to ask, stemming from just this last speech, but she confined herself to only one. 'Permission to have piano lessons, did you say? And *would* you like to have piano lessons, Janet?'

For the first time, Janet looked like her normal shy self. 'Well, yes, I would very much like to, ma'am. When I have saved enough.'

'Then you shall, my dear Janet. Gratis. That means for free. For being so brave. Because it took a lot of courage to come and say all that, and have so much faith too.'

Janet curtsied. 'I knew you'd be nice, Mrs Day. Everyone knows you're nice to people. Well, good-bye, ma'am.'

CHAPTER 16

It was extremely dark at three o'clock in the morning. It was however somewhat warmer than Harriet had expected it to be. Cloud-cover kept away the frost and the wind had dropped. She had wrapped herself in a thick duckdown quilt and sat next to the glow through the grate. Mrs Skipton and Daisy Etherington had long gone to bed. Harriet had set a single small lamp with a short wick to burn on the windowsill but made sure all the bolts were shot and the locks properly shut. The battered kettle had provided a little tea which she had sipped thoughtfully, both hands embracing the cup, looking into the coals.

Not quite sure still whether Janet Fairlight's behaviour earlier that day made sense, she had resisted the urge to rationalise it all away. Had it not been for the folded paper, written so long ago by Alexandra and of which she had known nothing, she would have doubted that the incident had occurred at all. She recalled how George Arden had once looked at the picture and said something like, 'Your life is full of secrets.' How had he known?

Dozing in the wooden armchair yet constantly alert for the church clock chimes, she knew at last that the hour was approaching. Why be afraid? Either it was all a strange series of coincidences and would lead to nothing – in which case there would be no knock at the door and she could go to bed; or it was just poor George, a harmless young fellow, accused of a crime he had not committed. Yet there was something so sinister in these circumstances, this darkness, that the very suspicions she had rejected clung to his image. Murder. A horrible word. Suppose Janet had set her up – and outside in the darkness a gang of thieves were skulking, waiting to force their way in if she answered the door?

The tap on the back door when it came therefore made her heart leap with fear and go careering in her chest. She went and placed a hand on the cold panels and said through the wood, 'Who is it?'

Naturally, the voice replied, 'Me. It's me!'

'You'll have to do better than that,' she said sternly.

The voice said, very low, 'Oh, sorry, Mrs Day. It's George.'

She set about opening the door as quietly as she possibly could. As soon as it was open, a thin dark figure slipped through and moved silently into the room. Harriet didn't turn to look at him until she made sure to lock everything up again. She had a wild fear that George had been followed here by footpads and rapists or that the police had been watching the whole time. When everything was safe, she took the lamp off the sill, shut the curtains across the window and placed it on the table. Then she took a good look at George Arden. Of course he looked terrible. She had prepared herself to see a fairly terrible sight, so she wasn't surprised. The most disturbing thing was the darkness sunk in his eye sockets. His lips were cracked. His face was bony. He smelt. 'George, dear George, just sit there. Don't say anything.' She hurried blindly to the pantry and returned with everything she could carry, laying her hands on the shelves randomly in the dark.

Back in the kitchen, the light of the lamp revealed that she had procured a stone bottle of ginger beer, some horseradish, a round porcelain jar of Gentlemen's Relish and half a very hard cheese. She shook her head at her own foolishness, stayed long enough this time to light a candle in a brass holder and set out again more methodically to get food suitable for an invalid. George meanwhile picked up the horseradish in mild confusion. Eventually, he was more suitably provided with a round white loaf and most of a roast chicken. All he wanted to drink was clean water. And before he ate, the still-warm water from the kettle, poured into a bowl, a bar of Sunlight soap and a clean towel made him so happy she wanted to hug him.

'This is wonderful,' he said after he had torn ravenously through half of the provisions. 'Thank you for letting me wash too. Water is a difficult thing, Mrs Day, but hot water is a miracle! You can't drink the river or puddles and you can't get clean. You have to use the horse troughs and the fountains for drinking. But there are lots of people about so you can't really get enough each time. Perhaps I could take this bottle if you don't want it and keep filling it up again?'

'You're surely not going off again?' said Harriet. She had already decided that he would stay with her from now on, hide in the attic or in a cupboard, until he was cleared of suspicion.

'I can't stay here. I have to run away, if possible right over the sea to another country. And that is why I had to come. I'm very sorry about it but I have no money and no clothes and things. Also,' he added, 'I hated the idea that you'd believe *him*. He is lying.'

'Albert Burroughs?' she asked. 'The one who claims to have seen you – seen the accident?'

'Yes, Burroughs is lying.'

'I am already absolutely convinced of it, Mr Arden. In fact, I never had a doubt of it. Would it be too difficult for you to tell me what really happened?' She added tentatively, 'Perhaps we could write it all down in a statement and then I could give it to the police.'

George looked at her. 'I don't think they would believe me.'

'Well, Mr Arden, I still think the best course of action would be to get your testimony written out fair and square.'

'Listen. If you were to go with a statement to the police, they'd know you'd talked to me and knew where I was. You can't do it.'

Harriet nevertheless went and fetched pen and paper and prepared herself to write. Unfortunately, George's memory was very patchy and very much mixed in with it was what Harriet called fancy. For example, he remembered being in a club and meeting a man who had lived in Thebes three thousand years ago; and then wandering about in the streets. He remembered Valentine standing at the very top of the stairs and how red and swollen his face had looked; and throwing the bottle, and the look of the bottle poised in the air and the crash when it landed; and then he remembered kneeling by the body, looking up at Burroughs who was looking down at him over the banister, and the shouting. And so he had run away.

Harriet wrote it down carefully and got George to make a mark at the bottom and then she witnessed it. She thought that seemed fairly legal but she had to admit privately that it would not necessarily strengthen the case for his innocence, although it referred to the fact that the bottle was smashed by being hurled down the stairs.

It was only after George had eaten some more bread and chicken and drunk more water that he remembered something else important. He produced a dog-eared calling card and handed it to Harriet. 'He was helpful,' he said.

She read aloud 'Dr John Watson, Surgeon, 221B Baker Street, London W. When did you meet this gentleman?'

'He was at the club that night too. And he was extremely kind to me, you know. I remember this. He walked with me through the streets even though the cold hurt his chest and he listened properly and suggested things. I definitely remember him saying that I should go to him if I needed help. It occurs to me that perhaps I should go and find him. What do you think?'

'He is a doctor,' said Harriet. 'That would be helpful if you needed some medical treatment. I expect that's what he meant he could help you with.'

'I think he mentioned other ways too, but yes, he was suggesting medical help,' answered George, carefully placing the last shreds of chicken on the last piece of bread and preparing to bite it. 'For my mind,' he added as an afterthought, with the bread paused halfway to his mouth. 'He thinks I'm a bit mad.'

'Oh, what are we to do with you?' Harriet asked, looking mournfully at the lamp in the middle of the table.

George regarded the lamp too as he neatly chewed and swallowed the food. Then he said, 'Money, clothes, food, a way of leaving the country. That's all. Transport. Or if I can't go now, then somewhere to hide for six months until everyone forgets. I'll go to France. It's a nice place. I can speak French very well. I was there once.'

'Ah. Could you find someone you know, to help you, give you shelter?'

'Not someone I know but there's usually a way.'

'So there's nobody you could go to? Very well, let's think then.' Harriet put her chin in her hand and tried to view the matter from as many points of view as possible. Finally she said, 'George, I really believe that you should take temporary shelter here until we can either prove your innocence or get you out of the country. Personally, I think it better to prove your innocence and we must think how that may be done. So I am going to stow you away in the attic for a little while, until we can find somewhere better. Mrs Skipton never goes up there because her knees can't cope with those stairs. They're a death trap, she says.'

So that was settled. There would be one or two items to smuggle up the next day but Harriet was confident that she would be able to sort everything out. George followed her silently up the stairs, past the door of the spare bedroom; up the next flight, past Mrs Skipton's and Daisy Etherington's rooms; finally up some narrow, almost vertical, stairs which led to a trapdoor.

Harriet handed George the lamp she had been carrying. Then with great care to avoid a clatter, she extracted a bunch of keys from her apron pocket. The trapdoor was padlocked because of the skylight in the roof. The space above was large and dry and surprisingly warm, smelling a little dusty and half filled with old furniture from the house below. George followed her up and placed the oil lamp and the bottle of water he was holding on a rickety rattan table.

'Help me, Mr Arden,' whispered Harriet, pulling at a rolled eiderdown. 'Look, you see, everything you need is here. You can sleep on these, and look, here's a cushion or two. And this chair just needs to have its struts tightened, but you won't break it, you're light as a feather ...'

George listened gratefully as she showed him the various treasures. It was like a palace after the horrors of the past days – he was by no means sure of how long he had been wandering. With the food in his stomach, his spirits rose by the second.

When they had spread out and arranged a bed and George realised that he was at last somewhere safe, he whispered, 'I actually don't know how to thank you. I really don't know how. You are so kind.' He held her hand, awkwardly shaking it from time to time.

'I just happen to want to help you,' said Harriet; and then to avoid sentiment, added, 'And look, there's a chamber pot in the corner – don't be shy, really, how silly! You once said you thought I had an idea in my head that you resemble my son, if he'd lived to grow up. Well, you were right. That is exactly how I think of you. So no need to be embarrassed about anything.' Harriet left the lamp with him.

She lay in bed, assessing the practicalities of food and water supply when she remembered that the skylight in the roof would give George access to a small leaded area among the chimney pots. This made her feel better. It would be less like a prison.

*

Later that same morning at the Adsullata hotel, Alexandra received some bad news.

'I know. It is a most tragically sad event,' said Minerva over breakfast. She was patting Alexandra's hand and her eyes were shining with sympathetic tears. 'And quite unexpected. What can I say? She was getting old, she was ill, she simply ceased to struggle. She left her body quite serenely, I believe, at about the midnight hour. She had a tiny smile on her face, or so it seemed to me. I was the one who found her in the early hours of the morning – I peep in on my residents before I retire (where appropriate, of course) - and in order to save the other guests any distress, I have already had the staff take care of everything. Her poor body is gone to the morgue. There, there, Alex. In a place like this, which caters for the infirm and the elderly, one must expect one's guests occasionally to depart for the greater life. She has gone to better things, she really has.'

Alexandra took the news of Mrs Halliwell's sudden death hard, considering their acquaintance had been so short. It got mixed up with Valentine's. It was setting her back: she could feel it. She spent the day wandering the valley, thinking about the briefness of this pause on the threshold of death. And perhaps it was her sadness and shock that gave her the impression that Minerva was watching her reaction with an almost scientific intensity. It was as though she herself were an experiment and Minerva was applying certain conditions to her, waiting for a chemical change to occur. There had been those hours of intense conversation in which Minerva was almost flirtatious, certainly very affectionate. There were hours when she was left in solitude. There was the sombre influence exerted by the White Stone Well, as they called it; and speculation about its ancient mysteries, which they discussed endlessly.

The next morning, Minerva received a letter from a prominent society hostess, a confirmed admirer of the Balm, entreating her to work upon a more concentrated form of the formula to provide a solution to the implacable arrival of freckles and lines. She laughed and read it aloud in mockery to Alexandra. 'Look at all this dignified polite nonsense hiding such a depth of terror,' she said. She glanced over at Alexandra's solemn face and said, 'Oh, but I see this is not amusing you. Listen, come and sit with me this afternoon, after I have dealt with all this tiresome correspondence. I have had to leave you alone far too much. We need to spend some quiet reflective time in each other's company. I know Mrs Halliwell had become a friend to you. I understand what it means to lose a friend.'

That afternoon, Minerva sat with her in the solarium and began talking about some work she had undertaken, research of a particularly interesting kind. 'I want you to become familiar with it, my dear Alex. It has a bearing on my entire philosophy of life. Let me begin to explain it.'

To Alexandra's confusion, she began not to explain a research project or even a religious conviction, but to tell a story. She determined not to interrupt but, looking quietly out over the greying valley as the evening drew in, fell into half-focused listening, like a child about to fall asleep.

'There was once a goddess who decided to visit her sister, the queen of death's kingdom. Before she set off, she instructed her servant to order everyone on earth to go into mourning for her – because she knew she was going to die, you see. You can't visit death's kingdom without dying, my dear. The servant was instructed to beg the gods at the appropriate moment to save her from death. I suppose the idea was that the extravagance of the mourning rituals would convince the gods to bring her back to life. You see, even divinities need to apply a little emotional blackmail to get their way. Anyway, the goddess passed through the seven gates of hell and as she went, her symbols of power, royal jewels and garments were stripped from her by the gatekeeper. Coming to her sister on her throne, without any earthly power left to her, the goddess demanded that she herself be placed upon the throne of death. The judges of the Underworld were outraged and they ordered that she be killed. And she was and her corpse was hung upon a hook for three days.'

'Dear me,' said Alexandra, feeling almost shaken into wakefulness. 'That is rather more gruesome than I hoped to hear. But she seems to have been usurping her sister's rightful power. Which I suppose is death itself. Is that the meaning of this story? It is the year's end and the mourning of Winter and then Spring returning, is it not?'

'It's a very old story,' said Minerva, 'and I do not think it quite follows our modern expectations. Or perhaps it has its own logic. For while the goddess is a corpse in the Underworld, the living upon earth carry on their extravagant mourning. Seeing this, the most powerful of all the gods is persuaded to invent a new magic to bring the goddess back from the dead. He must create an entirely new thing, a new way of being in order to get round the laws of the Underworld, and so he employs a trick. This is very interesting, you see. He has to imagine something which doesn't exist, beyond the laws of nature. So he finds the in-between space. He creates beings who are neither human nor divine, not spirit, not flesh, neither male nor female. They will not be bribed or turned aside and it is these messengers who bring the goddess back from death. Interesting, is it not?'

'Yes,' said Alexandra. 'So death itself is tricked by these

messengers?'

Minerva nodded. 'Not quite. A trick, yes, but it isn't enough for Death. Perhaps Death doesn't understand the new thing – I don't know. Perhaps it is so outside the laws of nature that it is unrecognisable. Do you think that might happen? If you or I saw an angel right at this moment, would we recognise it for what it was? You see, I think we would not, we wouldn't have the wherewithal to understand it. So Death sticks to the old ways and makes a bargain, an exchange. Something must be given in return to seal the compact. Oh, I so want you to understand! One day soon I'll give you my notebook. There is a lot to think about in this story. There is a twist in it, something a Christian would never think of writing. I hope you'll see what I mean when I show it to you.'

Alexandra did not fully understand and their talk passed to other subjects and she forgot about it. Later, she imagined it was Minerva's way of helping her to accept and mourn the deaths of Mrs Halliwell and Valentine; but the tale became an ingredient in the strange brew in Alexandra's mind. She thought about the letter Minerva had received from the society lady, desperately begging for a remedy for Time. She could feel that the soothing cream was affecting her own skin, but the sight of her improving face in the mirror paradoxically began to cause her more anxiety. She stared at her reflection closely, while half-articulated thoughts fleeted through her mind: this is just the effect of the Balm and it is temporary, it will go, this will go into the ground, under this skin is the skull. I am forty-eight years old. How much time is left to me?

She woke in the small hours of the morning with a weight on her chest. When she fell asleep again, she walked in graveyards, knowing that under her feet lay Valentine and Mrs Halliwell. Sometimes the earth gave way and she crashed in upon them, finding them entwined in a coffin, putrid flesh in each other's arms.

After these restless nights, she was very glad to receive a letter from Harriet. She hoped it would cheer and normalise things, but the subject matter surprised and worried her as she read it over breakfast. She instantly decided she could not share it with Minerva, although Minerva would certainly be affected by the outcome. The tug of old loyalty kept her true to Harriet's request for absolute secrecy.

She took the letter with her on her morning walk and sat to read it again on the very same tree stump from which she had made that first sketch of the house.

> *My dear Alexandra,*
>
> *I do hope you are well and continuing to improve in spirits.*
>
> *I am so sorry to trouble you, but things are not quite right here. I hardly want to refer to the death of our friend Mr Cabot but you will have to forgive me, as that is very much central to the matter in hand.*
>
> *Now, first of all, Alexandra, and before you get bothered and upset, I want to assure you that I am absolutely convinced of the truth of what I am about to write. Nothing could shake this conviction because I have seen incontrovertible evidence to support my belief, at least in part. The rest I am prepared to take on trust.*
>
> *The belief is that George Arden is innocent, that he did not hurt or even think of hurting Valentine Cabot. Albert Burroughs is lying. I believe he has an unknown reason to wish harm to George, which George will not or cannot divulge. Very well, that is the first thing I have to say. The second thing stems from the first and may not surprise you when you think about it: George is hiding in my attic.*
>
> *I imagine you have taken a deep breath and thought about this for a second or two before you carry on reading. If you haven't, please do so now.*
>
> *The third thing I have to say is going to follow easily from the first and second. Which is this: George needs a safer place to hide until we can find a way to prove his innocence. So. I know you're more clever than I, Alex, and you always were. So if anyone can find a way of keeping George at the Adsullata quietly, it is you. He needs to not draw attention to himself, that is all. I myself will make the booking by telegram to the agent's office in Bath just as soon as I have your agreement and I feel it is safe for him to travel, and he will arrive as a guest in whatever way is normal. Perhaps your beetle carriage will collect him at the station. You can pretend not to know him, or perhaps it's better if you do say that you know him as he may forget to remember that he should pretend not to know you! You know George is vague. Obviously, I will pay the fees in advance. I am thinking one month should be possible, as I have that much available until the dividends come in.*
>
> *Can you write to me and give me an answer as soon as you have thought it over. I just want to say again in the most convincing and persuasive tone you can imagine that he IS innocent. Think therefore how terrible, how unforgiveable and how tragic if he were arrested, tried and <u>hanged</u> as a result of the malice of Albert Burroughs! Help me, Alexandra. We must make sure that Justice prevails. (I am sorry to fall into cliché and I know you object to that kind of lazy thing, but really,*

my hand is shaking as I write and every hour I expect the police to knock at the door!!)

    Your loving friend,

    Harriet.

    P.S. I am going to be teaching piano to Janet Fairlight your maid. I hope you don't object. And thank you, dear friend, for the little note you put in the back of the picture you painted of me when I was fifteen on the jetty at Broadstairs.

Alexandra walked about thinking for a very long time that morning. As she walked, she kept sighing and wringing her hands together and then noticing that she was doing it and thinking of Lady Macbeth. Which in turn brought back the hilarious anecdotes that Valentine used to tell about incidents in the theatre, and she missed him anew.

Tiresome to have feelings, she found herself thinking as she applied the Beauty Balm to her face later that day. It soothed her. Just letting it sink in soothed her. She had been advised to put it on three times a day and then lie down and relax. Each time she did it, she had noticed a certain lessening of emotional intensity on any issue that the mind was overactive upon. 'It soothes the body and the mind,' Minerva had said with her little sidelong smile and dimple. 'I find it most serviceable.'

    Dearest Harriet,

    I am dashing this note off before the postman comes, so forgive my handwriting. We do have a good service here but all the same, I want you to get this as soon as may be.

    I have to believe that you believe whatever evidence you have seen. Please, please be sure that you are not deceived. My dear friend Valentine deserves nothing but the absolute, stern truth.

    If you are convinced that George is as you say, innocent of all crimes – except, if I may say so, cowardice - then yes, send him here. I will say that a friend from London is planning a visit on my recommendation. Be sure to send him with decent clothes, etc. because it will be very apparent that he is not a normal guest if he turns up dressed as Lady Macbeth. I am sorry, I know that isn't funny. I think my thoughts are disordered since the unexpected death of Mrs Halliwell here the other day. You'll remember her: we had become firm friends. I used to wheel her to and fro and we would discuss our memories of Egypt. She was only a little older than myself. Such a loss.

Anyway, Minerva will be glad of another guest, I think.
Yours affectionately,
A.
P.S. I had quite forgotten that note. However did you find it?

*

Madame Baranovsky was not overpleased to see Jerome Pollitt on her doorstep again.

She was just about to depart for a rather important meeting so his arrival was ill-timed, to say the least, although she was not entirely unprepared: her personal draw of cards this morning had warned her of delays and obstacles in the course of the day. Nevertheless, the ladies of the Spiritual, Astral and Psychical Research Committee would not be happy if she arrived late. They were depending upon her to explain how to enhance one's contact with one's guides. But Mr Pollitt looked remarkably down-in-the-mouth, standing there against the backdrop of drizzle and mist which was the London evening. His rather long blond hair was curling in loose rats-tails on his collar.

'Oh very well,' she said. 'I have precisely ten minutes to spare for you, Mr Pollitt. But if it is about mundane matters involving money and whatnot, I simply beg you not to ask. Mercury is still in retrograde. I will not discuss it at all.' She led the way briskly into the room where she did her sittings. It was unlit and the fire was low so she called for the maid to bring a lamp.

Madame Baranovsky carefully laid her umbrella and glittering black reticule upon the sideboard next to the decanters but did not remove her gloves, saying, 'I simply have no time for a full reading this evening, Mr Pollitt. The ladies of the Research Committee have engaged me to address them. Neither do I wish to disturb my aura by contact with overemotionalism, so I will thank you not to be too intense.' She shoved to one side a pile of magazines and they sat down opposite each other at the table. Madame Baranovsky took out a delicate gold timepiece and placed it where she could keep a good eye on it.

Poor Pollitt, who did not enjoy feeling overemotional at all, took a deep breath. 'It's just that I feel so – confused, Madame Baranovsky. I don't quite know what I want to do. There's someone I think I care about very much, and I don't know whether to stay with this person, but perhaps I don't really care enough about this person, and I'm not sure what to do,' he said, more or less in one breath.

'So,' said the lady, nodding. 'An affair of the heart is causing you confusion. You are contemplating a proposal of marriage to a sweetheart and yet you feel unsure whether she is truly the devoted wife of your future. Is it not so?'

'Well, in a very loose sense, you could say that,' agreed Jerome warily. 'But there's more, because someone else, a friend, is very ill and not likely to get better, if you see what I mean, and I feel that I should go to him. But he's in another country. It would take ages, and by then, you know, the – um – sweetheart might have gone to another country too. But if I stay with the sweetheart to sort things out, my poor friend might just die before I can see him again.'

'Ah. A bitter choice between love and death. How interesting.'

'Yes,' said Jerome, sounding a little choked. 'And then there has also been a most unpleasant incident involving a friend who has died unexpectedly – murdered, you see – in fact you know him, he came here – you'll remember him. Mr Valentine Cabot. He sat just there, in that chair not much more than a week ago. He's, you know, thingummy, passed over.'

Madame Baranovsky closed her eyes and put the forefinger of each hand to her temples. 'I see his astral form,' she announced. 'He is sitting just as he sat that day. He is telling me that the vision he shared was of himself entering the next spiritual plane.'

'Oh? Really?' Jerome glanced towards the empty chair at the far end of the table. 'But he also saw me and George in that vision. Does that mean we're all going to be entering the next spiritual plane? Because you know George might very well be doing that in the near future, if the police catch him, but I don't feel that I myself am ready to ...'

'What will be, will be, Mr Pollitt. Now I am very sorry to cut short this most interesting conversation, but may I ask you, what is your question on this occasion?'

Jerome hesitated. 'I suppose I just wanted someone to give me a clue about what choice I should make. Not to be overemotional about it, of course. I thought you might be able to help, I don't know why. It's the sort of thing Aleister might do, I suppose, but then Aleister is actually usually quite rude about fortune te ... um, he is, that is to say, he respects and values your opinion, but there are some people he says are …'

Madame Baranovsky's glare made him trail to a ragged end.

'Do you know, Mr Pollitt,' she said sweepingly, 'the only thing I can recommend for you is to go away for a period of quiet reflection. It is the most healing and nurturing thing you can possibly do for yourself. Find a place to make true Soul contact. Become aware of your deepest, eternal purpose. Leave aside these ephemeral considerations of love, money, death. For you are more than your appetites, more than your fears.'

'Am I?' asked Pollitt, impressed despite himself. 'Yes, I suppose I am. Aleister's not the only one with higher purposes and all that stuff. So would you recommend anywhere? Because I don't want to end up in a religious retreat with nothing but soup and a cell and monks and such like. But I think a few days' nice quiet holiday might be just the thing to set me up.'

Madame Baranovsky's glance alighted upon an advertisement on the back cover of the magazine topmost on the pile. She shut her eyes and once again placed her forefingers against her temples. She hummed a little bit as she had heard an Indian Yogi do. Then she whispered in a passable imitation of an Indian accent, 'It becomes clearer, clearer. The name rises out of the darkness. The Adsullata Spa Hotel. Find that place. The West Country. Most beautiful. Most healing.' She opened her eyes and nodded at Mr Pollitt. 'My guides have helped you, Mr Pollitt, and I advise you to take their wise direction.'

'Oh, I say, thank you very much, Madame Baranovsky. Adsullata. Can I just jot that down – yes, a pencil would be a help. I'll find it – are you sure it exists? Of course you are, your guides know all this sort of stuff. Adsullata. Thank you. I could do with a spa treatment.'

'Very good, Mr Pollitt. Now I must go to my meeting. And that will be five pounds. I'll take a cheque.'

CHAPTER SEVENTEEN

That evening, Minerva called Alexandra to one side just before dinner and said she had something to show her later and not to get involved in conversation with Lady Helena or they would never get away. So they left the Major to be distracted from his newspaper by the other remaining guest and Minerva led her towards her office. Alexandra was surprised to learn that it was in the further, more ancient reaches of the hotel. The main passage was roped off from the guests – as Minerva explained, there might be work going on and it was best that the public was kept away.

The corridor was dim here. It was part of Minerva's plan to have modern lighting fitted throughout these parts in the near future, but they were both obliged to carry oil lamps. Alexandra was impressed by the massive stonework of the walls as they walked towards the office, which lay behind a stout door. Minerva unlocked it and set her lamp down on the large desk in the middle of the room, and lit a further lamp for extra light, saying as she did so, 'No, don't blow the lamp out – you'll need it in a moment.'

Alexandra looked round the room. It bore more of a resemblance to a lost annexe in a museum than to the manager's office of an hotel. The walls were hung with framed copies of the kind of painted murals to be found in old temples: chariots and winged bulls and the impassive faces of ancient deities. Locked up in a glass cabinet there was a collection of cylinder seals set alongside modern tablets of clay indented with their close-written cuneiform text. In a heavy black case inlaid with mother-of-pearl lay a collection of what she took to be dusty oddments of pot or smashed tile, worn and fragile. Alexandra was curious to see that they were set out on purple velvet and when she peeped closer, noticed that they too revealed the blurred shadows of ancient writing. On shelves were crude figurines, hands, feet from ancient statuary. Half of a serene painted face from a broken statue was set on a plinth in pride of place above the wide fireplace.

'The beauty is in the lost half, don't you think?' said Minerva, standing next to her and viewing the face.

'Yes,' said Alexandra. 'The mind supplies perfection.'

'The mind does indeed supply perfection,' agreed Minerva thoughtfully. She walked away and turned back with a smile. 'I may use your clever comment to introduce my subject for this evening,' she went on in a mock academic tone. 'You will have noticed – because I told you to notice – the beneficial effects of the Beauty Balm on the tumults of the mind. Tonight, my dear Alex, I believe that your physical system is sufficiently habituated to the Balm to be able to begin to introduce the Supplements. But I must have your unconditional agreement to follow my instructions.'

'Well, thank you, then,' said Alexandra. She felt disorientated and not entirely sure if she liked what was happening; but she said, 'I think I would like to try the Supplement, if you're sure you want me to.' She shivered slightly. It suddenly seemed difficult to breathe. The office felt like an ancient tomb.

'Very well. In that case, I'm going to invite you to accompany me through that intriguing little door over there. Look, there in the corner. Is it not sweet? The doorway was bricked up and I had the way opened and that door made especially, by a dear little old carpenter from the village, just the size for fairy folk and for me to get through. Then, just to keep it dead secret, I chopped off his head.' She laughed.

Alexandra was jolted but laughed too. 'Of course you did, my dear Minerva. Exactly as I would have done myself. And did you plant it in a pot of basil?'

'Oh no, he was far too wrinkly and ugly for that. No, I just sent him home to his family with a fat fee and a roast beef sandwich. Never fear. Chopping off heads would be awfully messy, don't you think?'

'I hadn't thought too much about it. We can make it a theme in your portrait if you like though.'

'Well, what a charming idea!' Minerva laughed again as she approached a desk. Unlocking one of the drawers, she produced a piece of paper. 'Now, my dear, to be serious. You have to listen and read and think carefully. I have readied this little contract for you because, as I explained the other night, the Supplement is a preparation still in the final stages of development. I am sure it will not harm you, of course, but I need you to signify that you understand what I have told you. And of course, this binds you to secrecy too. A routine requirement in business, you know, rather like filing for Letters Patent to protect one's invention. You saw the other day how the P.B.s are always begging me for more intensive, more concentrated, more this and more that, versions of the Balm, did you not?'

Alexandra nodded and took the paper. Minerva did not interrupt as she read through the document. It began:

> *I, Alexandra Victoria Roberts, understand that all information pertaining to ingredients and effects caused by or relating to the Beauty Balm Supplement is to be guarded in the utmost secrecy…*

Minerva gave her a little ebony dip pen and she signed, despite misgivings at the reference to 'effects'. But in her current mentally exhausted state, she found herself thinking that the situation was so bizarre that a little more strangeness could hardly make much difference.

'That is excellent,' said Minerva, smiling as she took the paper and carefully blotting the signature. 'And now you have signed this, we have a compact between us. We're going to be in harmony. So delightful! You can't guess how much!' She seemed almost elated and began chatting like a girl, 'You know, I've been thinking I shall have two or three portraits done, and in each one I want you to paint me as a warrior queen or heroine. In the first of them I want you to paint me as Judith with the sword. In another I'll be Boudicca leading an army. Perhaps there will be more, because the third must certainly be your High Priestess of Ereshkigal,'

'Ereshkigal?'

'Is that not what you intended?' she said, picking up the lamp, ready to go through the little door. The light caught and reflected in her lovely long-lashed eyes.

'I have never heard of Ereshkigal. Pardon my ignorance, but what is it?'

'Interesting - but if you would be so kind as to follow me now. Let's go quickly. I'll tell you as we walk to the chamber at the other end. It's rather a long passage, you'll find. It was made I don't know when, but I've adapted it to my purposes. And listen, there may be some dust and so forth, cobwebs. Put this veil over your hair. Look, I always do the same.' As she spoke, she took a gauzy scarf from several hanging next to the door and draped it over her head. She handed another one to Alexandra.

On the other side of the door was a long narrow passageway. The air was close and smelled damp. Their lamps threw arcs of light onto the walls and floor, showing skilled hands had laid the paving and prepared the walls, but the stones were immensely large. Alexandra understood that this place was far more ancient than even the oldest parts of the hotel. As they walked along, Minerva continued talking softly. Her voice echoed off the walls.

'Do you remember the story I was telling you? Ereshkigal, that name you said you did not recognise, is part of that tale. I personally worked for years translating the legend with the help of my dear Joseph. It came into my possession, a version of the story of Ishtar's descent into the Underworld. It is far older, and tells not of Ishtar but of her foremother, Inanna. I often think of these words when I walk down this passage: "From the great heaven she fixed her intention on the great below." So the poet tells us. The name of her sister, the hag of hell, is Ereshkigal. Poor sister in darkness. She is old, you know, the dry barren one, but she was once the mother. Do you see?'

'Yes, I remember it now,' said Alexandra, thinking that the passageway was beginning to slope downwards and there was a rushing noise just on the edge of hearing. The air was warm and damp. 'Inanna is clearly a Persephone figure, visiting the underworld. Just as we discussed before, the apparent death of vegetation in Winter and its return in Spring. But you said there was some strange, un-Christian twist in the tale. I can predict it. She has to remain in hell for half of the year. Is that correct?'

'Oh, nearly. Not Inanna, though. It is a Sumerian tale and we have indications that the women of ancient times were far more powerful than their poor Greek sisters a thousand years later. Our goddess makes some interesting choices. In an angry moment, she throws her own dear husband to the demons, for example. I believe you'll enjoy studying the full myth, as I promised. Tomorrow I'll show you my work. For now, look, we have reached the end of our passage.'

She turned to look at Alexandra in the golden lamplight and whispered, 'And I would be prepared to wager a beef sandwich that your heart is beating faster now.'

Her bet sounded so ridiculous that Alexandra laughed. Minerva put her lamp on the floor. 'Now, this is the point where you can remove your shawl. Just bend your head, like so, and I'll do it for you.' As she took it off, Minerva said, 'And if you object to losing your head-dress, as Inanna did so long ago, and say "What is this, pray, what is this?" my answer should be, according to the poet, "Be satisfied, Inanna, for a divine power of the underworld has been fulfilled. You must not open your mouth against the rites of the underworld!" But never fear, all this extravagant mystery is simply to guard my work from spies.'

Minerva unlocked the next door and once again there was an office. This one was smaller, windowless, except for a kind of soft gash in the far wall from which a damp air breathed. It was a chamber cut out of rock; or perhaps, thought Alexandra, looking at its irregular shape and smooth surfaces, scooped over ages by the action of water. She guessed that they were near the hot springs forced upwards from the deep places of the earth: the thrumming noise was more audible here, like a pressure on the ears. If so, there was a quantity of water below which far exceeded the hot spring she had seen in the woods.

Minerva lit several candles. The light revealed one wall covered with rows of wooden drawers and glass fronted cupboards full of bottles and boxes, while on the other side there was a narrow laboratory desk and much chemistry equipment. Alexandra was told to sit down while Minerva unlocked one of the drawers and took out a blue glass bottle containing pills. She unstoppered it, smelt it, and then taking a pair of thin tweezers, extracted a tiny pill. It was yellowish in colour.

'This is for you, Alex. This is the first. Put it under your tongue and let it dissolve. Don't worry about the taste – you'll become accustomed to that, and anyway, that is a cosmetic detail I'll attend to in due course. That's it, just relax. Now, all you have to do is listen.

'You're going to feel a little bit odd at first. Perhaps sleepy and muddled. After that has worn off, in about six hours, you'll begin to notice a sense of vigour. You might even describe it as euphoria. But that will settle down too. You'll find your mind gets calm and clear and you won't get bothered very much by things that perhaps used to bother you. How can I say it? You won't get upset, for example, if you think about foolish sentimental nonsense – you won't be weepy anymore. It's a good thing! Don't look worried.

'At first, you'll need to take a pill every day, but after a while, I think your experience will be like mine, which is that your body stabilises at a certain rate and rhythm. I myself take a pill but once a month. I am pretty sure that the formula works by stimulating renewal everywhere, in your skin, for example. The effects look rather like growing younger. You won't get cold so much either as your entire metabolism changes. You'll start to feel the difference in your mind immediately and in a short while, maybe only a few days, you'll wake up in the morning and you'll begin to *see* the difference too.' She paused and looked at Alexandra closely. 'Yes, dear. I can see straightaway that you're going to need to lie down soon. Let's go back.'

Alexandra could not remember how she got back to her bed. The last thing she was aware of was Minerva blowing out the lamp and a darkness sweeping over her.

*

'I don't care,' said Jerome Pollitt, as he folded, rolled, then violently poked some of his best linen down the side of his trunk (someone would iron it for him at the other end). 'I deserve this, Aleister. I've just had it all up to here.' He made a throat-cutting gesture. 'I need a rest. Madame Baranovsky insisted upon it. Look at my hand shake!' He held a hand out to show a slight tremor.

'Don't you think I need you here?'

'No, I don't. I think I get in your way. And you know it. She said she could psychically sense that I am not appreciated and that I need to go somewhere and have a jolly good think about my life. And that's what I'm doing.' He walked off to the bathroom to find his shaving equipment and to rescue some rather nice cologne which he suspected Aleister had been helping himself to.

'I thought you said she was a fake?' called Crowley after him.

'She was a fake when she was taken in by Cabot,' said Pollitt firmly in the distance, 'but not a fake when she told me I need a holiday. Because I know what she said is simply true. I need to re-connect with *my* higher purpose.' He re-emerged with the shaving stuff and an ivory hairbrush which had fallen down the side of the bathroom cabinet, and packed them alongside his manicure set. He tried to decide whether to pop a spare wig in (you never knew – there might be evening entertainment and he was never averse to diving into character as Diane) and remembered to pack his embroidery.

Then he looked over at Crowley. He was touched to see him looking so mournful.

'Jerome, don't go. Haven't we had fun together? You can't just wipe out all these months like this. Think about it!'

'I don't want to wipe them all out, Aleister, you silly ass.' Pollitt sat down next to him. 'If anything, it's you who want to do that. And, by the way, now who's being emotional? Listen. I just can't compete with your distractions. Climbing mountains, and writing all night, and your peculiar friends turning up, and invoking "demons" in the most unpredictable way, and keeping that horrible thing in there and pretending it's alive. You're a little bit younger than me, Aleister - and by the way, you can stop telling everyone that it's ten years because it is only four and a bit – and I think that one day soon you're going to wake up and realise what rot it all is. Until that happens, I'm worried about you. It's like a mania and I don't know where I fit into it. Do you see? Quite frankly, I find the strain exhausting.'

'You know it was you who made me a poet, don't you?' said Crowley softly, not attempting to answer any of Pollitt's objections.

'Was it I?' asked Pollitt. He paused for a moment, anxiously remembering the verse about the octopus in the notebook hidden under the pillow. Wisely setting the subject aside without further comment, he went on, 'Listen, love, while I'm away, I'm going to think about things. Really think. You'll be alone – I presume – and if you get bored, look, this is the place.' He pointed out a leaflet propped up amidst a jumble of sticky champagne flutes and ashtrays on the cabinet beside his bed. He smiled a little sadly, 'I'm going to be relaxing in hot natural springs and lord knows what else, probably with dowager duchesses and major-generals and so forth. Major-generals hate me but dowager duchesses absolutely love me so I shall adore being adored. You can come and join in. For all I know there might be a mountain or at least some steep slopes nearby.'

Two hours later, Jerome sat in the train carriage watching the grey countryside sliding by. He had brought a carton of cigarettes, a bottle of mineral water for his hangover and the latest copies of The Sketch, Blackwood's Magazine and The Studio to amuse himself on the long journey. He was planning an extensive nap after lunch although he wasn't too sure whether he was to change at Reading or not, but he'd tipped the guard to sort everything out for him. He gave a sigh of contentment and let the whole concept of what Aleister might be doing all by himself, let loose in London, slip gently into the distance.

*

It was terrifying when the time came for Harriet to venture out of the house to take George to Paddington Station. She had visited it the previous day and bought a ticket for him and a platform ticket for herself; but she thought she was being watched even while she did those innocent things. She suffered agonies of apprehension on their way to the train, peeping out the windows of the cab, imagining that another cab was following theirs.

'You know, Mrs Day,' said George cheerfully, 'they've probably already forgotten all about it. They have much more important things to do than look out for me. Just think of all the real crimes all over London – that thing that's happening now in Chelsea, for example. You don't really need to worry about me at all.'

Harriet did not bother to ask George what he meant by the 'thing' in Chelsea. It was undoubtedly another imaginary scene. But although she privately agreed that the Metropolitan Police were unlikely to be watching her residence, she could not help imagining Paddington Station swarming with policemen. She felt faint and jittery, just as if she were coming down with influenza.

They stood in the shadow of a booth and she surreptitiously inspected George's appearance. She was glad to see that he looked decent – as Alex had said, he would stand out like a sore thumb if he looked like a tramp. He was dressed in one of the shirts she had obtained over the course of the last few days, with a grey silk cravat complementing a suit which fitted very trimly too. She had in fact borrowed most of the items from a friend whose son had outgrown them. She had been a little troubled about evening dress – a gentleman would absolutely require such attire when staying at a hotel – but had managed to get hold of a suit which, if a bit old-fashioned, would do. He was also wearing a hat she had discovered in a wardrobe, although she had no idea whose it had been. Certainly not her husband's. In fact, she decided, he looked really quite smart. His delicate build made it highly likely that he would be on his way to a health spa; and a tale of long illness would excuse his awkwardness.

'I want to say, again and again and again, how grateful I am to you,' he whispered as she looked him over. 'I promise to do everything you say, to the letter. And I like these gloves.'

'Good. Listen then.' She handed him a small drawstring bag such as might contain gentleman's toiletries. 'Some money is in there. Remember what we talked about: your name is Edward Day. Edward Day. You are my brother-in-law, the younger brother of my late husband. You have returned from Ceylon after working in the family business. Yes? You've been there for – oh, five years, no, that's too long. How old are you, George? Work it out so that people will believe you!'

George looked doubtful. 'Fifty years? Two years?'

Harriet sighed. 'Say three years. Three.' She held up three fingers. 'So what is your name?'

'Edward Day,' he answered. 'I haven't been to Ceylon but I'd like to go. I never got the chance.' Harriet frowned meaningfully at him and he continued, 'So now I can say that I've been to Ceylon. I have been in Ceylon for three years working in the family business – which is? Tea?'

'Yes, tea, exactly. Oh George, don't forget! Now, Mrs Roberts will be at the place you're going to. It's a hotel in the country and it will be ideal for you to rest and keep safe. Peaceful quiet and solitude. Try not to talk to the other guests though, George. Mrs Roberts knows you're coming and she will help you. Someone will meet you at the station – they'll call the name. What name will they call?'

'Geo - Edward Day,' said George obediently.

'Now, this is your ticket. The train leaves in five minutes and we need to go.'

They walked up the platform together. In their haste, he had to enter the first compartment they came to, which was crowded. Harriet quietly suggested he might get out at the next station and walk further along the train to find a better one later. He climbed into the carriage clutching his bags and stared back at her through the open window like an orphan.

'Oh, Edward,' she said suddenly in a rush as the guard blew a whistle. 'I nearly forgot. Mrs Skipton made some nice little pies yesterday. Here they are, for the journey, and this is something to drink, and some scones and apples.' She had been carrying a string bag of supplies, each item wrapped in newspaper, forgotten on her arm. She handed it through to him. 'Take care, dear. I'll write – oh, no, I'll write to Mrs Roberts. She'll tell you any news. Good luck.'

Once she had watched the train steam out of the station, she began to feel better. She then went to a telegraph office and sent a message to Alexandra to warn her that 'Edward Day' was on his way. Only after that did she allow herself a short period of nervous collapse in a tea shop. The next thing she did, which was to go searching for the man named on the tattered calling card, was completely unpremeditated. It might have been catalysed by the knowledge that she could not possibly keep on paying for George to stay at an expensive country hotel. She thought of it afterwards as the kind of last-ditch thing you do when you have utterly run out of ideas and nearly run out of money. Or perhaps she just wanted to share her troubles with someone.

Baker Street was broader and more busy than Harriet remembered and however hard she looked, she could not find number 221^B. The houses seemed to end at number 85 and she became quite flustered until she asked a postman who pointed her in the right direction. She approached the respectable-looking townhouse with some trepidation. She was not sure whom she was about to encounter – a medical man, for sure, but exactly what his connection with George was or what he would be able to do for him was not at all clear.

The door was opened by a sparklingly neat lady who said, in a voice which implied that Harriet might want to come back another day, that Mr Holmes was not currently available. At which Harriet replied that she had come to consult a Dr Watson and added apologetically that she knew nothing of a Mr Holmes. The parlour she was shown into at the top of the stairs was a large, airy room lit by two broad windows. It was however filled with a quite indescribable amount of clutter. Apart from the stacks of documents and the scientific equipment over in the corner, it did not look very like the consulting office of a surgeon. Scanning the assorted weaponry on the wall, she thought that this must be a rather strange sort of doctor.

'Good afternoon,' she said as a light-haired gentleman of about forty or forty-five years appeared out of an adjoining room. Not sure how to go about things, she went on, 'My name is Harriet Day. I hope you will excuse me for calling unannounced.'

The gentleman immediately shook hands and said, 'Delighted to make your acquaintance, Mrs Day. My name is John Watson.'

'Dr Watson?'

'That's right,' he said. 'Please sit down.'

Feeling a bit at a loss, and slightly concerned that there was no sign of a nurse or medical orderly in these consulting rooms, Harriet perched on the edge of a hard chair and proceeded, 'Let me say first of all that I have not come on a medical matter and I don't want to take up your valuable time. I'm sure you are very busy. I know the medical profession are always busy – my husband used to be.'

Dr Watson chuckled. 'I may as well confess that I haven't practised formally as a doctor for some years now. You might know my work in the field of literature? I am the 'Boswell' for Mr Sherlock Holmes, the consulting detective.'

'Oh? How interesting. But as a matter of fact, I came not to see a detective, but to see you, doctor, although strangely enough a detective might be the very kind of person who ...' she trailed off, realising that she was not explaining herself clearly.

She tried to start again: 'This *is* your name on this card, isn't it?' She held up the tattered calling card. 'I was given this by a friend of mine, a young gentleman who is in the most terrible trouble. He spoke of you as someone who might be able to help. So that's why I have come – on his behalf, although he doesn't actually know I'm here. And I can't say where he is either. I mean I don't know where he is.' Harriet, feeling that she had made a hash of this speech from beginning to end, gabbled, 'And before I go further, I want to say that he is innocent of the crime of which he stands accused.'

Dr Watson permitted himself a discreet sigh (how often had he heard that last sentence before?). 'Please go on,' he said. 'Perhaps with a little more information ...?'

Harriet said anxiously, 'I hope you can recollect my friend? I don't know when you gave him this card or why, but his name is George Arden. He's an actor. He is not tall, soft spoken, delicate in build, thin in the face - ?'

'Ah,' said Dr Watson, shifting in his seat. 'Yes, I believe I recall the gentleman.' He immediately decided not to disclose that he already had a pretty solid understanding of the particulars of the case. He decided to wait now and see what she herself revealed about the suspect; but to be fair to her, since she seemed a nice sort of woman, he felt he should give her a warning. 'Forgive me,' he said, steepling his fingers as he had seen Holmes do on countless occasions, 'can we just establish one thing? If the trouble of which you speak involves the police, I am sure I need not remind you that anyone who harbours, aids or abets a wanted suspect is committing a crime.'

One look at Harriet's face told him everything he needed to know. He added more kindly, 'So, on the understanding that you and I know absolutely nothing of the gentleman's whereabouts, we can discuss this case in a theoretical sense only, using your prior knowledge of his character.'

'Thank you, Dr Watson,' said Harriet. 'Well, theoretically speaking, what I wanted to ask your – and I suppose Mr Holmes's - opinion on was this: how might one proceed to clear his name?'

'Tell me, if you can, what the facts of the case are, Mrs Day,' he said.

Harriet then spoke at some length; but she did not add anything to what Dr Watson already knew. She confirmed George Arden's difficulty in recalling events, but her assertions that he was incapable of the crime did not appear to be based on any tangible evidence. She stated that she believed that the one witness to the event was lying, but she had no facts to prove this.

'The trouble is,' said Watson after he had heard her out, 'all you can really do for him is get a good lawyer. The police should do all the investigating and gathering of evidence. And I have to say that it doesn't help matters that the suspect ran away so precipitously. Is it in character that he should have done so?'

'He was frightened, doctor. Frightened by the accident, frightened because this man Albert Burroughs immediately began shouting. Or that's what I imagine must have happened, because of course I haven't talked to him about it. But he isn't – well, I won't say he is a simpleton, not at all – but he is unlettered and poor and timid. My belief is that he fled in panic, like a child would. Yes, that's the best way to describe him. Not a dunce but a child, an innocent.'

Watson nodded gravely. 'I recall his manner quite clearly, Mrs Day. But it still looks like an admission of guilt when a person runs away, I have to say. Judges don't care for childish young men who don't stand their ground and speak up for the truth. A good lawyer is what he needs.' He cleared his throat. 'I might be able to recommend a couple of names, should the time come when he needs a defence drawn up. Quite frankly, Mrs Day, I have very little other advice to give.'

Harriet sat up very straight as if having made a decision and looked Watson straight in the eye. 'I refuse to sit by and see this happen to him, doctor. And, therefore, I've decided. I know your colleague is not here at present but it seems to me an extraordinary, beneficial coincidence that he is a consulting detective and that you work with him. I have a cheque book in my bag here, and I would like to engage his services.'

'My dear lady,' said Watson. 'I am afraid that is quite impossible. He is away – far away, on a case which may engross his attention for weeks. I am very sorry.'

'But you, doctor, you say you work with him. You write about his cases, you must be familiar with his methods. Oh, please, if you could help, even if only a little bit – help me to find a way of proving that George Arden is innocent?'

'I am flattered that you ask me, Mrs Day,' said Watson hastily, for she was looking very crestfallen. 'But I am emphatically not a consulting detective myself and do not have the gifts of observation and logic possessed by Mr Holmes. I could bring very little to such an investigation.'

'But you do know *something*? You have some experience, surely, doctor? And you have met Mr Arden, he trusted you immediately and you know the kind of helpless creature he is. Would you not agree to be retained to undertake an investigation – call it a preliminary investigation, if you like - until Mr Holmes can take over?'

Watson shifted in his seat, feeling uncomfortable. He had never dared to usurp his friend's vocation before. He would certainly not have dared if it had been likely that Sherlock Holmes would walk through that door within the next few days. Moreover, he himself had been implicated in the case – for all he knew, there might be further last writings from the drunken hand of Valentine Cabot being deciphered at this moment. There were very good reasons to refuse to become involved. But here was Mrs Harriet Day, looking charming and flustered – and damn it. 'Very well,' he heard himself say. 'But please do not you go writing cheques and so forth. I will undertake to assist you on the basis that the final say is up to Mr Holmes. If he chooses to take up the case on his return, then that will be upon a business footing. And I can't predict, Mrs Day, whether he would take the case or indeed what he would charge.'

Harriet Day's face lit up. 'You are extremely kind, doctor. I hardly know how to thank you. If we could put this on a business footing, it might be better, but as you say, all that can be left until Mr Holmes returns.' She added timidly, 'Is he very expensive, doctor?'

'He is – unpredictable, Mrs Day, since he enjoys the game for its intellectual stimulation.'

'The game?'

'Oh, um, Holmes looks upon it as a pursuit, a fascinating puzzle, you know.'

'Oh.' Harriet looked as though she had a comment on the tip of her tongue, but she said nothing more than, 'Well, I hope this case is an amusing enough game for him – if he comes back. And that his charges are not too unpredictable for my limited means.'

'Never fear, I find he is usually flexible. He will never overcharge, that's for sure, unless you were very, very rich.'

Harriet told Dr Watson the details of her own address and everything she felt was relevant about George and Valentine. Then she left, feeling more hopeful and at peace than she had done for some time.

Watson paced the room a few times, glancing at the note he had made of Albert Burroughs's name and address. But: Harriet, Harriet Day. Something about her reminded him of the short years of his marriage, his dear lost wife. Perhaps it was her eyes: they were the very same blue. He found himself standing by the mantelpiece, picking up a calling card he had propped against the side of the clock late one night last week. He sighed again. Poor boy with the thin face. Three times he'd been approached about this case. Three times, as his old mother used to say, was the charm. Not without reluctance, he turned the card over to read Aleister Crowley's address on the back.

CHAPTER EIGHTEEN

The afternoon had brightened with a whisper of early spring as Dr Watson walked up the stone stairwell of the building marked 67- 69 Chancery Lane. He was not entirely sure what he was going to say to Crowley or even if he really wanted to involve the strange fellow in the case.

In his published works, Watson often played up the way Holmes was wont to amuse himself at the expense of his friend's slower intellect. It made for a lighter element in the stories, but the jibes were unjust - after all, very few minds could keep up with the intellect of Sherlock Holmes. But in truth, Dr Watson had the advantage not only of intelligence but also of shrewd insight. Consequently, he had already assessed Aleister Crowley in the following way: *headstrong; unusual mind; enjoys shocking the unwary; hates convention; (probably) uses certain substances.* Having lived for so long with his detective friend, who happened to share most of these characteristics (including occasional substantial cocaine use), Watson was quite prepared to deal with any combination of them.

Crowley seemed to be expecting him - or at least affected not to be surprised to see him. He was wearing a black silk dressing gown draped over his clothes and had clearly been engaged in writing: there was a thick sheaf of yellow foolscap on the desk in front of the window and a silver fountain pen lying on the blotter. A pile of books lay beside it, their spines turned towards the room as if on display. Watson studied them discreetly: *The Cloud upon the Sanctuary* and *The Book of Black Magic and of Pacts* were among the titles that caught his eye. Someone had also been burning incense and possibly something else, as there was a trace of a heavy fragrance with a strange tang. Watson's quick glance round the room registered an ornate sheesha-pipe or hookah on a low table in the corner.

The large room was elegant in an austere way, the walls hung with a plain gold-black Japanese paper. Leopardskin rugs were scattered over the floor. An ornate old silver lamp was suspended from the middle of the ceiling, a flicker of red glowing at its heart. Above the fireplace hung a large crucifix of ivory and ebony, while on either side of the chimney breast were alcoves, one draped with a black velvet curtain, the other shuttered with a white door.

'This is my London place,' said Crowley, removing a newspaper and several periodicals from an armchair so that Watson could sit down. 'I'm sorry Pollitt isn't here to greet you. He thinks he needs a rest in the country and he took himself off this morning. Anyway, bit of peace and quiet, gives me a chance to get on with my work. I'm thinking of moving in here, after I finish at Trinity. If I finish at Trinity.'

'A medical student, are you?' asked Watson. His quick eye had caught an oblique glimpse of the interior of the black-hung alcove: in a tremble of candlelight, a darkened human skeleton was arranged strangely within.

'Oh, no. Moral Science. But you refer to our friend over there?' Crowley walked across and casually twitched the curtain closed. 'No, that is entirely part of an on-going experiment in ritual necromancy. I feed him songbirds and little cups of blood. Call it a hobby.'

Watson knew that Crowley was watching his reaction closely so he just smiled politely. He got the impression that he was being observed as acutely as Holmes might have done, but with a razor edge of mockery. It made him feel uncomfortable.

'Do sit down!' Crowley said. 'Would you care for champagne, doctor? Absinthe? Cocaine?'

'For a man who ingests so much poison, Mr Crowley, you show no sign of muscle-wastage. I would hazard a guess that you enjoy a sport. Perhaps mountaineering?'

'Good guess,' said Crowley cheerfully, settling onto a couch. 'It's a hobby of mine, I won't deny it. No doubt you noticed the magazines I just stuffed into the rack?'

'I also will not deny it, Mr Crowley. Not to mention, if I may add, the equipment listed on the scrap of paper projecting from beneath your blotter. I notice the ink is smudged – perhaps it was not quite dry when you thrust it away? You need not be ashamed of good health and vigour,' Watson smiled slightly. 'But let us work together honestly. Let you not try to shock and terrify me quite so much and I will not force middle-aged medical opinion upon you. Does that sound reasonable?'

Crowley looked at Watson with an amused air. 'I predicted that you would come to me, Dr Watson. It is therefore reasonable to assume that you have information regarding George Arden.'

'Indeed. I have no further information. I am here because a friend of Mr Arden's asked me to take a closer look at the case. Since you've made it clear that you have a keen interest in it yourself, it seemed logical to speak to you. But before we proceed, I need to clear up a point or two regarding the conditions under which we can work, if you are still interested in joining me.' Crowley nodded, listening. 'We must bear in mind that both of us may get called as witnesses at Arden's trial. It is therefore particularly inappropriate for us to come into contact with the chief witness, this Albert Burroughs. We cannot attempt to influence him. You do see that?'

'I could call it another hobby of mine,' said Crowley.

'Mr Crowley, this is serious. Interfering with a witness is conspiring to pervert the course of justice - it's a grave offence.'

'I see.'

'I am glad you do.'

There was a short silence.

'So, what do you propose regarding the Arden case?'

'I propose first to investigate the witness,' said Watson.

'You've just said we must not do that.'

'No, I said we must not seek to influence him. I see no reason why we should not try to uncover information about him, perhaps discovering what motive he could possibly have to fabricate so maliciously a story likely to hang an innocent man.'

'Understood. I agree,' said Crowley. 'And we need to interview Arden himself. But we don't know where he is – do we?'

'No. If we knew where he was, we would have to inform the police. Better we don't know, just as long as we are convinced that Arden is innocent.'

'You *are* convinced, then? After our initial conversation, I doubted that you were.'

'My first concern is, as ever, to keep an open mind. But yes, I have been convinced that the witness's account contradicts the known *character* of the suspect. Nevertheless, I intend to make the theory fit the facts, not the other way round.'

'Ah yes. The detective I saw certainly seemed to be working the other way round, to make his facts prove his theories. He dropped plenty of hints that Arden has inherently criminal tendencies, is unstable, dishonest and so forth. Therefore, it strikes me as most amusing that perhaps the court might hear it was *my* hellfire-and-brimstone conversation that made him more unstable, and *your* nefarious offer of management that tempted him to be dishonest. And because of us, the whole thing devolved into murder. Imagine that, if you like! What will you say when they call you as witness?'

'They cannot prove any of that,' said Watson contemptuously.

'Oh, they don't have to: whatever we say won't affect the outcome because he's foreign and looks it, he has no friends and the officer who questioned me was very keen to bring Oscar Wilde into it all. His goose, in short, is cooked, if they get him. They'll just want to make out that it was a premeditated act of murder. By association, my dear doctor, we also become tainted. You do see that by clearing his name, our reputations won't come under public scrutiny?'

'My reputation is not in question,' said Watson.

'In that case, neither is mine. Anyway, if it comes to it, I look forward to indulging in some pretty good cheek in the witness box. I'll simply say I had to share the fruits of the holy seed planted by my father and watered by my mother's tears. I was thinking of writing it up in advance, expounding upon my upbringing among the Plymouth Brethren. I shall enjoy it. But, tell me, how do you fancy standing up in court and explaining your association with poor Arden? Remember, part of the case for the Prosecution may well be that he was – how can I put it delicately? – *un mignon* whose unmentionable profession was managed by Valentine Cabot. The victim's last written words record his suspicion that you had a wicked plan to usurp said management, which, alas, potentially involved more than the theatre. I think your cross-examination might be more interesting than mine.'

'Nonsense,' said Watson.

Crowley shrugged and lit a cigarette. '*I* was only supposed to have talked religion to him to dissuade him from his wicked ways. Very much in keeping with my character, I must say. Moral Science Tripos, you know.'

'Are you not planning to print certain immoral poems with a notorious publishing firm? Do you believe *that* reflects well upon your reputation? And are you not – by your own admission – engaged in necromantic experimentation with a human skeleton? Do you believe that reflects well too?'

'Why, no, now I come to think of it. But, one, I do not give a fig for society's moral chintz and chippendale; and two, my poems are not published yet, Doctor. And the skeleton is hidden away here. My reputation is *virgo intacta.*' During the charged silence which followed, Watson scowled at the young man opposite, who smiled back at him and said, 'It'll be good for both of us, won't it, now, Doctor? Everyone will benefit if we can prove George Arden is a lamb of innocence.'

Watson took a deep breath. This aspect of the case was nothing if not embarrassing and he would rather not dwell on it. 'To return to our plan of action,' he said, trying to take back control of the conversational drift. 'This Burroughs is a court reporter. It occurs to me that there may be something by his hand among the many crime records my friend Holmes keeps in the flat. I propose to begin by looking into his professional career.'

'Very well. Then I will undertake to follow him. Not *speak* to him. Just see where he goes and with whom he associates. Get to know his demons, if you see what I mean.'

*

I need to record these experiences.

Minerva's kindness in making me part of her extraordinary work still overwhelms me – the consequences are unimaginable - and I cannot hope to repay her. Indeed, what could I give her in return?

I noticed today on rising and looking at my hands in the morning sunlight that they appear to be changing somewhat. Certain ugly brown freckles which had begun to form have started to fade. The flesh is plumper.

As I write, I hear the breakfast bell sounding, so must shorten this: elasticity in skin improving, ache in lower back better & muscles more supple. The results of just a few days' supplement!

A strange side-effect: feeling distant from myself - curious sensation. I know that part of me still cares deeply (e.g. on thinking of Valentine) & can gain access to these feelings if I really try. Yet they seem to be fading away.

This effect is one I do <u>not</u> like. I fear that the more pills one takes, the less connection with one's fellows. Minerva warned me, but she said wd. be an advantage of the treatment. I suppose she was referring to what she calls 'sentimentalism'. Will I forget how to <u>want</u> to feel?

Will record comparison of results daily.

Minerva was not at breakfast again. In fact, she had been absent or busy elsewhere ever since the night she had administered the first dose of the Supplement. Alexandra had barely caught a distant glimpse of her since then; but it seemed typical of her modus operandi to leave her alone after a period of intense interaction. She had often noticed that Minerva enjoyed exercising the power of unpredictability; and this amplified the impression Alex had formed before, that she was the subject of an experiment.

She had woken up the day after the visit to the hidden office to find a small bottle at her bedside. It contained the little yellowish pills. She had started taking one each night before bedtime: it seemed the most sensible time because of the drowsiness which occurred within minutes of ingesting them. Each morning she woke with a sense of renewed purpose and energy. But the pills had a strange dusty texture and a stale taste. She recalled Minerva telling her that the sleepiness would begin to wear off as her body stabilised, so she was not alarmed about that; but she did not much like the way the flavour became more pronounced with each pill she took. She could taste it now, as if old breath were exhaling itself through her.

She would very much have liked to discuss the process with Minerva but all she had found waiting for her at the hotel reception desk on that first morning was a letter. It merely contained a short list of instructions with no mention of pills. Instead suitable activities were prescribed which, it said, would promote the beneficial aspects of the 'health regime'. She was to spend time in the hot water pool at a certain hour. She was to walk alone at a certain hour, eat certain foods in a strictly regulated diet which had been arranged for her, undertake certain callisthenic and mental exercises - even subjects for thought and contemplation had been prescribed – and above all, the letter ordered, talk as little as possible to the other residents.

The emotional numbness she had noticed creeping upon her began in a small way but almost immediately. The first symptom she noticed was the blunting of the pang associated with the thought of Valentine. A skin has grown over a wound, she thought wonderingly; and she could have pressed on it and made it hurt – indeed, she experimented a little on that first day and shed a few tears. But by the following day, she ceased to have an interest in that emotion, as if it were a dress she could assume at will and only if the weather demanded it. In its place, a sensation of steely lightheartedness occasionally took over. It felt like triumph. She wondered if this was how Minerva habitually felt. The time passed strangely, oddly elongated, without interaction with Minerva; and with this growing self-estrangement, Alexandra felt the life of the heart become muted.

Just after breakfast on Monday morning, a letter was given her by the hotel clerk. It was from Minerva and, after apologising for her absence, asked her in affectionate terms to do her the honour – if she had sufficient leisure - of giving an opinion on those curious notes which she had been meaning to show her. She then expressed her regret that her early departure for an unexpected business meeting had put it out of her mind; but now she had recalled it, she begged Alexandra to go to the desk clerk, show him the letter and ask him to give her the red bag from the safe.

Alexandra doubted that there had been a business meeting at all. But she duly went to the desk, showed the letter and was given a small leather portfolio from the jewel safe in the office behind the front desk. Holding it, she took thought and finally made her way to the one room she could be sure that Lady Helena and the Major would never come – the library. She settled herself at the reading desk and inspected it. The scuffed leather was held together by a worn strap with a little wonky brass buckle. Inside, further protected by an oilcloth bag closed by a drawstring, was a thick notebook. A first glance told her the leaves were written very close in black ink. She thumbed the edge of the pages and in the blur she saw sketches and diagrams.

She was a little disappointed. She had hoped that Minerva had been working on a novel or scandalous autobiography, but it appeared to be devoted only to a minute description of an archaeological curiosity, a cuneiform tablet she had purchased in her travels. A few lines dashed across the first page mentioned that this object had been bought in As-Samawah from a nomad; that it had been in many broken pieces and she had reconstructed it; and that she then laboured long to translate it using 'the work of Hincks and Rawlinson as a starting point'. Alexandra saw that some pages were mere lists of symbols or scribbled thoughts. Others were close-written. She could see no date anywhere although she looked for one, wondering how and when Minerva, among all her other studies, had had the time to pursue this hobby. Even a cursory glance showed her that it was a work of scholarship. She would have been astonished - if anything about Minerva could astonish her any more.

'This is a kind of daybook,' thought Alexandra cautiously,

'spanning several years. It will take a great deal of editing to prepare it for publication, if that's her intention in showing it to me. And I know very little about such things. I've been caught out. I'm afraid she mistook my interest during our museum visits for actual knowledge!'

She turned the pages curiously, thinking that most of it would be of interest only to a specialist in the field. Now and then Minerva's lively personality shone through but she skimmed lightly over many pages of discussion concerning possible alternative renderings of mark and symbol.

It is clear to me that the poem should be read not as a poem per se, but as the script for a lost ritual. Who can doubt the drama of the Seven Gates of Hell? Who would fail to shiver at the terrible fate of the Goddess?

'What is the terrible fate of the goddess? Is this the story she told me before, about the journey into the underworld?' murmured Alexandra aloud, glancing at a precise drawing of an uneven clay fragment. It showed a close pattern of tiny triangular marks, formed by pressure on wet clay. She recalled the display cabinets in Minerva's office. Below it there was a detailed discussion of how this had been fitted together with other fragments. 'There is such a lot to read here and I can't possibly manage all this before she comes back.'

Her eye was caught by a page which was blotted as if liquid had been accidentally spilt upon it, but she could still make out the words:

The mystery is maddening. What can she want to gain by entering her sister's darkness? I cannot make sense of the end lines of fragments V and VI, they are crumbled away to dust.

Curious about the 'maddening mystery', she read on, finding at last a rough summary written as numbered points and referenced against the different fragments. It was the complete version of the tale Minerva had told her on the day of Mrs Halliwell's death. She remembered now the 'terrible fate of the goddess'. After her impudent assumption of her sister's power, she had been struck dead and hung on a hook.

After this, as far as she could understand the story, other creatures – perhaps eunuchs or 'unsexed beings' as Minerva jotted in her notebook with a question mark – were made by another powerful god. These were instructed to revive the goddess and obtain her freedom: 'Go and make your way to the underworld. Flit past the door like flies. Slip through the door pivots like phantoms.' Minerva had made copious notes:

> *The Death Goddess asks if the 'gala-tura and kur-jara' (the newly created beings) who come to claim Inanna's body are male or female, gods or humans? Riddles in ancient contexts are always signs that one is dealing with the spirit realms. And here, Joseph's long study of the ancient cults is invaluable. His idea is that castrated or 'sexless creatures' were automatically believed to become liminal beings, <u>threshold dwellers</u>, able to cross between the worlds. This poem – so much older than anything else we have – may point to the rationale behind the practice of castration of males in Inanna's temples.*
>
> *In this tablet, the 'gala-tura' and 'kur-jara' are phantom-like, perhaps fleshless, while the later Ishtar story, as far as I am aware, identifies but one being, clearly described as 'the eunuch' and named as the Asu-Shu-Namir. I think this clarifies the meaning of the unknown Sumerian terms and hints at the millennia-long development of the myth. For the Akkadian empire rose as Sumer fell – and who can tell how long Sumer had endured before its end and for how many centuries Akkadia learned from its neighbour? And just as Ishtar embodies Inanna, so the <u>Asu-Shu-Namir embodies the magic of the gala-tura and the kur-jara</u>. These beings resist all bribes and regain the body of their queen, whom they then revive with sacred water and plants. In other words, they remember and are faithful – unlike Dumuzid, who forgets and is faithless.*

Alexandra yawned involuntarily and sat for a while, pressing her palms against her eyes. The close-written pages were a strain to read and it was an effort to guess what Minerva wanted her to learn. She suspected she would be tested in some way. She took a piece of paper and jotted down the words, 'Asu Shu Namir, eunuch, incorruptible messenger of gods' and various other terms in order to memorise them later. As she did so, she was interrupted by one of the staff bringing her a telegram. She opened it quickly and read the busy Civil Service handwriting of the local postmistress: *Bath Spa Station 7pm Tonight Edward Day Brother in Law Harriet*

'Oh well,' thought Alexandra with the mildest whisper of surprise. 'She managed to keep it under twelve words and only pay the sixpenny rate. But really! George Arden to be named Edward Day as if part of her family! Well, he must do whatever it is he does. He can't expect me to notice him, after his disgraceful cowardice. But as long as he leaves me alone, I don't think I much care.' And then she thought vaguely about Valentine for a moment; but quickly the memory was replaced by the idea that she should check that the desk manager had been informed that a guest needed collection this evening. She walked out to the desk, having replaced the book carefully in its covers and carrying it with her.

The desk clerk checked his records. 'Ah, that'll be the other booking arriving then. Customer wasn't sure of date preferred. There's another gentleman we're expecting too. Both from London, perhaps they are travelling together, ma'am?'

'Oh, perhaps,' said Alexandra. She thought no more of it. With her eyes so tired, she wanted to wander in the valley to refresh herself. She planned a walk to the well.

CHAPTER NINETEEN

When Mr Pollitt woke up and saw who was sitting opposite him, he gave an involuntary squeak of horror. If it wasn't the very last person he wanted to lay eyes on, that *creature* – confined in the same railway compartment as himself - what was he to do now? But George was alert and apparently waiting for him to wake up. He was fixing him with a solemn gaze.

'I didn't do it,' he said as soon as he saw that Jerome recognised him. 'I remember that he threw the bottle and it smashed at the foot of the stairs. And then I was next to him and then I was running.'

Jerome stared at him implacably.

George noticed this and continued, 'I wanted to help him but I couldn't. He had to go out. He was very angry but it wasn't my fault.' His words began tumbling out a little faster as he realised that Jerome was unimpressed by his story: 'He came back and spoke to Janet but after he'd done that, I told him there was no need for him to stay. So he's gone on because it was far preferable to staying there with the gentlemen in the wigs. They are very gloomy company and quite obsessed with the fate of some cousins who fell foul of Robespierre.'

Jerome shook his head in an effort to clear it. George Arden seemed to be speaking English but it made no sense at all. The first thing he thought with any clarity was how annoying it was not to have brought any champagne in his hand luggage. Then he remembered that he had a whole hipflask of brandy somewhere about his person. He recalled Aleister making a big fuss when giving it to him and telling him twice that it was a special gift as he had been planning to drink from it on the Matterhorn or some such place. Probably with a friendly Saint Bernard. Jerome rapidly extracted the silver flask and began to dose himself in order to get over the shock of waking up with a murderer sitting opposite him. Why, he could have been killed several times over right there and then in his sleep! The murderer continued to watch him placidly. After a while, Jerome felt fortified enough to begin to ask questions. 'So, I gather you have no intention of doing me in right here and now. I'm obliged to you. Thank you very much. Anyway, you know Aleister would certainly come after you and give you what-for if you laid a finger on me. So put any thought of that right out of your mind.'

George nodded.

'And where, may I ask, are you going?'

'I'm going to stay with Mrs Roberts,' he said without further explanation.

Jerome sighed. 'And where – and indeed who – is Mrs Roberts?'

'She is my landlady. I don't know where she is because I'm to be met at the station and taken to her. Somewhere in the countryside, Mrs Day said, where it will be peaceful and quiet.'

'H'mm,' grunted Pollitt, taking a genteel sip of brandy. 'Am I to understand that I have nothing to fear from you? That you didn't conk Valentine on the head with a brandy – yes, well, with a bottle?'

'I really didn't. I know I didn't.'

'Let us put the matter to one side for a moment,' said Pollitt. 'Tell me how you come to be in this blessed train and particularly in my private compartment.'

'Yes, certainly,' George said, seeming to relax and curling up by the window of the carriage to watch the land rush past. 'Because this is an interesting coincidence, isn't it, Mr Pollitt? I was in a compartment at the back which I had to get into you know because we only had five minutes to spare and it was very, very crowded and it had us all squashed together, and one of the pies got broken. I think it leaked a bit. And when we stopped at a station to take water on, I thought it was a good time to go for a little walk up the platform. And I saw this compartment had only one person sleeping in it so I crept inside. It's very funny, isn't it, to find ourselves in each other's company again. Did we actually talk on that night at the club?'

'First, this compartment was occupied solely by myself because I had arranged it to be that way and paid rather a lot extra to the guard to keep it like that. Second, no. I don't believe we so much as exchanged a word when we first met. And incidentally, I would like to ask you a few frank questions about what happened that night.'

'Oh, yes, very well,' said George.

'Why was Aleister talking to you so intimately? Don't think about it. Just answer, quickly. None of your wriggling out of it.'

'He was talking about things to do with magic and spirit memories and spirit journeys. I understand that better now because I've started unbuilding the wall. It took a long time to put up so it's taking a long time even to make a crack in it. Little bits are seeping through now. Your friend has a long, long past and I saw a little bit of it and told him about it.'

'He's only twenty-two and a quarter, you know,' said Pollitt.

'It is a very strange thing that he spends so much effort opening a door and I have spent so much effort shutting one.'

'You do understand that I have not the least idea of what you are talking about,' said Pollitt. 'Now, listen here, Mr Arden. Are you telling me once and for all that my friend's only interest in you was that dreary magic and spiritualism or whatever it is? Astralism. Ghostism.'

'Yes,' said George firmly.

Pollitt sighed in relief. 'Very well, I will condescend to believe you. And I am prepared to believe that you are quite incapable of killing anybody or anything, now that I see you in the flesh again. I feel that we can converse like gentlemen. Now the next question is why. Why are you suspected of having done – you know, that horrid thing?'

'Because of a lie.'

'May one ask why?'

'He's lying because he hates me and he wants to get rid of me to make sure I shut up.'

'Ah,' said Pollitt. 'A person takes a dislike to you. Naturally he tries to get you arrested for murder. I see.'

'I don't really want to talk about him,' said George.

'Well, that won't help, will it, if the police come asking you questions? You've got to know what to say. It really is important these days, it's all become very uncivilised and dangerous at present. So this friend of yours, he is lying about you because you annoyed him. You must have done something quite dreadful to him.'

'He never was a friend,' said George.

'Very well. Have it your way. But I can tell you I've experienced it an awful lot. At school, for example, the worst of the bullies were always the ones who, you know, got very hot and bothered when I demonstrated my sweet dances, and then got very angry as if I'd done something to them. Their reaction was not my fault though.'

George listened carefully. 'Yes. Exactly. Only he was worse than that.'

Pollitt fanned himself with his hat. 'I need only to look at you to know your story,' he said.

'Really?' said George.

'Oh yes. The story of beauty and the beasts. There are a lot of beasts, my dear, a lot of beasts.'

They remained silent after that, Pollitt finding the brandy had lulled him into a sense of repose. They both looked out of the window while the train rattled and shook gently on its journey. Gradually George's eyes began to close and his head slid down the pane a little. Pollitt watched him silently falling asleep and decided to have another little nap himself.

By the time they arrived at Bath Spa station and stood together outside in the dark of a February night, looking about for their connections, Pollitt had almost forgiven George for being a little younger and perhaps just a little prettier than he was. He found that he could easily lead and dominate him, which very much suited his style – he would be able to show him off to any dowagers he might encounter, especially if he polished him up a little. He had also begun to instruct him in the relative merits and influences of Toulouse-Lautrec, Beardsley and Felicien Rops in the last part of the journey. In this way, he would become a perfect foil in conversation and might even be schooled to introduce Jerome's own favourite topics. All in all, Pollitt decided that George was perfectly harmless. It was not an unpleasant surprise therefore when they heard their names called by the same coachman. It seemed they were both bound for the Adsullata Spa Hotel.

*

Dear Harriet,

I thought I'd better let you know that your brother-in-law arrived here last night. He is accompanied by another gentleman – name of Pollitt – I had no idea you had arranged this, but it is most convenient from my point of view as they keep each other amused. It saves me from conversing with him as I have a lot to do. I am sorry this letter is short. I find myself much occupied with various activities. I am feeling very well. The hot springs, I expect, are the cause. Minerva is not here at the moment and I don't know where she has gone. I hope she returns soon. I will keep you informed of any further developments.

Yours affectionately etc.

After Alexandra had sealed the envelope, she recalled that there were certain letter-writing conventions required of one, concerned with enquiring about other people's health and so forth, which she had not fulfilled. Never mind, she had mentioned her own health and that would have to do for now. She would be more thorough next time.

She wandered through the salon and out into the solarium. Enough weak morning sunshine got trapped here for an invalid to sit and enjoy the view down the valley, but nobody was doing so at present. Walking together down the slope among green daffodils, she could see the two new arrivals. They looked companionable from this distance. She found herself quite equanimous about the presence of the one who had been accused of killing a friend of hers. She supposed that Harriet was probably right and it was all a mistake. The other one, Mr Pollitt, seemed personable enough: rich, educated, not very interested in anyone at the Spa but willing to engage in conversation. As they passed out of sight, she dismissed them both from her thoughts.

She had brought the notebook with her and now sat down to return to her reading. She had lost her place but the page she opened at random caught her attention and she read on.

Of paramount interest: It is extraordinary and I am more excited than ink can express that the text here differs substantially from all other known versions of the myth of Ishtar's descent. Here, the loss of her husband is not the motive for her journey to the Great Below. Joseph agrees that the Babylonian story is so much later, perhaps by a full ten centuries – and our Inanna has by then become Ishtar. The later tales present Ishtar's motive for her journey to Hades as a search for her lost love, like the journey of Orpheus. But here, in this older text, Inanna's motive is not to find Dumuzid. It is nothing less than to gain immortality, to depose death itself! Why did this intention become obscured in the later versions? Did this confrontation with Death have to be rationalised, explained away in terms of common family bonds? To me, this hints that the rituals had not only become widespread and diluted but that a priestly hierarchy deliberately chose occultation to preserve their mysteries. I hope to reconstruct lines 293 to 350 and that these will offer up clues.

Overleaf Alexandra read:

Disappointment! This last fragment does not elucidate it. Sadly many lines on fragment IV are lost and little can be inferred from the broken words and exclamations which remain. I fear that the corner fragment (XVII) I had hoped fitted on the lower right hand side would reveal further information - but is not at all related to the others, seeming to refer to business matters, beer and barley and so forth, although invoking the name of the goddess as keeper of the grainstore. She is clearly marked holding the reed bunches. There even may be a king name, if I can make it out.

The great grief of Inanna for her lost love, Dumuzid, is yet another of those peculiar inconsistencies in the story. For it is she herself in her wrath who consigns him to the underworld in the first place. Finding he failed to mourn her as she had instructed, she gives him to demons who have accompanied her out of hell. Shortly thereafter, she is overwhelmed with grief and makes a very beautiful lament out of it all. It is impossible to prove – but in my opinion, this lack of logic within the poem points to several traditions having been conflated. If only I had the provenance of the fragments, whether uncovered in tomb or temple, wherever it might be, I would travel there to look for the rest and unravel this mystery. Joseph said today that if only his health permitted, we would go together and search through all of ancient Sumer to find clues. If only it were possible – but hope of any more such journeys together fades daily.

There followed a long discussion as to whether the disappearance of Inanna and her reappearance was a symbol of the journey of the planet Venus. It seemed that Minerva's husband Joseph had made a study of ancient astronomy.

I believe Joseph's suggestion is correct: that the period of three days which marked Inanna's 'hanging on the hook' is symbolic of the loss of the Evening Star - for Inanna is everywhere represented by the planet Venus. Joseph says that the ancient people believed the Morning Star and the Evening Star were twins, rather than one and the same body. They watched the star of sunset in the West disappear and then, apparently, her twin reappearing days later as the star of dawn in the East. The Morning Star is warlike and active, the Evening Star emanates harmony and love. Reflects the contradictory aspects of Inanna. And of ourselves: our anger and regret.

Alexandra noticed some scribbled words in the margin next to that entry, apparently written with a different pen at a later date:

It is heartbreaking to remember J. sharing this, the wealth of his research, already knowing what I did not: that time was so short.

Alexandra paused, wondering, and read on.

*

After his talk with Crowley, Dr Watson began that same afternoon to research Albert Burroughs; but he found it difficult to get very far. He started by looking for examples of his work as a court reporter. He spent almost the whole of the next day working his way through a small tower of dark-grey files, tracking down various pieces in the crime sections of newpapers such as Lloyd's Weekly and The Daily Mail. Glancing through Burroughs's work, he found that it displayed a notable bent towards the disturbing, detailing criminal activities with clinical accuracy – but then, thought Watson, since the Ripper, editors encouraged court reporters to pander to the libidinous moral outrage of the newspaper-reading public. Perhaps the man was simply following orders. It was interesting, however, to come across an admiring report of a case investigated by Inspector Miller and which mentioned Miller by name. He sighed and placed the file on top of the growing heap beside him, wondering how to proceed and deciding that a cup of tea would be just the thing to enhance his powers. Mrs Hudson, the landlady, happened to appear at that moment. She was accompanied by Aleister Crowley.

'Ah,' said Watson. 'I was just thinking of you, Crowley, and speculating how your side of the work was coming along.'

'Yes,' said Crowley, 'I thought it was time to compare notes.' He sat down opposite Watson. 'I spoke to several people about Burroughs and I am rather pleased with the results.'

'I hope you conducted your questioning discreetly? It won't do to let him know we are trailing him, you know.'

'Yes, yes. I can be very discreet when necessary, Doctor. I discovered that Burroughs is careful, regular in his habits, very clean. He goes daily to various courts such as the Old Bailey, follows proceedings and then takes his copy to Fleet Street in time for the morning edition.'

'Yes, I've been digging out his reports.' Watson flicked a finger at the pile of cardboard boxes and files near his feet.

'Have you found some? Good. Well, Burroughs often has to wait about for verdicts and so on before he can write up his pieces, but he's known to keep to a routine, as far as he can – where he dines, the colours he wears and other strange little things, such as how many times he taps on the desk.'

'Taps on the desk?'

'It's been noticed by the clerks at his editor's office – he always taps on the desk in a certain pattern before a conversational exchange. Tap, tap, tap …tap. A nervous tic, you see! They've got a private, rather disrespectful name for him: Old Tick-Tock. Shows they're scared of him.'

'Surely this shows rather that he is considered methodical and trustworthy?' said Watson. 'Not very promising for our purposes.'

'No? Do you not think it shows he is expending a great deal of energy in maintaining rituals to block a hidden shadow?'

'What on earth do you mean by that, Crowley?' asked Watson.

'I have set myself to find this shadow,' answered Crowley, as if it were the most obvious of facts. 'The man is dogged by demonic entities, attracted by the turbulence he generates.' Watson raised an eyebrow and Crowley explained, 'By the interplay. The turbulence generated by the repression of and subsequent rebellion of this shadow – do you not see it? Oh well. Think of it as a geyser throwing up a rock. Even quite ordinary people sense this disturbance in him and keep away. He is, you might say, a loner.'

Watson nodded. 'Go on,' he said. 'I think I see what you're driving at.'

'As I said, he is also a man of rigid habits. It represents an attempt to impose order on the entities feasting on his confusion.'

'Mr Crowley, there may be merit in your ideas, but it would help me a great deal – would help George Arden a great deal too – if you could refrain from thinking in terms of demons, entities and energies. But, please, continue.'

Crowley looked at Watson with his head on one side for a moment and then went on, 'Very well, I will confine my comments to the mundane, Doctor. After several boring hours spent watching his movements after he had left court and trekked over to his editor's office, I was interested to observe last night that he was approached by a ragged, disreputable fellow. Burroughs seemed not to be particularly pleased at the sight of him but – and this is the thing that interested me- he was by no means surprised either. It was as if they had an appointment. The ragged man followed him. They disappeared into a side-alley. Naturally, I followed.'

'Yes?' said Watson. 'Blackmail?'

'Maybe. I received the distinct impression that the ragged man had been an associate or employee of Burroughs. I immediately thought that, as a journalist, he would likely be in the habit of paying criminals for information so I slid myself into a shadowed recess between houses and listened. There was some kind of tiresome dispute about money and I think the beggar or whatever he was tried to put pressure upon Burroughs for more than usual. Then it became quite delightful. He began reminding him that he himself had protected Burroughs from the law – even that he had served time in prison and had protected Burroughs's good name. Interesting, isn't it?'

'Well, well,' said Watson. 'So Burroughs has got a shady past. But whatever this man went to prison for, you may be sure that evidence to link Burroughs to him will only be his word against Burroughs's. I don't hold out much hope of catching him out there – but still, this is a very promising beginning. Good work!'

'Ah, but there's more, Doctor. For then I heard the word that made me prick up my ears: 'resurrections'. You know as well as I do what that means. As a medical man, you'll be familiar with the generally superseded practice of digging up and selling fresh corpses. And that got me thinking. Was our Mr Burroughs indeed a burrower? Was that their association long ago? Could they have once supplied corpses for dissection? No great crime in my eyes – nor probably in yours, doctor – but still a something-staining for a reputable journalist to have been involved in. What do you think?'

'It's rather a long shot,' answered Watson. 'And any such activity would have been quite some time ago, Mr Crowley. Nowadays, there is no need for the foulness of grave robbing to supply fresh corpses.'

'Indeed. But I'd add that there is still a brisk trade in body parts, you know. Plenty of competition for a fresh corpse and the teaching hospitals and schools of anatomy turn a very fair profit from selling-on unwanted anatomical bits and pieces. And skeletons.' Crowley met Watson's curious stare without a flicker. 'I just happen to know it is quite impossible to get a corpse for oneself – legally, that is. Anyway, from this I infer that the resurrections undertaken by Burroughs and his fellow were for a different buyer, an illegal one.'

'Well, this is all very valuable, Mr Crowley. I congratulate you! If only we had a name for the ragged man.'

'Ah, but wait! It gets better. Burroughs kept hissing at him when the fellow was pressing him for money, "Go to the devil, Bateman!" It was most convenient of him. I almost broke from the shadows to thank them both.'

'Splendid! Bateman, Bateman. Then I have a name and a possible crime to search the records for. Thank you, Mr Crowley. That really is a help. Holmes is an avid reader of every kind of crime record, whether it is agony columns or official crime reports, and searching this entire archive would take me a year at least without a name to go on.'

Crowley sat back in a satisfied way and lit a cigarette. 'I say,' he said lazily. 'Has your friend left any of that seven per cent solution in the jar over there?'

CHAPTER TWENTY

It took many hours – with Watson regularly asking himself whether it was worth wasting so much time on this case - but by the middle of the next morning he had discovered a pasted-in newspaper clipping of a court report concerning a Charles Bateman. It did indeed involve grave robbing, and Holmes might not even have bothered to index such a lowly crime had it not been for the rather grisly details. Bateman had been apprehended in the act of removing heads from fresh corpses. His assistant fled on hearing the approach of a sexton and Charles Bateman was discovered with a bag containing three heads. He was sentenced to six months imprisonment.

As nothing had been stolen from the grave and Bateman claimed to be supplying a medical student, the case might have been dealt with more leniently but for the desecration involved. On being questioned on the identity of his customer, Bateman had declared that only his 'assistant' had had all the details of the student for whom the heads were intended; but the assistant could not be apprehended.

Watson assumed that the assistant in question had been Burroughs – what else could have made the man vulnerable to blackmail? Why might he have needed a private supply of human heads? Since the Anatomy Act, there had been a plentiful supply of paupers' corpses available to medical students. Had the man perhaps been thwarted in his ambitions to become a doctor? He made a note to investigate – might Burroughs have been expelled from one of the teaching hospitals, for example – and if so, for what offence?

He took a turn round the room and stopped at the window, looking down at the bright street below. He had agreed to go to Chancery Lane once he had uncovered further information, so he stuffed his notes into his inside pocket, took his cane and made his way there on foot, feeling in need of an hour's gentle exercise. The weather had cleared and warmed up considerably, unusually mild for February. He was fortunate to arrive just as Crowley was leaving. They met on the very doorstep. 'Mr Crowley, I came to talk about the Bateman connection,' said Watson.

Crowley nodded. 'Yes?' he said energetically. 'Then you can talk as we go. I have something in mind that needs to be done this afternoon.'

They made their way along the busy streets. Watson disliked shouting complicated information over the noise of the horses and wheels and street vendors. He was also ready for a rest (his chest was by no means completely sound). But Crowley was rather maddeningly mysterious about their destination and led the way determinedly to the Embankment. When they came to Cleopatra's Needle, Watson absolutely refused to go a step further until they had sat down and talked things through. The bench faced the rippling brown river. Sunshine sparkled on the water. It was far quieter here. A blackbird singing somewhere among the branches of the plane tree above their heads was competing with another, hidden in shrubbery across the road. Watson carefully reiterated the Bateman story, handing Crowley the newspaper clipping.

'So,' Crowley said, having listened again to Watson's information in the quieter environment. 'Delightful. Three heads in a bag. What are your thoughts?'

'My first thought is that, in terms of clearing George Arden's name, it is promising but leads nowhere as yet,' said Watson, stretching out his leg, which sometimes became stiff from an old wound. 'It is a side issue; but it might usefully call into question Burroughs's veracity if it could be proved that he was the escaped partner. It would have to be argued as admissable evidence, which is doubtful; but it does make it more likely that there are other hidden things in his past. He seems to want to keep this Bateman sweet, at any rate, so I think the next move is to track the fellow down and have a quiet word with him. He needs money and will probably become responsive with the right inducement. Aside from that, I hope you will now tell me why you've dragged me all this way without explanation?'

'Apologies, Doctor. I can get pig-headed from time to time,' said Crowley without the least sign of regret. 'My plan is to visit Burroughs's house now at this hour when he should be at work. I want to get in there and explore some ideas of mine. Now that you're here, I hope you will aid me? I would appreciate your assistance in interviewing whomever among the servants cleared up the mess on the night Cabot died.'

Dr Watson had no particular objection to looking at the house in question. It would be worth taking a peek at the staircase. There might be some issue relating to line-of-sight, for example. As long as they did not impersonate police officers or suborn witnesses, it should be perfectly legal. 'What about Burroughs? Are you sure he will be out?'

'That is the advantage of his being predictable.'

It was Janet Fairlight who answered the door. It had been she who had let Crowley in when he visited the house before and she recognised him. When he explained that he had brought a doctor with him to look into the circumstances of the late Mr Cabot's death, she explained that Mrs Roberts had gone away. As she was speaking, the rather gangling figure of Dafydd Williams emerged from the parlour and asked to know what was happening. The upshot was that Janet agreed to run down and ask Mrs Jenkins for permission to talk to Crowley and Dr Watson, since he was a respectable medical man.

They were shown into the parlour where they sat by the low fire. Mr Williams, when he found out that the two visitors had both known the deceased and the suspect, began to talk at great length and in a very low voice about the terrible accident (they learned that he himself now referred to the 'murder' as an accident). Williams said he wondered very much about the fate of poor George Arden and so Dr Watson took the opportunity to ask questions about Arden's general behaviour. Crowley said very little. He seemed to be becoming impatient and more than once rose and walked about the room.

Finally, Janet returned, sounding breathless, and announced that Mrs Jenkins said it would be all right to talk to her but that she herself would have to be present. This suited Dr Watson. When Elizabeth Jenkins, looking quarrelsome, ascended from the kitchen, they went aside into the morning room. Crowley, to Watson's surprise, did not accompany him but opted to stay with Dafydd Williams. Watson settled down with his notebook and, while Mrs Jenkins looked sternly on, began to question Janet as thoroughly on every detail of the evidence that she had cleared up from the floor that day as he hoped Holmes would have done.

Meanwhile, Crowley had made a split-second decision regarding the inconvenient presence of Dafydd Williams. Part of his plan had been to go quietly up to Burroughs's room and have a look round but he could not very well wander about the house unsupervised. 'Now,' he said, once Watson and the others had left the room. 'I need to speak to you, Mr Williams. Would you do me the favour of standing up?.'

Looking uncertain, Williams did as he was asked. Crowley positioned himself in front of Williams so as to look directly into his blue, rather startled eyes. With a little unexpected gesture of his hand, he drew Dafydd's attention away to one side. At that moment, Crowley, very swiftly and in one smooth and sudden movement, put a hand on Dafydd's forehead and pushed him backwards into the chair, preventing him from falling too fast with another strong hand positioned at his back. At the same instant, he began to speak into his ear in a low murmur.

The reaction of Dafydd was to go limp. Crowley, murmuring smoothly a stream of reassuring words, gradually took his hands away. He withdrew a little to stand observing him, his head on one side and a slight smile on his face. Dafydd Williams sat perfectly still with his head hanging forward, his mouth open and his eyes closed.

Softly, Crowley continued, ' – and in a moment when you open your eyes, the first thing you'll want to do is show me the way to Albert Burroughs's room. And you'll want to open your eyes when you hear the sweet old tune of Greensleeves.'

Crowley left him there and walked over to the window. After a moment, very quietly he began to whistle. When Dafydd opened his eyes, he saw him standing with his hands clasped behind his back silhouetted against the window, looking out onto the street, whistling Greensleeves to himself.

'Do you know what I think, Mr Crowley?' said Dafydd clearly after a moment in which he wondered if he had fallen asleep and hoped he had not snored, 'I think we should search that Albert Burroughs's room. I am sure there's something not quite right about him, you might say. If you will accompany me, we can bear each other witness on what we find. What do you say?'

'Why, Mr Williams, what a bold idea,' said Crowley, feigning surprise. 'Lead the way!'

There was a dense energy in Burroughs's room. Crowley sensed it before he went in. The place felt shrunken, as if something had sucked out the space and light and left only stale air. He perceived a kind of charnel grey filtering everything. Even the afternoon sunlight was sickly here. There was a hint of a smell which he could not immediately identify.

Dafydd Williams shook his head as they entered the bedroom. He felt so odd he half thought he was sleepwalking. 'There's something about this room, and I don't know what it might be, but I'm very glad that mine is on the other side of the house,' he muttered.

Crowley noticed that he was looking unhappy. 'It's good that you had this idea,' he said softly. 'This will certainly help George. Where shall we look first?'

'I suppose in the desk drawers, or in the wardrobe.'

'Yes, good. Where else?'

'I don't know what it might be,' repeated Williams, 'but something is telling me I don't want to look under that bed. I'll start on the drawers.'

'Yes, good,' said Crowley. 'I'll look under the bed then.' He pulled out a padlocked black leather box from beneath the bed. 'What shall I do, Williams? Should I open the box?'

'I don't know,' said Williams. 'I don't like the box.'

'Yes, you needn't be troubled about that,' said Crowley. 'This will certainly help George. Would you like me to open the box for you?'

'No,' said Dafydd, his eyes widening. 'Don't. Don't open the box.' Williams seemed to snap into full consciousness. 'Good lord, Crowley. There's a stink coming from that thing.'

'Don't you think we should open it, Dafydd?' said Crowley softly. He took the brass paperknife from the desk and slid it under the hasp of the padlock. He applied pressure. Gradually, although the metal of the padlock held, the old leather of the box itself began to split. After a little work, Crowley levered open the lid.

The bottom of the box was littered with index cards of the type used in an office. To each card, attached neatly with a brass split-pin, was a dried and blackened human ear.

Detective Browning had finished making notes. The box and its contents had been removed. Burroughs's room had been inspected. An officer had been despatched to interview him at his place of work; and Inspector Miller, who had drifted in and very quickly drifted out again, had long gone home for tea.

'The Inspector doesn't think there is *necessarily* foul play involved in all this, you know, sir,' said Browning reassuringly to Dafydd Williams who was still in shock.

They were all sitting in the parlour making use of Mrs Jenkins' most generous tea pot, and Mr Williams was being dosed with strong sweet tea. He was feeling ashamed of himself because he had had a kind of ridiculous fit when he had seen the contents of the black box. He was not entirely sure how it had happened, but he remembered running into his own room and crouching in the corner. It was embarrassing. He assumed that Crowley had gone straight downstairs for Dr Watson and that a servant had been despatched to fetch the police, but the details were not clear. He remembered being questioned by a policeman in a perfunctory sort of way, and then questioned again in much more detail by Browning.

He could not satisfactorily explain his motives for suggesting that they look inside the box. Crowley had jogged his memory by asking him if he didn't remember complaining about the smell? And then he remembered that had been the reason, a search for a strange smell. He had racked his brains for further details but everything before the discovery was so vague. The smell was the best explanation; so he had agreed that it was the smell which had troubled him. Crowley and Watson said they had happened to be passing the house and had popped in to see their old friend Dafydd Williams. Dafydd was so confused he was not even sure whether he had met them before today, but he went along with it all. His strange loss of memory made events unpleasantly vague.

Browning went on, 'Mr Burroughs is quite a well-known reporter, you see, Mr Williams. He studies crime and criminals. There is every reason to assume that the human remains found in the case were purchased or obtained legitimately. Nobody *owns* dead bodies, sir, legally speaking, so there is no such thing as stealing one. Stealing items such as jewellery from a grave or a corpse, yes, that's theft, but not stealing the body itself. I know, funny, isn't it? You'd think there'd be a law. But there ain't.'

Dr Watson added, 'Quite right, Detective. As a doctor, I know that the 1832 Act put a stop to the whole trade in Burking. You'll have read about the case, I'm sure, Mr Williams – Burke and Hare, the pair who murdered a good number of innocent victims in order to sell their bodies? One of them turned Queen's evidence and got off scot-free. The other was hanged.' Watson sipped his tea, made a face and added a sugar lump. 'We also do not know how old the ears are. I detected a smell of preservative in the box. They could have been preserved by an antiquarian – or if modern, been reduced to their current state by the use of drying salts and so forth. The external ear or pinna is made of ridged cartilage, you see. Egyptian mummified remains, many centuries old, often retain portions of ears or even complete specimens.'

'Yes, sir. Exactly what Inspector Miller said: how do we know that these ears ain't straight from old Egypt? He also said that if there was anything criminal about them, he'd expect to find them under the bed of the suspect rather than under the bed of the witness and was it quite certain where they was usually stowed?'

'Well, luckily you have two witnesses to the opening of the box and other witnesses, the housemaids, as to its habitual presence under that bed. No doubt their owner will have a plausible explanation,' said Watson, with flicker of a glance towards Crowley. 'By the way, while I am here, detective, I have heard that the housemaid is a very observant young person. I believe it was she who cleared up the scene of Valentine Cabot's death. She mentioned certain interesting facts which I think should be noted by the police. I am only a medical man, of course, but I would strongly recommend you interview her.'

'Thank you for your advice, Doctor,' said Detective Browning, 'but at the station I think we probably have some notes from the girl.'

Watson felt that they were in a delicate position. He and Crowley had had a hurried consultation on the subject before calling the police in and had decided to keep their own investigations to themselves. Browning had not personally interviewed Watson before and the doctor now made no mention of his association with the famous Sherlock Holmes. As for Crowley, the detective remembered him all right, but it seemed perfectly natural that he would be acquainted with Dafydd Williams – who was after all a fellow boarder with Valentine Cabot - and that passing the house, he would have called in for a visit.

'Well, what do you think?' asked Crowley later as they left the premises and walked down the front steps of the quiet house. The early evening sky was a pure cobalt blue. The bare trees were clotted with the untidy silhouettes of roosting birds.

'I have not yet formed an opinion, Mr Crowley,' said Dr Watson. 'If Holmes were here he would no doubt be conducting experiments on these poor remnants of humanity and cross-referencing cases and discovering a wonderful tale of abominable criminality. Sadly, it's just myself. The police have got the evidence, although it may merely be evidence of a macabre taste in collectibles.'

'H'mm. I did retrieve a little of that evidence for myself,' said Crowley, 'in the shape of some paperwork in the box, which I took the liberty of removing. Oh, did I fail to mention it to Inspector Miller? Ah, dear me.'

'Well that is unfortunate and not good practice, to say the least,' said Watson. 'But now they have been removed, we might as well take a good look at them ourselves, I suppose – but then they must absolutely be returned to the police. They may be important evidence.'

'Well, of course, Doctor. That is precisely why I did not want to leave them in the hands of Inspector Miller.'

'And, by the way, I too have struck gold, Crowley. It was after all rather a good idea of yours to call this afternoon.'

CHAPTER TWENTY-ONE

Alexandra adjusted her lamp to spill light across the close written pages. Here in the library, lettered gold glinted in the recessed shelves. Only the night porter was at his desk and the hotel was silent except for the innumerable small noises an old house makes at night, stealthy creaks on empty floorboards or the brush of a curtain in the night draught. It was very cold, for although the porter had at first made the library fire blaze up, she had not called him to put on an extra scuttle of coal as it began to burn low. She kept telling herself that she planned to go to bed. But the clock said it was past midnight and she read on.

> *It is also interesting to note the insistence on balance, barter and guile: in the ancient world, one bartered with the forces of nature, one either tricked or appeased the gods. Ereshkigal makes it very clear that she expects a life in return for releasing Inanna from hell. Q. Is there a hint here of a requirement for a male sacrifice?*

The next page she turned over appeared to contain some personal reflections written alongside quotations from the body of the poem. In the margin was written:

> *But Inanna knows - before she begins her journey she knows - that she cannot take her sister's place and her rebellion must fail. Her plot is not to outwit Death by usurping that throne but by tricking the gods into making a new thing, an unprecedented magic. But Death cannot see it, Death repeats the old way, Death imagines that she can satisfy her emptiness by taking another living soul. Like Joseph's.*

There was a gust of wind at the casement and she shivered, despite the thick shawl wrapped round her shoulders. Her thoughts now barely engaged with the fact that George Arden was in the hotel this very night. It seemed less and less interesting to her that an old friend of hers – how long ago it seemed now – had fallen downstairs and, ridiculously, died of it. It seemed equally preposterous that the silly fellow now skulking about this hotel had been accused of murdering him. With the objectivity which followed the complete subsiding of emotion, she saw how unlikely it was that such a thing could have happened. And she wasted no time thinking about it. All her interest was confined to the pages of Minerva's notebook, intrigued and a little horrified by what she was reading.

The entire day today, more or less, had passed in poring over books that Minerva had listed for her to consult. They all related to ancient Near Eastern mythology. She had learned enough to confirm that the broken tablet was indeed unique, for in all these academic studies, Alexandra could find little about the ancient shadow behind Ishtar, Sumerian Inanna. She realised that the field of Mesopotamian archaeology was in a state of constant - almost breakneck - development, and further discoveries were being made with every dig. Minerva's tablet seemed therefore to be of the utmost importance, for here was a lost, more primitive form of the myth. And the goddess shown in it was so much more daring, autonomous, capricious – dangerous. The story dated from impossibly distant times, was the rarest of discoveries and Minerva had done an excellent job of translating it. Why had she not published her findings?

Alexandra left the books on the table to be consulted again tomorrow, but gathered up the notebook. Carefully, as usual, she placed it first inside its drawstring bag and then within the leather portfolio and carrying it like a holy thing, she retired to bed.

*

Watson and Crowley went back to Chancery Lane by cab. On the way, Watson outlined the results of his interview with the housemaid. 'She's the only person to notice the configuration of the evidence at the scene, Crowley. I cannot conceive that Inspector Miller or indeed Detective Browning could be aware of it and not see that her testimony completely contradicts Burroughs's story. This is the concrete detail we needed. She said that she clearly remembers seeing the body lying upon the broken glass. In other words, Cabot must have fallen and landed on top of the smash. And if she saw it, then surely all must have seen it. After Cabot's remains were removed, she cleaned the floor, of course. I hope they made a record of it!'

'And if they did not?'

'But they must have done.'

'And if the other witnesses' statements either omit these details or contradict the girl's story, what then?'

'My guess is that nobody even asked them whether the body lay on or near the glass – they were all persuaded by Burroughs's insistence that he had seen a fatal blow being struck. They did not doubt his story and did not look for a reason to do so.'

'Yes, they would adjust their perceptions to conform to his more dramatic report. And what if the girl's statement has simply been filed away or lost?'

'How do you mean?' asked Watson.

'Oh, you noticed Miller today – he came and went – and showed no interest in pursuing good Mr Burroughs.' Crowley laughed. 'If that box had been under Arden's bed, a great deal more would now be made of it.'

'Bias. You believe Miller would stoop to suppressing evidence?'

'Why, yes, of course, Doctor. Did you not see his ring? I understand that Burroughs is a Freemason too.'

There was a fire already laid in Crowley's sitting room which they lit themselves and as it began to draw and flicker up, they settled down with a sandwich and a bottle of red wine. Watson silently raised a glass towards the curtain behind which he knew the skeleton sat.

'Toasting the demons, Doctor?' asked Crowley, noticing the gesture.

Watson snorted. 'I trust you're joking, Crowley.'

'Oh no, not at all. They're swarming all round it. It's rather stained with blood – you wouldn't like to see it - so I think of them like blowflies. If you pay attention to them, they'll pay attention to you, so I wouldn't, you know. I told you, it's an experiment - and things aren't going right with it. But I know you dislike any talk of such things.' He got up and turned up the light. 'There. Nice and bright for you.'

'Are you mocking me, Crowley?'

'Not at all, my dear Watson.'

'I am not intimidated by your demons, you know. Holmes and I hunted a monstrous hound on the moors – and a more hair-raising adventure you cannot imagine. It was all a trick in the end.'

It was Crowley's turn to snort. 'There, let's turn our attention to these documents, for I fear we'll be stymied in the matter of the servant's witness statement, however precisely you write it all down. She'll be overturned in court and stamped upon.' He brought over a lamp each to allow them to have a good look through the sheaf of papers that he had smuggled out under his waistcoat when poor Dafydd Williams had fled the room. Watson had mixed feelings about this theft but said no more of it. It would be difficult to explain the absence of the documents from the box if they proved to be important. He was already trying to invent a plausible excuse.

They decided to go through the bundle, taking half each. For a while, the room was silent except for the shuffling of papers, the occasional crackle of coal in the grate and the tick of the clock.

'My papers are dated and appear to be records of cash transactions,' said Watson. '"1 item delivered, received 5 guineas, 12th July 1895." That seems fairly typical.'

'I would be prepared to wager,' said Crowley, 'that the items in question were human heads, considering these records were stored along with the ears. I am also prepared to wager that the ears were taken from heads that he and Bateman had stolen.'

'Disgusting to think of. And more than likely. Unfortunately, there is nothing to support that presumption within the body of the text and since the papers have been removed from the box, we cannot prove that they ever were ever *in* the box and are related to those objects. Nor is there a receiver's name. It would be interesting to know why Burroughs felt it necessary to remove an ear from each head, wouldn't it? Or both ears. We don't know if there are pairs of ears in the box …'

Crowley, who was reclining in his favourite position on the couch, looking through the sheets of paper one after another then letting them drop carelessly onto a leopardskin rug, now paused and peering closely at one, held it up. 'Ha! The man is a pornographer, doctor!'

'Such vileness,' said Watson. 'Put it to one side, Crowley. Don't offend your sensibility.'

Crowley raised an eyebrow. 'Oh, please, doctor. The bourgeois ambition to get through life without unpleasantness seems to me the lowest vileness.'

'I do not wish to see any part of that,' said Watson.

'I won't show it to you then. But come, you *are* a doctor, so I would not have thought you so very shockable.' Crowley continued scanning the papers. 'Do you know, I think he's been elaborating upon the crimes he reports on? Presumably details the newspaper didn't feel suitable for public consumption.' He peered closely at a page and remarked, 'How strange. There appears to be a little drawing of Arden here.' He held up a torn half-sheet. 'And this all goes back to what I said about him in the very beginning. His shadow is immensely strengthened by its suppression. If he had not been forced to pretend to be what he is not, he might simply have followed his inmost desires in harmony. Now he is a force of disharmony and unbalance.'

Watson had a burning desire to point out that some shadows were better suppressed but he confined himself to saying, 'A picture of George Arden? Really? Why would Burroughs have that?'

'Isn't it obvious?' said Crowley.

'Is it his own work, do you think?'

'Unsigned. No, signed. It's a scrappy thing, dashed off quickly but there's an initial, A.'

'Standing for – Arden?'

'Maybe. Burroughs has made the effort to keep it though. Evidence of something or other, don't you think?'

They fell back into silence, continuing to study the various papers.

'This is curious,' Watson said at last. 'It appears he never paid his own rent. It was paid by a third party. Here is a contract. "As agreed between us this day of 22nd October 1896, your rent and a monthly stipend not in excess of twelve percent of your yearly expenses will be paid wherever you choose to lodge. In the event of your reneging on the terms of our agreement, no further payments will be made." And the bottom of the page has been torn away. No address, no indication of where it came from.'

'Interesting,' said Crowley. 'I wonder what the "terms of agreement" were?'

'Whoever pays this stipend would be of interest to us,' said Watson, looking relieved that something straightforward had finally come to light. 'How would one discover the man's identity? But it brings us no closer to implicating Burroughs in actual wrongdoing.'

'It's useful to be able to tarnish Burroughs's reputation – and to have these papers in *our* hands, not Miller's, is also something.'

'But can't you see? The letter doesn't actually tarnish anything. I very much hope you were not referring to these other improper documents as a kind of leverage' said Watson. 'They are useless to us without proof that they came from the box. You can't even prove authorship. The letter concerning his financial supporter merely shows that somebody was paying rent and a monthly allowance to Burroughs. For all we know, the fellow could have saved a man's life and have this as a reward for valour. The letter being in our hands is simply proof that we meddled in Burroughs's private affairs. The improper material was for his own use, one assumes.'

'The anonymous benefactor may be a medical man who bought heads from Burroughs, though,' said Crowley with a yawn. 'Or he might just as well be a magician. The human head is particularly sought after. I came across an interesting recipe which calls for the cooking of eight full ounces of fresh opium, sesame oil and a freshly-killed human head. I haven't had the opportunity to try it out.'

'I shudder to think, Mr Crowley. But just for example, can you tell me what one would hope to do magically with a head?'

'The process I am referring to produces an oil. The oil, when burned in a lamp or applied to a person, supposedly confers the power of vision. Personally, I think eight ounces of opium rendered into oil, with or without the sesame, let alone the entire substance of a human head, would certainly do *something.*' He laughed.

Watson nodded. "It certainly would. Opium resin dissolves flesh. I have seen it done on mutton. But I think that would be a very vile concoction indeed. Whatever spiritual vision one would hope to experience would surely be tainted by the very process of making the oil designed to achieve it.'

Crowley smiled and sipped his wine. 'That surely depends on your overall goal. Visions need not be morally edifying in order to be true.'

'But, Mr Crowley,' said Watson, sitting up a little straighter, 'is not the origin of magic one and the same as the origins of science? Was not the alchemical process the very beginning of our chemistry? And therefore are not such experiments – if they ever had the slightest basis in fact – repeatable, with repeatable and observable results – and could therefore be tested now?'

'Perfectly right, doctor.'

'And *ergo* have been proven to be mere mumbo-jumbo, Crowley! Do you see what I'm getting at? The true facts have turned into modern science and the superstitions have been weeded out.'

'Well, that is one way of looking at it. And the majority of old magical rituals are either purposely unintelligible or actually puerile nonsense. But I will say this, Doctor, if one does not understand anything about electricity, one cannot construct a dynamo; and having failed to do so, one cannot get oneself electrocuted. In other words, magical formulae are perfectly harmless to the average person even while they *are* repeatable experiments - if you are in possession of both the skill and the components.'

'You mean eye of newt and so on?'

'Not in the slightest! A sigil, a gesture, a word – something to intensify a particular energy. But these components are never written down.'

'Very convenient,' said Watson, thinking his usual thought about Crowley, which was that he had read too much of the wrong kind of speculative literature. 'And for myself, I will stand on the firm ground of observable phenomena and repeatable experiments.'

'Of course you shall, Dr Watson,' murmured Crowley, returning to his perusal of the documents. 'But it rather depends who is doing the observing, don't you think?'

'And, may I add, I think there are very few of your 'magicians' currently in practice,' said Watson, annoyed that Crowley was unperturbed by his objection.

'And that is truer than you know,' said Crowley.

The evening drew into night and at about midnight, Dr Watson decided to call it a day. They had established very little, except that Burroughs had been supplying something to someone and had an ongoing financial agreement, possibly with the same someone; and that he had a particularly elaborate perversion. But there was still no explanation for the ears.

As Crowley bade goodbye to Watson, he suddenly said, 'I wonder how Williams is getting on with Burroughs? The poor fellow will be better off moving elsewhere, having tampered with that box. Burroughs is strong, or looks to be. Williams may be at risk from him. What do you think?'

Watson thought for a moment. 'I can think of no excuse for us to intervene, Mr Crowley. If we turn up on the doorstep like a military guard, what would it accomplish but to imply a conspiracy between us? No, better he sticks to the tale of an offensive smell which required investigation.'

'I don't know,' said Crowley. 'I feel a little responsible. After all, it was I who suggested that we look in Burroughs's room and open the box.'

'Indeed?'

'Did I not mention that?'
'No, you didn't.'

*

Dafydd Williams steeled himself for the appearance of Burroughs that evening. He practised what he would say, which would be the thing about the smell. As it happened, Janet had mentioned a smell a while ago – he remembered her very words, 'like pigs' trotters' – and although he did not wish to go calling upon a child to support his testimony, it was still a comfort to know that he had not imagined it.

His stomach was crawling with dread as Burroughs's habitual return from work loomed. The fellow frequently smelled of alcohol when he came home. The alcohol usually had the effect of making him more pompous and fastidious – but surely, a man who valued a collection of human ears was not one to baulk at violence, Dafydd thought. He very much wanted to run away and lock himself in his room, but by physical exertion, he stuck to his post in the parlour. There was no point looking scared and guilty. He had to face up to the consequences of his curiosity. After all, it was he who had suggested to Mr Crowley that they look in Burroughs's room.

When the front door announced his return, Dafydd experienced a momentary flash of panic but he held firm. Burroughs stalked into the parlour, met his eyes briefly, almost sorrowfully; and without a word, positioned himself at the fireplace, leaning upon the mantel. He seemed to think while he drummed a tattoo with his fingers on the wood and then began to speak, staring down into the hearth. His voice was controlled, tight, but Dafydd could see the hand at his side clenching and unclenching as he stood there. As if reading from a list, he related that the police had come to his place of work at the newspaper offices and questioned him about the box. He said his good name had been besmirched. He said he could have lost his job. He said the collection was purchased legally from a dealer in mummies and Egyptian amulets in Museum Street and he himself had been attempting to catalogue them. He would provide a receipt in due course and at that point would reclaim the box.

Dafydd was given no opportunity to say anything, not even to apologise. At the end of the speech, Burroughs threw a piece of paper on the table, which he said was notice of his intention to sue

Williams for defamation of character, adding that he should also be charged with criminal damage for ruining a treasured box of great sentimental value. Then he marched out of the room and slammed the door. Whereupon Dafydd crept upstairs to his own room.

The next day, Janet was intent on wangling an opportunity to discuss things with Lily and Amy. While Mrs Roberts was away, these two had arranged to come in early each day and go home each night to sleep. Both of their mothers had new babies so they were a help at home of a night. They unkindly told Janet that the real reason was to avoid getting the creeps from sleeping in a 'house of death'.

Janet, whose dream encounters with poor Mr Cabot and sweet Mr George had faded into the realms of fantasy, was not particularly happy about this. She had begun to rely instead for news and moral support on nice Mr Dafydd. He was not at all stuck up; and, best of all, was good friends with dear Mrs Harriet Day who had promised Janet the most heavenly piano lessons. The lessons were a reward for some help she had given her, but Janet, whose only memory was of sitting in her parlour and getting down a painting, imagined she had dusted all the pictures or something. Exactly why was a hazy detail. Now, although she could not positively say that the Welshman had replaced the more exotic Mr Arden in her girlish heart, she was nonetheless very fond of him.

Amy had been engaged in floor-scrubbing in the hall and Lily had happened to come down with an armful of linen, coinciding with Janet coming out of the dining room at the same moment, where she had been seeing to the coal scuttle. Mrs Jenkins was making pastry in the kitchen. Mr Williams had gone out to see Mrs Day and Mr Burroughs was at his newspaper offices. It was an unmissable opportunity for a chat.

'Well, listen to this! Mr Williams, after breakfast, he told me something about that box under his bed,' whispered Janet. 'Mr Burroughs's bed, I mean, the one that smelt like pigs feet what the officer took away yesterday. He said it *was* something horrible - not just socks and unwashed stuff like *you* said, Amy.'

'And what was it then?'

'I dunno. He wouldn't precisely say.'

'Then what are you talking about?' demanded Amy scornfully, who always disliked being the last to hear a rumour.

Lily put in, 'I believe Mr Burroughs cut up a lady and put her remains in there, like in the *Mystery of the Murderous Mansion*.'

'Oh what rubbish, Lily!' said Amy. 'If he done that he would be under arrest and in prison. And the box weren't big enough neither.'

'But what *was* the horrible thing then? Nobody tells us nothing! And what about that argument last night?' retorted Lily. 'The one you said Mr Burroughs had with Mr Williams and there was a lot going on? *You* said, Janet, this morning when we come in.'

'I don't know what was said,' conceded Janet reluctantly, 'because Mrs Jenkins would not allow me to go cleaning the fitments on the door, which I said at the time really need a polish. You can see for yourself.' She indicated the dim brass of the fingerplate on the parlour door. 'But I can tell you that Mr Williams didn't go into the dining room for his supper. He took it upstairs in his room.'

'Mr Williams is scared, anyone can see that,' said Amy.

'Course he is,' said Janet. 'And there's something else too. Yesterday when that nice doctor come – before the police turned up - and talked with me all private, he was asking what I cleared up that day, all about the glass on the floor under Mr Valentine's poor body, and he was very exact and particular about it. And he said it might mean that Mr George gets off free if I was to stand up and give evidence. And that would prove that Mr Burroughs was a liar. And he wants to collect information so he can give it all to a posh lawyer.'

'Should have took a photograph,' said Amy. 'That's what I would have done.'

'They didn't ask me much, did they you? The police, I mean,' said Lily, 'after Mr Valentine died. Just what was the habits of him and Mr George.'

'Me too,' said the others in unison.

'They could'a asked better questions, if you ask me,' agreed Janet. 'That doctor said they was too busy.'

'Ooh!' said Lily. 'But listen to this! Me and Mrs Jenkins saw an horrible man hanging about by the railings opposite, like he'd been sleeping in the Square. And he was looking at the house, and up at the top windows, but we looked at him, and he slunk away.'

'He was just an old vagrant looking for money,' said Amy.

'You know what I think?' said Janet vengefully. 'I think that vagrant is waiting outside to murder you girls on your way home and cut up your remains.'

CHAPTER TWENTY-TWO

ime speeds by. I find it hard to keep up. I realise I planned to keep a daily record of the changes but it becomes difficult to remember why. I am full of energy at times. I know also that my body desires a great deal of rest. It is paradoxical. I believe the others here are beginning to treat me differently although I am fairly certain that my behaviour has not changed. Perhaps I am too stand-offish but the two young men can supply my place in conversation. One of them seems to be able to make people laugh. The other, I remember he was a boarder of mine and never did speak much even then. I think it was Cabot who did most of the talking in those days. Now this one sits in a corner, shivering like a – I don't know, a lost child. When I take the pills now they don't send me straight to sleep. So I have begun taking them in the morning. The sensation as they begin to work is like a piston in a great machine sinking deep into its cylinder: and I know that the work is beginning and once that feeling starts, it won't stop. Then I go out into the valley and walk and walk. The man saw me walking and he looked at me too with his mouth open. It makes me want to laugh to think of what they think they know.

Jerome Pollitt tried, but he could not prevent himself from annoying Major Farnsworth. He was doing it now while they played whist. Lady Helena and the Major made up a pair, while Jerome and Mrs Roberts made the other. His game was to pretend that the gentleman was in secret communication with himself. He would respond to a comment with a fleeting bat of his eyelashes or a tactful finger to his lips as if advising prudence, keeping well within the bounds of discretion so that nobody but the Major noticed. The poor man, unsure whether to burst with military indignation, was reduced to muttering from time to time that he had a gun in his bedside cabinet.

The evenings did drag on so, though. They could make up a rubber of whist; and the piano in the salon was put to good use. Pollitt had bashed out a fair number of tunes and Lady Helena had her own extensive if lugubrious repertoire. The Major sometimes sang with her in a wobbly baritone. Mrs Roberts would clap politely and Pollitt always sighed exaggeratedly, 'Oh bravo, sir, bravo! Encore!' as if each love song were secretly directed at him.

Mrs Roberts was physically present for the evening's amusements but her mind seemed disengaged. She seemed to want to say very little, whatever anyone did. Jerome wondered if she had taken a vow of silence. She only answered direct questions, in as few words as possible, and never volunteered a comment of her own. He didn't quite know what to make of her – a couple of times he'd glimpsed her actually running through the woods, like a wild woman. And her eyes looked glassy. He decided that the reason for her presence at the spa must be to recover from the mental disturbance caused by Valentine Cabot's death.

George was no good. He had evinced a strange aversion to Mrs Roberts as soon as he met her again on his arrival at the hotel. Pollitt knew she was his landlady because he had mentioned this fact when explaining his journey to the Adsullata. Jerome assumed the coldness was caused by the imaginary dead body of Cabot between them, but he observed no dread in Mrs Roberts. She simply looked through George as if he were a table or a chair, as if she remembered him with no emotion whatsoever.

Jerome looked over at Arden where he sat, frozen in a corner, and wished that he could force alcohol down his throat. It had also been something of a trial for them both to remember to call him Edward all the time. Jerome occasionally changed it to Teddy or Neddy according to whim. This confused George too. 'I am surrounded by idiots and misfits,' Pollitt thought sadly. And it was all very well having a peaceful place in a peaceful valley if you were ill, but it was not much fun if you were fit as a fiddle. He had forgotten entirely that his aspiration had been to meditate upon his deepest life purpose: he was secretly planning to come down one evening for dinner in his finest Diane outfit, pretending to be a new guest, just to see what the Major did.

Aleister had once said, in a rather lovely and memorable moment soon after they had first met, 'Hippolytus, your hair is pale gold, like spring sunshine, and its texture is of the finest gossamer.' Recalling that comment always made Pollitt regret that to complete his stage toilette it was the convention to cover up its natural glory in an extravagant wig. Here, in the slow death of the hotel salon, he fought against an urge to perform an extemporised version of his celebrated 'Serpentine' dance for the pure joy of watching their faces. There wouldn't be enough room, of course, but it occurred to him that perhaps George could be taught to join in. He noted the weedy way the boy shrank from contact with the other guests and the idea was killed stone-dead before it took flight. It was difficult to believe that

the fellow had been touted as the new star of that dreadful play –
Hamlet, Prince of Darkness, or whatever it had been called.

In addition to these dissatisfactions, he was never sure if he really
liked old things or not, and the hotel was horribly old in parts.
Everything must have been so cold, he thought, back when it was
built. And no doubt they had dungeons and oubliettes and
thumbscrews. There was a whole section of the place that was under
repair and when you looked past the roped-off end of the old
corridor, as far as the eye could see, shadows receded into winter
darkness; and you could feel a cold draught blowing from somewhere
as though someone had left a blessed window open. He avoided the
routes which took him near the shut-up quarters of the place.

'So, Ned, what do you think of this God-forsaken place?' he had
asked George after their first twenty-four hours in the hotel.

George had thought this through and then answered, 'That it is a
God-forsaken place.'

'You know that you are completely maddening, don't you?' said
Pollitt sincerely. He decided before another twenty-four hours was
up that it was time to contact Aleister and get some more company
in. So he took up a pen at the front desk and wrote on a piece of
hotel stationery:

> *Dear A. - I have been here about a hundred years now – I actually do
> not know how long as time drags by in a blur of tiresomeness - and have
> been thoroughly baptised in the waters of Jordan. I am clean and
> completely free of sin and, far from helping me to feel better, it is
> becoming <u>exhaustingly boring.</u> The hotel has champagne and all
> necessities, but it does not have decent conversation. Outside there is
> only Scenery. I need you, immediately, now. Come and amuse me if you
> can bear to leave the horrid skeleton. - J.*
>
> *P.S. After some consideration, and as a sign of my forgiving nature, I
> have decided to let you into the secret that George is here. I did think
> that perhaps I would not tell you; but quite by the most extraordinary
> chance, he and I actually get on rather well - although he needs some
> lessons in the perfect gentleman's toilette. I have offered to teach him
> the art of maquillage just as soon as he cheers up. Anyone who says he
> killed Valentine is off his head, by the way, as I always maintained. He
> definitely did not do it.*
>
> *P.P.S. Now I think of it, I probably shouldn't have written the above
> (about G. I mean) but I am too exhausted to scrub it all and start
> another letter.*

*

Jerome's letter lay, along with several others, unopened on the breakfast table next to a cup of cooling black coffee. Aleister Crowley had been up late into the night. After talking to Watson, he had continued working on into the early hours in preparation for a meeting of the Order. This morning he had a headache. He was jotting down a record of a scrying session in his Grimoire which had rather segued into some scathing opinions of the others in the Order and their misapplied conjuring. He had so many fundamental disagreements with them that things would tend to burst into open warfare over the slightest details.

He paused, losing his thread to remember with satisfaction how he had recently offended Yeats with horrible and unjustified criticism of his poetry. After a while, he returned to his coffee and finding it undrinkable, lit a cigarette instead. Then he slit open the envelopes waiting for him. Bills: tailor, membership of a club, tobacconist, wine merchant. Letters: one from his mother (he threw it towards the bin - he abhorred her brainless religious bigotry, which obliged her to perform daily acts of the most senseless atrocity upon herself and others); one from his friend Allan Bennett, which was probably mournfully detailing his current state of health; one from Pollitt.

He ignored the others and read Pollitt's letter. Damn, he thought after reading the body of the letter, why did Jerome think he could just drop everything and go and play at an obscure hotel in the heart of – oh, Somerset? It was entirely his own fault that he was there. Ridiculous. Since he had been gone, Crowley had found himself after all more than equal to the solitude. Indeed, when immersed in writing, he remembered, he always found Jerome a severe distraction and would banish him from his rooms in Cambridge. He had his experiments to tend, he wanted to talk to Watson about some things he had discovered about the use of human ears and other appendages in magical practices; and his desire to question George Arden was becoming something of an obsession.

He was about to fling the letter aside, also in the rough direction of the bin but without quite the same vigour, when he took the time to read the two post scripts. He paused, savouring the knowledge that sublime synchronicities were at work, then jumped up, thinking to go to Watson and tell him the whereabouts of Arden.

*

George was wandering alone on the slopes of the valley. The treetops boiled with rooks jeering at each other over the evening roost. Now and then he looked up at them, swallowing down the hot fear which kept rising to his throat. All he wanted to do was run away. Ever since he came to the house, ever since he stepped into the black coach at the station, he had felt the strong presence of the woman with the knife. And whilst sitting in the salon, watching the others sing and play their card games, he had been kept constant company by a lady with bandaged feet, always, sitting near him, dumb and staring. She would not talk, she would not signal. As he left the salon to go up to his own room, she would be there, standing at the roped-off entrance to a dark corridor. He knew she wanted him to go down there but he did not want to. That way led to a shade of horror: the same emanating from Mrs Roberts now. He had hardly recognised his landlady through the overwhelming sense of something deep inside her, silently going wrong.

At some point, the lady in the portrait, the lady with the knife, would return and they would meet. Her very presence in Mrs Roberts's house had made him flee (it seemed such a long time ago, but it was a matter of no more than a month) and now he knew he was in *her* house and had nowhere to go. He had a little money given to him by Mrs Day but he couldn't go back to London. He was wanted by the police. There was no shelter here, nowhere to scavenge food, no friendly tumbledown buildings to hide in, just the bald winter hills and the rooks. His only companion was Pollitt and he found it impossible to communicate his terrors to him. He was kind and funny but he wasn't like that friend of his, Crowley. George had perceived that one like a multiplicity, a pack of playing cards. He could have understood. Jerome was different: charming, funny, but easily bored, sometimes impatient, often anxious.

George had left the hotel in order to get away from the lady with the bandaged feet. She seemed tied to the boundaries of the walls and couldn't follow him. The valley itself was a brooding place. He avoided the hot springs of Erecura and the angry guardians, disturbed since the removal of their totems. That had been another cause of terror for George. The three white heads, set up in the salon like frivolous souvenirs from a holiday, telegraphing to him the terrible details of their creation. George had had to shut out this information at every turn, while waves of sound dashed at him from the piano and he saw the odd distorted shapes of the mouths of singers, separated from the music and meaning. He wished he was safe in Harriet Day's attic again as he picked his way back towards the hotel as the light faded. Yellow-looking storm clouds were brewing at the head of the valley.

It was late, maybe past midnight, and Alexandra was restless, unsleeping. She paced about her room, going to the window from time to time and staring out at the eclipsed valley. She wanted to go and walk out to the place of the rising water and feel its heat as it came out of the ground. She would be alone. She would slip her clothes off entirely and stand right in the deep part of the spring, in the total blackness. There would be darkness and noise, freezing air and hot water and that gaping, pumping funnel from the underworld.

She imagined herself doing that, getting herself dressed, coat, shoes, explaining to the sleepy night porter that she needed to walk, carrying a lantern through the woods. It made her shiver, fearful; and almost as if just by thinking of it she had made a pact to do it, she began to hurry to get dressed with nervous fingers. Suddenly the window shook and a great rattle of hail was thrown against the glass. The branches would be tossing in the gale. Should she still go out to the well? She opened the window to feel the sting of ice on her face.

Sense prevailed and with an idea of having cheated someone out of something, she assumed her night clothes again. After some thought, she opened the drawer in the bedside cabinet and took out the battered black notebook. She had not finished reading it. It was both precious and difficult. She had meted it out to herself like the yellowish stale pills. But she was nearing the end. She brought the lamp close and sat on her bed, propped up by the pillows.

In this section of the notebook, ideas had been jotted down apparently in a great hurry.

And this is the remarkable conclusion. The formula hinted at within the invocation has become clear and I think I now understand the meaning. The apparent discontinuities and contradictions within it are deliberate, an occultation. Or they are scribal errors. For it is not merely a poem, it is not empty religious diorama, it is not quaint theatre: it is *technology of a sort that we have forgotten how to use. Far subtler than a combustion engine or the electric telegraph. It is a step-by-step guide to the correct procedures for invocation and use of a certain kind of <u>energy</u>. What the nature of that energy is I do not know – magnetic, electrical, etheric? My dear Joseph believed there is one thing missing, however, a component only hinted at in the text - and although he had definite ideas as to how the missing piece is to be obtained, I will not set them down here.*

Alexandra paused. She felt strange. Looking up, the room was spinning before her eyes. She did not feel well enough to read on. As she closed the book, it dropped from her hands, falling face down on a page towards the end. Picking it up, she saw a rough pencil sketch. It was dated 1876 and signed with the initials M.A. It showed a naked woman, flanked by lions and owls. In each upraised hand, the figure held what she now knew to be a twisted knot of reeds, symbolising the doorposts. Her feet were the talons of a bird and wings drooped from her shoulders like a cloak.

CHAPTER TWENTY-THREE

After his long conversation with Crowley, Dr Watson found it difficult to sleep for the remainder of the night. The more he thought about the strange box and its contents, the more his chest tightened. He had to sit up, dozing and waking through the small hours. In the end, he tried to alleviate his breathing by burning a powder recommended by a Dr Beverley of Scarborough. Watson read through the ingredients:

> *Datura tatula, stramonium, cannabis, and lobelia, with 4 drachms of nitre and ⅓ drachm of eucalyptus oil. A teaspoonful to be burnt occasionally and the fumes inhaled.*

He coughed during treatment; but was able to go to bed, feeling pleasantly floaty, just as he heard the milkman's cart rattle in the street below and Mrs Hudson stirring in the room above.

There was no doubt about it: he needed a good eight hours sleep these days, he thought to himself, as he tried to clear his head over coffee. Mrs Hudson was not sympathetic as she too had been disturbed in the night - by himself trampling up the stairs at a late hour, she said. She made it clear that she expected a quiet life when Mr Holmes was away. Watson was not too sure if she had been charged with keeping an eye not merely on his health but on his general behaviour. He resented the schoolboyish feeling which occasionally swept over him under her eye.

He received an enigmatic note on the back of a picture postcard from Holmes in the post this morning. The note merely said, 'Greetings, S.H.'. He put it wistfully onto the mantelpiece. It was stamped 'Eastbourne' and showed a picture of the pier with some solid-looking ladies promenading nearby. Holmes had connections in the area but Watson knew better than to imagine his friend might really be staying there. The postcard would have been posted by a go-between. He knew it was a routine part of a ruse to build an alibi — Holmes was, after all, engaged in a case of the highest diplomatic moment. If something were to go wrong, it would be typical of him - and Her Majesty's Government - to make sure there was a cover story in place to exonerate all concerned of complicity. Nevertheless, it was still a secret sign between them.

The postcard combined with his lingering ill health and tiredness to make him feel a little low. He cheered himself by imagining sitting opposite Holmes and telling him, in a measured, assured manner, of the Mystery of the Stolen Heads in the Graveyard. No, that was too clumsy. The Case of the Graveyard Decapitations. The Mystery of the Ears in the Box. No, better: The Box of Ears. Yes, that produced the necessary frisson. Watson's literary agent, Dr Conan Doyle, would appreciate that. He went, in a kind of author's trance, to his desk and began writing:

THE BOX OF EARS

In the first cold months of 1898, Mr Sherlock Holmes was called away on an urgent matter of national importance, leaving me ~~suffering alone from ill health~~ *in sole possession of his rooms, his documents and my usual modest armchair at his fireside. My peaceful sojourn was, however, swiftly interrupted by a series of sinister events: events which made me sorely miss my friend's flame-like intuitions. It happened that a curious coincidence threw me into the company of a strange young man who ...*

Watson stopped himself. The fact was he did not know the end of the story. In order to solve the mystery of the ears and the heads, he would have to wait until Crowley had sought out the man called Bateman again; and he would probably need to give him some money. Money. Was his cheque book still locked in the drawer? Had Holmes got the key? He made a little investigation of his finances and found all was well. After that, he stuck his head out of the window to determine the atmospheric conditions and whether it would be safe to breathe in the streets today. There was indeed a cold, yellowish look to the air. Visibility was poor. The buildings opposite, glimpsed through the mist, looked like ruins of an ancient, lost London. He sighed and decided that it would be safer this morning to continue his researches inside, in the hope that later the fog would clear. Being confined to the house when there was so much to do was not to his taste at all.

*

'George, Edward, whatever you're calling yourself today. Wake up!' Pollitt tapped on George's door more loudly. Then, finding it was unlocked, he went in. George was not in bed. He was fully dressed, sitting on the window seat with his knees drawn up, looking out over the valley. He turned his face to Pollitt.

'Well, *you* look ghastly,' said Jerome placidly. 'In fact, I'd go so far as to say that for a place which is supposed to promote health and happiness, it seems to be doing the absolute opposite for you. You look,' Pollitt regarded George with his head on one side, 'you look frumpy. I mean that in the nicest possible way; but take it as a warning. So come down for breakfast. I can't stand it alone. The Major will be harrumphing and Lady Helena will throw egg and bacon everywhere and Mrs Roberts will drift past everyone like a snowy cloud atop Mount Fuji; and for that matter, you'll sit there shivering without so much as a squeak. In fact,' he finished, sitting down on the side of George's bed with a deep sigh, 'this entire holiday is becoming simply horrible. If it weren't for the fact that I'm making a point by staying here, I wouldn't stay here. I am so bored I could kill myself.'

George watched him and said nothing.

'Why are you so damned passive, George?' Pollitt allowed himself to sink backwards onto the bed and addressed the ceiling. 'Why do you never speak, never share an emotion, never discover, never run, never play, never – never live? Are you, in fact, dead, George? Is that the problem? It is, isn't it? Tell me, then, you died twenty years ago and at night you sleep in a coffin on a pile of your native earth. You are a vampire in negative, then. Don't contradict me. I know I'm right. And I know you'll say nothing at all to this monologue, however rude I am; and I might as well be talking to myself. Do you know, you confirm every bitter, hopeless, anguished, despairing thought I have about this universe and our place in it?'

He turned his head to see how George was taking this and was surprised to see that his companion had his face in his hands. Immediately, Pollitt rolled over and off the bed. He went and stood in front of George, putting his hands on his shoulders and shook him gently. 'Oh, come now. I was joking! What's the matter with you? Tell sweet little Polly. Is it just because you're being hunted by the police for murder? Never mind about that, it'll all get cleared up, one way or another. Either your good name will be restored or they'll hang you. It's perfectly straightforward. Nothing to worry about. Oh come on, I'm joking, George! You have absolutely no sense of humour.'

George emerged from behind his hands.

'I once read of a case, you know, of a man who really did believe he was dead,' said Pollitt, sitting down next to him on the window seat. 'Did you know I was going to be a doctor once? Well, I was. In fact, I would have been a resoundingly good doctor but life and the theatre got in the way and I didn't put quite as much effort into my studies as was required. So, anyway, I read this extremely interesting case study and the gentleman in question *was* dead in a sense, dead to the world. And it turned out the reason for it all was giving in to despair on regular occasions.' He put his arm in a brotherly fashion round George's thin shoulders. 'Now, I am the last person to lecture anybody on how they should live their lives and I think that melancholia is a horrible thing (and I should know). But I'll tell you a secret. Listen to me, George. The cure for melancholia is threefold. One, singing. Two, dancing. Three, love. That's it. And there is a fourth. Four, breakfast; also known as regular and sufficient nourishment. So come, put on your shoes. Come and watch Lady Helena juggling.'

As they passed a roped-off corridor at the bottom of the stairs, George paused and looked intently into the unlit passageway. 'She's there again, but this time she's signalling to me. Oh, Pollitt. Do I have to go down there?'

'What?' asked Pollitt, glancing from George's face to the empty corridor and back again. 'Who is signalling? Has Lady Helena gone off her rocker and taken to wandering about the hotel like a frightful chimpanzee in a red wig?'

'It's the one with the bandaged feet,' said George. 'She won't leave me alone. She sits so close, staring into my face whenever I'm in the salon. Now she's gone further down the corridor than ever before. She's pointing at a door. Pollitt, I don't want to go down there. I really don't.'

'Do you know what I think?' said Jerome. 'I think that *hunger* and lack of sleep and worry is causing you to create some very imaginative phantoms out of naturally-occurring shadows. Particularly hunger. Once you've been fed and watered, you'll feel so much better. I'll trot you round the valley later, like a little pony. In fact, you *are* similar to a pony, George, being so small and short but not so shaggy.'

'Will you come with me, Jerome? Will you just walk a little way down here with me, so that I can see what she wants?'

Pollitt was alarmed at this development, but he was also genuinely kind-hearted and upset by George's distress. 'All right, we'll walk a few steps down the corridor, since it's daytime and there's plenty of light coming through the windows. Though it does look somewhat misty down there. It must be dust from the stonemasons or something. If there are stonemasons here. I haven't seen any but it's the sort of place where stonemasons would lurk.'

The pair slipped past the dividing rope and began pacing slowly along the passageway, Pollitt gripping George's arm. He kept up a running commentary as they proceeded. 'These old doors are massively thick. Look at the arches, George. They are in the Norman or Romanesque style, do you see? This place is even older than I thought. The bit we're all in, it's no more than Mad George – not you, George, I mean His Majesty King George. But this, this is an abbey or some such devastatingly grim building. I can feel the holiness infecting me. There was probably one solitary monk here and two hundred peasants to keep him stoked up with sufficient head of steam to perform the prayers and keep the devil from jumping on them in the dark. Oh, George, is this the place?'

George had stopped at the end of the corridor outside a door of black oak. He pushed the latch down and simultaneously turned the handle but the door only rattled.

'George. A large keyhole requires a large key. Can't you see?'

'She says there is a way in,' answered George with a bewildered glance at Pollitt. 'If there is a way in, it isn't through the door here. You'll have to show us.'

'Me?' asked Jerome.

'No, the lady there.'

'But the lady there *isn't* there, George. She is in your head, waving and suffering with her bunions or whatever you imagine is wrong with her. And now is definitely the time for food. Nothing else will do, not even a troupe of – well, never mind. Come on, come on.' He pulled George back down the corridor.

They walked through the hall. Glancing into the library through its half-glazed doors, Pollitt saw that Mrs Roberts was seated at a table in a kind of trance, furiously writing in a notebook. 'Look, George,' he said. 'This just proves that every single person in this hotel is stark staring mad.'

George looked unhappily in the direction that Jerome pointed. 'Yes,' he agreed.

*

Dr Watson's morning confinement had been alleviated by a brief visit from Crowley, who had flapped a letter from Jerome Pollitt triumphantly in the air and said it revealed the whereabouts of George Arden; and announced he planned to track down Bateman today if he could. They sorted out sufficient bribe-money between them after a slight altercation - Crowley was rich and overestimated what inducement should be offered. After he had left, Dr Watson reflected that his opinion of the young fellow was improving – he was at least energetic and determined. At the same time, Watson did not care to be outdone and, remembering that it was his duty to share information with his almost-client Harriet Day, took a cab to Pimlico.

The air was clearing at last although fog still veiled the church spires with an illusion of unguessed height. To add to the broil, some workmen in Baker Street were breaking up stones for the road and there was a strong smell of tar. On the way, he debated whether to ask Mrs Day directly about the whereabouts of Arden, reveal it himself or let her do so in her own way; and whether to tell her about the ears and the box or if that would be too shocking for a lady.

Harriet was in the middle of a piano lesson. It would be a good fifteen minutes before he could interview her. Since he had come so far, he decided to wait and was shown into a room where early daffodils in a crystal vase adorned the table. There was a small but vivid portrait over the fireplace which he readily identified as the lady he had come to see. Inevitably, Watson found himself comparing her with his late wife, Mary. He had to remind himself sternly that he was in no position to become sentimentally attached again. Holmes would simply kill him.

Watson could detect that Mrs Day was pleased to see him; but after they had greeted each other, she surprised him by turning to a cupboard in a business-like fashion and pulling out a file containing notes. When they sat down, she balanced it on her knee. 'Well, Doctor. Thank you for coming to see me. You've saved me a journey, because I was thinking I should come and see you. I have a great deal to tell you.'

'Indeed?' said Watson.

'I expect you have something to tell me too,' said Harriet kindly with a nod. 'You go first.'

Dr Watson cleared his throat and summarised yesterday's events at the house of Alexandra Roberts, optimistically mentioning the housemaid's testimony as well as the discovery of the ears. He then returned to Crowley's report about Bateman and the case of the human heads. Mrs Day listened intently. When he had finished, she said, 'That is quite encouraging, isn't it? Doesn't it imply terrible things about Burroughs?'

Watson explained about the law relating to human body parts, how Burroughs could simply have employed Bateman in a journalistic capacity and all the difficulties of proving that there was any kind of wrongdoing associated with the ears; and then the impossibility of getting any of that information to prove that his testimony about Valentine's death was false.

Harriet considered this for a moment. 'Like a Chinese Box,' she murmured. 'Let me tell you some of the things I've been discovering. First of all, I need to tell you that Mr Williams came to see me. He told me about the box, of course –' (Watson nodded, now realising why Mrs Day's reaction had been so muted); '- and he told me something else interesting. He said that Burroughs has stolen - or borrowed, I suppose one must allow - an oil sketch from the studio of Alexandra Roberts, a portrait, and placed it in his own bedroom. Actually removed it from Mrs Roberts's studio! The cheek! What do you make of that, doctor?'

'Strange perhaps but I fail to see – unless it is particularly relevant to our problem with Burroughs? Is the subject matter apposite?'

'Well, the subject matter has relevance to what I will tell you in a moment. It is the preparatory sketch of a woman known to my friend Alexandra. It's uncharacteristic of the man – have you met him?'

'No, I have not, and would like to keep it that way for now.'

'Yes, I can understand that. But to explain my point further: Mr Burroughs is a cold, fastidious kind of creature. Doting on a sentimental portrait isn't at all the behaviour I would expect – one would hardly consider him capable of such a thing.'

'Well, perhaps it is worth making a note of,' said Watson.

Harriet held her hand up. 'Wait, please. I took it a little further. I have a particular interest in the subject of the portrait. She is a powerful woman, Minerva Atwell by name. As I say, she is not personally known to me, except by repute. Mr Williams was quite incensed at the thought of Burroughs making himself free in Alexandra's studio. He's even been hatching a plot to remove the portrait and put it back where it belongs.'

'Why would Williams remove the portrait, Mrs Day? We don't know, presumably, whether the artist gave her permission to Burroughs to put it in his room.'

'Mr Williams is rather protective of Mrs Roberts's property – and believes, as do I, that Burroughs is lying about George. Anyway, I was alarmed – and I can't quite tell you why at the moment. So I looked up the address of Minerva Atwell's business, Atwell Beauty and Health.'

'Very well,' said Watson. 'And?'

Harriet went rather pink at this point. 'I know it may sound odd to you but I personally dislike Mrs Atwell intensely. I don't trust her, I believe she tells lies and I don't think she is a good influence on my friend Alex; and – well, I went to the British Library to check the diplomatic records in the London Gazette. Yes, I know, Doctor. You are going to say that I have overstepped genteel behaviour. Well. So be it. I discovered a single fact which means that more or less everything she has been telling Alexandra is a tissue of lies.'

'Ah? What exactly do you mean?'

'It began as a paltry thing really. Mr Williams told me about it: just a silly boast she made to Alex, that she was present for a particular event which, it turns out, she simply could not have been. It stuck in my mind. In researching the thing, I proved to my own satisfaction that the man she claims was her first husband was either really her father or perhaps an uncle. Joseph Rupert Atwell C.M.G. of Her Majesty's Diplomatic Corps – Alex spoke endlessly of Minerva Atwell's adventures with him. Well, he died of a long-drawn out illness in 1876 - and Mrs Atwell must have been born about that year. It's all in here,' she said, patting the file.

'You've been very thorough, Mrs Day,' said Watson, a little non-plussed.

'Yes. There's more than that, though. Finding that this Atwell is associated with Burroughs, on behalf of my wronged friend George Arden I had every intention of finding out as much about them as I could. Yesterday, I went over to the offices of Atwell Beauty and

Health in Camberwell to see whether they would answer some questions.'

'Remarkable!' exclaimed Watson.

'Yes, well, I pretended to be trying to trace a relative – in fact, I said I was Mr Burroughs's aunt, who had returned from abroad, and that this was the last address I had for him. I asked if there was any record of the man having been employed there. To my considerable surprise, I was able to discover some rather interesting details. Burroughs *was* employed there a few years ago – I don't know in what capacity. I spoke to a very obliging lady called Mrs Shelley, in charge of the general office. She did not have much detail about Burroughs, though she remembered him. Said he was proud, not given to mixing socially, and then said he had access to Minerva Atwell because he was related. Related! When I asked how, she asked in surprise, didn't I know he was a step-brother or half-brother or some such? Obviously, I couldn't ask more as it rather showed up my deception. I had to leave at that point rather than expose my ignorance any further.'

'That really is interesting, Mrs Day,' said Watson. He regarded Harriet curiously. 'I hope you won't be offended,' he said. 'I am just wondering why you have gone to such trouble to research this connection between Burroughs and Mrs Atwell?'

'Well, I had to – because of George.'

'Why would George Arden be known to Mrs Atwell though?'

Harriet cleared her throat, leaned forward and said in a low voice, 'Very well, Doctor. You have guessed. The truth is, I sent George to hide in the country at a place where Alexandra is staying: it's called the Adsullata Hotel. And it is owned - or at least is run by - Minerva Atwell. When I discovered there might be a connection between Atwell and Burroughs, well, I feared that I'd sent Mr Arden into further danger. What if there should be a chance of Burroughs turning up there, for example?'

'H'mm,' said Watson. He looked towards the door for moment and held a finger to his lips. He said clearly, 'I'm afraid I didn't hear any of the details of your last speech, Mrs Day. I sometimes suffer from temporary hearing loss.'

Harriet nodded gratefully. 'It was nothing of importance, Doctor. I shan't weary you by repeating it.'

*

While Dr Watson was visiting Harriet Day, Aleister Crowley was scouring the alleys near Fleet street. There were innumerable ragged figures in the streets of London and, dynamic and impatient as he was, he quickly became frustrated at the tedious complexity of the task. How was he to find Charles Bateman in all this vast city? He had decided to stay in the vicinity of Burroughs's newspaper offices, thinking that he was bound to return to file his stories and perhaps Bateman would emerge in due course.

As he looked out of the window of the A.B.C. Tea Rooms in Fleet Street, he wondered what would happen to Sherlock Holmes's readership if Watson told the truth and filled page after page with accounts of loitering on street corners, walking miles and sitting in foetid coffee shops? He was just sighing to himself as the afternoon dimmed and reflecting that he could probably float a small battleship in the quantity of threepenny tea he had drunk today at the Aerated Bread Company, when Albert Burroughs walked straight past the window. Luck, at last.

The cold air hit him after the warmth of the shop. He followed the figure of Burroughs as he strode rapidly along the crowded pavements, hoping his guess was right. After a little while, Burroughs cut down towards Victoria Embankment and the Thames. Beyond the line of streetlamps, the slippery unstable skin of the river was dancing with points of lights. It was here that Crowley paused by a tree and spotted Bateman slinking along the railings of the darkening gardens. He saw him approach Burroughs, saying something. He put a hand on his arm. Burroughs, who was holding a thick file of papers, shook him off. The man touched his forearm again, talking urgently. Burroughs looked angry but seemed to offer some kind of compromise because Bateman suddenly let him go. He stood hunched up in his thin jacket, watching Burroughs stride away, the coat tails of his heavy black overcoat flapping as he went.

It was already nearly dark in the narrow side street leading back up to the Strand where Crowley caught up with Bateman. He noticed how the small man made to duck aside as he heard footsteps catching up with him. 'Mr Bateman?' called Crowley pleasantly. 'Don't be alarmed. I am a friend of Albert Burroughs. I need to talk to you.'

Bateman turned. The twilight lifted his thin face out of the gloom.

Crowley could see that it was a little streaked with soot and deeply lined around the mouth. His expression was fearful. 'Burroughs sent you? Then say straight away what you want, or I'm calling out for help. Quickly. I give you five seconds.'

Crowley realised he had played the wrong card. He said, 'Well, Burroughs is not a friend, as such. I see he is not a friend of yours either. Give me an opportunity to explain, Mr Bateman! I mean you no harm.' He went on as Bateman waited, half turned away as if ready to run, 'I think I may be able to help you. I work with a friend of Mr Sherlock Holmes. You may have heard of him? No? The celebrated consulting detective? Well, anyway, we are trying to trace all previous associates of Mr Albert Burroughs. There may be financial compensation to be claimed.'

He laid emphasis on the word *compensation* and was rewarded with a slight change in Bateman's expression. He went on in a steady, matter-of-fact voice, hoping that the deductions that Watson and he had made were correct. 'We understand that you, Mr Bateman, had to endure a term of imprisonment as a result of carrying out the instructions of Mr Burroughs and that you were left without adequate financial redress.'

'You can say that again,' said Bateman in a more decided voice.

'You worked with or for Burroughs?' asked Crowley.

'For him. To my cost. And I have very much gone down in the world, sir, because of him. And all through doing what he asked, I lost my job. A good job I had. One of the Mortuary Attendants at Barts I was. It's a good, respectable job.'

'So what was his purpose in employing you?'

'I never understood his purpose. He never offered to tell me neither, just said that he had been commissioned by a very important scientific body, but he would never give me particulars or proof. He was very persuasive.'

'How did you come to be involved with this – this business?'

'Which business?' said Bateman suspiciously.

'Are there many businesses for which you have served time in prison, Mr Bateman?' asked Crowley. 'We're talking about providing heads, getting heads from a graveyard and being apprehended with them in your possession.'

'Ye-es,' said Bateman. 'Yes, that is the business I had in mind too. How did I come to be mixed up in it? Well, he sought me out.

Burroughs sought me out, came on all friendly, got me involved almost before I knew it. And now I think of it, if you're so interested in my financial situation, you should be paying proper rates for this information.'

'Quite right, Mr Bateman,' said Crowley. 'I was just going to suggest the same thing. Will half a sovereign be sufficient this evening?'

'That's more like it, much more like it,' said Bateman. He began to relax. His shoulders looked less hunched and he faced Crowley squarely. 'Money beforehand please.'

Crowley handed over a small gold coin. He hoped that Bateman would not take off with it without imparting a little more information. Bateman muttered apologetically something about 'just making sure 'tain't snide, no offence' and took care to bite the coin, weigh it in his hand and then stow it deep inside his clothes.

'So, tell me, how did this Burroughs take advantage of your good nature, Mr Bateman?'

'He hung round the mortuary, didn't he? Took me to dinner, out to Simpson's, all very nice. Then before I knew it, he got me a little way into it, getting him a souvenir. It was a strange thing to ask anyone, but he was forceful – I can hardly tell you how he drew me in. Perhaps it started when he did me a favour, unasked like, gave me an advance on a sum of money I needed, and in return, a bit later, he insisted on this souvenir. You know, I never drink myself, not more than a pint; but he got me stupid drunk one night. Mixed something in with it, most likely, said I'd agreed though I had no memory of it. Said he'd taken a fancy to it and it was a sign we could work together in the future, like, a sign of trust between us. *Now* I understand what he was doing but I didn't then. It was a way to draw me in, sir, under his power and influence, for once a little way in, you know, you can't just go back.'

'What was the souvenir?' asked Crowley fascinated. 'From a corpse was it?'

'Yes, it was. An item from a corpse. A finger.'

'How very curious,' murmured Crowley. 'And I suppose he then had an incriminating item he could say that you alone could have provided?'

'Exactly, sir. He kept it and said he would tell my superiors that I had been boasting about it when I was drunk like.'

'Yes, yes, I see. I understand how his mind would work,' said Crowley. 'And I suppose he forced you to provide what he wanted. What was it, heads? And in the end, they found out?'

'Of course — them bodies are for the medical students, not for outsiders. I lost my job, as I said. He still wanted more and employed me for it. Well, what could I do? Where was I to find honest work after getting sacked and without a character reference? And when the parts weren't good enough, how could I change that? By the time they reach the graveyard, they're days old. He said he wanted them hours old, minutes old. Not possible, I told him. And those paupers' graves are deep and, though open to the sky while they get filled, tainted with dangerous gases. A man can die — twenty feet deep, some of them! I scrambled about doing the most atrocious things for him in the dark after the sexton had gone home but they were never fresh enough. You won't be able to imagine it, sir, you really won't.'

'Oh, I can,' said Crowley. 'But tell me what happened then? You were caught with three heads in a bag, I understand?'

'After they got me, I was very good to him. Very loyal. Not a word I said, thinking to get my reward for that in good time. You'd think he'd make it up to me, but no. Barely five shillings at a time he gives me. What's that, five shillings? Five guineas more like! And keeps me hanging around, hanging around, having to beg for it too. My profession all ruined along of him.'

'He wanted them fresh, you say?' said Crowley, trying to steer him back to the matter of the heads. 'Freshly killed?'

'No, not freshly *killed*. What do you take me for? Just freshly deposited, new dead, if you see what I mean. But they are the very ones as the students need the most from the morgue. You can understand why, can't you, sir, because who would want something old and dug up? No, they come fresh enough for the students into the mortuary from the workhouse, but once I lost my position, sir, it was just the leavings of the graveyard. And they weren't fresh enough for him.'

'I wonder why?' said Crowley. 'Did he ever say what would happen to those heads, Mr Bateman?'

'No idea, no idea. Don't care neither. Anyway, he never told me nothing about it. He just wanted heads for experiments, I suppose. For scientists, like Doctor Frankenstein. That's what I presumed and he never contradicted me.'

'Very well,' said Crowley. 'So you don't know the purpose for which these body parts were needed. And what is the significance of the ears?'

'Ears?'

'Burroughs was instructed to remove the ears, is that not correct?'

Bateman made a sound like a laugh on a nervous intake of breath. 'No! Not he. He just liked doing it. He liked the sound it made when he snipped them off, that's what he said. He carried a particular pair of silver wire cutters for the purpose.' His eyes flashed as he looked stealthily behind him, checking the darkness. 'When I recall the look on his face at the time, it scares me,' he continued, turning back to Crowley. 'That man is a man with no natural feeling. I would prefer to get right away from him. I would prefer a sum of money to seek out another life altogether. I'd take myself off to the Americas or Australia if I could. But he keeps me dangling, dripping out my life, drop by drop, because he likes it. He's cruel. I begged him to ask *them*, them scientific gentlemen, for fifty pounds to buy passage out of England. He could do it, but he don't. He likes to torment creatures. I am a creature he is tormenting.'

Crowley suppressed a desire to point out that if Bateman gave up blackmailing Burroughs, he was free to seek a life elsewhere. He said, 'And is there anything else you can recall about a connection Burroughs might have had? No name, no place? Where for example did he take the things once you had provided them?'

'I don't know, sir. It was not a matter I cared to ask about. Burroughs, you know, he is a cold man but forceful when crossed.'

'I see, Mr Bateman. Your information is invaluable.' Crowley took another gold coin from his pocket. 'Take it and this too, this calling card. It is the address of the detective I mentioned – any further information you happen to recall will, I am sure, be adequately rewarded.'

Bateman took the gold hastily as though he thought the offer would be withdrawn and then inspected the card. 'Very well. I won't lose *this.*' He put it away and continued to stare at Crowley as if expecting him to do a conjuring trick. Crowley enjoyed his amazement for a while and then said, 'Well, thank you. I'll not keep you longer. I wish you a good evening.'

'Wait a minute, sir. If you was to find a way of getting to them, these scientific gentlemen, and telling them about me - for they may not know my story - tell them to help out an old employee who suffered for their business. Tell them about my sorry state! You can find me at The Ram in Shoreditch – round the back, there's a stable loft I sleep in.'

Crowley answered, 'It is highly unlikely that I'll be able to do any such thing, Mr Bateman, I will not mislead you. I am not working for the scientists, although I would be fascinated to hear about their work. If you do recall any clue or crumb of information, please bring it to the address on the card. And, if you would take a word of advice for your own self-respect and sanity, remember, you still have your health. You have your limbs. You can take yourself away from here, leave this arrangement which keeps you weak and vulnerable, find any honest job. Even settling South of the River would take you beyond his influence.'

Bateman shook his head. 'It's more difficult than you can possibly imagine, sir. And you can't just walk into another parish. Every street is somebody's possession. You have to fight. I can't fight no more. You can't think how hard it is, once gone wrong, to go right.'

CHAPTER TWENTY-FOUR

After Dr Watson left, Harriet began to wonder wrily if perhaps she herself could find employment as a consulting detective. She sat down at the piano to think things through. Alexandra had clearly got herself tied up with a dangerous woman – Mrs Atwell was a liar, unstable, manipulative; and, as Mr Williams had informed her and Dr Watson had confirmed, had a step-brother who kept a box full of mummified ears under his bed. Appalling! After a while, she rose and went to the writing desk.

> *My dearest Alexandra,*
>
> *I am so grateful for all that you are doing for Edward and I do hope that it is not at all a burden to you. I am glad too to hear that he is accompanied by another young man.*
>
> *I want to discuss so many things with you, Alex my dear! I too am becoming quite fascinated by the history of the Near East. I wonder if you could tell me, where was Mrs Atwell's husband stationed and what other digs did she visit? It must be so exciting to see treasures such as the Jewels of Helen actually in the process of being discovered, especially at such a young age!*
>
> *But perhaps I will have the delightful honour of talking these things over with her myself. I have quite decided to take a holiday and I am convinced that there can be no better place than the place where you are. It will take a few days to arrange things with my students but I am delighted to announce that I will be joining you at the Adsullata as soon as may be.*
>
> *I am so enchanted to think that soon I will again be in person*
> *Your affectionate friend,*
> *Harriet.*

Harriet rather shocked herself when she wrote the last paragraph. She had not been planning at all to go to the hotel but her pen had simply chosen for her. She left the letter open on the desk and decided to think for a good hour before she sent it. She was conscious of the malicious undercurrent in what she had written and had to read it through three times to see if Alexandra would be horribly offended. She would know that Harriet had been gossiping with Mr Williams and she would know that Harriet wanted to point out the conflict in dates. Well, she could always re-write the thing, she thought as she went down to the kitchen and informed Mrs

Skipton that she planned to go away in the course of the next few days.

*

'So, to summarise,' Watson said, after he had made detailed notes of Bateman's words (with the private intention of turning them into dialogue in his write-up of the case), 'it looks as though the heads were obtained by Bateman for Albert Burroughs in order to pass them on to a private scientific establishment. *Looks* like that - except that any reputable establishment would be able to apply for a licence and could legally obtain what was required. Obviously, he was lied to. And as for this habit of removing the ears, well, that is a disturbing feature to say the least. What on earth motivated Burroughs to do that?'

'You might need to read his pornographic papers to find that out, Doctor. Also, Bateman mentioned Dr Frankenstein,' said Crowley. 'Are there, to your knowledge, secret organisations of medical men intent on stitching body parts together to learn the secret of life? Is such a thing possible?'

'You are mistaking science for sensational novels, Mr Crowley. Or possibly for your own necromantic experiments,' said Watson drily. 'And please put those ideas aside. You are however quite right about the improper writings – I shall study them. It strikes me that the man is –'

'–working very hard to suppress a shadow. Perhaps you will finally listen to my ideas? Look, it fits beautifully: he pins those things to little catalogue cards, pigeonholes them in a box and writes up reports! He's filing stories on his interior struggle like a – like a war correspondent from the front line, like a journalist would. It remains to be seen whether his reports are based on fact or are merely a safety valve - but when this filing system fails him, my instinct tells me that he will become more dangerous.'

'H'm. You have an unusual view on the matter. Perhaps it has some virtue, Crowley.'

'Generous of you.'

'But perhaps the system, as you put it, has already failed him? At least, it is no longer under his control, because his box is now in the possession of the police. How that will affect him I cannot guess. I think Bateman needs to be persuaded to speak to Detective

Browning as quickly as may be.'

'Very well, Doctor. I'll undertake to go in search of the fellow again tomorrow. But it's been a long day and I don't feel inclined to trek over to Shoreditch tonight.'

Watson nodded. 'Good. Let's see now. Aside from that, the other thing in your report that intrigues me is the requirement that the heads be absolutely fresh. A student who simply wished to study the organic structure, layers of the dermis, for example, would be satisfied with a body part a day or so old, especially in winter.'

'Then what do you deduce, Doctor?'

'I do not know. I will have to think about it.' He studied his notes.

'What about that servant girl's evidence, Doctor?' asked Crowley, leaning back with his hands behind his head and staring at the large 'V' that Holmes had once shot into the wall. 'Suppose he finds out that she has shared information with you which flatly contradicts his story? What then?'

'You think she could be in danger?'

'I don't know! You're the experienced detective's assistant. What is your opinion? Should she be removed or can we trust that Burroughs is still a rational actor?'

'Are you thinking that he would threaten the child to stop her testifying, Crowley? It would be tantamount to an admission of guilt. Think what he has to lose if she went to the authorities! No, a servant girl's testimony is not worth so much, not compared to that of a respectable fellow like Burroughs. Not until the man feels genuinely threatened would he take such a course. But then, who knows? Unpredictable once he stops being predictable, don't you think?'

'Oh very well,' said Crowley. He yawned and stretched. 'I can't think about this any more. When "Old Tick Tock" loses control, his shadow takes over, that's the only thought I'll leave you with. I must be getting home. Just tell me, what do you intend to do next?'

'I might do a little investigation of Burroughs's history, I suppose. Where he comes from, where did he live before, that sort of thing. Somerset House is a good place to start.'

'I see,' said Crowley doubtfully. 'So this is the even more boring bit of detective work, is it?'

'Regrettably, yes,' said Dr Watson.

When Crowley got back to Chancery Lane, he found Pollitt's

answer to his last letter had arrived. It was an unusually thick envelope and he settled himself on the couch to read it. Jerome rarely wrote so much these days – not like those significant letters they had exchanged when they first met. He recalled that on one occasion, Pollitt had walked in as he was registering at a hotel desk and called out loudly across the foyer, 'Hullo, Monkey Tricks!'

He unfolded the letter and read:

> *Hullo, Monkey Tricks.*
>
> *Thank you for your insultingly brief letter. In answer to your question, I have to tell you that I believe George is going madder. He said this morning that there was a lady, visible only to himself, with bandaged feet, who was trying to get him to break down a door at the end of a corridor. And all this before breakfast. We have just been out for a walk and he insisted on following a path which took us to a cliffy, tangled bit near a river. It was the kind of mess I don't like to approach without galoshes. You know me: I don't like climbing things. Anyway, George ~~forced~~ begged me to come with him and we found a narrow cleft which requires a good lantern to investigate. Now this is the bit that you will find unusual in me. I have agreed to acquire the aforesaid lantern and galoshes and accompany George in an exploration of the cave this afternoon! I will conclude this letter with an account thereof, when we get back in time for dinner.*
>
> <u>*Later*</u>
>
> *Aleister, I think you would have enjoyed this. I won't go into all the details of our journey. Suffice it to say, the cave led to a tunnel and it was cold, slippery and terrifyingly horrible and there was a place where skeletal hands were definitely trying to seize me. Anyway, we reached this kind of caved-in hall where there was a brownish, spidery kind of light and an eerie rushing sound. George wanted to go on down a further tunnel and I let him. When he came back, he seemed – well, shaken, I suppose, as when one gets the bill from the tailor. Wouldn't say what he had seen. Then we made our way back and I came straight up here for a hot bath. There, aren't you impressed with me? You should be. I did it to show you I can survive amidst the scenery too sometimes.*
>
> *Do pack your bags and pack in your studies for a bit.*
> *J.*

Crowley read the letter through twice then lay back, tossing it onto the table in front of him. He thought for a little while and finally wrote back:

> *Dear P.*
>
> *Please do not break George. I need him for my experiments which are going very well, since you asked. I will not tell you anything more, except to say that the skeleton is now becoming covered in a kind of viscous slime. I expect that is probably the soot of London, though I have noticed the presence of an increasing number of demons. It does smell a little bit, so you are probably best not to be near it.*
>
> *Expect me when you see me.*
>
> *A.C.*

*

Alexandra sat alone in the library, partly to be alone, partly in obedience to Minerva's instructions and partly because she felt obliged to conceal the laughter which frequently welled up at the sight of the oddities, the inconsistencies, the pointlessness of the other guests' behaviour. They were after all every one of them destined to get older and older and more and more infirm. And then they were going to die. What on earth were they doing, singing at the piano, playing whist, walking about conversing with each other about the food they would eat or had eaten? Lady Helena, for example. She looked more and more risible every day, tottering about, her face all powdered and rouged. And those long clattering strings of pearls at her crêpey neck, highlighting the unnumbered creases in the skin, the disorders of pigmentation as the tiny veins broke down. Alexandra was compelled to clench her fists sometimes to stop herself from shaking the woman by her bony shoulders. But did she want to say, 'Look, old woman, the grave is waiting for you. You might as well give up your share of air and space now, just go!' or did she want to shriek, 'Help, help, help me!'?

As she finished her study of Minerva's work, she had to force herself to sit still now. Although a tremor would run through her body from time to time, like the flank of a horse flinching under the bite of a horsefly, she would hold steady, sitting at the desk. Some of the prescribed reading challenged her established ideas on human nature, power and morality. She read slowly, making notes, trying to wring the meaning out, distil the drops. And she continued her journal. Today she wrote:

It is so wonderful: she was never attempting to conceal anything. She left me hints and clues at every turn. I now see that she is at least as old as I am. The date in the book tells me. The fact that she saw the Jewels of Helen in person told me too. I wonder when it was that she developed the formula? Did she experiment upon herself, did she try it on guinea pigs, people? The thought makes me laugh. Curious that the disparity in our ages should have been a dampening factor in our friendship. Now I understand that she is my contemporary, now I can truly call her friend. I am going out now to enjoy the cold. The sun is out, each and every twig and stalk is glistening, the sunshine is resting on everything. No words for these extraordinary energies.

CHAPTER TWENTY-FIVE

Jerome was filing his nails, swivelling on a stool at the reception desk of the hotel and chatting with Billy Sandford, the desk clerk. It was early afternoon, shortly after lunch, when sensible people were just getting up or even better, just going to bed. Outside, the 'scenery' looked sort of greeny-grey and damp. The uncertain sun threw slices of watered light onto the marble floor and floated a dim wash of colour down from a high-up window. The stained glass picture showed an unidentifiable woman kneeling at a stream with a pitcher. Jerome supposed that the hotel proprietor had commissioned it to represent the healing spa waters. He thought it was plebeian and in poor taste.

Major Farnsworth and Lady Helena were having some kind of treatment involving wraps of hot mud, mushrooms and lichen (or so Jerome imagined); Mrs Roberts was probably running wild like a young doe in the forest; George was hiding in his room, staring out of the window and could not be persuaded to come down. All that was left to amuse him was the hotel clerk, who was Irish with a charming accent.

'So who is the old bird in the window?' asked Pollitt, looking up at the stained glass. 'It is terribly substandard and really quite generic. Modern, of course, imitative of that pallid painted style: so very last century. A lazy thing with none of the vibrancy of a Burne-Jones.'

Billy Sandford looked admiringly at Pollitt. 'Well, yes, I should think you're correct, sir. That, as I believe, is only the work of a local artist who designed it himself. And it is a depiction of a very holy woman, very holy indeed. A poor holy anchoress who was praying and living and counselling the poor people and healing the sick right here in this very place. She had her cell somewhere in the old part of the building.'

'Oh really? How perfectly sweet,' said Pollitt. He yawned discreetly behind his hand and, to change the subject, began enquiring whether there might be any more visitors soon.

Billy told him that he had received notification that more guests would be arriving in the next few days. Jerome hoped that one of them would be Crowley – he had received a grumpy sort of letter promising a visit - but was wondering whether the others would be yet more invalids, and Billy kept explaining that yes, some of them might well be invalids as it was a health spa; and Jerome kept pretending that Billy had said something vaguely improper so that the clerk was forced to explain it all again. This *divertissement* had been going on for a good five minutes when the clerk glimpsed the black coach with its sturdy horses clopping along the road towards the hotel.

'Ah, yes,' said Billy. 'Mrs Atwell has arrived. You'll excuse me, sir. I must assemble the staff for inspection.'

The clerk rang a small but surprisingly eardrum-rinsing gong three times. Shortly after that, various members of the hotel staff began hurrying in to present themselves at the desk, adjusting caps or aprons or buttoning up collars. They were still lining up as Minerva Atwell swept into the foyer.

The first thing she did was greet Jerome with an inclination of her head in its magnificent hat. Her outfit was a sombre yew-green and to Pollitt's eyes, the effect against the white sunlit lobby of height, a trim outline and swift movement was like an alarming tree rippling towards him in the wind. She murmured a request to the clerk for an introduction to this honoured guest.

'I hope you are enjoying your stay, Mr Pollitt,' she said as they brushed fingers in a distant handshake. He felt as though he was greeting a poplar.

'Yes, thank you, Mrs Atwell. It's an interesting old place but could do with a better billiards table,' said Pollitt with a helpful smile.

She inclined her head again, but not as if she were particularly pleased by the information. 'Thank you, Mr Pollitt. Any suggestions will be most welcome. Please inform the manager of anything you lack.' She then diverted her attention to the staff, inspecting each individual. They looked tense.

Watching her, Jerome thought that although she was an exceedingly beautiful woman, there was something about her he didn't like. Perhaps there were no cracks in her façade to exploit, or qualities for him to mock or seduce. It was an odd thing (and he supposed that everyone possessed the same ability to a greater or lesser extent) but he was usually able to tell at a glance whether someone was likely to be in sympathy with himself. Minerva Atwell was not. She's got a steel mask under that lovely face and a heart of flint bouncing about in that bosom, he thought.

He left the staff lined up being inspected and looking unhappy about it and, with a wink to the clerk, wended his way to his room. His plan was to take a well-earned snooze. He thought he'd look in on George as well. After he tapped on his door, he tried the handle and found it locked. He called through the panelling. After a short while, the door was opened and George peeped out. '*She's* here now, isn't she?' he whispered.

'You'll be meaning one of the following,' Jerome said, trying for the cheerful lilt of the desk clerk and holding up a hand to tick names off his fingers, 'Mrs Roberts, Mrs Atwell, Lady Helena or your mother.'

'Yes,' said George. He let Jerome in, walking backwards in front of him as he advanced and talking with unusual fluidity, as if he were slightly feverish. 'That's right. Mrs Atwell. We thought the dead had bird faces.'

'What?'

'The ones who are trapped.'

'George?'

'Yes, what was I saying? The back wall was all sheeted with gold. We got it from Aratta, that and the silver, bringing it over the mountains on donkeys. Because the king answered the riddles...'

'George? George! Stop it at once! You are talking nonsense. Really!' Pollitt tried to feel George's forehead. 'Are you ill?'

George looked confused, then shrugged and shook his head.

'I think you should just go to bed, love. Don't worry about anything. I'll tell the staff and they'll send a nurse up.' He took George by the elbow and led him gently to the bed. George lay down obediently.

'Is it nearly finished?' he asked, closing his eyes as Jerome covered him lightly with a blanket.

Pollitt was suddenly reminded of Aubrey's exhausted face. 'Don't you dare talk like that,' he said. 'Just calm down. It's a reaction to the excitement of yesterday, all that darkness and danger, the tunnel and the odd place underground, and you got upset about something. I got upset, for that matter, and *I* still feel peculiar from it all. And cold, it was very cold and entirely unnecessary. You're just tired to the bone.' He walked to the window and looked out, twitching aside the heavy red curtains. The winter afternoon lay over the valley. Feathered, wind-torn clouds were saturated with light. With the ice of anxiety in his throat, he glanced over at George again and saw that he was already asleep. He tip-toed out of the room.

At dinner that night, Pollitt missed him. He had made sure that soup and other invalid-style food was sent up but he did not feel equal to sitting anxiously next to a sick man. He hated sickness. He had to endure instead a bizarre party at dinner. The company seemed more mismatched than ever with Mrs Roberts confirming at every moment that she was besotted with Mrs Atwell. Jerome watched the way she mimicked her every move, laughing with the same annoying tinkling laugh - the kind that he particularly despised among the P.B.s. Mrs Atwell, on the other hand, seemed merely to tolerate Mrs Roberts, as though she were a toy she had wound up too tight a while since but whose antics had gone on too long. She seemed restless and once cut short the Major by talking over one of his Indian anecdotes.

After dinner, the four of them played cards while Pollitt sat himself down at the piano and tried to recall some pieces. He was not a great pianist, never having applied himself sufficiently. He played softly, stumbling through phrases he half remembered.

'What is that you are picking out?' called Lady Helena. 'I feel sure I know it, but I cannot now recall its name.'

'A piece by Chopin, ma'am,' answered Pollitt apologetically. '*The Raindrop*. Have mercy on me for committing a murder.'

Lady Helena nodded, 'Yes, that is it. I met her, you know. Aurore. As an old lady.' She waved her blue-veined hand towards the sofa, as if Chopin's celebrated lover were sitting there listening. 'She told me of his words, *Ah, je savais bien que vous étiez mort - I knew well that you were dead!* A most terrible storm. He played in a kind of dream.'

'Yes,' agreed Pollitt. 'I have heard the story. And was she very beautiful still, even in old age?'

'Beautiful? No, no, no. It wasn't beauty she had. What does that matter? It was strength of intellect, strength of character, dignity. Such a relief to leave the game, young man, still holding the card of wit.' She looked at her hand of whist. 'Consumption carried *him* off, you know,' she added vaguely.

'Did you know him too, ma'am?'

'No, no, of course not. I was just a young thing when he died.'

Her attention was called back to the card game and Pollitt wandered over to the french windows to look thoughtfully out at the dim-lit terrace.

*

'No luck,' said Crowley. He stood shaking the rain from his hat at the door of Dr Watson's sitting room. 'He's not there, not in the stable loft of The Ram, anyway. They didn't know where he might be. Sweeps the yard in the morning but goes all over, apparently.'

'Well, that's a disappointment,' said Watson. 'Come in, come in, my dear fellow. You're very wet, take your coat off. Sit down by the fire. Well, I had hoped to be able to take him down to the station. My plan was to present the papers from Burroughs's box along with Bateman himself to tell his story.'

'Yes, it rather weakens the case, doesn't it? Not having Bateman, I mean. What will you do?'

'I will take them down to Browning and explain everything we know. The more I think about Burroughs, the more uneasy I feel. You were right about the improper writings – they do point to a fascination with the macabre, such as the Ripper cases. I didn't like the feel of them at all.'

'And when you put this tendency together with his nervous tics, his strangely rigid behaviour and his apparent obsession with Arden, I suspect there's far more to discover about him.'

'Yes, the obsession. I noticed that. The little picture, obviously, which, now I think of it, is probably the work of Alexandra Roberts. The 'A', you know. No name in the written passages, of course, but adequate descriptions to tie them together. You noticed, did you not, that there is an account of a particularly vile crime against the Arden character?'

'No. I barely glanced at the stuff, Doctor, if you recall. Shocking if so. But not surprising. I said he wanted to kill part of himself, didn't I? Is this the evidence we need, then, the motive for his trying to get Arden arrested?'

Just then there was a tap at the sitting room door and Dafydd Williams walked in. He had a folded dripping umbrella in his hand which he had failed to leave by the front door and which, at Watson's urging, he now stood in the fireplace. After he had apologised for bringing in so much wet, he explained that he had been passing this way on another errand and had decided to combine it with a visit. He produced Watson's calling card as if to justify his presence and then replaced it carefully in a little morocco card case. 'I hope you don't mind my taking the liberty, Dr Watson?' he said as he sat down, steaming slightly in the warmth of the fire. 'And it is very charming to see you again too, Mr Crowley. That was quite an unpleasant adventure we had the other day, wasn't it? Made things tricky at home, I can tell you.'

'It must be difficult for you,' said Watson. 'Tell me, is Mr Burroughs sticking to his story that the ears are mummifed remains?'

'I presume so, not that I have discussed it with him. He wouldn't speak to me about it. Doesn't speak to me at all. But that is no doubt what they are, mummified,' said Dafydd, 'though it was still an almighty shock to the system, seeing them there. So, anyway, I should explain myself. I thought it right to draw your attention to this and I know I probably shouldn't but it seems of interest.' He fished inside his jacket pocket and found an envelope. 'I borrowed this, gentlemen, and I must bring it back to the house with me. If he sees it's gone, I think *my* ears will be in danger.'

Watson looked curiously inside the envelope. It contained a long thick strand of hair of a particularly rich Titian red and a scrap of paper. He uncurled it and saw that it was a signature torn from the bottom of a letter: Minerva Atwell was the name written there. 'This is related to the portrait that Mr Burroughs has taken into his room, is it not?' said Watson.

'Yes, it is. How did you know?' asked Dafydd.

'Because I went to see Mrs Day yesterday and she told me all about it – and that you objected strongly. She said you were making plans to remove it and replace it in Mrs Roberts's studio. Is that correct?'

'Yes, he has stolen the thing. I don't care for the portrait myself - I don't know that it's particularly Christian, you know; but that won't be Mrs Roberts's fault. She just works to please her patrons. And Burroughs took it for himself as soon as poor Mrs Roberts had gone on her rest-cure. To be honest with you, I have since thought better of taking it back. I was all for picking it up and carrying it upstairs and then locking it in. Taking the studio key, you know, and giving it to Mrs Jenkins. But then I thought to myself, just as I was preparing to do it, I don't rightly know if he did get permission to have it there. Anyway, I noticed this. He had it tucked away behind the canvas. Like a little shrine, I thought. And you know, seeing we know what was under that bed, I found it disturbing.'

Watson handed the envelope to Crowley, who stared at the hair and the paper fragment. He nodded to Watson, saying softly, 'I like this.'

'Do you mind for one moment, my dear fellow? I must just get something to show Mr Crowley.' Watson left Dafydd being offered a cigarette by Crowley, and went into his room. There under his own bed was the file containing the documents Crowley had removed from the black box. He rapidly extracted them and began to thumb through the leaves quickly. Yes, there it was. He returned to the sitting room. 'Excuse me for leaving you so long,' he said. 'Crowley, just to refresh your memory.' He passed over to him the note from the box of ears which promised payment of Burroughs's rent. The thick creamy paper exactly matched the torn signature. Crowley nodded and handed it back.

'Mr Williams,' asked Watson, 'I wonder if you would permit me to hold onto this envelope?'

'I don't think that would be possible, Doctor,' said Williams, flinching slightly at the thought. 'Albert Burroughs would go stark-staring mad if he thought I'd been poking about in his room again.'

'Yes, no doubt he would.' Watson thought for a moment. 'Here. You had better after all replace this where it was. I don't want it destroyed, that's all.'

Dafydd tucked the envelope into his pocket and continued rather laboriously to smoke the cigarette Crowley had given him. It was a notable cigarette, being black with a thick gold band at one end. Watson hoped it was not tainted with opium. Poor Mr Williams, now looking a little forlorn, said, 'I wonder if you gentlemen happen to know of any families requiring drawing tuition? I seem to be losing my regulars – leaving town they are. It is rather disheartening. My poor mother is very much hoping that my career prospects will be brighter soon but it all seems bleaker and bleaker. I don't know what I might do if I have to return home.'

'You are at loose end, Mr Williams?' asked Watson, an idea dawning.

'Yes, I am. I would rather not be but I am.'

'Would you care to undertake some research for me – be my assistant for an afternoon? It is very important work and I can pay you for your services.' Watson was aware out of the corner of his eye that Crowley threw his cigarette end into the fire with a short laugh.

'Well, that would be very interesting and quite to my taste,' said Dafydd, immediately perking up. 'Tell me what I have to do.'

Dr Watson had frequently helped his friend Holmes by investigating records in the North Wing of Somerset House. It was here that he sent Dafydd Williams with a covering letter from himself, to find out as much as could be found about both Minerva Atwell and Albert Burroughs. He gave him the name of a particularly helpful clerk. It was tedious work and he was glad to pass it on to the young drawing master.

'I feel that we are at last onto something,' he said after Williams had departed. He held up the note in one hand and the signature strip in the other. 'I am ready to admit the force of your example, Crowley. I secreted this scrap in my shirtcuff. Disgraceful. But I felt justified in keeping it. The lock of hair remained in the envelope, of course, and is tucked away in Mr Williams' pocket.'

'Excellent,' nodded Crowley. 'Minerva Atwell. Beauty Balm no less. And that is the lady you spoke about, the one hated by Arden's patroness, Mrs Day, who discovered a relationship to Burroughs. Half-brother, was it? Looks like he is part of the family business.'

'We might assume too much, you know, Crowley.' He indicated the documents on his lap. 'There's nothing here linking any of the payments to Atwell, nothing to associate the firm with the heads. Moreover, she could be paying him to stay away, if you think about it.'

'Or paying him to do her dirty work. Wouldn't it be beautifully appropriate if those balms and creams and so on had all come from a laboratory full of grisly human heads? You know, in general, I am not at all interested in ladies' skincare products: they are all full of repulsive ingredients boiled down to a grease, but this is pleasantly ironic.'

'The sex glands of the civet cat make the finest perfume,' agreed Watson, 'but the women who dab it behind their ears don't seem to care in the least.'

'But it occurs to me that one could not build an extensive business based on human ingredients without a copious supply of heads.'

'They would need the help of a Genghis Khan. It is an impossibility. However, there would undoubtedly have been an essential step in the development process which necessitated study of the cell structure of the hypodermis, just as an example. Perhaps there was a stage when Burroughs was supplying his sister's business in a limited way. There are after all those employment records.'

'Quite disappointing,' said Crowley, thoughtfully regarding the jack knife which skewered a sheaf of correspondence to the mantelpiece. 'Rather mundane. Beauty research does not pique my interest very much.'

'No, and it doesn't go any further towards clearing George Arden's name.'

'Which reminds me, Doctor. I got a letter from my friend Pollitt this morning. Now that you have a new assistant, I feel able to take myself off to the spa.'

'A new assistant? You mean Mr Williams? Is that why you laughed when I sent him off to Somerset House?'

'Well, I knew you were no keener than I to go and search through those records. But listen, don't you think I should interview Arden urgently? With a little delicate questioning, I could get evidence to throw light upon the writings you discovered. If they depict what I suspect, an abominable assault upon Arden, then it is the very thing we must establish in order to provide a clear motive for Burroughs's lies.'

'Yes, yes, I quite see that.' Watson shuffled his notes for a few seconds before he looked up and said gruffly, 'Well, if you must go, then at least be aware that it immediately puts you in a difficult position. You should by law inform the authorities where he is.'

'Oh, I shan't trouble about *them*,' he answered serenely.

CHAPTER TWENTY-SIX

When the coach brought a guest from the station, Pollitt was disappointed. It was not Crowley but a lady; and not a very handsome one at that. But she at least had a kindly face. He encountered her as she arrived at the front desk because he had been hanging about pestering Billy the clerk again and hoping for a letter. She was middle-aged, dressed in sensible clothing and not at all fashionable. Pollitt looked sidelong at her deep-chocolate travelling dress and thick boots. The modest luggage which the coach driver dumped beside her on the floor was worn, the brass fitments at the corners well-rubbed.

After she had gone through the procedure of signing in and had her bags taken up to her room, Pollitt heard her asking for Mrs Roberts and her 'brother-in-law, Edward Day'. His heart, which had been oppressed since George's sudden illness yesterday, lifted. 'Good morning,' he said. 'May I introduce myself? I'm a friend of Edward's,' he said. 'My name is Pollitt, Jerome Pollitt.'

She turned to look at the slim, rather dandified young man who was proffering one graceful hand in greeting. She said, 'Any friend of Edward's is welcome to me, Mr Pollitt. I am his sister-in-law, Harriet Day.'

'I am absolutely delighted that you've come, Mrs Day. Yes, delighted. We've had some adventures, I can tell you. But I'm afraid there's been no sign of Edward so far this morning. He came down with a dose of something yesterday afternoon. I think the nurse gave orders that he shouldn't be disturbed. Nothing serious and I expect he'll be down later.'

'Oh dear me. How awful. I do hope he gets better soon – I was so looking forward to seeing him again. But it's delightful that he's had someone to talk to here, Mr Pollitt. My friend Mrs Roberts wrote to me saying that he had a companion.'

'Look, there's the nurse I spoke to earlier, oh, excuse me, Miss! Nurse! The gentleman in Room Thirteen, Mr Day, how is he this morning?'

'Ah, Mr Day, sir?' The nurse, who was wheeling a vacant bath-chair over towards the pump room, left the chair where it was and walked over to them. She inclined her head politely and continued, 'Mr Day is very poorly. Mrs Atwell gave orders that he is to stay in his room and see no one for the time being. He is fevered, and Mrs Atwell looked in on him herself, like she does with all the sick ones, and she said as he has spots such as made her think of a contagion. We hope he has not the measles, sir, but if such is the case, we must keep him away from the other guests.'

'Oh, rotten luck!' said Pollitt.

'How unfortunate,' said Mrs Day. 'But he *is* my brother-in-law, you know, and I myself have had the measles many years ago. It will be perfectly safe for me to nurse him. I should like to see him as soon as may be.'

The nurse bobbed her head politely again. 'I'm afraid that won't be possible, ma'am, not without Mrs Atwell's express permission. She is very specific about care of her sick guests, which you will appreciate is how the Adsullata Spa maintains a good reputation.'

'I understand, nurse. Don't trouble yourself. I'll talk to Mrs Atwell myself. Once she understands, I'm sure she won't object.'

The nurse agreed and went on her way. The wheels of the bath chair made a tick-tick-tick sound as she pushed it across the white paving of the vestibule.

'That really is rum,' said Pollitt. 'And I hadn't got George – er - Edward pegged as a measley sort of fellow. '

Harriet Day gave him a shrewd look at the name of George as she picked up her handbag and umbrella from the counter top. Then she nodded. 'Poor George,' she agreed very quietly. 'And by the use of that name, I understand that you really do know my brother-in-law. Perhaps we can speak later. But now I *will* go and tap on his door, whatever Mrs Atwell might think. Then I must search for Mrs Roberts. Where might she be, I wonder.'

'Oh, Mrs Roberts?' said Pollitt. 'She'll be galloping over the mountain tops. Either that or soaking in the hot pool, or maybe talking to Mrs Atwell. If you wait a while she'll return because she always takes her meals at fixed intervals, things like grilled chicken with dandelions, garnished with tree roots or something. She is admirably consistent. And very well-exercised.'

'Mrs *Roberts?* asked Harriet. 'Well, this spa has certainly done her good then. She has always been the very opposite of what you just described. Still, perhaps I had better wait here for her rather than go exploring the valley. It looks as though rain clouds are rolling in. If she's abroad, no doubt she'll return shortly.'

After Harriet had been up to her room and freshened her toilette, she returned to wait downstairs, a little sobered by a thwarted visit to George's door which had given her no further insight into his condition. Jerome naturally drifted over to sit with her, leafing through the newspaper, drinking coffee and finding that they rather enjoyed each other's company. He had such a relaxed and charming manner that Harriet soon felt completely at ease in his company. She was spellbound by his tale of how George and he had explored an old monastic way from the riverside.

'How interesting,' said Harriet. 'I should like to explore the house – and especially that tunnel. I have a particular fascination with that era. I expect Mrs Atwell has looked into the history of the place. I'll ask her later.'

'Oh, you can try,' said Pollitt. 'She's a society lady, if you know what I mean. Lots of shallow, steely conversation. Doubt that she cares much about the place as long as it makes a profit.'

'Really? I had heard that she was something of an historian.'

Pollitt shrugged. 'Looks can be deceptive, as I'm ready to concede. At first glance, she didn't strike me as the kind of person who would like to get her hands dirty by taking her silk gloves off.'

Harriet looked doubtful. Noticing her expression, Pollitt said, 'Am I being offensive? I am so sorry. I am sometimes inclined to speak my mind without thinking. Just high spirits, you know - which I assume, like a mask, to hide my extremely low spirits. I am actually a very serious person.' He laughed. 'But perhaps she is a friend of yours?'

'I have never met her,' answered Harriet. 'But I do know Mrs Roberts doesn't enjoy being confined by convention. She's an artist.'

'I wouldn't have guessed. We might have more in common than I thought. If she is a friend of yours, I am very happy to think so. I have a natural sympathy with artists.'

'Why, Mr Pollitt, are you an artist yourself?'

'I have natural sympathy but alas, no natural talent. I do a little acting from time to time though. That's how I came to meet our Edward Day. His manager was trying to sell this play to me, you see, Hamlet meets the Pirates of Penzance or some such rot. He wanted financial backing. Sadly, as a leading man, George failed to make much impression.' Pollitt paused and searched in the pocket of his jacket. 'Do you mind if I smoke?' He extracted a cigarette from a japanned case and lit it, adding, 'Poor chap struck me as someone who would frighten an audience. They'd go home wondering who they were and why they were here.'

'Yes,' said Harriet. 'I can't say I disagree. I've often wondered how he ever came to be on the stage. He seems so lost most of the time.'

'It's because he's empty. That's what I think. After I'd been with him here for a bit, I thought to myself, he's such a good listener. Then I realised it wasn't so much that he was listening, as that he had nothing coherent to say about himself. Yesterday, when he was fevered, he began talking such rot, things about gold walls and silver donkeys.'

'Really? It sounds like a Nativity scene.'

'Yes, all mixed up.' Pollitt shook his head. 'He'll be all right though, don't worry about him.'

They were silent. The afternoon darkened and the storm that Harriet had predicted began. Soon there were rivulets coursing down the windows and the sashes rattled in the wind. They moved closer to the fire. Harriet was expecting Alexandra to come rushing through the door at any moment, laughing at having got wet. The minutes ticked by. Perhaps after all she was somewhere within the hotel? Perhaps she was painting Mrs Atwell's portrait? Harriet became restless and decided to walk through the hotel, hoping to find her. Pollitt said he would accompany her.

They walked round the salon and the lobby, peeped into the pump room and the pool, walked the gallery and then, trying a little door and finding it open, ventured along the cloister which ran along the exterior of the south side of the building. Rain streamed from the roof but the wind was thwarted by the house and although it curled round the ends of the walk and flung wet leaves and twigs onto the tiled way, they themselves remained dry. The cloister had been added recently to the modern building to allow guests to take the air. They watched rain sheeting across the paving stones and earth of the bare rose garden and listened to the drumming of the water on the roof. They returned through another door and carried on exploring.

Eventually, they exhausted all possible routes in the modern part of the building (Pollitt refused to venture beyond the ropes into the ancient sections) and did not, as Harriet had hoped, come across her friend sketching by a window. They peeped into the library. The room was empty. It smelt of lavender polish and new books.

'Well, if I can't see Alexandra, I am determined to get more information about George,' said Harriet at last. 'All I got was a polite dismissal from the nurse up there and no news.'

'I wonder if they'll put a guard on his door,' said Pollitt, as they turned away.

'Guard? They wouldn't do such a thing!' laughed Harriet, half alarmed.

'No, no, but he might go wandering out. You know George. He can get very … get overwhelmed by subliminal uprushes.'

'What is a subliminal uprush, Mr Pollitt?' asked Harriet, laughing.

'I have no idea,' he answered, 'I've never had one.'

'Well,' said Harriet. 'Thank you for your company, Mr Pollitt. It has been a most agreeable hour. I hope to see you again at dinner.'

She left a note for Alexandra at the desk and went along to tap at George's door again. This time, a rather grim-faced woman opened it. She assured Harriet that Mr Day was still fast asleep and being well looked-after and that there was nothing at all to fear. Harriet had no choice but to retire to her own room. She lay down on the bed, wondering where Alexandra was and disturbed that George should be ill enough to require a nurse.

*

After Crowley had gone, Dr Watson decided to venture out for a stroll. By the time he got home, he found Dafydd Williams waiting in the sitting room, holding a cup of tea provided by Mrs Hudson. He had been there for some time.

'I am so sorry, Mr Williams,' said Watson. 'I hardly expected you so soon.'

'Oh, no need to apologise, Doctor. Your landlady is very kind and gave me a cup of tea and a piece of really excellent Parkin when I told her what a headache I'd got. Well, I mustn't delay you. I just wanted to hand all this over. I didn't come up with very much – but then I'm not entirely sure what it is you might be looking for.'

Watson was glad when Dafydd Williams had gone. He now had a headache of his own and wanted to think quietly. He had also paid the young man ten shillings for his help which was probably far more than an afternoon's work in Somerset House could possibly be worth. Dafydd Williams' notes read:

Joseph Rupert Atwell married Minerva Anne Pargeter 1860.
Joseph Rupert Atwell, born 1836, died 1875.
Minerva Anne Pargeter born 1839.
Albert Horace Burroughs born 1857.
No trace of further family for Burroughs.
No death certificate for Minerva Atwell.
No further records pertaining to M.A.

After he had read through this information twice, he realised that he was sorely missing another mind to bounce his ideas off. The more he looked at the dates, the more obvious it became to him that Minerva Atwell had taken on another woman's identity. Born in 1839: she would now be nearly sixty years old, which clearly was not right. Dafydd Williams had not got the wrong birth certificate because the marriage made sense. He found himself wishing that Crowley was here, and then was annoyed with himself for needing him, even feeling a little disloyal to Holmes. The best thing to do, he thought, was what he always did. He took to paper and pen.

Sitting at his orderly desk in the privacy of his bedroom, looking out beneath the brown bobbles which trimmed the blind and seeing the usual smooth yellow fog sliding across the day, he jotted down the questions he would have asked Holmes. Unfortunately, he could not imagine the answers he would have got from Holmes.

Q. Is the real Minerva Atwell dead and her identity taken by another? Or is the old Minerva the mother of the younger? If so how foist this imposition on the company? A. A complex and elaborate fraud.
Q. Is Burroughs working for his sister or being paid to keep away?
A. Both possible.
Q. Is he actually related to Minerva Atwell in the first place?
A. ?
Q. Would the firm of Atwell have any use for human heads or is that entirely unrelated?
A. Maybe.

He sighed and shut his notebook, remembering as he did so that the ink was still wet and that it would all smudge. Damn.

*

The dining room was cold despite the fire in the hearth. Mrs

Roberts's shiny table, polished meticulously this morning, had only one place setting. There was a dinner waiting for Mr Williams, to be sent up to his room or taken in the kitchen when he came back; but Mr Burroughs liked to eat slowly and deliberately in state. Amy was busy downstairs and Lily had gone home. Janet was alone, checking that the table looked perfect. Mr Burroughs disliked the slightest smudge on his silverware or any informality in the folds of his napkin. Tonight there would be mulligatawny soup, plaice, lamb, queen of puddings, cheese with port. Mr Burroughs would have various wines with each course too, sipping slowly, a different kind of glass for each one.

Suddenly, Janet, making sure everything looked fresh and perfectly placed before she left the room, knew that she was being watched. She decided to act as if she did not know. She even pretended to give a little jump of surprise when she turned and saw Mr Burroughs standing in the doorway.

'Good evening, Janet,' he said. Janet dropped him a curtsey and said nothing. He went on, advancing a step into the room, 'The table looks perfect. I have often noticed you. You are so efficient and so very neat, tripping about the place like a little fairy.'

Janet did not know what to say so she said, 'Thank you, sir,' and began to plot a route out of the room which would give her a wide berth round the man. This conversation might lead to one of those inexplicable situations she had been warned about so often, the details of which were obscure but the outcome of which could lead to dismissal if not ruin.

'Oh, don't go, my girl. No need to be so formal. You've been here how long – let me think, it was December you joined us?'

'Yes sir, just a week before Mr George turned up …' Her voice swallowed itself, aware that she should not introduce that subject. But Mr Burroughs ignored it.

'Yes, the beginning of December. And in all that time, you have kept a very laudable demeanour. Respectful and quiet. And I like that in a girl.'

'Thank you, sir.'

'And when you cleaned behind the portrait in my room and picked up the envelope I had inadvertently dropped behind it, tell me, Janet, did it occur to you that you should never ever spy?'

'Spy, sir?' Janet went very white. 'I never!'

'Did you like the colour of the hair?'

'I – I don't know what hair you mean, sir. I never seen no hair.'

Burroughs looked at her for a long moment and his black eyes were as shiny and hard as buttons. Then, as if the spell was broken, he looked away and said, 'Why the pretty lady in the portrait. Her hair, of course.' And he moved past her to seat himself at the table. He looked round as he helped himself to a glass of wine. 'That is all,' he said, abruptly dropping his friendly manner. 'Tell Mrs Jenkins I am quite ready to dine now.'

CHAPTER TWENTY-SEVEN

Assembling for dinner in the salon that evening, Harriet finally encountered Alexandra. But it was nothing like she had hoped and imagined. She remembered meeting her for the first time, a spindly, dark-haired girl of eight, already self-possessed, glowing from the long sea voyage she had made with her Ayah. Harriet herself, a year younger, plump and blonde and used to the predictabilities of London life, admired her immediately. The girls had formed the closest of friendships which, particularly in the months preceding Alexandra's early marriage and their separation, became romantically intense, and the intimacy between them had lingered.

It was a shock then, when Harriet witnessed Alexandra enter the room. She was dressed in a beautiful gown of silvery-grey taffeta, a single black rose at the shoulder and long black evening gloves on her arms. She looked – Harriet had to admit it – indefinably, she looked *young again*. Her face was so much closer to the face she had had twenty years before that Harriet had to blink. Had she dyed her hair? What had she done to herself? There was a faint blush to her cheek, a definition to the jaw, a plumpness to the flesh – subtle but visible to Harriet's familiar eyes. The even-younger looking woman who entered with her was tall and dressed to show off a spectacular figure, with a flash of diamonds at her throat. They walked in together, arm in arm.

With sinking heart, Harriet rose to greet them. It seemed that Alexandra's eyes lingered on her with a hint of bewilderment, as if trying to refresh her memory. She reached out and took Alexandra's arm after exchanging greetings and compliments with Mrs Atwell to draw her away to the sofa to sit down together. Conversation was stilted and she worked awkwardly to revive their intimacy. Words kept slipping into troughs of silence. And Alexandra's eyes constantly slid beyond her to Mrs Atwell.

Minerva Atwell: there was no doubt, she was unusually beautiful, particularly in this grey company. And even years later, when Harriet thought back on that moment, it stood out in breathing colour: the line of her throat, the sparkle of the jewels and the wine-coloured velvet of the dress . She was talking loudly to her guests, standing by the fire, flattering and charming, making Major Farnsworth bark with laughter and Lady Helena cool herself in the old-fashioned way with a little ivory fan. Even Mr Pollitt was listening to her, unconsciously slipping into her circle. She was making everyone laugh with her story about the Duchess of Fenwick, a plumed hat in the wind and an unfortunate debutante.

At the dinner table, Harriet found she was near enough Mrs Atwell to ask about George. It had not been possible to ask Alexandra whether she had revealed George's history to Minerva. She would just have to trust that she had respected her request for secrecy. She began, 'I came in the hope of seeing my dear brother-in-law, Edward. I am so grateful that your staff are taking such wonderful care of him in his sickness. Your establishment is admirably careful of its guests,' she said.

Minerva said, 'Thank you. That is the highest praise, coming from one so rich in experience as yourself.'

Harriet was uncertain what she meant, suspecting that it was a jibe against her years. She chose to make use of it, however, continuing, 'Yes, experience. Exactly. I should like to nurse dear Edward myself, Mrs Atwell. I am very used to the sick room and I feel sure he would be more comfortable and therefore recover more quickly if I were to take care of him myself.'

'Ah, I regret to say that it is quite beyond my power to accommodate you, Mrs Day. The hotel maintains the strictest of medical supervision. All cases of fever or suspected contagion can only be dealt with by the staff. I would simply be unable even to allow you to enter your brother-in-law's room.' She touched Harriet's hand in sympathy. 'Imagine, dear Mrs Day, what would happen if the residents here − weakened in health as they are - were to suffer because of a simple lack of careful management? No, it cannot be. I cannot allow any of my guests to be endangered - for what would I do without dear Major Farnsworth to tease?' She said the last part of the sentence more loudly so that he could hear and respond. As she had planned, the conversation became general and more lighthearted.

Harriet was annoyed. She tried to hide her disappointment. Looking at Pollitt in the hope of an ally, she saw that he was involving himself rather inappropriately in the banter between Mrs Atwell and Major Farnsworth. She sighed and returned to her dish of *Poulet à la Marengo,* knowing that Alexandra's eyes were fixed exclusively upon Minerva Atwell.

*

By the next morning, Dr Watson had reluctantly come to the decision that he would have to hand the Burroughs papers over to the police without the support of Bateman's testimony. It was either that or delay the handover for an indefinite period while he himself tried to track down an itinerant, of whose appearance he was by no means certain. He could at least inform Detective Browning and perhaps persuade him to bring the man in for questioning. Now that Crowley had gone, he felt strangely disarmed – he had begun to lean on him a little too much.

Somebody had spilt something sticky on the counter at the police station. Dr Watson unfortunately rested his hand upon it and regretted taking off his gloves. While he waited for an opportunity to see Detective Browning, he tried vainly to wipe his palm with a handkerchief. In the middle of this, the desk sergeant announced that Browning would see him now and to come this way please.

The detective looked, as usual, too youthful, very alert and slightly confused, as though twelve different thoughts were crossing his mind at the same moment. And busy. When Watson entered his office, he was writing laboriously in a ledger. He held up a hand for him to wait until he had finished his entry; and then he threw down his pen and stood up to shake hands.

Ignoring the stickiness, Browning burst out, 'I must say, Doctor, I am particularly glad to see you. I was most fortunate to be given quite a few backcopies of *Harper's Weekly* and *The Strand Magazine*. I read through the lot, and the experience was really quite an eye-opener. When we spoke before, I had no idea it was you! I'd read but one of the stories and could not know that you were *the* Doctor Watson! But as I was reading last night, I put two and two together and realised there can't be more than one medical man called Watson in Baker Street. Will you be writing any further accounts, doctor? I'm just asking for a friend.'

'Well, yes, as a matter of fact. I have quite an interesting story in preparation,' said Watson, not displeased to be asked. 'Based on a case in Dartmoor a while back. I'm thinking of calling it *The Howl of the Baskerville Curse.*'

'That sounds proper blood-curdling. And Mr Holmes is -?'

'Ah, I can't say, I'm afraid. He's elsewhere. Not able to say where or what he is engaged upon. In fact, I may say that I personally have been taking on a little of the investigative work in his absence. And in fact, it is in that respect I've come here today. The, er, Box of Ears case. I think Mr Holmes would probably show an interest in it if he were here.'

'Ah, yes. But, you see, Mr Burroughs is insisting he can obtain proof of where those ears came from.'

'Indeed?'

'Of course, Inspector Miller is inclined to believe him – about the proof, I mean. But between you and me, I'm not, not now we find the earrings and perhaps a connection to a missing person. '

'Earrings?' asked Watson.

'You haven't heard, doctor? No, how could you? I'll tell you then. Your opinion would be very welcome. I set one of my men to recording the contents of that box very carefully, of course, and in the process, he notices a mended rip in the canvas lining inside the lid. He takes a look, undoes the stitches with a little scalpel, like, and what should fall out but a ball of tissue paper. And there's this little pair of earrings in it. Well, we were very interested in *them*. They have little portraits painted on them. I thought to myself on inspecting them that they was likely to be identifiable. And I was right. We aren't as stupid as people are led to believe. And to be fair, Doctor, as your stories would sometimes lead people to believe. I say that with the greatest respect, sir, I really do.'

'Ah,' said Watson. 'Do you mind if I sit down, Detective?'

'Where are my manners?' asked Browning. He scrambled to clear a heap of files off the chair on the other side of the desk. It was rather a small, dingy office and the door was propped open by a box full of papers. He pushed it out of the way with his foot so as to shut the door and give them some privacy.

'So the earrings?' asked Watson.

'They belonged to a missing person, Doctor. Or if they don't, they're exact-same copies of a pair she had on when she went missing. But hers were very particularly identifiable, according to her mother, because these little portraits was painted by the girl's own sister. Name of missing person: Miss May Dutton. Went out six months back, never came home.'

'And when did you find this out, Detective?'

'We took the earrings round to show Mrs Dutton yesterday

morning and got a positive identification from her. It took us a long time going through the files – stolen goods, missing persons, lost items – but I am glad to say it paid off. Being thorough and using our powers of observation, as you, above all people, will appreciate.'

'Thank you. I commend you on your thoroughness, Detective. So you have arrested Burroughs?'

'Well, let me tell you the end of the tale – and it's a sorry end. We had him in yesterday afternoon. As I privately predicted – I said it to myself as he walked through the door - Burroughs was supported by my Inspector. He personally undertook the interview and I was there to hear it. It was all very nicey-nicey. A lot of compliments flying about. And Burroughs said as how he bought the earrings from a man in a public house and had intended them as a present for someone.'

'And could he produce proof of this?'

'Nah. Course not. But did that bother my Inspector Miller? Well, it seems that Miller is in the habit of occasionally visiting the same public house near the Bailey, and Burroughs described the fellow who sold the earrings and Miller said he recognised him by the description. Some kind of travelling salesman. Well. That stymied that.'

'You sound unconvinced, Detective, and rightly so. The fact that Miller supposedly recognises the man's description does not prove one iota of Burroughs's story. Was May Dutton's body ever found? Did it have its ears? '

'Ah, you're thinking of the Ripper, aren't you? Strange mutilations, bodies disposed in perculiar positions. No, we never found May Dutton. We didn't look too hard in the first place. You see, her mother had originally made a statement that she thought the girl had gone off with the Postman: they had been a bit too interested in each other and Mrs Dutton forbade her to talk to him. So we treated it as a Missing Person, and that's it. Did she sell her earrings? There's no proof, no trace. She could have gone to Gretna Green; or her ears might be in this box. And the case remains filed under Missing Person.'

'I suppose Miller made much of the mother's previous statement?'

'Yes, of course. He said it supported Burroughs's tale of buying them. I could not say this to anyone at the station, Doctor, but it is becoming my considered opinion that there has been some conspiratorial goings-on to the advantage both of Burroughs and my Inspector. Don't bother to look for evidence, though, because there won't be none.'

'So Burroughs is not under suspicion?'

'Not by Miller, it would seem,' said Browning. 'But by myself? Yes, one hundred percent. Why would he stitch them into the lid of the box, if they was an innocent purchase? Why would he keep those ears? Egyptian my foot!'

'Yes, those earrings were of significance to Burroughs for some reason; although it could be argued that a murderer would not keep hold of anything so identifiable.'

'And that a murderer would not be so stupid as to keep ears he'd snipped off under his own bed. Inspector Miller made that point several times.'

'I'd answer that point by saying that murderers are not entirely rational in their behaviour. You yourself just mentioned the Ripper. And may I ask,' put in Watson, 'whether any of the ears in the box are pierced?'

'Quite right, Doctor. And the answer is several. And all have been deliberately treated with some kind of preservative which leaves them blackened and dried and old-looking. Almost pickled or painted on, it looks. I maintain it would be hard to prove their age, but the association of ears and earrings – well, to me it looks very fishy indeed.'

'Yes,' said Watson, uncomfortably aware that he had postponed the purpose of his visit for far too long. 'And I have to hand over to you some papers which came into my possession. They were originally in the infamous box found beneath Burroughs's bed.' Watson sighed. He produced an envelope from a deep inner pocket of his coat and handed it to Browning. 'There are also records of financial transactions.'

'Indeed?' said Browning. He looked shocked, weighing the envelope in one hand. 'Before I look into this further, Doctor, I have to ask, did you personally remove these documents from the box? Because if you did, you were tampering with evidence. I hate to say it, but I have noticed a tendency to do so on the part of your Mr Holmes too. Brilliant as he is – and well, I would very much look forward to making his professional acquaintance, if the chance ever arose – but, as I say, removing evidence from the scene, that is a serious matter.'

'I know, Detective. And I myself would not have done so. It was another person who was present on the day, a young, inexperienced person who had no idea of correct procedure. Truly. I did not come into possession of these until after the box had been taken away by your officers.'

'H'mm. That young Mr Crowley, was it?'

'Well, the papers were given into my keeping; and after I found what they were, I brought them straight to you.'

'I see. And that wouldn't have been on the same day as that box was opened, would it, now, Doctor? Because, let's see, you would have been hanging onto these for three full days. When did you look at these and know what they were?'

'When did I discover the import of the papers? It was only yesterday evening that I truly began to put two and two together. It becomes complicated. I have come across information that associates Burroughs with a man called Charles Bateman, who served a prison sentence for having stolen some heads of corpses from a graveyard. I believe that the financial transactions you'll see referred to in these papers might have some bearing on the sale of body parts illegally to the firm of Atwell Beauty and Health.'

'And you think the ears in the box came off of them heads, is that what you mean? And the firm of Atwell – that will be …?'

'Offices in Camberwell. They make lotions, creams for the skin, cosmetic products. And Minerva Atwell is the director and, it seems, Burroughs is her close relative.'

'Whoa, there, Dr Watson. Let's go right back to the beginning. Burroughs has an association with a fellow named Bateman who did what?'

Browning took a sharp pencil, turned over a fresh leaf in his pad and prepared to take notes. Dr Watson then embarked on an account of all his dealings with the documents. As he spoke, he decided to leave out all mention of George Arden and Burroughs's apparent obsession with him, concentrating instead on the case of Bateman and the heads. He thought he could return to the matter of Arden in due course, gently introducing the subject of his and Crowley's amateur enquires. His wariness had good foundation, for too close examination into Watson's involvement would quickly lead to Harriet Day and perhaps suspicions about Arden's whereabouts.

'Clipped them off with wire cutters, did he, according to this Bateman? I absolutely would like a word with *that* fellow,' commented Browning as he made his notes.

Watson fudged over exactly how he had connected Bateman with Burroughs, vaguely referring to Holmes's extensive crime records; although he realised that he would have to mention it eventually. He laid emphasis instead on the probable financial arrangement with Burroughs's half- or step-sister, Minerva Atwell, and the possibility of an elaborate fraud based on identity theft. He described how the signature to the letter had come into his possession but specifically requested that Browning not reveal Mr Williams's involvement, should he need to discuss this with Burroughs. He emphasised that he thought Burroughs was a dangerous man.

After half an hour, Browning sat back and said, 'Thank you for all this, Dr Watson. It is a very serious matter, however, having hung onto this evidence. You must leave us to do our work and we can't be hindered by this kind of thing. And, may I say, in *The Adventure of the Blue Carbuncle,* you describe how Mr Holmes takes it upon himself to allow a thief to escape justice. It's that kind of thing that sticks in my craw, if you get my meaning.'

'Oh, understood, understood,' said Watson. 'I do take some liberties with the tales, you know, Detective, to make them flow, to avoid unnecessary detail, for example. I would not suggest you take them as absolute gospel truth. It would, um, probably interest you perhaps to see some of my original notes, you know, compare them to the finished stories? It would put your mind at rest about Holmes's methods.'

'I see,' said Browning, looking very much appeased at the suggestion. 'I won't deny that that would be very interesting indeed. But I still feel that there are questions to be answered on this matter, but we can leave that till later.'

Watson left the station feeling rather chastened, not to mention annoyed with Crowley for lifting the papers in the first place and for departing for the countryside at exactly the point when his presence would have been useful – although he had to admit that if the documents had fallen into Miller's hands, they would have been unlikely to see the light of day. He decided to go straight over to see Dafydd Williams and tell him about the earrings. It would be useful to have him keeping an eye on Burroughs. When he arrived, he found Mrs Roberts's house was quiet and empty, apart from Williams himself sitting nervously in the parlour.

'Good morning, Williams,' said Watson abruptly as Janet opened the parlour door to show him in. 'I don't mean to intrude but I feel I have a responsibility to inform you of certain facts.'

Dafydd had jumped up as soon as the door opened, looking alarmed. 'Indeed, Doctor?'

'And to thank you again for your work yesterday. Sterling, very useful,' added Watson in a more soothing tone.

'Oh, yes. Thank you.' Dafydd sat down again as Watson took a seat opposite him, adding, 'That has been preying on my mind a little bit, you know. It makes me feel guilty somehow, like a conspirator. And I don't normally sit in here, not in the evenings now, nor any time I'm likely to run into Burroughs, see. I just got fed up with staring at my bedroom wall. If I look a bit less perky than my usual self, that'll be the reason. I thought you might be *him* returning early from work.'

'Why, is he so very dangerous, Williams?'

'I'll admit I feel as if he is, but I'll also admit I haven't got a reason to. Strange, isn't it?'

Watson regarded Dafydd for a moment. 'Not strange at all, my dear Williams. He has caused a great deal of disruption in the house and we, between us, have reason to believe he – well, let me tell you. I've been to the police, spoken to that Detective Browning first thing this morning. Now, he revealed something I'd like you to keep very quiet. Absolutely secret. Can you do that?' Watson hesitated. Dafydd Williams stared at him with his pale blue eyes wide and his mouth slightly open. He nodded wordlessly. 'Very well. The police found a pair of earrings in the box alongside the human ears, stitched into the lining. Belonged to a missing girl.'

Williams pressed his hand to his stomach.

'Now, before you jump to conclusions,' went on Watson, holding up a hand, 'there is no evidence to link Burroughs with a murder. The girl went missing but may have eloped, may have sold her earrings on the way to Scotland, for example. Burroughs was questioned yesterday afternoon and that was his story – that he had purchased them.'

'And do you believe that, Doctor? You believe he's the kind of fellow who goes about buying second-hand jewellery? He is well off, he doesn't need to.'

'They were particularly attractive – unique. Painted with little portraits. I suppose he could say that was his reason for buying them. There'll be a thousand excuses, Williams. But I myself? No. I don't believe his story. That is why I've come to inform you. It makes sense if you keep an eye on what he does, when he comes and goes. Anything, anything at all out of the ordinary that comes to your notice, please inform me.'

'Inform you, not the police?'

'Unfortunately, the man in charge, Inspector Miller, he is not inclined to pursue matters related to Burroughs. But Browning, yes, he'll listen, so I suppose you could request to speak exclusively to him. I leave it up to you.' He paused. 'Did Burroughs evince any signs of distress yesterday evening, say anything out of the ordinary? He had, after all, been questioned about the earrings.'

'I wouldn't know, I'm afraid. I avoid him, completely. I take my meals in my room or in the kitchen sometimes. Mrs Jenkins is very understanding, see. Like my Mam-gu.'

'Mam-gu?'

'Grandmother, sorry, a bit of Welsh creeps in sometimes.' Dafydd fell silent and stared mournfully at the little wonky unicorn above the fireplace. 'In only a few short weeks, all the life has gone out of this house. A few short weeks! The first week of January it was, that we were all sitting here in harmony: me and Mrs Roberts and Harriet Day and Valentine Cabot and George Arden, yes, and even Albert Burroughs. And Mr Cabot was laughing about death that evening, I remember. At the time I thought, you shouldn't go mocking death. Death won't be mocked. And I was right.'

'We-ell,' said Watson, as he rose to go, 'a little laughter is no bad thing.'

It occurred to him as he was about to leave that it would be well to summarise recent developments in a letter for Aleister Crowley, who was presumably on his way to the Adsullata Spa Hotel or shortly would be. There was a chance he was still in Chancery Lane; but the thought of bursting in upon him feeding canaries to a skeleton was rather too much for Watson's sensibilities. He asked to use some of the note paper on the desk and sat himself down to write a brief account of the finding of the earrings. Then, saying goodbye to Janet, who was polishing conscientiously in the hall, he left Dafydd Williams drooping in the cheerless house.

He walked a long way before he felt ready to take a cab, making a diversion to post his letter to Crowley and paying extra to send it Express. The busy streets were damp. A freshening breeze ruffled plumes on ladies' hats and sent a posy spinning along the pavement, tumbling past his feet.

Meanwhile, Dafydd Williams was drinking a cup of tea in the little housekeeper's room with Mrs Jenkins. He sat for some time, staring at the toe of his boot, feeling that he might burst with the information inside him. At last, he took a deep breath. 'Mrs Jenkins, I feel it is my duty to inform you that I –'. He paused. He had unconsciously mimicked a form of words used by the police in stories he'd read. 'Well, I mean to say, Dr Watson who called just now, he told me something I think it would be well if you understood. It's about Mr Burroughs, you see. In that black box, you might not know – no, in fact, you wouldn't know because as far as I know the Detective didn't want to inform the rest of the household. Did he?'

Mrs Jenkins patiently stirred her tea. 'Mr Williams, I am more than happy to have a genteel chat with you, but I am not too sure what you are in fact talking about. The police, the box, yes, I understand, there was a smell, the box was removed, the police were not interested – in fact, Mr Burroughs himself told me that it was part of some work he himself is doing in the way of criminal investigation.'

'Oh, I say, is it?' said Dafydd, taken completely aback.

'Yes, he told me it was top secret. In fact, I should not be speaking of it to you now.'

'I am astounded, Mrs Jenkins. Astounded.'

'It's of the highest importance. Works secretly for that Sherlock Holmes, the famous consulting detective, he told me.'

'Well I never,' said Dafydd. He sat back in his chair and frowned at the teapot. 'I'd never have thought it.' After a while, he shook his head and continued, 'In fact, I can't believe it. But then, if it don't quite all fit together, it's because we don't see the full picture. In that case, I'll say no more. Perhaps there's layers in this business I don't know about.'

Upstairs, Janet had torn through the house searching for Amy and Lily. They were now all hiding in the larger linen cupboard to have a private consultation, ''Cos we can say Tiger got in and messed it up and we're folding it all up again,' said Amy in the dim light. She was holding the door shut, all but a sliver.

'Listen, listen,' hissed Janet, flapping her hand for quiet. 'I got to tell you this instantly. I heard something awful, terrible, about that box. It was full of ears. It was full of humin ears! And more than that, there was a pair of earrings in it! Belonged to a missing girl, a girl called May Dutton, lived local to us, not been seen for six months!'

The girls held their hands over their mouths to suppress their cries of horror, but anyone passing by would have heard a sudden commotion from within the linen cupboard.

'Burroughs, he cut off ears and put 'em in the box and hid the bodies somewhere in the house? All over the house?' whispered Lily in a shaking voice when they had stopped babbling at each other.

'I didn't say no such thing,' said Janet intensely.

'Listen, listen,' said Amy. 'Janet says she heard the box was full of ears and there was earrings, that's all. Nothing about bodies in the house. Where would he hide bodies anyway?'

'That cupboard at the top of the stairs,' said Lily. 'Mrs Roberts's studio. The attic. Under the floorboards.'

'Sshh, sshh, stop it. Someone will hear you!'

The girls froze, straining to listen. A floorboard creaked.

'He's outside, he's outside the cupboard listening to us!' whispered Lily suddenly.

At that, quite without warning, Janet went into hysterics. Amy tried slapping her face and shaking her shoulders. Lily tried to put a pillowcase over her head to keep the noise down. The sheets came tumbling off the airing shelves like a flock of ghosts and fell upon the floor. Nothing calmed her. In the end, Amy went down to tell Mrs Jenkins that Janet Fairlight wasn't well and might need smelling salts. As a precaution, they decided to keep the terrible information (gained through Janet's habit of eavesdropping) to themselves, in case it got her and them into trouble.

'Well, I don't know what got into the child,' said Mrs Jenkins to Mr Williams as she served him his lunch. 'I've had to send her home. Mrs Fairlight can talk some sense into her. Seemed to have taken fright over something – but I'd be surprised if it was just a mouse, like the girls say. Tiger got in among the linen and a sorry mess he made of it, chasing the creature. A day or two off won't hurt though. There's only yourself and Mr Burroughs to look after, and though it's a big house, I think we can manage without her for now.'

CHAPTER TWENTY-EIGHT

Harriet was in the process of sighing at her reflection in the mirror and plumping her hair into shape when she fell to wondering exactly why Alexandra's face had looked so different last night. What was it? Perhaps happiness, perhaps that was the difference. Completing her brisk toilette with a dusting of the Beauty Balm Compact, she noticed its fragrance did have a curiously refreshing effect on the mind. Nevertheless, despite the slightly rosy glisten it gave to the cheeks, lines fanned out from the corners of the eyes quite unchanged. She studied them critically for a moment and thought how merciful it was that just as wrinkles appear, the eyesight fails. Feeling beyond all such concerns, she left her room in search of Alex.

The early hotel was quiet. There was a sound of remote clattering from the direction of the kitchen and a parlour maid with a wooden punnet was walking briskly towards the salon, trailing a scent of beeswax polish. Out of the front door, she caught a glimpse of a donkey cart carrying milkchurns away up the road out of the valley. The clerk, who was just taking up his pen at the front desk, smiled brightly on her enquiry and told her that Mrs Roberts was already up and about and could be found in the library. Harriet found her sitting in a chair by the french windows. She was holding a thick battered-looking book and there was a wondering or thoughtful look on her face when she raised it to see who was approaching. The extinguished lamp at her elbow hinted that she might have been reading there since before daylight .

Harriet immediately sat herself down opposite her friend. Despite last night, she wasn't ready to give up just yet. She began by praising the refreshing morning with its hint of spring and the clean air of the place. But Alexandra looked at her with the atmosphere of distant recollection that Harriet had noticed before. 'And it is,' she said. 'Very clean air.'

'And one can do so much walking. We used to love a scramble over the rocks. Didn't we? Remember our holiday in Lyme – you found more fossils than I did that summer, Alex. That time you slid down the rock, lost your footing and rolled into that gigantic puddle! It was so comical.' Harriet laughed, trying to draw her in. 'Donkey rides! Remember?'

'I do a great deal of walking,' Alexandra answered. 'Healthy.'

'Well. I suppose that's what the place is for, health. Quiet though. Not many visitors.'

'Winter seasons are always quiet in country hotels. People go to town, do they not?' Alexandra returned her gaze to the book.

'Have you seen George?' asked Harriet after a moment of struggling with intense disappointment. 'Is he well, do you think? I have so much to tell you, Alexandra. You know, about the things that happened at home?'

'George Arden – or I suppose I should say Edward Day, since that is the name you gave him - is under the special care of Mrs Atwell,' said Alexandra. 'He will get the best attention possible for his condition.'

'I mean to see him today,' said Harriet. 'I shall take a battering ram to the door.'

Alexandra looked alarmed. 'No,' she said.

Harriet regarded her for a moment and suddenly decided to go ahead and say what was uppermost in her mind straight out. She could not prepare the way by keeping up this strange pretence. 'Listen, Alex. You must listen to this. I researched your friend Minerva. You know she said she saw the Jewels of Helen when they were dug up? She insisted upon it, didn't she?'

'I understood from your last letter that you know this, but I do not understand how you know this,' answered Alexandra coldly.

'Dafydd Williams told me. That you had been told this story by Minerva. And you must know that those jewels were found in 1873 or 1874 or something like that. And that would make Minerva Atwell no more than a baby at the time. Her husband, Joseph Atwell, or the man she says was her husband, he died in '76 or '75. Oh, I can't remember the exact dates. But do you see what I'm getting at? She is telling stories about herself which cannot possibly be true. She's leading you on - '

'No,' said Alexandra decidedly. 'You are quite wrong, Mrs Day. You really are. You cannot possibly imagine how very wrong you are.'

'My dear Alexandra, is everything – are you in good health?' asked Harriet anxiously, trying a new tack.

'I have never been in better health.' Alexandra said with the wisp of a smile.

'I can't neglect to tell you this, Alex, then, if you really are quite well. And I know you'll hate me for it for a little while, but you'll thank me in the end. Listen, really listen. I researched Mr Burroughs. Do you realise that they are brother and sister, he and Minerva? Either step- or half-, I couldn't establish. Doesn't that make you wonder? Why didn't she say? Doesn't it make you wonder if she chose you to paint her portrait only because Burroughs lives in your house?'

Alex's face did not change. 'I am not at all bothered by it, if it is true. I don't see that it makes any difference. Minerva – well, you might as well learn it now – Minerva and I are very fond of each other. She wants me to be her companion and travel the world with her. We have been making plans to set up an establishment together.'

'Is that why you imitate everything she says and does then?' Harriet wanted to bite her tongue. She stopped the impulse to be unkind: it wasn't her place to dictate whom Alex should love. After a sigh, she said, 'That is your own affair. I shan't speak of it again. And I've said my say. But I feel that something is different about you, Alexandra. Nobody has – um – hit you on the head or something?' Because you talk like a kidnapped bride. Seriously. Like a mesmerised heroine. Please stop. It's upsetting and you don't need to do it, especially not with me. If you don't like me anymore, if you don't care for my friendship, then just tell me straight out. It would be so much kinder of you.'

When Alexandra responded with that tinkling society laugh that she had recently adopted, Harriet hastily rose from her seat and excused herself. She decided as she left the library that one or both of the following were true: Alexandra had retreated into a monstrous delusion; or her infatuation with the Atwell woman made her now despise Harriet.

'Well, I *am* going to see George today,' she said to herself. 'That is for sure. If this is what Minerva Atwell does to an intelligent, independent woman, what will she do to a confused, slightly idiotic young man?' She marched upstairs but as she went, something warned her to be quiet and careful. If she were to bustle in, demanding things and making a fuss, Minerva Atwell would have every right to exclude her from the hotel. Mrs Atwell had, anyway, every right to keep George in quarantine – if the tale of a contagious illness were true. And George was here, she reminded herself, under an assumed identity and was wanted for murder. No outside physicians should be involved and no police called in under any circumstances.

It just happened, as she walked along the thick red carpet of the passageway, that from a distance she saw the maid knock on George's door with a tray of breakfast. The door was opened and the tray taken. So there was a nurse within. Harriet sat down on an oyster-coloured sateen chair next to a little desk in an alcove halfway along the passage towards George's room. A billowed curtain caught up by a fat gold rope and tassel partially masked the alcove.

She pretended to be using some of the crisp hotel notepaper with which the desk was furnished and distractedly began making a shopping list. She wrote 'Sausages, Eggs, Bacon, Sausages, Apples'. Opposite the alcove, a brass-faced longcase clock showed the hour to be five minutes past eight. Its ticking pendulum had a discreet footfall like the measured tread of a policeman. Harriet added the words 'Bacon' and 'Eggs' again to her list, noticing that the loops on her 'g's were quite disorderly under the pressure of her nervous fingers; and at that moment, she heard the door of George's room open. Footsteps went along the passage away from her. The nurse had left the room. Harriet sprang up, leaving her list and the dip pen she had used on the blotter. She hurried to the door and found it was open. She got herself hastily into the room. The key was in the lock on the inside and she turned it. Her heart was beating so extremely fast, as if she had run up many stairs, that it was actually difficult to make sense of what she was looking at.

There was a window, two windows, with drawn curtains and the early light spilling round them. Between them was a dark chest of drawers. To her left was a bed, an old-fashioned one with curtains. The curtains round the bed were also drawn. The room smelt like a sick room, acrid and medicinal. The first thing Harriet wanted to do was open a window, but she crept instead towards the bed. Peeping round the curtains, in the gloom she saw damp, dark hair on the pillow. She reached in and felt George's face. Cold, sweaty. He was not well, that was for sure. She whispered, 'George, George dear? It's me. Harriet Day. Can you answer me?'

George sighed and seemed to want to turn over but Harriet could see that he was sunk in a dream. She decided that after all it was true, she would be able to do nothing. All she wanted was to sit by his bed;

but she had best get out of the room or risk expulsion from the hotel. She kissed the end of her fingers and put the kiss onto George's forehead. Then she swiftly retraced her steps to the door, turning the key to let herself out and gliding silently away. She walked back to the alcove, retrieved her absurd shopping list and then, hearing a rustle and footsteps approaching from the other end of the corridor, emerged from the alcove and walked in that direction as if by chance. Politely, she enquired of the returning nurse about her brother-in-law's health.

'I believe the worst is over, ma'am,' said the woman with a beaming smile. It was a different face and a kinder voice than the other she had encountered. 'Mr Day's been sleeping peacefully this night, after one or two intervals of delirium late yesterday evening, apparently. I came on at midnight and Mrs Atwell personally came and administered a calming draught at one o'clock in the morning. Devoted, she is. She will have her say, of course, but I think he's on the mend.'

'And is it measles, nurse? Or the smallpox? Nobody has been very specific about his illness. I have been to enquire frequently but no one tells me anything and just shuts the door in my face.'

'Measles, ma'am? Smallpox? There's never been a spot or a rash on him. Just heats and cold sweat and a heaviness. But he's young. He'll pull through.'

'No spots, did you say?'

'Not one, not that I can see,' said the nurse with a smile. 'But if you'll excuse me, ma'am, I have to sit by my charge. I'm keeping him in the dark to be sure not to hurt his eyes when he does eventually wake. You never can tell in such cases. Brainfever is unpredictable in the extreme and I don't want to set him back.'

'Brainfever?'

'Well, in *my* nursing experience, which I may say is thirty years, when a poor soul rambles and raves and is fevered, we call it brainfever. Patience will see him clear. Mrs Atwell gives him the medicine regular too, very calming.'

Harriet gave the nurse her heartfelt thanks and walked away, pondering what she had said.

CHAPTER TWENTY-NINE

It was one of those evenings when you don't go out without a big scarf wrapped round your mouth. That's what mother said anyway. Janet had been despatched to buy some fish and chips. Now that she was home for a day or two, there was a mildly celebratory air in the Fairlight household which had led to the suggestion of a treat from Mrs Jones's shop.

Janet's little brother begged to accompany her and so she had set out, holding his hand, to make the journey along the road, round the square, along the next street and all the way to the corner. You could get the loveliest, most generous bit of cod here and chips, all crisp and hot and salted; and wrapped up twice, in a piece of white paper and then big sheets of newspaper. When she got them home, they would eat them off the paper because that way it tasted nicer, her mum said. Her brother set about bargaining to carry the package home because it was warm; but he would squash it and so there was a bit of an argument when they first set out. The streets were wet and misty and not many people were about. Dark of course; but it was only six o'clock and Mrs Fairlight was not at all bothered that Janet would run into any trouble so near home.

'Look, over there, Chrissy, that's where I work, in that big house.'

'Cor,' said Christopher. 'But that's not as big as a proper house.'

'Yes, it is. It must be as big as a proper house, because it is a proper house. You numpty.' She gave his hand an affectionate shake.

'A proper big one would be like the Queen's.'

'Oh. Well, yes, that would be a proper big one. And I'm going to take you to see the Guards changing there soon, Chrissy. When I was eleven, Father took me to see the Changing of the Guard at eleven o'clock, and it was the eleventh day of the month! All elevens. What do you think of that?'

'But I'll be seven,' Christopher protested.

'Yes, Chris. Next birthday I am going to take you and maybe mother can come too.'

'And will it be at seven? Because I'll be seven and will it happen at seven o'clock?'

Janet gently explained the timetable for the Changing of the Guard at Buckingham Palace as they walked along and Christopher decided that quite a number of toys might need to come with him, particularly a red fire engine which he did not actually possess but which a friend might lend him for the occasion.

The fish shop, run by Lily Jones's Auntie Pippa, was banging with noise and light. People were waiting for their orders, gazing out at the misty night, chatting together or reading the evening newspapers which Mrs Jones left out for them. There was a wonderful smell of frying food sharpened with vinegar. Big glass jars of pickled eggs and pickled onions, swimming mysteriously in green depths, glinted next to shakers of salt. Everyone seemed cheerful because, thought Janet, what can be more cheerful than fish and chips on a cold, misty evening?

Mrs Jones was a lady of immense dignity, with arms like hams and hands as red and mottled as minced meat. She recognised the Fairlight children and paused to give Christopher a little twist of crispy batter drops for him to amuse himself with while they waited. There was no time to talk but Janet would have liked to know how Lily was getting on at the big house.

She herself now felt recovered and had steeled herself to go back tomorrow. They had all been frightened and tense that day; and because of Lily's silliness, Janet had over-reacted. Her hysterics had ensured that she was given a weekend off, which had given her time to think things through: what she had really heard was perhaps not what she thought she had heard. Mr Burroughs collected odd things, old mummies, and had bought a strange pair of earrings. She remembered that nice Dr Watson's voice saying, 'The girl went missing and may have eloped'. That was it, then. May Dutton ran off with the Postman, just like rumour had it. Shocking mad thing to do, but not a murder. After all, the Postman could have come forward, couldn't he? But maybe he had done? Janet could not be sure now.

They paid their money over and Mrs Jones winked and said she'd 'put in extra' for good luck; and then Christopher tussled briefly with his sister to be allowed to carry the warming package and they departed into the night. The mist was thickening and Janet made a point of positioning her brother's green muffler carefully over his mouth. He hated it and said it tickled and was unbearable. She put her own tartan scarf in place and explained through the wool that it was to keep the moths out. Since Christopher had a fear of moths, he protested no longer.

They came to the railings of the square, looming up through the fog, skinny and crooked where generations of boys had worked them to create a bolt-hole. The gates to the square were locked of an evening of course 'to keep the place respectable', as Mrs Jenkins said, but the children knew that really anyone could get into the place and hide under the bushes. It was just as they paused to inspect the bent railings, in a kind of ritual devotion to the inspiring effort of so many children, that a man's voice caught Janet's ear. It was speaking low beyond the railings, inside the square and among the bushes. She quickly put a finger to Christopher's scarf-covered mouth to show him to keep quiet. She recognised the voice.

'And so I'm giving you due warning. '

'Why do you think the worst of me, sir? I protected your interests in the most horrible circumstances, and you know it. You know I stood by you. You'll remember that till your dying day.'

'Yes, since you constantly remind me of it and I am constantly paying you for it. But if such a thing were to happen, well, we'd have to think what to do about it.'

'What do you mean, sir, think what to do? You mean what might happen if – say, a gentleman was to come asking questions?'

'Why do you say that?'

'Just because you said it, sir. You said "if such a thing were to happen" in such a way as to suggest that such a thing *might* happen.'

'You simply need to keep your mouth shut. That is the beginning and end of the matter.'

'I am not under any obligation to. You robbed me of my living and I have every reason to expect -'

'Think! Any question of the earrings, it all devolves upon you. I need only say that you offered them to me and I bought them from you. Whom will they believe, little man?'

'You'd lie like that, would you? Maybe I've got my own friends now. '

'Oh? How interesting,' said the first voice: Mr Burroughs's voice - and Janet imagined him leaning in and perhaps looking coldly into the other man's eyes. 'I wonder who *your* friends are? Perhaps you'd like to tell me?'

'I told you, I'm not afraid of you. You're as vulnerable as me,' the second voice said stoutly. 'And if there *is* all this money, then why am I left to rot in this manner? 'tin't fair. Ask your rich men to help a poor man who suffered for their research. If they want me to keep silent then I say they should pay for it.'

'Oh, Mr Bateman, I would not go along that road. Not with me, my dear fellow.'

'Very well, but this is not blackmail, it is wages, and so pay up. Not five shillings, five guineas. Twenty-five guineas!'

'Ridiculous.'

'Not ridiculous if you was living where I am living and putting up with what I am putting up with. I know what I want now. Next time, twenty-five guineas.'

'I suggest you think long and hard before you make me angry.'

'Threatening me, Mr Burroughs? You might as well know, there *has* been a gentleman asking questions. And when I say a gentleman, I mean a real gentleman, not like you, with lovely shoes, beautiful clothes like real gents have. Ow! Leave off!'

There was the sound of scuffling and the laurels heaved and were pressed suddenly against the railings as if a body had been pushed into them. Janet and Christopher jumped backwards off the kerb and into the road. Just at that moment, a small dark man appeared and squeezed his way between the bent railings and went dashing off into the thickening fog. Within seconds a more bulky and slow figure followed, stumbling as he extricated himself from the gap. The children stood silent. He cast them an angry distracted glance as he picked himself up, flicking at the knees of his trousers, and quickly disappeared in the direction of the departing footsteps.

'Cor,' said Christopher. 'That was int'resting.'

'Let's get home,' said Janet, trying to hide the shake in her voice. She was very glad she had put that scarf up so high and tight, and with her tartan tam o'shanter pulled low, there had been little of her face to see. Mr Burroughs would not know who the girl was or if she heard all that strange talk.

Janet did not tell her mother that she recognised one of the men from the incident when Christopher took it upon himself to explain it eloquently over the fish and chips. He was particularly interested in the fact that two grown-ups had burst out through 'the Naughty Boy Gap' as he called it; and that Janet had promised to take him to see the Queen on his birthday.

Later that night, as she dried her hair by the fire, she asked her mother about May Dutton. The answer was simply that the girl shouldn't be discussed: she was a disgrace. No more information was forthcoming, without tempting the wrath of Mrs Fairlight. It was better not to enquire and lead her mother to deliver one of her terrifying sermons upon girls who brought shame on the family. After all, Janet had settled 'beautifully' into Mrs Roberts's house, Mrs Jenkins said. She had good friends now in Lily Jones and Amy Matthews. She had wisely kept quiet about how much she had adored poor Mr George – that would certainly have led to a lecture – and she said nothing about nice Mr Williams now; she did not want to have to change her position. If she left, there was no guarantee that she would find work locally. Suppose she had to go miles away and not be able to see Christopher on his birthday or her sisters when they came home? No. She kept her mouth shut.

The next morning, she walked over to resume her post at Mrs Roberts's house. She was all ready to start the new day, dressed warmly against the freezing morning air, with the brightly-coloured hat and scarf disposed in exactly the same manner as last night. Mr Burroughs happened to glance out of a window as she crossed the road from the square and approached the house, ready to descend the area steps and knock on the backdoor. He watched her.

*

Dr Watson was not surprised when Detective Browning was shown into the sitting room. It was the day after his visit to the police station so he assumed Browning had come to discuss the papers. And perhaps to avail himself of the offer of a little sight of his stories.

'Delighted to see you again, Detective,' said Watson. 'Do sit down!'

'Thank you, Doctor. Well, well, so it's all true!' he said, surveying the parlour. 'There are the bullet holes in the wall, as large as life! And the Persian slipper!'

'Yes, yes, it is all true,' said Watson. 'You may look at it all, as long as nothing is touched. I would never advise anyone to lay a finger on Holmes's papers or work. Nor his tobacco.'

'I quite agree, Doctor. And I do certainly appreciate the opportunity to inspect the working environment of Mr Holmes. He strikes me as a very interesting mixture, Doctor, if I may say. I think you said somewhere in one of your tales that it was a good thing he never turned to crime. I have to agree with you there. It would be most unfortunate for us all if he did.'

'Thankfully, he will not, Detective.'

'But can one ever be sure? Can one ever be sure of anything?'

'In this life, no. But I think I will continue to trust in the basic goodness of Sherlock Holmes.'

'Ah,' said Browning with a philosophical look on his young face, 'you see, I think nothing can be a hundred percent cert. Not in the horses, not in crime, not in love.'

'And what has led you to say that?'

'I came partly to see the rooms, I won't deny, but also to share with you some thoughts I've had on that Albert Burroughs. I wanted your opinion. I would also like Mr Holmes's opinion, but since he isn't here …' He looked hopefully towards the closed doors of the bedrooms.

'No, he isn't. He is abroad, as I told you yesterday. I have not heard from him for some time. But do tell me, what have you learnt?'

'Well, I had a good look at them papers,' said Browning, 'and I'm afraid I had to discuss the details with Inspector Miller. He wasn't too keen to have Burroughs into the station for questioning again – said he was a respectable gentleman and that it would be impolite to keep ruffling his feathers -'

'Ruffling his feathers?'

'Those were his very words. But he did give me permission to call at his offices and interview him again, which I did, very private and discreet. He is more than a little fed up with being interviewed, there's no doubt about it, and was remarkably short with me. And to deal with the unsavoury aspect first, you'll mind that there were some writings among those papers which dealt with remarkable filth; and I felt it my duty to ask him about them. He said he is making a study of criminal perversion and that these are his notes. He keeps them locked up because he wants to protect the innocent from such things.'

'Well, that makes sense, Detective. I myself have had to suppress some of the cases that Holmes and I have worked on. The world is simply not prepared for them. And what about the missing girl? What happened to the man she was supposed to have eloped with?'

'Disappeared along o' her, it's thought. Never turned up for work on the Monday. Supports the theory that they went off together.'

'Ah. I see. Unless it was a double murder … no, no, you're right, Detective. I am introducing fictions to support my hypothesis. They are probably living in bliss somewhere. Let's not get ahead of ourselves.'

'Agreed. Anyway, leaving aside the Dutton case and the earrings, as I looked through the documents, it occurred to me that they show a most unhealthy and long-standing obsession with that foreign gent he went on to accuse of immorality and murder.'

'Well, yes,' said Watson with a pondering air, trying to sound as if this point had never occurred to him before. 'Your insight does you credit. How did you deduce that?'

'Description of a certain character in his stories fits description of Arden; little pencil sketch matches the one we borrowed from the artist-lady as owns the house; several rather disturbing tales in there. I won't go into detail but – well, it was all a bit distasteful to be honest and not something I would want to talk about.'

'I don't suppose you mentioned that to him?'

'No, I have to say I didn't personally but Burroughs himself brought up the subject. Odd that, isn't it? Asked if we had any clues to Arden's whereabouts. Was very severe about it. It struck me that there was a strange edge to his talk and I didn't like it. If I were a lawyer, I'd make a good deal out of these papers and argue that Burroughs had a kind of monomania about him, and that his testimony on the alleged murder of Valentine Cabot should be treated with caution.'

'That is an excellent point, Detective. And what about the financial transactions? I hope that, as we discussed, you were able to protect the source who brought the Atwell connection to my attention?'

'Yes, I was. I was able to make out that our information was the result of a constable looking inside an envelope. Burroughs looked flushed though when I said that. I thought at the time, that's got him. Hit a nerve.'

'Interesting.'

'Anyway, I asked what these transactions represented and he said it was merely the family way of supporting him – paying his rent, paying for articles he wrote anonymously in the newpapers, puffs for the firm, that sort of thing.'

Dr Watson sat forward, resting his elbows on his knees and chin on clasped hands.

'You're not praying, are you, Doctor?' asked Browning interestedly.

'No, not at all. I am trying to think. I am lost without my Johnson!'

'Ha. Who would that be now?'

'I merely mean Mr Holmes, Detective. He calls me his Boswell, so I call him … oh, never mind. I am just trying to think how we can prove a connection between the theft of body parts and the firm of Atwell.'

'You'll not get to the bottom of all those transactions without a court order to search through the Atwell finances and you won't get that with the slim bit of evidence you have. It's all surmise and circumstances. Oh, and I should have mentioned, Burroughs has got a shopkeeper to vouch for the sale of the ears. Said it was Museum Street, that antiquities shop – I've seen it myself, Roman pots, bits of this and that, dusty old place. Even saw a mummified cat in the window once. He says the shopkeeper will write a letter to confirm that he purchased the ears as part of his ongoing interest in ancient history. So that's another dead end.'

'I don't believe it, Browning. I don't believe that Burroughs is a collector of Egyptian mummies. Where's the rest of his collection then? Also under his bed?'

'Oh, you may be sure that a "collection" will be found, somewhere conveniently far away, and it will all be vouched for. And Burroughs said he used to hang about round excavations and the like when he was a young fellow, out in Cyprus and Mesopotamia, being illustrator or something to a Mr Hogarth. It's a fact. No, Miller won't want to waste time and resources on investigating an upstanding fellow like Albert Burroughs.'

CHAPTER THIRTY

The days and nights blended into each other. There was darkness; and candlelight or lamplight, shaded red, in the far corner of the room; and an acrid smell of dust in the curtains round the bed, which shook out into his nostrils when they were drawn back. He forgot where he was. For a long time he was walking along a hard, baked-white path and the shimmer of heat detached the earth and floated it into the sky. A small pool was tepid and green and slimey. At night the insects sang. You had to hide from the sun. When it came on, at the time of year when the summer was at its height, that was when Dumuzid had to die.

In the cracking heat, he felt his lips parch and his whole body dessicating. He heard the ritual words again which must be spoken to the Gala-Tura:

> *The sweepings of the city streets be thy food,*
> *The gutters of the city be thy drink,*
> *The shadow of the wall be thy abode,*
> *The thresholds be thy dwelling-place;*
> *Drunkard and sot strike thy cheek!"*

'George, George dear,' said a voice speaking over the voice of the Gatekeeper, shimmering across the wavering desert air.

When he opened his eyes a long time later, he saw the red light over there, and the curtains round the bed, and he gradually recognised where he was. The voice had been his mother's voice, but she had used the wrong name, but time had looped in upon itself and brought her here, so perhaps it didn't matter.

*

At mid-morning, the black coach with its heavy black horses drew up at the hotel. A single passenger descended with a modest valise, unhurriedly scanned the building before him and then the landscape around it, and stepped into the vestibule. The first thing he saw was Jerome Pollitt sitting on a stool at the reception desk, talking to the clerk. Pollitt looked up, saw him and rose. 'Hello, Crowley,' he said. They shook hands, looking slightly confused as if surprised by each other. Crowley signed in at the desk and sent his bag up to his room.

He and Pollitt then walked out into the valley to talk privately.

Harriet saw their departing backs as she came down the stairs. She had been to George's door again since her secret visit this morning before breakfast. She had sat in the little alcove and read a novel as she waited hopefully for the nurse to leave the room, but nothing had come of it. Neither could she persuade the attendant to let her enter. Then she thought of sending in a little note to be read to George if he were able to listen. She sat again at the desk and wrote, 'Dearest Edward, I am here at the hotel. I shall come to your door often to find out how you are. I know I will see you again soon. Your affectionate sister-in-law, Harriet Day.' It troubled her that he would perhaps forget who he was supposed to be – or even who she was – but she could think of nothing else to do. She gave the note to the nurse who promised to read it aloud to him as soon as he showed signs of comprehension. Wishing she had some flowers to send in, she went downstairs and asked that nice Mr Sandford at the desk to arrange to send up a basket of sugarplums with a note thanking the nurses. Not knowing what else to do with herself, she decided to settle in the solarium and read the rest of her book; but it bored her and half an hour later she was quite glad to be interrupted by the approach of Mr Pollitt and his friend. 'Delighted to make your acquaintance, Mr Crowley,' she said as they were introduced.

'And yours, Mrs Day,' said Crowley with a little bow of the head. Pollitt had brought him through to find this lady, saying that they had become great friends. He was relieved to discover that she looked like a person of intelligence and stability. He had been extremely disappointed to find that the object of his visit was confined to his room; and rather vexed that Jerome seemed to have spent most of his time with the desk clerk. He was also somewhat distracted, as he sat down, by the stone heads on plinths he could just see by peering through to the salon.

'Don't you, Crowley?' said Pollitt.

Crowley found he was being looked at by both Jerome and Mrs Day. 'Don't I what?' he asked.

'Write poetry,' said Pollitt.

'Yes, yes, I do,' he answered. 'It is very gorgeous and solemn. But is it the kind you think Mrs Day would like? Actually, it probably isn't. But it is excellent.'

'Do you recite it, Mr Pollitt?' asked Mrs Day.

'No, I don't. But I could. Why don't I, Crowley?'

Crowley knew that Pollitt was being mischievous. 'You can't embarrass me,' he said. 'I am perfectly beyond any kind of shaming. My verses are not for the general public. They are erotic and some might think satanic.' He waited to see the effect of this upon the rather frumpy middle-aged lady sitting opposite him, with her cup of tea in one hand, half raised to her mouth, and a saucer held underneath it in the other. If he had hoped that she would spill her drink or blush, he was disappointed.

'How interesting,' she said. 'I am not especially familiar with erotic literature, Mr Crowley, but I am an admirer of the liberating thoughts of the Langham Place circle. I believe that social equality will go hand-in-hand with sexual enlightenment.'

It was Jerome Pollitt who almost choked. He had not expected such a reply from Harriet. But Crowley's eyes lit up. 'Yes,' he said. 'What is necessary is not to seek after some fantastic ideal relationship, utterly unsuited to our real needs, but to discover the true nature of those needs, to fulfil them, and rejoice in them.'

'I do so agree,' said Harriet, putting down her tea-cup and saucer on the table. 'And - don't you agree? - the creation of a better society absolutely demands that each individual goes into him- or herself and makes peace, so to speak, with all the forces found there.'

Jerome began to think that Harriet was somehow more in tune with Aleister than he himself. He had an overwhelming urge to interrupt. 'What's the news about old George, then?' he asked. 'Still confined to barracks, all spotty?'

Harriet frowned. 'First I was told it was contagious spots. Then this morning that it is brainfever and he must be kept in the dark and not allowed to see anyone. Before breakfast, I took it upon myself to sneak in when the nurse was absent. He is clammy and apparently unconscious, so something is wrong, but it isn't at all clear what. No fever that I could tell, but sweating, yes. He did not respond to my voice. The nurse I spoke to mentioned episodes of delirium last night. Well, that *is* a sign of fever, is it not?'

'I am sorry to hear that he is so ill. I very much hope to see him recover fully within the next few days. It is of the utmost urgency that I speak to him,' said Crowley, lowering his voice. 'Dr Watson and I believe that we have discovered clues to Burroughs's motive for trying to do away with him.'

'Indeed? What is your line of enquiry?'

'Impossible to discuss just now, Mrs Day. But concerning a serious criminal act on the part of Burroughs.'

'Which George witnessed?'

'Only Arden can elucidate that,' said Crowley gravely. 'But that brings me to the letter I found waiting for me here. It's from Watson. Would you care to read it?'

Harriet read the letter which contained information concerning the earrings in the box. They fell into a discussion of what it might mean and how much Minerva Atwell knew.

'I really don't care for her, you know,' said Pollitt. 'Her character is such a strange mixture of flirt and assassin, I hardly know how to talk to her. Do you think that just by coming into the hotel she made George collapse? An overwhelming personality!'

'Overwhelming. Yes, I think you might have hit upon something there,' said Crowley.

'Oh?' said Pollitt.

'I mean that for a mind organised like his, just a little extra strain may be too much and it will manifest physically. I see it all the time with Bennett. The stronger his powers, the weaker his body.'

'It's just asthma, Aleister,' said Pollitt with a little roll of his eyes.

'Just asthma? There is no such thing as "just" an illness. Besides, I have seen Bennett cast a force towards another person so intense that the other was blasted to the floor and took hours to recover.'

'That sounds extraordinary, Mr Crowley,' said Harriet. 'You are speaking of a friend of yours? How did that come about?'

'Oh, somebody questioned the usefulness of wands.'

'Very nice way of making a point, I must say,' said Pollitt.

'But Allan Bennett is in fact the soul of kindness,' explained Crowley, ignoring Pollitt. 'And he is to be my magical tutor in the autumn.'

There was a charged pause.

'Oh really?' asked Pollitt sternly. 'Your magical tutor? You need one of those too now, do you? And where might that be going to happen? In your rooms at Cambridge? In Chancery Lane? Or some other little hidey-hole. Up the Alps perchance? Excuse me, my dear Mrs Day, but I feel the need to take a turn about the room.'

Harriet cleared her throat and, to distract from the brewing argument, she forced herself to discuss the changes she had noticed in Alexandra. Crowley listened attentively despite the patrolling up and down of his friend within earshot. 'Another thing,' she went on, 'and this will sound ridiculous, but she looks a lot younger than she did a few weeks ago. I mean noticeably younger, younger by ten years.'

'Extraordinary,' said Crowley.

Jerome, circling in the vicinity with an aloof, slightly suffering expression but becoming interested despite himself, deigned to seat himself graciously on the chair next to Harriet. 'How useful,' he said, with a shoulder turned away from Crowley. 'May one enquire how old she is then?'

'First tell me how old you think she is.'

'A lady's age, h'mm, impossible to guess. If you want a completely honest opinion, then I say approximately thirty-five years of age. Not what you'd call young, but not by any means old. Will that do?'

'She is forty-nine. Nearly fifty.'

'By Jove,' said Pollitt. 'That is extraordinary.'

'And this has happened in the space of weeks?' asked Crowley incredulously. 'Mrs Roberts must no doubt have been using the famous beauty products – but they could never produce this effect. It is too marked. In fact, it is impossible. Are you sure it is not merely an illusion, the product of cosmetics, hair dye, and so forth?'

'I don't think so. At least, I cannot detect their presence,' said Harriet. 'I use something of Atwell's myself. It is just the powder form, the Compact. It does have the advantage of conferring a bloom of course but its best effect is a calmness. Something to do with the fragrance, I suppose. I find I miss it if I don't use it.'

'You miss it if you don't use it? Like a narcotic, you mean?'

'I'd hardly call it a narcotic, Mr Crowley.'

'It's a thought though,' said Pollitt. 'I say, Mr Crowley, let me have one of those.' He paused while Crowley gave him a cigarette and lit it for him. Jerome seemed to cheer up. 'Yes, what was I saying? Like these dratted things – if you don't have one, you notice yourself getting nervous and irritable. Is it like that?'

'I suppose it *might* be,' said Harriet.

'Very clever,' said Pollitt.

'And there are other products?' asked Crowley, nodding to Jerome in agreement.

'A cream, I think. I know Alex has used the cream, because she mentioned it. You rub it in three times a day and have a little rest, or something.'

'How delightfully decadent,' said Pollitt. 'I should like to try that.'

'There'll be more than that,' said Crowley. 'An injection is my guess. I wouldn't be surprised if your friend's arms were all over puncture marks.' With a glimmer of a smile, he added, 'Like Dr Watson's detective friend, apparently.'

'Really?' asked Pollitt with interest.

'Yes, I'll tell you later. But now, Mrs Day, I hope you won't be offended if I ask this: is it possible that your perception of Mrs Roberts's appearance might be affected by whether *you* are using the compact yourself?'

'Are you implying that the calming effect might interfere with my eyesight?'

'Or expectations.'

'Well, I think the idea is very interesting,' said Harriet. 'But I personally don't expect to look younger just with a dab of powder and I didn't expect Alex to look younger either. I feel sure, however, that a neutral observer would see that Alex's appearance has changed. If only one were here who knew her before – George, for example. Did he not notice or comment on the change in her appearance, Mr Pollitt?'

'*George?* I am afraid George was simply useless when he was awake and functioning. He became a complete infant when Mrs Roberts was about the place. And then, of course, he had the Lady with the Bunions to cope with too, the one he said was always staring into his face. Did I tell you about that, Aleister?'

'I remember you did mention a lady with bandaged feet in your letter,' said Crowley.

'Bandaged feet?' broke in Harriet. 'Well, that is something I recall from Alex's first letter – back when she first arrived here and she still wrote human letters, she mentioned a woman with whom she had made friends. Yes, I remember the phrase, *hobble on bandaged feet*. Alexandra was very upset because she died quite unexpectedly, the lady. She passed away before George came to the hotel.'

'Well, well,' said Crowley, almost to himself. 'I think Arden was being told something. I wonder what it was?'

CHAPTER THIRTY-ONE

In London, the day was dreary. The morning had thickened steadily to yet another fog and Mrs Jenkins was inclined to say Drat under her breath. She had heard from Old Stokes that the butcher had had to close up today because of a bereavement and none of the orders were going out; and that there had been a fire at the fishmongers, of all places. She had nothing in the larder but a pint of cream, some brawn and half a dozen eggs. That would not feed the gents and the girls and herself. 'Janet! Get down here now,' she called up the stairs. 'Put your coat on. You need to go down to the market and get some things for me.'

It was a relief for Janet to be able to leave the house. Mr Williams was in his room and that was all right, but Mr Burroughs was in too – in the parlour. It made her uncomfortable to know he was sitting so unnaturally quiet by the fire. She did not want to go in there. He kept clearing his throat – she could hear him as she polished the brass fitments on the front door. It got right on her nerves and made her jump each time.

When she had returned to work, she found that Amy Matthews had declared everything Janet had overheard was 'rot'. She made this assertion on the authority of an oblique conversation with Mrs Jenkins which, she said, cleared Mr Burroughs of suspicion but enforced secrecy concerning all his doings. Janet was inclined to allow this to go unchallenged. Nevertheless, she kept away from him.

The fog made it dangerous in the street. You couldn't see more than a yard in front of you and it did something odd to the sounds too: noises were difficult to place. Crossing the road was risky – once or twice a horse and cart came looming suddenly out of the wall of mist, almost on top of her. After a bit, she realised that footsteps were following her. Nothing unusual in that, except that they slowed down when she slowed down and speeded up when she did too for a little while as if someone wanted to keep her in sight; and then vanished. She thought no more of it. There was a little side street which she always took as a shortcut and it was here that she unexpectedly met Mr Burroughs, coming along towards her from the other direction. He stopped and smiled at her.

'Ah, what a coincidence!' he said, tapping his shiny fingernails on the handle of his cane. 'I had no idea you were out shopping, Janet. A thick day, isn't it?'

'Yes sir,' she agreed.

'I'll just turn back with you for a moment. I am very busy, of course, but in fact you have been on my mind today.' He spoke in a friendly manner but she thought he had a way of swallowing his voice as if his throat were drawn in too tight. 'I was just thinking that I needed to consult with you about something. Now, I hope you don't mind my saying this, but the other evening, I saw a girl and a young lad standing near the square. The girl had on exactly the same hat and scarf as yourself and it wasn't until I was thinking about it later that I realised you might be able to help me. What a fortunate chance! You see, Janet, I work with the police. I was investigating a criminal and indeed, I was in the course of an important interrogation in the square that night. He escaped me, but it would be immensely helpful if I had a witness to what was said.'

'Oh?' said Janet. She brightened up. So that was what Amy was hinting at: Mr Burroughs worked with the police. Could that be the explanation for all the weird things going on? 'Yes, it was me as was standing there with Christopher. I didn't like to mention it, it weren't my place. I didn't know you are with the police, Mr Burroughs.'

'No, I like to keep it very quiet. Undercover. Don't tell anyone else.' Almost playfully, he placed a finger on his thin lips and Janet noticed with a slight shudder that they were wet. 'That's what I was doing that night, you see.'

'Like Dr Watson and that Mr Crowley then,' she said.

'What's that?' he asked a little sharply, glancing down at her as they walked side by side into the market.

She noticed his tone and became wary again, suddenly remembering a strange dream she once had about old Mr Valentine. 'Oh, nothing, in a story I read.'

'Yes, but those kinds of stories are nothing like as exciting and dangerous as the real thing. My work is very important.'

'Yes sir.'

'Well, Janet – oh but look,' he said as they walked slowly along, 'that poor woman over there has a tray of my very favourite kind of confectionery. Have you ever tried this? I've never seen this on sale in London before. This is called baklava. I used to eat it when I was a young fellow on my travels.' Without waiting for an answer, Mr Burroughs suddenly purchased one of the sweetmeats wrapped in a paper from the Turkish lady and Janet found herself tasting the delicacy for the first time. He stood leaning on his cane and watched her consume it. She was embarrassed but could not refuse. It was like eating heaven. She thanked him but was not so disarmed that she lost all her caution. Nevertheless, the glorious combination of honey and nuts and pastry warmed her all the way through, leaving her bolder, if a little stickier.

'Well, I won't keep you,' Mr Burroughs said pleasantly. 'I'm sure you are running errands for Mrs Jenkins, and she can be very ferocious. But I almost forgot! Silly of me! While we're chatting let me ask, did you by any chance hear that bad man, the one I was talking to that evening, say something about crimes – about murders? He is a suspect, you see.'

'No, not really, Mr Burroughs. I just heard talk about money and stuff,' said Janet. 'And I don't eavesdrop, you know.'

'Well, good, I'm glad to hear that. Your honesty impressed me before too. But it would be most helpful for my investigation if you could remember whether he said something about – well, certain earrings. That he had sold me certain earrings.'

'No, I remember you saying that that would be what *you* would say and that would make trouble for *him*,' said Janet. She said it with the intention of letting him know that she was astute and investigative. But his face took on a closed look as if something inside it had withdrawn itself and she wished immediately that she had simply denied hearing anything.

'Thank you, Janet. But you're wrong, you know. Your memory is at fault. Anyway, get along and do your errands.' He turned and walked away through the sparse crowd until the fog closed in upon him.

*

In the afternoon, Harriet ascertained from the nurse coming off duty that George was improving. She gave Harriet a sunny smile which confirmed the efficacy of the sugarplums. Feeling reassured, she wandered outside and came unexpectedly across Jerome Pollitt standing by the front door in the sunshine, looking at the sky.

'Good afternoon, Mr Pollitt.'

'What a lovely afternoon it is,' he answered. He looked unusually calm and peaceful. 'I hope you had a lovely walk this morning. I am sorry I didn't see you at lunch. Aleister and I decided to have a tray in our – I mean in his room.'

'And what are your plans for this afternoon? The weather has brightened up, hasn't it?'

'A long walk in the woods, I think, away up there on the ridge. It will be charming in this sunshine.'

'Delightful,' agreed Harriet.

'Are you ready then?' asked Crowley, coming out of the door. 'Oh good afternoon, Mrs Day. We are just off to explore the tunnel. Mysteries, you know!'

'*Tunnel?*' protested poor Jerome. 'I thought we were walking gently among the trees and listening to the birdsong? That's what *I* suggested we should do.'

'Yes, I know. But then I thought it would be more fun and a lot more exciting to go down the tunnel. Come on, Polly, get your boots on, you can't go out in those silly city things.'

'I don't want to go down that tunnel. And I haven't got any boots, just horrible galoshes.' He turned appealingly to Harriet, saying only half in jest, 'It is genuinely hair-raising, Mrs Day. He can't make me. Don't let him take me.'

Harriet laughed. 'I think it sounds fascinating.'

'There you see! Mrs Day thinks it would be interesting. Let's get going!'

Pollitt's brow darkened and Harriet said, 'May I suggest something? Why not explore the tunnel this afternoon and take your ridgeway walk tomorrow? Why, Mr Pollitt, you could arrange for a picnic luncheon to be prepared and you could take it up to that lovely spot with the beautiful view.'

The idea seemed to appease Pollitt whose face now brightened. He went over to his friend the desk clerk and began a long conversation about the potential contents of a splendid picnic basket, to include, of course, champagne along with as many delicacies as the kitchen could offer.

It was Crowley who now looked impatient. 'I can't bear waiting about,' he said. 'I want to be off and doing. We need to explore. There is something deep beneath this valley. I tried to explain it to Pollitt, but he dismisses all such stuff out of hand. Thinks he's realistic when in fact he's just pessimistic.'

Harriet looked out over the yellow-grey of the wintery trees in the sunlight. 'There *is* something odd about this hotel, this valley, the hot spring. The stone heads, for example, the strange feeling of the place. It would be interesting to know more.'

'Then come with us this afternoon, Mrs Day,' said Crowley, surprisingly.

Harriet, rather flattered, agreed and went to get her own stout boots on. When they all reconvened and Jerome learned that Harriet was to be one of the party, he seemed relieved, as if her presence would somehow stop it from being quite so cold and dark down there. So ten minutes later, the little group followed a footpath leading away from the White Stone Well, which led first round towards the back of the hotel, glimpsed through the trees, then along a fold of the land and finally struck a path running along the bank of a little river. Its rolling brown waters were deep and cold and it was clearly navigable. A mile down the bank they came upon a square cutting which in some remote time had been used to moor boats. There was even the hint of a landing stage with broken stone posts, one still with half a rusted skeleton of a ring attached. Ancient slimed steps descended into the water.

'Has the river risen over the centuries, do you think?' asked Pollitt, peering distastefully at the submerged growths rippling and fanning out from the crumbled stone in the current. The steps were visible a foot or two under the surface of the river and then disappeared into deeper murky water. A small brown fish swam into view, flicked its tail and vanished.

'I shouldn't think so,' answered Harriet. 'Wouldn't the winter rains have swollen it? A summer visit to this spot would probably be very different. '

'I don't like the look of steps going down under water. I don't know why. It makes my hair stand on end, it really does,' said Pollitt.

Crowley said, 'Well, that would be an old fear, Jerome. You should find out your past life and lay it to rest.'

Pollitt winked conspiratorially at Harriet as if to confirm that they both agreed this was nonsense.

The mouth of the tunnel had been hidden and partially blocked by an old landslide. Trees and bushes had planted themselves on the slope, forming a labyrinth of boughs and trunks. In summer, the entrance, hardly more than a diagonal slash of darkness, would be invisible from the path. The smell of damp earth breathed out of it.

'There's a sound, isn't there?' said Harriet, as she lit her lantern. They had brought the sturdy bulls-eye kind, provided by the hotel, which could direct a beam through the magnifying lens at the front.

'Yes, there is. Can you hear it, Polly?' asked Crowley, peering into the gloom.

'It's that half-heard thrumming. I remember it from last time. It's horrible.'

They made their way carefully through the gap. Towards the entrance, the floor had been much affected by the old landslip and although there were traces of paving, it was so cracked and disrupted as to almost be unidentifiable. As they proceeded, this became smoother. The tiles were in places whole and fine, a slick terracotta colour with occasional undamaged runs of glazed cream and brown squares at the borders. Feet had worn a shallow channel along the middle. Although the patterned floor lent itself to a familiar timescale, the tunnel walls showed no working. As Harriet thought this, a hint of its immeasurable age crept upon her, age not just of the rock but of the darkness. Sunlight had never stepped into this place.

A twist of the tunnel took them out of reach of the light from the entrance and they became dependent on their lanterns. The air felt close and damp and if they stopped to listen, it was silent except for the occasional drip of water. After a while, Pollitt halted and held up a hand. They had come to signs of workmanship: a little round-headed doorway. Pointing his beam forward, Jerome showed them that they were at the foot of a spiral staircase. A hint of greyness in the dark above suggested natural light was seeping in somehow.

'I absolutely hate this bit,' he announced, his voice echoing slightly. 'I remember it so well from last time. It was worse then, because George was leading the way and he seemed to walk in a dream without due regard for health and safety. I think this spiral is possibly worse coming down than going up. Just telling you now, in case you have second thoughts about going up at all – I say, Crowley, come back! Would you credit it, Mrs Day, he didn't even listen?'

Crowley had slipped past Pollitt while he talked and was half way up the stairs. The light of his lantern could be seen above them. They began to climb, Harriet first, Pollitt bringing up the rear.

'Take care, Mrs Day,' said Pollitt. 'This is the crumbliest bit of all.'

'Yes, I can see,' said Harriet. 'And very steep.'

'And this is where skeletal hands might come poking out from those places, those there, where the spiral is falling in, look, be really careful!'

'I like the fact that you are so solicitous for *my* health and safety, Mr Pollitt.'

'Well, to be perfectly frank, since we are on an adventure together and therefore must trust each other to the death, as Aleister invariably tells me when talking about glaciers and such like, if you were to break an ankle, it would be encumbent upon me to carry you home. And I am not sure I have the necessary muscular equipment to do so, so I'd rather you didn't.'

'We can use Mr Crowley as a packhorse, don't worry,' whispered Harriet.

'What's that?' came Crowley's voice from the shadows above. 'No rescues available today. Anyway, Pollitt is more likely to break his ankles than you, Mrs Day.'

At the top of the spiral staircase, they stood in a little knot, out of breath, all holding up their lanterns to see where they were. As Pollitt had described in his letter, they were in a kind of subterranean hall. Above, choked windows let in a dim light. A great deal of debris on the floor in front of them indicated that long ago the ceiling had fallen in. They were looking upwards to a higher roof too gloomy to make out, while at ground level, maybe twenty feet above their heads, ivy had a deathgrip on broken mullions, masking the daylight.

'You know, I think this is an undercroft,' said Jerome. 'See, that above us would have been the Refectory, the floor of which is now down here; and in here was cellarage and storage space. Yes, look, over there. The monks would have kept their barrels of wine and stuff.'

Various deep alcoves were visible on the further side, although nearly impossible to reach due to the mounds of earth, stone and timber which now bulked up the floor.

'It must have been jolly inconvenient to bring the stores up that spiral staircase,' said Harriet.

'Maybe there's another way,' said Crowley.

'Listen to that eerie voice now!' said Harriet. 'Like a vast copper of seething water.'

'Or as if there were a Niagara Falls under the earth,' said Crowley. 'Where do we go from here, Pollitt? Ah, yes, I see. There's an entrance blocked up with modern bricks over there on the other side.'

'Looks recent, doesn't it? I think one could have got through from the hotel to here,' said Pollitt.

'And the wall was built from the other side,' said Harriet. 'See the way the mortar is sloppy and has oozed out between the courses on this side? A bricklayer would have finished this side better if he could see it. They must have put it up because it would be far too dangerous to allow guests to explore this way.'

'Good point,' said Pollitt, then added like a tour guide, 'and then we have this other way, this perfectly sweet little Stygian way, which George Arden insisted on exploring. I suppose now it's our turn.'

Harriet looked where he pointed and saw another arched doorway and inky-black entrance. They scrambled over the mounds of rubble, compacted as they were by damp years of settling and hardening, and showing signs of animal habitation everywhere.

'Wolves and foxes and bears and badgers,' said Pollitt, shining the beam of his lantern into a burrow-like hole full of spiderwebs.

'Don't be ridiculous,' said Crowley. 'Nothing has been here except perhaps the badgers and foxes. We haven't had wolves in England for two centuries, and as for bears, you'd have to go back even further. There might be a few wildcats hereabouts though ...'

'Oh don't try to scare me with that. I'm from the wilds of Westmorland.'

'And don't pretend that you've ever been anywhere *near* wildcats, Jerome. Or indeed the wilds. I know the nearest you ever get to them is a charming view through your windows.'

At the entrance, they all naturally paused. The rumble was louder, but still so low that it was a sensation inside the chest rather than a sound on the ear.

Pollitt put his hand on the wall. 'Feel?' he said. 'It's all through the stone.'

'Small wonder the undercroft fell in upon itself,' said Harriet. 'That vibration has been constantly affecting every brick and stone and scrap of mortar and timber since the place was built.'

'Is there a remote chance, do you think, that the rest of it might fall down *today?*' said Pollitt.

'This is solid rock,' said Crowley. 'Don't dwell on it.'

'And now you've said, 'Don't dwell on it', of course all I can see in my mind's eye is this tunnel collapsing on our heads.'

'Nonsense,' said Crowley.

They walked down the tunnel which was far lower and narrower than the way from the river. It became apparent that the place was in its natural state, although the floor had perhaps been smoothed. The bulging walls glistened with moisture and here and there the lamplight showed disconcertingly odd formations where the rock had ballooned strangely or pleated and folded in upon itself, or slid down in cascades of waxy melt. It felt warmer as they progressed and became more steamy so that their lantern light was veiled and diffused. Bands of mist pulsed by them. Pollitt was just remarking that it felt like being in a bathroom when Crowley, who was leading and tapping the ground with his walking stick, barked, 'Stop!'

He stooped and cast the beam of his lantern towards the ground before him and revealed an abrupt end to the floor. The surface had split and slipped, sloping towards a chasm several feet across.

'I think we've had an earthquake here,' he said. 'Look at this! The floor disappears.'

'That surface looks dangerously unstable, and the further gap is far too wide to jump over,' said Harriet, also directing her lantern beam at the mass of cracks across the rock and the gaping hole a few yards ahead. The steam which rose from the gash was thicker and their light filtered through it like a filmy curtain. 'I don't think we should attempt even to walk upon it, Mr Crowley. There is every reason to suspect that the floor will crack and fall into this chasm if we put weight upon it, and that chasm may be bottomless.'

'The landslip or earthquake which opened this up was long ago, I would say. Look, there's evidence that there was once a bridge – a rough thing, and several centuries ago, but here's the remains of rivets and wood.' He peered over the edge. 'No such thing as bottomless, you know. But yes, in the sense that the bottom is quite probably a very long way down. Impossible to see. It could be twenty yards or a thousand. I would not care to attempt getting across that without some ropes, although I would be prepared to try it with the right equipment – a piton in here perhaps...' He peered upwards. 'It's no worse than a fissure in a glacier. I feel sure I could manage that.'

'No, you couldn't,' said Pollitt firmly. 'If you are to take stupid and pointless risks, Crowley, you had better do it far away from me.

Foreign glaciers are all very well, but this is England and this rock is crumbly.'

'We could cross with a long plank though,' said Crowley. 'Look, you can just make out that the tunnel continues on the other side. There's quite a wide space over there. If only these lanterns were more powerful or we could penetrate this steam, we'd be able to see.' He formed a trumpet round his mouth with his hands and sent a hard sharp call across into the darkness. The echo bounded off unseen rocks far away. 'That way goes on, who knows where? Perhaps to a series of magnificent chambers. There will be stalagmites, stalactites - think of it! – we are after all, in the foothills of the Mendips. You do know that human remains have been found recently at Cheddar showing signs of cannibalism and head hunting?'

'Oh really?' said Pollitt. 'How perfectly sweet. Just what I wanted to know.'

'A treetrunk perhaps could be used to bridge the gap,' continued Crowley thoughtfully.

'Beams or planks from the ruins in the undercroft?' suggested Harriet. 'I noticed several oak ones, but they would be massively heavy, even if still sound.'

'Oak would probably be sound, but as you say, immensely weighty, and there are only the three of us, if you can count Polly.'

'Well, I like that! But anyway, despite your rudeness, no oak beams this time, please!' said Pollitt. 'Mrs Day, you are a lady and therefore really ought to be tired and hysterical by now. If you will not fulfil that office, I feel that someone should, and that someone will be me, unless we turn back now. I want something to eat. And a cup of tea.'

'But what did George Arden see here?' asked Crowley, lingering. 'He could no more get across than we can. What exactly did he say to you, Pollitt?'

'He didn't say anything. He looked ... not very happy.'

'You said it was like someone who had had bad news. Is that an accurate description?'

'Yes. He was perhaps disappointed that he hadn't been able to cast himself headlong into this convenient abyss. Or he met a head-hunting cannibal. How should I know why he had a long face? Who can tell what he was thinking? And quite frankly, I don't see why we should trouble ourselves. This has all been very interesting, thank you very much, but I feel a definite need to get out into the fresh air and see the sun in the sky.'

'Yes, let's go back now,' said Harriet.

'Very well,' said Crowley. 'But I think,' he added, loitering very near the edge of the first cracks in the tunnel floor, 'with a little careful reconnoitre, one could use this lip for an actual descent and view where the so-called abyss bottoms out. One would have to test carefully first, of course, but think of it! The depths of these potholes can be tremendous, why, Gaping Ghyll in Yorkshire is over three hundred feet deep. I suspect from the steam that we would find some very hot water down there, so your idea of a copper boiling up is perfectly accurate, Mrs Day.'

'Please don't talk about it,' said Pollitt. 'Come on, for goodness's sake, let's walk back .'

After a while, they were back in the undercroft, then picking their way carefully down the spiral staircase and finally retracing their steps to the river. The sun was shining on the water outside and the air felt pleasantly fresh after the warmth of the tunnel. They each had a lot to think about and were silent for the most part as they walked back to the hotel.

CHAPTER THIRTY-TWO

'I thought you might be interested, Doctor,' said Detective Browning.

'And what are we to make of it? That he took his own life?' The foggy night was cold and penetratingly damp. Watson could almost sense tiny flakes of soot entering his lungs – or was that just his imagination? A sheen of glistening moisture masked the fine woollen fibres of his greatcoat and the waterproof capes of the policemen were slick in the light of lanterns.

'So, we know this is Charles Bateman,' said Browning, leafing through some damp papers. 'Hold that light steady, Taylor, good lad. He has identifying documents in his coat – an old letter, see, various scraps and your calling card. I wonder if he was on the way to see you?'

'Why would you think that?' asked Watson, looking down at the shape under the tarpaulin. The metal tracks nearby glinted, feeding into the tunnel up ahead. Under the bridge there was a scuttling and squeaking of rats.

'Well, the card was in a different place, you see. Not in the man's wallet but in his pocket, where he could easily pick it up and look at it. Doesn't that suggest he was wanting to find his way to you?'

'And if he was on his way to visit me – or Holmes, as no doubt he would have hoped - why would he have taken his own life by jumping off that bridge?'

'Precisely, Doctor. Just what I thought. But perhaps he fell. He'd been drinking heavily.'

Watson paused at that, remembering something Crowley had reported of this dead man. 'Perhaps he had something to add to his previous story.'

'Ah, who knows? If he had, it's a pity the rascal could not have come forward sooner.'

It began to rain. The first drops spattered on the tarpaulin just as the officers came with a stretcher to remove the body.

'Drunk, you say?' Watson knelt besides the corpse and lifted the edge of the tarpaulin. He did not pay much attention to the state of the face. Instead, he noted the fumes of strong drink assaulting his nostrils. He reached out to touch the damp clothing. Bringing his wet fingers to his nose, he detected the alcohol. Watson bent closer to smell the mouth. 'H'mm. I suggest you take a look at the contents of this man's stomach, Detective Browning. My first impression is that the alcohol has been administered to his clothing. The smell seems rather to emanate from that than from his mouth.'

'Ah,' said Browning. 'Interesting.'

'Yes, isn't it?' said Watson, standing up. He removed his hat as a mark of respect as the body was carried away. 'It makes it look rather deliberate, doesn't it?'

'Would you mind accompanying me to the station, Doctor?' asked Browning blandly.

'Now then. I am a great admirer, I've made that clear, Doctor. But when you tell me that you've been suppressing yet more important evidence, then I begin to lose a little sympathy for your methods.' Detective Browning's young face was disappointed as he read from his notes, summarising, 'You tell me that you first heard of the connection between Burroughs and Bateman from your friend, Mr Crowley – he seems strangely mixed up in all this. Now then, Crowley overhears Burroughs talking to Bateman and Bateman mentions prison. You go and look up Bateman and discover the case of the heads. Then we get to the day Crowley and you go and look under Burroughs's bed and find the ears. Right. Crowley takes the papers away. You bring the papers back. We find the earrings. Dr Watson, I have to ask: why not just come forward and let me in on your investigations? We could have been collaborating every step of the way.'

Watson cleared his throat. Midnight at the police station was not the most pleasant place to be, but it was not the first time he had been in such an environment. He was not alarmed by the distant roaring of drunks and the sharp voices of ladies of the night. He said, 'I am quite prepared to share my misgivings, Detective. It's Miller. I realised that Burroughs had written in praise of your Inspector and after discussion with Crowley, we decided that we would only present our evidence when it became incontrovertible.'

'Yes, I gathered that. But you and I, Doctor, *you and I* have discussed Miller's shortcomings. You could have been a little more trusting at that point, couldn't you?'

'Very well. There is another factor. Both Crowley and I might be called as witnesses in the Arden trial. You'll recall that my name came up in Cabot's last writings and I had – well, I had made a point of drawing official police attention to the disturbing influence of Aleister Crowley on the suspect. I hasten to add that neither Cabot's accusations against me nor my speculations about Crowley's conversation have any basis in fact, as I now well know. But at the time, it seemed, it seemed less than perfectly legitimate to undertake our own enquiries, although they were entirely amateurish and simply to satisfy our own curiosity.'

'Really? Doesn't sound amateurish to me, sir. Sounds like you put a great deal of time and effort into the matter. And by the way, I *do* seem to recall something about your wanting to manage Arden. Actor or something, wasn't he? Or was there some other suspicion attached? I'll send for the file to jog my memory in just a moment.'

'No need, no need,' said Watson hastily. 'The charge of wanting to manage Arden's acting talents is completely false. I am not – never have been – associated with the theatre. Writing, yes, not acting.'

'Mr Holmes is interested in acting, isn't he?'

'Only in assuming disguises for professional purposes,' said Watson sombrely. He began to feel tired.

'Let's leave all that for now. Let's get back to poor old Charles Bateman. We'll get a report from the morgue in due course and hear about stomach contents. I am inclined to treat this death as suspicious, but until I have it confirmed that he weren't drunk - or anything else comes up to convince me this weren't an accident, I have no grounds to act. I know what you'll say - '

'What will I say?'

'You'll say that Bateman knew too much or had asked for too much; and that his death might be a result of certain gentlemen wanting him got rid of.'

'Gentlemen?'

'Scientific gentlemen. That's what your ideas imply – a Freemasonry conspiracy to cover up secret labs and research, a kind of Dr Frankenstein affair. Am I correct?'

'I hadn't thought about Freemasons, Detective. My ideas were less ambitious. I simply see some sketchy clues to indicate that a brother and sister have perpetrated a fraud upon a large firm, somehow passing the sister off as either the wife or daughter of the original owner. The brother meanwhile undertook to supply certain body parts needed in the course of product development.'

'Ah,' said Browning, shaking his head. 'You see, I believe that Miller is a Freemason and that so is Burroughs; and basically, they are sworn to help each other out. Aren't they? That's their way, and has been for centuries. It's all in a novel I was reading.'

'I am afraid that's well beyond my ken. I am frankly more concerned that the late Mr Bateman was prepared to offer me some information about Burroughs. Did Burroughs find this out – and if so, how? And finally, if he did, might Burroughs have had a hand in Bateman's death?'

'And as this is all hearsay and there is nothing to connect Burroughs with Bateman, *except* the hearsay, there is no likelihood of my getting a warrant for his arrest. Miller would go mental. It would be difficult to even justify interviewing him. I think we need to get a statement from your Mr Crowley. If I presented that to the magistrate, I might get a warrant, but not without it.' He paused expectantly, looking at Watson. When nothing was forthcoming, he said, 'I'll check Mr Crowley's address then, if you haven't got it to hand.'

Watson nodded, trying to keep the fact that he knew Crowley was staying at the same hotel as Arden out of his mind.

Browning sat back, tapping his teeth with his pencil. After a while he said, 'And all this shenanigans is because you felt moved to prove that Burroughs was lying his head off. And have you got any further in that respect, Doctor?'

'Sadly, no. We can't prove that Arden did not commit murder, although the testimony of the parlourmaid is of the utmost importance. I trust you have checked that you have a record of it? She confirms that she saw the body of Cabot lying upon the broken glass, in a manner to suggest he fell upon an already-smashed bottle.'

'She *confirms* does she? And have you been interviewing the servants too, Doctor?'

'It seemed appropriate to have a word, while we were calling on Mr Williams the other day. I think I mentioned it to you at the time?'

'You did mention *something* but you never mentioned that you had conducted an interview. And once again, I have to object. How do I know you haven't influenced her?'

'No, no, I merely wrote down her exact words. I can pass my notes over to you, Detective.' Watson cleared his throat. 'Anyway, to continue, we tried to prove that Burroughs might have a motive to lie about him. And I think you may have found it yourself, in Burroughs's papers.'

'Ah, yes. You're referring to the improper written material in the box. Yes, I see your drift. Very well, Doctor. I'm sorry to have kept you so late. I won't say I haven't felt upset tonight but I'm determined to rise above it. I'm sure not all Sherlock Holmes's cases are so shoddily handled. Anyway, I'll keep you informed.'

They shook hands and, once again, Dr Watson left the station feeling chastened.

*

That evening at the Adsullata Spa Hotel, the guests were low-spirited and rather quiet. Neither Minerva Atwell nor Alexandra Roberts were at dinner and Major Farnsworth and Lady Helena missed them sorely: particularly Mrs Atwell. George Arden was also missing, although nobody much noticed his absence. Added to that, while Harriet and her friends explored the tunnel, three more new guests had arrived at the hotel.

There was a mother with a sickly son, a boy of twelve or so called Frederic, who was thin and milky-skinned and short-tempered. Frederic's mother was a combination of overbearing and infantilising, and her one topic of conversation appeared to be how much she had sacrificed. Her name was Camilla Ives. She conveyed an impression of vigilance, like a frigate patrolling choppy waters.

The other new guest was an immensely fat gentleman called Mr Slindon. Mr Slindon claimed he was to undergo a system of weight loss involving a régime of hot mud wraps and steam. He maintained that the treatment was due to begin tomorrow; and had more or less eaten his own weight in pork chops at the dinner table that night. After the meal, Frederic was retired to his room by Camilla Ives, who promised to return in due course. The original guests became gloomy, partly because the new guests looked to be grim future company. And Crowley's gimlet stare did not bode well for their whist games.

'One does hope, one really does hope that it is not a contagion. We are far enough away from the city to be spared a great deal of the foul airs there, and so one thought one would be safe,' said Lady Helena of George Arden's illness. 'One is particularly careful not to breathe foul airs.'

'Quite right, madam,' said Major Farnsworth vaguely. 'Quite right.'

Farnsworth had sat with Crowley, Slindon and that queer fellow Pollitt over quite a lot of port after dinner. He had missed having a companion to talk over his old campaigns and conquests with and had rather attached himself to Slindon. The Atwell was a fine subject for discussion. Even better than the laundry maid, who had a very neat waist, plenty up top and was not averse to flashing an ankle from time to time. Now, however, further talk of nags and titties had to be postponed. He was sunk into a sofa opposite Lady Helena, partially listening to the conversation, but mainly wondering about a game of cards with Slindon and planning to get out his private collection of French postcards later.

'I'm not sure that foul air is the cause of contagion, Lady Helena,' said Harriet. 'There is a mounting body of evidence to show that disease is frequently caused by micro-organisms, invisible to the naked eye, which pass into the system and multiply.'

'Yes, yes, they are carried by the foul air. That is what Sir Gerald always said. That is the very smell *of* the foul air, you see, my dear. That is why I never breathe foul air.'

'Oh, I see,' said Harriet, not particularly clear on the details of the new Germ Theory herself.

'It's all nonsense,' said Mr Slindon. 'Invisible organisms! It's just a way of the quacks getting more money out of us. Disease is passed down from the mother and father, like criminal inclinations, that's all. And lack of good nutrition in childhood is what sets up the course of the illness. And who is it you are discussing, may I ask? Do we have a contagion here in this hotel?'

'Nobody. Just a silly fellow with a headcold,' said Farnsworth, discreetly burping.

'It's a guest who has been confined to his room for three or four days now,' said Lady Helena. 'I do hope he is on the road to recovery.'

'So do I,' said Harriet.

'A rubber, Slindon? Lady Helena?' said Farnsworth. His eye slid over Jerome Pollitt and alighted on Aleister Crowley. 'Join us for a rubber of whist, sir?'

Crowley's face remained completely impassive. 'No.'

'Mrs Day? Whist? You *must* play?'

Harriet was saved from having to join the card table by the arrival of Camilla Ives, who had freed herself from the cares of motherhood and looked as though she had every intention of making her presence felt. She instantly volunteered to join the game and Harriet took the opportunity discreetly to move elsewhere. She sat a little way off and was joined by her friends, Pollitt and Crowley. They seemed naturally to have formed a kind of anti-whist clique. Harriet, aware that she had gathered round her all the eligible batchelors, felt a cold emanation of dislike from Mrs Ives.

'You didn't smoke those gold-tipped ones before, did you, Aleister?' said Pollitt lazily watching Crowley light a cigarette. 'Someone told me Oscar always says charming people should smoke gold-tipped cigarettes or die.'

'Sshh,' said Crowley, blowing smoke towards him. Then he added, 'You were mercilessly accurate in your correspondence, Jerome. It *is* very boring here. I think I'll take a little walk round the old part of the building after everyone's gone to bed. Want to come?'

'Absolutely not. I don't believe in ghosts but that is no reason to go into places where you might meet one,' said Pollitt.

'You, Mrs Day?'

'I am afraid I am quite tired out after our adventure this afternoon. I'll be delighted to hear an account of your explorations over breakfast though.'

Crowley sank back in his chair in thought; Pollitt began flicking through a magazine and Harriet stared at the black windows, wondering how George was getting on.

CHAPTER THIRTY-THREE

There was a disturbance of voices at the door and George's attention drifted back into the desert. He was still travelling. He had been travelling for days. He was walking beside a line of asses, and they were loaded with bales of coarse woven stuff, and deep inside one bale was a little chest of pearls; and these carried tortoise shells and belonged to the merchant Teoma, but the one carrying cinnamon, cardamom and medicinal syrups packed in straw was fussy Djehut's.

Now it was evening and the enormous stars were blazing overhead. They were walking past an abandoned village in the dusk, roofs and walls slumping back into earth after half a millennium of earthquakes and rains and parching heat. He didn't like the shadows. It was getting cold and he had on the felted cloak stitched round the hem with golden salamanders; and they were going to push on along the Royal Road to get to the next fortified inn; and Walagash cursed that ruffian Vidarna who delayed them by fighting: he would be sacked without his fee for making them walk in the dark.

'When will it be, then?'

George understood that the voices had been speaking to each other again for some time. He tried to listen but the words just made painfully-bright pictures in his mind which would shatter and reassemble into something else.

'I think we need to prepare ourselves and learn our parts and things. So for that purpose, I propose that you and I lock ourselves away in my inner sanctum. No, I'm joking, don't look glum! It will be fun. There are certain preparations to do, but they aren't tedious. But we'll have to think of a way of keeping your friend away from here. Why did she have to come here?'

'I don't know, Minerva. I didn't encourage her. It was this one, I think. She followed him. She left a note, sent up sweets, always knocking at the door.'

'Well, she is ridiculous. Dowdy and repulsive, like a toad. Did you say you once felt something for her?'

'As a girl, yes. But it's this person, George Arden, he is the cause.'

'Yes, yes, annoying that she's come to take an interest. Always interfering with the nurses. It was after you told me about this fellow being friendless and in hiding that I began to think he would do for our purpose.'

'Why? Why him?'

'Because I thought he wouldn't be missed when you told me his history. It's too late to go back on it all now. We won't find another like this one. Anyway, I refuse to wait. I have set other preparations in train, you know, that can't be changed either. We must just work round the inconvenience. But there's something else about him, I can't put my finger on it. As if he's already ... well, I don't know. Anyway, we needn't trouble about that. I'm a scientist – I don't go in for melodramas personally, though I am obviously expert at making them happen.' Laughter again.

He slid into a dream.

Over there, the old man said, the hills were pocked with caves and every cave was rammed full of robbers. When the robbers came later and killed everyone else, George would be taken away with them, along with the tortoise shells and syrups and the little chest of pearls. He already knew the end of this story. But right now, he was back at the part where he could see the terror of realisation opening up Walagash's eyes. He knew now that those guards he had hired in the market place were all complicit with the robber gang. George choked and coughed as the knife drove into the old man's throat. A strong hand hauled him upright and banged his back.

'No, just some water. It's the effect of the medicine. Sometimes it relaxes the smooth muscles of the pharynx and they can't swallow.'

He drank from a cup and was repositioned on the pillows. With his eyes shut, he quickly drifted back into his dreams.

*

Dr Watson sighed and threw his pen down in disgust. The account was stubbornly unsatisfactory. It was all very well if it had been Holmes: then he would have been able to praise his friend's extraordinary genius and intuitions. But, damn it, he did not feel like making a song and dance out of young Crowley's arrogant ways. He wondered if he could re-cast the whole thing as a Holmes case. That would be dramatically justifiable: after all his readers were accustomed to the character of Holmes and expected him to behave in a certain way. It would be impossible to have a case with both

Holmes and Crowley operating in the same space. No.

He wrote, *With long nervous fingers, Holmes opened the lid of the black box. "Good God, Holmes!" I exclaimed in horror. "Steady, my dear fellow," said Holmes, laying his hand on my arm …*

Watson crossed it all out in exasperation. No, he could not do it, and it showed how incredibly vexing Crowley was to have had the audacity to appear in the place of Holmes. He turned instead to his notes on the Dartmoor case: *The Curse of the Baskerville Howl.*

At that moment, the door to the sitting room was opened and Mr Dafydd Williams walked in. He was holding his hat in his hand and peeped round the room at first, looking a little fearful. He grew bolder when he saw that Dr Watson was in possession of the parlour.

'Oh, that's a relief,' he said. 'Dr Watson, I was a little bit afraid it would be the famous detective returned and I was getting quite nervous thinking about what to say to him.

Watson shook his hand warmly. 'Very pleasant to see you this morning, Mr Williams. No, regrettably, my friend is still absent. Please sit down and tell me how you are and how I may help you.'

'I am very well, thank you. The household is as quiet as when you last visited – in fact, quieter. I just thought I should come and discuss recent developments.'

'Yes?' said Watson, sitting forward.

'As you might guess, it's about Burroughs again.'

'I am at your disposal,' said Watson, his conversation with Detective Browning last night and the death of Charles Bateman at the forefront of his mind.

'I'm surprised you can't tell me more, Doctor,' said Williams cannily.

'Beg pardon?'

'He's one of you, isn't he? Very clever. Remarkably convincing, but then I suppose that's part of the game. Like spying.'

'I don't entirely understand …'

'Mrs Jenkins told me. Your Mr Burroughs, a colleague. Makes sense, court reporter, known in legal circles. But however much I think it through, *I* can't make it make sense. Is it something to do with being undercover to investigate a fraud at the Atwell place then?'

'Burroughs is emphatically not a colleague of mine, Mr Williams. *Who* told you he was? Dear, dear me.'

'Am I wrong?'

'Completely, my dear fellow. Burroughs has pulled the wool over the eyes of your redoubtable Mrs Jenkins. And that in itself is very significant: he knows the pursuit is drawing closer.'

'Is it?'

'Yes, it is. But I cannot divulge any further details. Utmost secrecy, you see.'

'Same as he said to Mrs Jenkins, apparently.'

'Please, Mr Williams, tell me what developments you have observed.'

'Well, first of all, he came home later than usual last night. There was a letter waiting for him since the last post. I saw it on the hall table so I knew it was there. And you know I stay well away from him, so I assume he read it in the parlour – which is more or less his territory now, since as you know, I never go in there when he is at home – and after he had read it, I assume, he went stumbling up the stairs in a great hurry. I heard him because I was in my own room. And I heard him sobbing, I swear. Now that you tell me he's no colleague of yours, I suppose I shouldn't feel concerned for him - but I am not a hard man, Doctor, and it does occur to me that something in that letter touched his heart. You know such things happen – a chance word or act can be an opportunity for Grace to enter the darkest soul. You understand my meaning, Doctor?'

'Yes, yes, my dear fellow.'

'So when I heard his door open and footsteps going down the stairs, I crept out onto the landing to see what might be happening and I looked over the banister and I saw him standing at the bottom step with a suitcase in his hand. So I called down to him, "Burroughs, what is the matter?" And he looked up at me and I swear his eyes – I don't know, Doctor, it was such an odd look, a mixture of looks. But he just said very calmly, "If you'd been so quick a few weeks ago, you'd have seen the truth. But you can't change that now." It was such an odd thing to say, don't you think? Almost like he was taunting – or regretting. I still can't tell which. And then he looked towards the front door and marched out. With his suitcase and all. What do you make of that?'

'That he has probably gone on a holiday, Mr Williams.'

'But what of the sobbing and the taunting?'

'It sounds uncharacteristic, as far as I know him, but then I don't know him at all, except by report.'

'Perhaps we have rather made him into a devil, Doctor? Do you think he has a heart after all? Might we be mistaken?'

'That's a long shot, I'm afraid. He's deceived you and Mrs Jenkins, all of his journalist colleagues, not to mention a police inspector.'

'No, I just mean that … I don't know what I mean.'

'That he might be a confused, hurt kind of person rather than a malicious devil?' said Watson.

'Perhaps his story about the ears is perfectly true.' said Williams. 'Perhaps it is we who have judged unjustly. Perhaps we should be turning the other cheek.'

Watson looked surprised and dubious. 'Believe me, I am in possession of information which points rather to the malicious devil explanation.'

'Oh yes,' said Dafydd. 'I just thought there might be a bit of light in his soul, like at the very end of a story when there's a twist, like in *Great Expectations,* when the benefactor turns out to be the convict.'

'I think the twist is that he's gone without giving us the satisfaction of proving anything incriminating against him yet,' said Watson drily.

*

Over breakfast, Aleister Crowley reported that his explorations last night had been rather dull. The corridors and rooms in the old part of the hotel were in a state of disrepair, empty and dusty, stacked here and there with builders' equipment. One interesting fact was that one remote passage ended abruptly in a brick wall with a slot in it. He guessed immediately that it had been the cell of the famous anchoress. Apart from that, he said, it was not very interesting. 'The whole place seems to have an air of waiting,' he added. 'It's the build up – you know, since they interfered with the energies of the holy well. I shall go and have a good look at it today.'

Crowley took Pollitt with him – unwillingly, it seemed to Harriet, as she imagined that he would have preferred to inspect the place alone. But Jerome had arranged the glorious picnic and insisted that they go together to eat it even though the weather had turned chilly and overcast. Harriet felt rather sorry for him.

She walked along George's corridor again and again. Once she paused at the door and thought she heard voices talking. They stopped instantly as soon as whoever was inside heard her. After a moment, she knocked and was surprised to be answered by Mrs Atwell.

'I am administering medicine to poor Mr Day,' she explained with the air of an exhausted saint. 'As you know, I am always personally concerned for the welfare of every single one of my guests. The dear boy, he is so brave. But fevered, you know, fevered. You may have heard him murmuring in his dreams. I attempt to calm him, reading from the Holy Book. It brings such solace. I always feel that the words alone bear a benison in their sound, healing the sick in mind and body, or so I have observed.'

Harriet could hardly object to these words. Although she asked, as usual, to be allowed to see 'Edward', her request was denied. Sadly, she busied herself that day writing letters to Mrs Skipton and Dr Watson to enquire how things were going at home; eating and walking and wondering. She found herself agreeing with Crowley's assessment: the whole place did have an air of brewing intensity. It was partly atmospheric pressure, she decided: there was a dirty look to the weather. When Pollitt and Crowley returned from their picnic, she wasn't entirely surprised that it had been something of a disaster. Pollitt disappeared to his room. She decided to spend the afternoon with a book but was once again disturbed by Crowley coming to find her in the solarium. Another letter from Watson had arrived with the late afternoon post.

'Look at this, Mrs Day. Watson writes that Bateman has been found dead. Fell onto the tracks from a bridge but suspicion of foul play. His body was soaked in alcohol but nothing of the sort in his stomach. Watson says they need me to return to London and make a statement, if there is to be any chance of getting a warrant for Burroughs's arrest.'

'Will you go so soon?'

'What else is to be done? Arden is unreachable – and even if I could reach him, he is uncomprehending. I will leave in the morning.'

'Mr Pollitt will be unhappy,' said Harriet; adding sadly, 'unless he chooses to return with you.'

That evening, not willing to get caught up in the gravitational pull generated by Mrs Ives in the absence of Minerva and Alex, Harriet wandered over to the piano and began to play. Pollitt immediately came and leaned on the side and after a while, Crowley joined him.

'Thank you, Mrs Day,' Pollitt said. 'I feared Camilla Ives was about to suggest charades and parlour games.'

'Why are you thanking me in particular? You should thank Major Farnsworth for nobly volunteering to play cards.'

'He does it every night though. It's what he lives for. But if you keep playing, we might be in danger of dancing instead. That Camilla Ives looks like a dancey kind of woman. She won't last long at cards tonight, you'll see. She doesn't like Farnsworth because he is too old and not rich enough; nor Slindon because he is too fat and not rich enough. She'll be after *you* shortly, Aleister.'

'Or you,' said Crowley.

'No, wait,' said Jerome. 'She's sneaking little sidelong looks at you. She's already calculated the price of your clothes and shoes, you can see. She is sensing husband-potential. Even though my heart is free as a bird at the thought of returning to London with you tomorrow, Aleister, I would be very mortified if forced to jig about with her.'

'Nobody could make you,' said Crowley with half a smile. 'But perhaps you would enjoy it if you did.'

'I should like to sing later,' said Pollitt, suddenly turning towards Harriet. 'And as this shall be my last evening here, it behoves me to sing a pathetic air. Or I could quite happily revisit my triumphant rendition of 'Di, Di, Di' from 'Go-Bang' as a personal *hommage* to Miss Letty Lind. Would you prefer that?'

'I'll accompany you in whatever you wish, Mr Pollitt,' said Harriet gravely. 'Although I believe 'Di, Di, Di' is less elegiac and more along the frivolous line.'

He thought for a moment. 'Do you know *Annabel Lee,* Poe's poem set to music?' he asked, looking rather pleased with the idea.

'No, actually.'

'Well, that is no obstacle,' said Pollitt, 'because I happen to have it in my luggage. And I shall go and get it forthwith.' Jerome practically skipped out of the salon at the prospect of performing.

'I will be sorry to see him go, I won't deny it,' said Harriet. 'But he tells me he has been utterly bored since he came here.'

'Yes, he tells me that too, all the time. He hated the picnic and complained all the way; and I had to carry everything because he *would* wear that cream suit. Yet it was his own idea, just as it was his own idea to come here. But boring or not, once I've made a statement regarding Bateman, I will come back to the hotel and talk to Arden. Don't despair – you won't be left alone here for long.'

'I do rather feel a need for moral support.'

'At least Mrs Atwell seems to have decided to ignore her guests.'

'I wish she would ignore George,' said Harriet. 'She pretends to be practically a doctor from the way she talks, but it's all fake. Something's not right, Mr Crowley. I fear I may need to call in a doctor from Bath to get a second opinion. But would that be safe? I cannot think straight about what to do. I wish I could get him away from here.'

At that moment, Jerome returned bearing some sheet music. He handed it to Harriet and said, 'Well, I don't know what's going on but The Atwell just received a rather late-night guest. A gentleman too. Ho, ho.'

'A guest just arrived, did he?' asked Crowley. 'Did you see Atwell then?'

'Yes. I don't know where she's been hiding herself but she came down as I went up and then she was coming up as I went down again. We exchanged frank and bitter smiles but she didn't introduce me to her gentleman.'

'Taking a gentleman up to her room?' asked Harriet softly, looking shocked.

'Well, I wouldn't go so far as to to say that, you know,' said Pollitt. 'The porter was carrying the suitcase and Mrs Atwell was showing the chap to his room, I suppose. Nothing more, sadly. But let's sing. Look, can you do it in A Flat?'

After Harriet had played a little run through of the simple tune, Pollitt began singing: *It was many and many a year ago In a kingdom by the sea …* They got on very well; and although the card players paid him almost no attention, Jerome looked happier and more relaxed as he sang than at any time since Harriet had met him. His face, which easily became grave and anxious when he was lost in thought, naturally brightened and cheered with the music. But as she played, Harriet caught sight of Crowley slipping out of the salon.

And neither the angels in Heaven above
Nor the demons down under the sea
Can ever dissever my soul from the soul

Of the beautiful Annabel Lee …

By the time Pollitt was singing the last lines, *In her tomb by the sounding sea,* Crowley was back again.

'Well, that was really rather rude,' said Pollitt, turning to him after the final chords. 'I chose that because I thought you might like the eeriness of it, but you slithered out in the middle of it. Aleister, don't you care for Art? You mayn't care for Poe but Art, surely?'

'It was magnificent, Polly,' said Crowley quietly. 'I had to go out because I wanted to check something. I could hear you all the way out there – I was only talking to the night clerk at the desk. I wanted to check who arrived, saying I was hoping a friend of mine had come in late. Guess who just signed the register?'

'The Archbishop of Canterbury,' said Pollitt sulkily.

'Albert Burroughs,' said Aleister Crowley.

'Burroughs?' asked Pollitt.

'He's the man accusing George,' said Harriet in a low shocked voice.

'He's been flushed out! This is proof positive that he's come here to get away. I need to send a telegram to Watson.' With that Crowley went out again to the front desk.

'Oh Lord, I'm so worried for George,' said Harriet to Pollitt. 'This man is extremely dangerous for him. We are going to have to think how to get him away from here. And he's too ill to be moved.'

'Horrible bad luck, isn't it?' agreed Pollitt. 'But I have a very sensible idea: we do nothing. We leave him exactly where he is, shrouded in darkness in his room with a big nurse to see off any intruders, and he should be safe. Especially if he really is contagious.'

Crowley rejoined them, glancing across at the card game and taking out a cigarette from his case. 'They'll send a boy on a bicycle to the Post Office, but it won't be open until tomorrow morning.'

'What can Dr Watson do though?' asked Harriet. 'There is no action any of us can take – you said yourself, you are the only witness to Bateman's story and your statement needs to be heard by a magistrate. I am afraid you'll still have to return to London, Mr Crowley, even though Burroughs is now here.'

'But you'll be left here alone, Mrs Day,' said Jerome in concern. 'Is this man safe to be near?'

'I've argued with him in the past, Mr Pollitt, yes, but he's no danger to me. It's George I worry about.'

Crowley said, 'Don't worry. I have every intention of keeping my eyes on Burroughs. Watson can decide what is best to be done but until I hear from him, I'm going to stand guard here with you.'

Jerome gave his arm a discreet squeeze while Harriet looked markedly relieved.

Just then Lady Helena called over to them. 'Oh do play again, dear Mrs Day. Poor Mr Pollitt made such an effort to give us some Chopin the other night, but it was dreadfully difficult for him. It would be so lovely to hear a Nocturne or something like that. Your touch is so delicate and precise.'

Harriet bowed towards Lady Helena and began a quiet piece but before she had played more than four bars, Camilla Ives approached them, her voluminous skirts swishing. She had left a trail of destruction behind her, with Major Farnsworth and Mr Slindon quite distracted from their game by the acreage of white bosom and arm she was displaying.

'I have come to sing. The Major is very taken by the idea of my singing, I can't think why. I do hope you won't mind accompanying me? In fact, I see there is a volume of very agreeable parlour songs here.' She picked up some of the music on the piano lid and flicked through it. 'Yes, here we are. *The Wreck of the Hesperus.* And look, *I'll Sing Thee a Song of Araby.* And here are a number of beautiful duets. Surely, Mr Pollitt, you would lend your voice to strengthen mine?'

Crowley kicked Pollitt slyly on the ankle.

'Oh,' said Pollitt with a smile of genuine delight. 'I would be charmed.'

After the guests had retired at an early hour (earlier at any rate than Mrs Ives thought normal), Harriet, desperate to talk to Alex, tapped loudly at her door. There was no answer. She tried again. Then she ran down the stairs to the library and looked through the door – all was dark inside. She made a circuit of the salon and the dining room where servants were clearing and straightening and raking out cinders. Lastly, she went once again to George's door and knocked very softly. This time a nurse came to the door suppressing a yawn. Asleep, of course. Mr Day is asleep. Harriet took herself wearily to bed, not expecting to sleep herself.

CHAPTER THIRTY-FOUR

It was with trepidation the next morning that Harriet came down to breakfast. She dreaded seeing Albert Burroughs face to face. Her night's sleep had been just as she predicted. Quite apart from her fear of Burroughs - and her imagination running riot - she felt in some unaccountable way that she should try to catch the nurses in some wrongdoing. She even crept along the corridor with a shawl round her shoulders and her hair in a plait at three in the morning, slipping down the little flight of steps which took her to the passage on which was George's room. She listened for a while and tapped lightly on the door but this time there was no answer. The door was locked. Why is the door locked? she wondered. Why would a nurse lock herself in with a sick man? Has he been left alone in there?

She dithered, shivering, in the corridor for five or ten minutes; and then was struck by an intense fear that Burroughs would come along at any moment and find her. It was such a vivid picture in her mind that she became almost sure she could hear footsteps nearby, climbing the stairs at the other end of the passage. If he found her hovering outside this bedroom, how would she explain herself? This stupid behaviour is the quickest way to draw attention to George, she told herself. She just hoped and prayed that Alex was not so vengeful as to tell Burroughs where he was.

She went back to her room with the beginnings of a plan to bundle him up in a blanket and take him to the railway station with the help of Jerome and Aleister. Pollitt had mentioned that his family home was in Kendal. That would be a lovely place to take George to recuperate – rather wet at this time of year, but she could read him some Wordsworth and feed him on the famous Mint Cake and he would get better and fatter by the day. Back in her bedroom, she lit her lamp, set herself up in bed, opened a 'creeper', a mystery novel, and forced herself to concentrate.

When she woke with the pillow at a strange angle and her neck aching, the early sunshine was bland and white at her window. She went to breakfast to find that none of the people she dreaded seeing - and none of the people she wanted to see - were there: just the sickly boy refusing to eat the porridge because it was too lumpy (Harriet privately assigned him the name Frederic Goldilocks). Camilla

Goldilocks (as Harriet automatically named his mother) seemed rather to enjoy causing work for the staff by demanding instead eggs in various complicated states of softness, discussing them knowledgeably with Lady Helena. Mr Slindon had a sombre look on his face as he contemplated his scanty breakfast. Harriet had an urge to go to each individual guest and slap them. She settled for a piece of toast and marmalade instead.

*

'Listen! there's someone trying to come in.'

'Oh, is that the nurse at the door? Tell her to go for a walk, take a breath of fresh air. Tell her I am personally taking care of the patient this afternoon. Now, in theory, once we have everything in place, a supreme explosion of will can set forces in motion which cannot be invoked in ordinary circumstances. The most repulsive rituals might in some way be the most effective, do you see?'

'I think I do, in a way. But you told me it will just be a kind of theatrical show.'

'Don't worry about the detail. Just learn the part and everything will work. I am convinced it will. I have studied every detail.'

George hardly listened anymore. The two voices came and went all the time. When he found himself talking to his sister, it was very pleasant to sit together in the shade. She was telling him a lot of things he had forgotten.

'You see,' she said, 'The Lady of Heaven is very sad when she condemns him and sends him away with the demons. That's why it can't be forever. There's more to it than anger, because there's also love. She was only angry because she loved him. Everyone else missed her but he just carried on having fun. Think how hurt she was! She regretted it afterwards and then she showed mercy.'

Then George thought, with a little affectionate chuckle, Bilit Taauth always secretly yawns during the long rituals. The heavenly blue of the stars glows against the golden wall behind her.

The day wore away. Rain came down in sheets and the lights had to be lit at noon. The rooms brimmed with the dim electric tension of thunder. There was no sign of Alexandra, no sign of Minerva Atwell. Harriet's dread of bumping into Albert Burroughs only subsided when Crowley reminded her that Burroughs had his own reasons for having fled to this God-forsaken place and was undoubtedly intent on lying low. He would no more want to bump into her than she into him. Nevertheless, it inhibited her from hanging about near George's room or drawing attention to him.

Crowley stationed himself like a watchdog just inside the salon in an armchair facing the stairs and refused to move. He had a pile of books from the library on a little table at his elbow and appeared to immerse himself in a thick work on Natural Philosophy. The storm cleared at last. Pollitt got cross and bored and went out for a walk. He returned at about three o'clock. Crowley, looking serene and determined, settled himself to read yet another book. Jerome, peevish and tired, took himself up to his room to quietly do some embroidery, he said, and change his socks which had got wet.

Harriet, realising that Crowley was waiting for a telegram from Dr Watson as well as keeping an eye on the entrance hall, retired to her room too, thinking to rest on the bed. She found she was too ill at ease to lie down. The conflicting information she had kept being given by the nurses kept running through her head, with the sense that there was something else she should be doing for George. But what? A dose of Coca Wine did not soothe her nerves and she found herself wandering restlessly from window to door and back to window again.

'I am simply not going to allow this to go on,' she said aloud, having worked herself into a state of agitation. It was something to do with being confined in the bedroom and her tiger-pacing to and fro. She had paced like this night after night in terror over Peter's health. 'It's driving me mad, for one thing. I'm going to find Alex right now. Minerva Atwell must be forced to give an explanation – or a physician must be called in. I know that Mr Burroughs must be kept out of it in some way, but at this rate, George is in more danger from incompetent medical care than from the law.'

Harriet could not find Alex or Mrs Atwell anywhere. There was nobody at the reception desk, so she walked through every public place in the hotel and peered down the roped-off passageway into the gloom. Finally, she returned to Alexandra's room, knocking once more at the door. The polished wood reflected the last glow of a stormy sunset from the tall window behind her. Harriet knocked again, this time turning the handle. To her surprise, the door opened.

The room was disordered. There were clothes flung onto the

ottoman, bed and across the little gilded chair by the dressing table. A wine-coloured velvet dress was crumpled next to it on the floor. Harriet looked at the evidence of haste. Alexandra was never particularly tidy, but she was not wild like this. In the grate, she noticed the fire had burned down to ash and been left. It was as though the staff had been told to leave the room untouched, and yet the door was unlocked. More evidence of a hurried departure, perhaps.

At the back of the grate, there was a heap of blackened cinders where a large amount of paper had apparently been burnt. Harriet did not know why she felt compelled to disturb it with the poker – an action perhaps suggested by the plot of the creeper she was reading – and as the ash turned to grey powder, she saw that a single white leaf remained underneath, half-burnt. Alexandra had been disposing of some private writing, it seemed. She pulled the paper out and shook off the ash. She went to the window and stood by it, trying to make out the words in the failing light. The entirety of one side of the document had been destroyed.

> *of an energy, a kind of catalyst, which she believes will build… spiral through all physical points at the climax of the proced… worth all the sacrifices she… her Inanna ….fluid must be extracted within one hour of death …was wasted on useless corpses). The pituitary gland is reached by a surgi…the nose or lip through the sinus cavi… ong syringe she had developed for the purp…suffi*

Harriet read the words through several times. What were these references – 'useless corpses', 'within one hour of death'? Harriet hastily rolled the paper up and left the room.

She dashed down the stairs. The whole building seemed to be listening as she hurried along the passages, past the stairs leading to the kitchen, past the roped off entrance to the empty, ancient corridor; until she heard the sound of a piano being played in the salon. Thank God. She had not felt the place so oppressive before. Now it seemed vast and cavernous and menacing.

In the warmly-lit salon, she saw that it was Jerome Pollitt at the piano. He was tinkling through some popular tunes and singing quietly to himself in his pleasant voice. Crowley had moved to a couch and was lying full length, apparently giving his attention to a book in his hand. The sky beyond the windows was a wash of royal blue. There was no sign of the other guests; but then it was early, only four-thirty or five o'clock.

Harriet hurried over to the piano. 'Help,' she said. She could not think of anything more appropriate to say. 'Help! Mr Pollitt, Mr Crowley, please. Can you look at this?'

Pollitt, still sitting at the piano, alarmed, automatically held out a hand as she thrust the flaking page at him. A fall of cinders dusted the piano keys. He blew them away before saying, 'What on earth is the matter, dear Mrs Day?'

'The paper, I found it in Mrs Roberts's grate. In her room. Her room is a disorder of clothes as if a whirlwind had struck it, and this was in the fireplace along with a lot of others which had been completely reduced to ash. Read it, please.'

'Has her room been burgled?' asked Pollitt in astonishment.

'No, well, no, I don't think so. It looked more as if she had emptied her clothes out and not tidied.'

'Well, she does have terrible handwriting,' murmured Pollitt. 'Crowley, can you make it out?'

Aleister Crowley had come silently to stand next to Jerome and look down over his shoulder at the paper. He took it and Harriet watched his face as he read it. 'Does any of this make sense to you, Mrs Day?' he asked.

'Not a word,' answered Harriet. 'Does it to you?'

'We need to send this paper to Watson. Look, this reference to pituitory gland, corpses. I think we at last have here an account of the Atwell modus operandi.' He read over the few words again. 'Yes, syringing the gland through the sinus cavity. That's the answer. This must be what she did with the heads – but see, they had to be fresh – presumably within one hour of death. Poor May Dutton! And who knows who else?'

'Unspeakable,' said Harriet. 'Do you think this might be enough to convict her - Atwell, I mean? - although this is written in *Alexandra's* hand. She must know about it all, she must be familiar with all the details of the crimes. She must be a co-conspirator.'

'Wait, wait, wait, Mrs Day,' said Crowley. 'We are not yet at that point. The use of human body parts, as you will recall, is not actually illegal.'

'Murder, though? The girl May Dutton in London? What about Mrs Halliwell here at the hotel? She died unexpectedly! Suppose the woman has been taking advantage of the death of guests here or even, God forbid, hastening their end? How could Alex even bear to be in the presence of this woman if that were a possibility?'

'There is absolutely nothing here which indicates that your friend is aware of any wrongdoing – even if she is clearly aware of the extraction process. But these words here intrigue me. They refer to a magical ritual.' (Pollitt made a little sound like 'pfft' which Crowley ignored). 'Look, energy spiralling from one physical point to another, the name of a goddess form.'

Harriet said suddenly, 'She's going to kill George.'

Crowley said, 'I think we need to go immediately.'

Pollitt got up from the piano stool and joined them as they moved towards the door. 'I doubt very much that old George is in any danger really, you know,' he said.

It was a jarring shock to discover, when they got to George's room, that the door was standing open. In the dark interior, they could see by the light from the passage that the bed was empty. The window was propped open but apart from that, the room was as it had been when Harriet had crept in. She gave a little cry, going to the bedside table and picking up the half-filled water jug which stood there, as if it could tell her what had happened. Pollitt sat himself down on the side of the bed and shook his head in confusion. Crowley left the room. Harriet heard his voice down the passageway.

'Absolutely I am demanding an explanation. How can this be?'

A lighter voice was murmuring in response. Harriet went out and saw one of the nurses she had seen before, the kind-faced one. It felt dream-like as she approached the two of them facing each other, as if she were seeing things from the wrong angles. Fear, she supposed, was playing tricks on her mind.

'Yes, sir, I agree. It was a tragically unexpected development. He was on the mend at dawn when I come off duty. I swear. Early afternoon, Mrs Atwell said for Miss Frampton, the nurse on duty at the time, to go and take a good long rest. When she come back, the Mistress says he's gone. Miss Frampton she came and woke me and I run down here. Gone? I says to the Mistress. But at dawn, he was well, he was cool and rested! No, she said, with such a sad, tearful face, he has gone. He is at rest in the Lord. I couldn't believe it. Slipped away in his sleep this afternoon. Poor young man. So uncomplaining.'

Harriet could see the woman's face reflecting her own helpless disbelief. George? George could not be dead.

'And where is the body, nurse? Our friend is very dear to us. We would like to pay our last respects,' said Crowley.

'Oh, Mrs Atwell has a special arrangement with the undertakers in town. She will have sent for to take the body away. The guests here are vulnerable, ill some of them, easy to upset them, easy for them to take a sickness.'

'So poor Mr Edward Day's body will already be gone to town to be laid out? That is impossible!' said Crowley. Harriet was speechless and could not have made a sound.

'I have no information about it, sir. Mrs Atwell manages all such things. I'm most surprised that she hasn't already informed you. That's something she usually takes care of personally too. With the greatest sensitivity, she usually tells all the guests individual-like, takes each one aside and counsels them with words of comfort from the Holy Book.'

'It won't do, nurse. Whatever she usually does, she hasn't done it this time. This is our friend, I repeat, our very dear friend. Mrs Day's brother-in-law, no less! It is not right to spirit his body away. And there must be a coroner's report, a doctor to sign the death certificate – how are these things managed in this hotel? I fear the police will have to be called if these procedures are not followed.'

The nurse curtsied. 'If you don't mind, sir, all I can do is repeat that these things are managed by Mrs Atwell and I have no information to give you. I am sorry if we haven't given satisfaction. I can assure you I personally gave my best to nurse the gentleman. It is a terrible thing to lose a patient, and one so young. I feel it very deeply.'

Pollitt had joined them by now. He was as silent and his face as white as Harriet's.

The nurse was allowed to go on her way, having agreed to tell Mrs Atwell that they demanded to see her as soon as might be. Crowley led the way back into the room. 'We must examine everything,' he said. 'Before they strip it bare. There must be a clue.'

'A clue? What – a clue to what?' Harriet said, sitting down on the nurse's armchair. She was far too shocked to cry but her legs were giving way. 'Oh my poor boy. No, not dead.'

Pollitt too sat down, perching on the bed. 'My legs are giving way,' he said. 'The shock.'

Crowley ignored them. He began to open drawers, look under the bed, in the wardrobe. He stood on a wooden chair to reach the picture rail and the lintel and above the swags of the window dressing. Finally, in the canopy of the bed, above the curtains, he discovered a little bottle. 'This. This is it,' he said with satisfaction. He unstopped the bottle and held it some distance from his face for a hint of the scent. 'I guess we have here a form of dwale – the old hemlock, henbane, mandrake mixture that Juliet used. A drop or two has kept him quiet – sleeping, apparently. The mandrake will have produced the raving of brainfever you told me the nurse had mentioned. Get up, Pollitt! He isn't dead. Mrs Day, don't give way. We need to find him.'

'Is he in the hotel, do you think?' said Harriet. 'Oh, please God! Let us find him now!'

'Why on earth would he be drugged and – well, kidnapped, I suppose is the only word to describe it?' said Pollitt, shaking his head.

'Because of this! Listen to this!' Crowley read aloud from Alexandra's paper which he had thrust into his pocket. '*...of an energy, a kind of catalyst, which she believes will build... spiral through all physical points at the climax of the procedure.* Do you see? An energy, a kind of catalyst. What did I say to you, Polly? He is a voltaic coil. And she knows it.'

They left the room and began walking rapidly down the passage.

'The obvious thing is to look in the old part of the building,' said Harriet as they went.

'Agreed,' said Crowley.

They descended the stairs. The desk clerk was writing in a ledger. Pollitt put a finger to his lips with a meaningful glance at Harriet and Crowley. They lingered at the foot of the stairs while, with a solemn face, he approached the desk, holding his pocket handkerchief to his lips.

'Billy, Billy Sandford, my dear fellow, what a ghastly thing it is,' he said in fragile tones. 'I am distraught. There is no pain so great as the memory of joy in present grief. Aeschylus. But what I wondered was, what firm of undertakers was it that Mrs Atwell used today? I would like to compliment them on their speedy assistance. You know how dreadful it has all been.'

339

The clerk looked alarmed. 'Why, what is the matter, Mr Pollitt?'

'The recent death,' said Pollitt, lowering his voice. 'I understand that you have to be discreet about these things, Billy, especially in a place like this with so many guests teetering on the verge of eternal slumber, but tell me, who does Mrs Atwell use to collect – you know, collect the remains of the dear departed?'

As he spoke, Jerome signalled for them to go down the roped-off corridor. They scurried into the passageway and as fast along it in the dark as they could, with the sounds of Pollitt's conversation with the clerk receding as they went. They stopped by a door near the end.

'Locked, of course,' Crowley said. 'We must break it down.'

'And be apprehended and stopped before we can search? Is it likely that they will be keeping him in the office here?' asked Harriet.

'We can try to force an entrance quietly,' said Crowley, 'but I agree. It's not likely he is in here. I think we urgently need to search through the rest of this old part of the building.' He took a knife from his pocket and pulled up various implements from the nested blades. He tried to turn the lock mechanism with no success and then put his shoulder to the door. It was massively built and hardly shook in its hinges. By the light of a match, Harriet then noticed the second keyhole set further down the door. They gave up.

'I'll come back with an axe,' said Crowley, 'if we can't find him in the hour. Very well, this is just one option. The passage leads off that way.'

They were just about to go through a low doorway further down when they were joined by Jerome, Billy Sandford and, surprisingly, Major Farnsworth.

'I've explained everything,' said Pollitt, with an air of triumph. 'Billy believes me and - well, Major Farnsworth was passing by and sort of got involved. He's quite interested to see what happens next.' He added in a quieter tone, 'But I'm not sure if he's grasped who we're searching for, you know, but he's enthusiastic and even says he can get his gun if we need it.'

The little group followed a twilit passageway with darkening glazed windows along one side. It was too gloomy to see much but when Jerome struck a match, they were delighted to find several hurricane lamps left on the floor by the door, along with folded sheets and various pieces of equipment belonging to masons or glaziers. Taking a lamp each, they walked rapidly but carefully onward.

The place was a warren of connecting passageways and empty rooms. Scaffolding reached to the roof in some areas. Other rooms had no glass in the windows and were boarded up. There was no sound anywhere and Harriet quickly began to feel that this entire wing was empty of life. At the furthest end of the building, on what they presumed was the outer wall, they came to a door which had been bricked up. The work was old, the bricks tiny. A slot, now shuttered with a wooden board of great age, was visible at eye level. The little door with its stooped sense of secrecy immediately suggested the story of the anchoress.

'I don't think he's here,' announced Crowley to the little group, 'but we know he's somewhere in the area. Mr Sandford has already assured us that no visitors have come or gone from the hotel this afternoon and no one has called the undertaker at all. Therefore, he is in the valley but I think there is another way, down to the undercroft perhaps or to another hidden room. We know there was one door bricked up down there. There may be a number of other ways. I'm afraid we must go down the tunnel.'

'He's in the tunnel?' asked Pollitt. 'Oh, don't ask me to go in there again. Please, Crowley.'

'Thank God I don't take you climbing with me, Pollitt,' said Crowley in exasperation.

'All right, all right!' said Pollitt. 'Billy will come with us and help, won't you, dear? And the Major.'

Major Farnsworth, looking more keen and active than Harriet had yet seen him, assured them that he was ready for anything. As they hurried back to the modern part of the hotel, they all agreed to get dressed and be prepared for the conditions in the tunnel. Billy sensibly suggested sending one of the kitchen assistants on his bicycle to get a constable from the nearest village.

'Absolutely,' said Crowley. 'The rest of us, five minutes at the front door.'

'Don't forget, you'll need galoshes,' called Pollitt as everyone dispersed.

Harriet heard him complaining rather pitifully to Crowley as they walked towards their own rooms, 'You know I don't like climbing things, Aleister. Of course I wouldn't be any good up the bloody mountains. Whoever said I would be?'

CHAPTER THIRTY-FIVE

Harriet stood nervously at the edge of the chasm, holding her lantern up and peering at the twisted shapes of mist rising out of it. The journey through the rainy evening along the path next to the river had been dream-like, as had the tunnel and the stairs up to the hollow place above. No daylight had come through the ghosts of the distant arches now. Their idea was to find some beams with which to bridge the gaping hole in the floor – Crowley was convinced that beyond it, the tunnel would go on to join another hall or cave; and that this would connect to the old hotel itself. His energy inspired everyone to follow his lead. But Harriet, in nervous agitation, opted to go on along the tunnel and keep watch at the edge of the fissure. She left the men searching among the old rubble of the fallen ceiling.

As she waited, she saw a bloom of light approaching on the other side of the fissure. Suddenly, as if the bearer of the lamp had spotted Harriet's own light, there was a cry. It was a woman's voice, full of terror. Beyond the misty chasm, Harriet could just make out the spindle shape of a figure, a solid piece of dark vapour, standing just beyond the edge, holding a candle or lantern. The voice wailed again and this time there were words in it: 'Help me, whoever you are! Help!' There was a sob.

Harriet darted forward as near the cracked edge as it was safe to go. She held her lantern at arm's length, trying to direct the beam at the figure. 'Alex? Alex, darling, stay there! Don't move a step nearer. There's a big hole in front of you.'

'Harriet? Oh thank God, thank God. Who is with you? I can't see anything.'

'Listen, Alex, you need to stay still. Don't take another step. The edges may crumble away. Can you see the light of my lantern? I'm on the other side of a chasm, six or seven feet across with a good yard or so of unstable cracked stone this side, probably the same on your side. I am with Mr Crowley and Mr Pollitt and Major Farnsworth and Mr Sandford. We are trying to work out a way of crossing the chasm and they're finding beams and planks and things and then they'll need to get them in place. Then we can rescue you, darling.'

'It's not just me, it's George and Albert Burroughs too,' Alexandra said. She went on in a shaking voice which carried through the swirling vapour with the whisper of an echo. 'She's mad, Harry. I don't know how to describe what she's doing. I don't think she knows herself. She's trying to play-act an old ceremony but at the end of it, she's going to – she's going to extract a – a fluid from the human brain, a living human brain! While he is alive, Harriet! I can't stop her!'

'Oh dear God. George!'

'No, no, Burroughs! He doesn't know what she's planning. She has persuaded him it's some kind of ancient wedding ceremony and that she loves him again.'

'Loves him again? I thought he was her brother?'

'No, no, her second husband – a thing that went wrong, a mistake she said, hastily done and undone abroad.'

'And George? What about George, will she do the same to him?'

'No, he is to be another character. It's all mad, Harriet, I don't know how to explain it. I seem to have been living in a strange dream for days and weeks and inside the dream, everything made perfect sense but now this shock has broken through the skin of it.'

'What is George doing? Can he help you, can he help stop this thing happening?'

'No, I don't think so. He is so weak and dazed and almost out of his mind. She's been poisoning him, she's been keeping him drugged. She's dressed him up in odd ceremonial robes and persuaded him that he is a character from an old legend. And he believes it, he is just acting exactly as she wants him to.'

'We must stop this thing happening,' repeated Harriet almost to herself.

'What can I do?' wailed Alexandra. The figure in the mist appeared to begin pacing to and fro.

'The best thing you can do at this very moment is stand still,' said Harriet. 'Let's think. Is she armed, has she a weapon?'

'Yes. She has a knife and a revolver. That's what I know of. She showed the revolver to me and said she needed it in case anyone suddenly changed their mind. Can you understand how mad this is, Harriet? She has this old story in her head, she's been brooding on it for years, ever since Joseph died.' Alexandra's voice broke into a sob like a cough. 'She's convinced that there is a way of permanently cancelling out the effects of Time. And the odd thing, Harriet, the oddest thing is that George acts as if he understands it.'

'It's a delusion, Alex. Mr Crowley said that Atwell has used things like hemlock and I don't know what else to drug George. He will be very susceptible to suggestion. Atwell has talked him into it.'

'Yes, of course. You're right,' said Alex. 'How long will this take? Should I go back?'

'I don't know – would she come looking for you? Does she need you?'

'Yes, she needs me to play a part, or several parts. But she was taking a long time sweet-talking Burroughs, getting him to trust her – they talked all day about it and finally she's getting him to agree to sitting in the chair and I left her securing him to it. I noticed a narrow door in a dark corner. I took a lamp and crept away.'

'What exactly is in there? Is it far?'

'It's a big cavern and it's not far, maybe twenty or thirty yards from here. She's used it for a long time, she said. It's got candles and lanterns in place and paraphernalia which I suppose – I don't know. The place connects to the old part of the hotel. I don't like to think of it but do you suppose that she has been extracting this fluid from guests at the hotel? Like Mrs Halliwell?'

'It does occur to me that that was the probably the reason she began this venture of the Spa in the first place,' said Harriet.

'I must go back, mustn't I? I must go back and stop her, or delay her. Protect George. Stop her from killing Albert Burroughs.'

'Stay there! Don't go back, don't go back!' insisted Harriet urgently. 'She's got a gun, she's got a knife. She is obviously insane.'

'I have to go back, Harry. I helped make this happen. I encouraged her.'

'Oh, God! Please stay there. They're coming soon with the planks, they'll be able to cross, we can all go together and put a stop to it.'

'I'll try to delay her. If I stay any longer she'll suspect something is wrong. She thinks that nobody knows she's here. Goodbye, Harriet. I didn't know until this moment what you mean to me. I will never not love you.'

Harriet choked but she managed to say, 'We'll see you very soon. Don't take risks!'

Asu-Shu-Namir had not been his name at the beginning. That came a lot later. In the beginning, they had been of the Gala-tura, the Kur-jara, the sexless beings who flitted between life and death. Those who played this part were the beautiful ones, chosen for ritual castration and bound in service to the temple of the Lady of Heaven. He and his sister Bilit had been dedicated to the temple at the earliest possible age. It was a great honour to their family and a guarantee of the favour of Inanna. His life from that moment became a long repetitive dream of ritual and chanting, just one of the many temple servers, learning the prayers and acting out the ceremonies. As the years passed, gradually it was observed that, alone of all the servants who had ever been in the Temple of Uruk, he had received a unique blessing. For it seemed that just once in the history of Time, the Goddess had truly come. Perhaps every gesture and step of the ceremony, every atomic pulse of death-energy from the sacrifices, every call and response and tone in the long complication of the chants, had combined with perfect planetary alignments; or perhaps it had simply been Her whim. But it was he who had received the gift, quite by chance it seemed, given capriciously as was Inanna's wont. He had never aged. He had not been able to.

The priestesses kept him as a token and symbol of divine power. They carefully recorded everything he said and did, for they told him that his inner eyes had been opened and he could prophesy and see the truth everywhere; and every moment of the ceremonies in which he continued to participate was observed and remembered and sung about throughout the land. Kings and warriors and priestesses came to consult him, touch his robe, kiss the dust of his feet, hoping that his presence would persuade the Goddess once more to bless Her servants; but never again was a human being touched by divinity as he had been. Years upon years passed, a thousand years; and wearily he withdrew into the inner sanctum, rarely emerging, until it was rumoured that he had never been, that it was but a succession of young men who took on the role of the Asu-Shu-Namir. But there was only ever one.

Eventually, invaders came from far away, looking for new land and wealth. Uncouth and indifferent to the outlandish wonders around them, they casually destroyed the temple, sacked the city. The priestly ways were forgotten. He escaped and became a wanderer – but the threshold had always been his dwelling place. Gradually it became easier to forget than to remember. Gradually he built the deep-founded wall round everything he knew so that he could hide it; and hide away from it.

And now, tonight, he was back in Sumer, in the city of Inanna. He knew his robes were wrong and the place was wrong and the language was wrong; the very temperature and smell were wrong; but the Goddess was coming. He could feel the promise of her presence, like the first puff of wind in the stillness before a hurricane. The woman called Atwell, she had begun it. She had spun out the fibres, she had sung the words again and again. She knew what to assemble, what to lay bare, she knew when to plunge in the copper knife. She had dressed herself in a loose gauzy mantle over her gown, embroidered to glitter in the candlelight. Her long hair was hanging free under a twined diadem of gold wire.

He picked a thread from the sleeve of his robe and wondered at the strange cave in which he found himself. He could see a throng of people, whispering and moving in the background, in the dim places between the pillars of rock. Some were recently dead – he saw the woman with bandaged feet mutely signalling to him – and some were ancient memories from this cold alien land, dressed in skins with smoking torches in their hands, holding out ceremonial knives of flint, mammoth tusks, magical herbs. This cavern was old. It was the deep memory of Time itself: thought, intention, emotion, coiled and woven, stored by the valley people for ten millennia, twenty millennia. He was not sure whether the woman understood or could see what he could see, but it did not matter. She was just an instrument.

He looked at Albert Burroughs and could see everything about him, everything he had ever done. This man was also insane. Although his crimes – among them, those against the girl May Dutton and against himself – were layered like bricks of hot darkness on his heart and head, he sensed his raging, helpless longing for the woman and was sorry for him. 'The great bull held by a little ring through its nose,' he thought. 'This man thinks he will get his woman back. He has come here because she promised to keep him by her forever.' There was trust and hope in his face, even while the woman slowly, lovingly, bound his arms and legs with iron and whispered to him of the chains of lust and delight.

When Alexandra returned to his side, he barely looked at her. She had disappeared through the little door in the corner but he did not care. He was preoccupied with his own thoughts, riding billows of memory, millions of grains of sand, as if the sea were silting up and surging through his mind and the little permanent point of consciousness that was himself barely managed to stay on top, somehow, almost by chance, whirling and rising and sinking. When she spoke, he hardly understood at first. She spoke again and then again. In the end, he heard her.

'Harriet Day and others are going to come and rescue us, George,' she whispered, keeping her eyes fixed on Minerva where she stooped over Burroughs. 'We must delay this terrible thing. She will try to do something horrifying to Mr Burroughs there. We must try to stop her.'

'She will give him to the demons in exchange for her own life,' he said. 'It has to be done like that. Sometimes the Goddess favours her servants and gives a life gift in return. Such was my blessing – or perhaps it is a curse. Yes, it is a curse.'

He spoke slowly and clearly in answer but all Alexandra heard was gibberish. 'George, I don't know what language you're speaking,' she said out of the side of her mouth, 'but it isn't any language I have ever heard. Please, concentrate. Speak in English.'

'Do you not want this thing done?' he asked. His tongue seemed clumsy but this time the words were comprehensible.

'This thing, this thing is murder! How can I want it done?'

'It is the bargain,' he said in some confusion. 'We have to make the bargain with Ereshkigal, a life for a life. And Dumuzid was unfaithful.'

'Oh, George, she has led you into a maze. She has been whispering this story to you, again and again, while you slept or raved in delirium. It isn't true. Listen to me: it isn't true. She has persuaded you that you are part of this ceremony, that you are a creature called the Asu-Shu-Namir, but you are not. You are George Arden. You are from London. You are my friend. And we must save that man, Albert Burroughs.'

'Why?' asked George, still unsure. 'He killed a girl. He hurt me. He has hurt a lot of people. Is it not time for him to be hurt and killed too?'

'We must hand him over to justice, yes, but this isn't justice. This is just another crime.'

'Oh?' said George. 'Then what must I do?'

'You must … you must play along but do it slowly, do it wrong and I will do the same. Or we can try to attack her. Why don't we rush her now and overpower her?'

'I'm afraid I am very weak,' he answered. 'I can hardly stand up. I don't think I can do much more than walk.'

At this, she looked at him and saw that he was leaning against the wall with his head against the stone. His eyes were wide and dark in the candlelight but his face was shining with sweat and his hair was lank, sticking to his cheeks.

At that moment, seeing that he could do nothing, Alexandra decided to act. She strode decisively down from the rocky area upon which she and George had been placed, supposedly in contemplative preparation for their roles in the ceremony. She approached quickly from behind Minerva, intending to reach out to take her round the neck. Burroughs looked beyond Minerva and saw her. He cried out, 'Watch out!'

Minerva turned. Almost instantly, it seemed, she was holding the revolver. She gave a short laugh, took aim and with cold purpose shot Alexandra in the foot. The echoes clamoured in the cavern. She watched impassively as she rolled in agony on the floor, moaning and breathing in laboured gasps.

'I thought you might do something like this,' said Minerva without emotion. 'Don't imagine that this changes anything. You will take part in the ceremony as I instructed you. The only difference is that you will receive no benefit from it.' With that she turned back to Burroughs. 'There, darling. Do you like this? Are you firmly held in place? You like this restraint at the throat, don't you?' She caressed his neck and down his chest to his groin. 'I remember well how you enjoyed this. I have often thought of it. And soon we can be fulfilled in passion, very soon. Look, I have prepared a special device for you.' Delicately, she fitted a kind of cage helmet over his head which connected to a ring in the chairback to restrict his movements. 'I can make you long for this, more and more.'

Burroughs smiled and licked his lips. 'Just get rid of the old hag,' he breathed. 'Stop her noise. I want you now, I want you right away.'

'Oh, yes, I know you do. And him?' Minerva nodded her head towards where George had sunk to the floor. 'You want him too? I kept him for you. There's nowhere he can run.'

'Mmm,' moaned Burroughs and bit his lip.

'After the ceremony. Soon we'll belong to each other again. Just wait a little while.'

Minerva stepped round Alexandra and the pool of blood she was rolling in. She went to George, who had begun to try to crawl towards Alexandra, and with surprising strength, she pulled him up. 'Stand up. Walk over here,' she said in a soft, almost kindly voice. 'I need your help.'

They made their way to Burroughs in his chair. With sudden strength, Minerva ripped the sleeve from George's robe. 'Good,' she said. 'Use this to bind it up. Quickly, before she bleeds to death. Yes, a tourniquet, like that. Tighter.'

George did his best but the blood continued to flow at an alarming rate.

'She has made herself useless to me,' said Minerva in an aggrieved voice. 'How can you be Ereshkigal for my Inanna, idiot? How will you remember the lines? Sit her up, sit her against the stalagmite.' She went across to Alexandra and crouched in front of her. She slapped her face several times, trying to make her open her eyes. 'You are not to give in like this. You are deliberately fainting.'

George said, 'This ceremony won't work, lady. All the parts are wrong. The energy is dissipating and the Goddess has lost interest. She will not come.'

Minerva turned on him. It only took a push to send him sprawling backwards. 'Don't question me. Don't speak until it is required of you. We shall make this work. I alone shall make this work. I need nothing more than my own will.'

Minerva placed herself in the middle of the cavern and began to chant. She intoned the words of the tablet according to the phonetic values she had ascribed to them. George wanted to tell her that her interpretation was wrong, it was jumbled up, the emphases were wrong, the thought was wrong. She went through it all as a substitute for the ceremony she had devised and which could not now be performed in full.

Alexandra could hardly bring herself back to awareness. The darkness in the cavern seemed to deepen. Every now and then, her mind dipped into the shadows and Minerva's barbaric chanting disappeared. The pain of her wound got blotted out in the shadows and she was glad of that, that it could lessen for a while before it had to come back, and she thought of Mrs Halliwell and her bandaged feet and her kind smile. She seemed close beside her, offering drink in the cool darkness.

George pulled himself upright again and stood holding the wall. His head spun and his legs were trembling. The heaviness of his long drugged sleep hung on him. His limbs felt like those of a dead man. He listened to Atwell's chanting, thinking how useless, how pointless this all was. The witnesses, the ghosts in the cavern, were blank, yesterday's news, nothing but wisps of lost information, storm water trapped in a drain. No greater power than ghosts, after all, would come to this place now.

Minerva began to walk towards Burroughs, still intoning her garbled words, and she took out a long metal object. It was a little spear of lamplight as she held it up. Burroughs watched her, still lustful, ready to play her game in order to get her and keep her, as she had promised.

'This is useless!' shouted George. 'It will not call the Goddess! Do not do this terrible thing!'

Minerva looked at him once and said plainly in English, 'What goddess, you little idiot?' And then she walked purposefully towards Burroughs, whose head and neck was clamped firmly in place, straddled his lap and kissed him deeply. As he sighed and moaned, she suddenly brought the syringe up and began to pierce his nasal cavity, pressing the sharp point of the needle mercilessly through the fine bones at the back of the nose and into the brain. He screamed.

'Help me!' she shouted at George. 'He is struggling, this is delaying me. Hold him still, hold him still!'

The shrieks of Albert Burroughs reached Harriet and the others where they stood by the pit. Everyone exchanged fearful glances. Aleister Crowley maintained his concentration however as he inched his cautious way over the misty abyss. This was no time for distraction. The horrifying sound ended abruptly.

Harriet had shared every detail of Alexandra's story with the others. Now she looked at the way they must go. They had laid three narrow heavy oak planks side by side across the gap. The weight of the things was immense – each one ten feet long and six inches wide – and it had taken all the strength of the four men to free them from the rubble, bring them up the passage and then lay them across the chasm. They had made use of the rope and grappling hook, hauling and pushing and lifting the beams over the uneven floor.

Pollitt held onto Harriet's sleeve. 'Stay here, please, stay here. We know she has a gun, we know she has shot someone, we know she is doing something awful. You heard that scream …'

'All the more reason to go,' said Harriet. She stepped in front of Billy Sandford, who had been preparing to walk across. She had seen how the old beams wobbled under Crowley's weight and she found herself wishing there was something to hold on to. Crowley called to stop her as she was about to step on. He threw the rope across – the grappling hook clanked on the stone at their feet.

'Put it round your chest, under the armpits, and hook the grapple onto the line. I'm braced with the rope secured round a rock,' he said.

Harriet was glad she could not see the bottom, only the white steam twisting in the beam of the lantern she held and the increasingly solid figure of Crowley taking up the rope as she approached. She was soon standing behind him, projecting the beam forward to peer along the passage in front.

'I beg you to wait a little longer,' said Crowley curtly. 'Shine your light back along the beams. It's dangerous, we need to be together.' He looped the rope, swinging the hook and releasing it skilfully towards the shadows and lights on the further side.

'Got it,' came Billy Sandford's voice.

'Come on then, Billy. Round your chest, walk straight over, looking ahead. I've got you.'

In due course, Major Farnsworth arrived over the bridge. 'Good lord,' Farnsworth whispered to her. 'I haven't had this much fun in a quarter of a century.'

'Have you got a firearm, Major,' Harriet asked him.

'Yes, indeed I have. A very trusty service revolver. Never without it.'

Jerome Pollitt was now over. They began the journey along the tunnel. It curved ahead in the beams of their lanterns, disconcertingly throat-like and wet, with its smooth floor and bulbous folds and distensions. Billy hit his head on a pendulous udder of stone and cursed softly. When they were halfway along, they began to hear voices. There was also a moaning noise, low and anguished, which Harriet instantly identified as Alexandra's voice. The shock of hearing that sound caused her such terror that she almost reeled against the wall.

Major Farnsworth stopped and said in the hoarsest of whispers,

'We don't know if she is about to shoot someone in there. We must take our time and reccy properly or somebody might get killed. She might be shocked into action, d'you see? Understand, all? No rushing in. Quiet approach. It's a cavern, Mrs Day's friend says, so we need to hide ourselves in the shadows, get behind rocks, find cover, that sort of thing.'

They crept nearer, the tunnel shrinking to little more than five feet in height. It ended abruptly in a low doorway, covered with the remains of a crude wooden door; and through it they could hear George Arden's voice.

'If you kill her, you will have to kill me too.'

'Well, that is no trouble to me,' said the voice of Minerva Atwell. 'In fact, that is the most convenient solution to the problem of what to do with you both, now that you've betrayed me.'

'I know you have no conscience, no normal functioning heart, Mrs Atwell, but I want to tell you something. It is important for you to listen. You took it upon yourself to torture Dumuzid to death, pretending first to believe and then not to believe in the power of the goddess -'

'You talk like a simpleton, boy. The power of the goddess, such nonsense. Yes, there is power. There is an energy, but it is not a being, not a person. You might as well say that lightning is Thor the Thundergod. The ceremony was a formula which would have worked, were it not for her betrayal.'

'You have called on Ereshkigal, you have sacrificed Dumuzid,' said George's voice steadily. 'But you have not fulfilled your part of the bargain.'

'My part of the bargain? I never made one, except the compact I made with that woman, bleeding to death on the floor. I had a purpose. My purpose was to harvest this – this fluid here under certain conditions. Those conditions were not entirely fulfilled because of her. It would be perfectly just to finish her off. She's old and therefore useless,' – here she laughed – 'and nobody would miss her.'

In the dark outside the little door, the group paused. Major Farnsworth, for all his age and trembling hands, was not lacking in courage. He gently slid past the others, holding his lantern, one finger to his lips. He placed the light on the ground, pointed to his own chest, nodding, as if to indicate 'Me first,' took out his revolver and delicately passed through the doorway. He took a number of careful steps into the cave. They held their breath. Then they heard a rattle as his foot kicked a loose stone.

Instantly, Minerva Atwell turned towards the sound and shot. The bullet struck the wall and sparks flew. Major Farnsworth also fired his revolver but the shot went wide as he lost his balance. Crowley, Sandford and Pollitt all ducked through the doorway and there was a scurry as they dispersed into the shadows. Harriet was left outside, standing indecisively by the store of lanterns, listening. She could hear echoes of movement dying away. They must have found cover and now be lying silently in hiding, waiting for a chance to attack. Major Farnsworth was the only man with a gun. Where was he? She wondered if he had been hit, whether perhaps Aleister Crowley could get hold of his revolver and use it. It seemed that he should have been entrusted with the first shot. Now Minerva Atwell might pick them off one by one, or take George hostage. And where was Alexandra?

She peeped round the door. The chamber was lit by lanterns and huge church candles clustered in three different places, but it was a flickering, confusing mesh of shadows. It was large with an arching darkness above. The roof lowered in a sweep of wet rock until it met the floor, and here and there dripping waxy teeth of stalactites merged with their mirror images growing from the cave floor.

But the wonder of the cave was of no importance at that moment because Harriet saw two things that made her blood run cold: a chair and a silent figure held rigid by metal bonds; and the body of Alexandra on the floor. She was not making a sound and there was a slick of blood all round her. George Arden was crouching on the floor nearby with his arms encircling a stalagmite, wide-eyed, peering into the darkness. Minerva Atwell was nowhere to be seen.

Harriet crept into the cavern and crouched her way over to George with difficulty. At that moment, in the further darkness, there was another gunshot, the echoes making it impossible to pinpoint where it had come from or who had fired it. Harriet ignored it and on reaching George, embraced him like a child. 'George, dearest, what has happened to Alex? Where is Atwell?'

George started violently at being hugged so tightly. Then he understood who it was and whispered, 'Hello, Mrs Day. Mrs Roberts has been shot in the foot. I think she has fainted because of losing blood. And Albert Burroughs is standing over there, looking very wrathful.'

'Burroughs is dead, George. I can see his body in the chair.'

'Yes, his body is there. He wants to make Minerva Atwell keep her bargain.'

Just then there was a disturbance on the far side of the cavern. It seemed that Minerva had been making her way quietly to a hidden way leading back to the hotel, skirting round the walls; and she had encountered one of the group in the darkness. There was an angry scream, the discharge of a gun and then a scramble of feet slipping on pebbles.

'I've got her pistol,' came Crowley's voice out of the dark.

'She's heading towards the other door,' cried Pollitt, emerging into the light of some thick candles far over the other side of the cave.

Billy Sandford was suddenly there, jumping up to try to stop a shadow flying past him. There was a scream. 'She's stabbed me! She's got a blade, a very sharp blade, oh my God.'

'Billy!' said Jerome, hastening across the open space in the midst of the cavern.

'No, it's just my hand where I went to grab her, she didn't get much of a blow in,' began Billy.

'Never mind your bloody hand, Sandford!' yelled Major Farnsworth. 'Damn it, I've dropped my service revolver, can't find the bloody thing...'

'She's getting away!' shouted Crowley at the same moment. 'Stop her, somebody!'

Minerva Atwell fled through the door leading to the undercroft and the river before anyone could catch her.

'Now,' said George. He stood up, swayed, took a second to gain control of his limbs and began walking towards the door. 'This way,' he said to thin air. He passed swiftly through, picking up an abandoned lantern on the other side as he did so, and without waiting for anyone else, limped resolutely along the passage.

The others, hastily picking their way towards the door from their various hiding places, were hindered by the rocky floor and the darkness.

Harriet left Alexandra and hurried to catch him. 'George, what are you doing?' she called after him. 'We must help Alex! George, I need you right now!'

'Then go to Alex,' he said, half turning round. 'I know she needs you and that's where you can do the most good.'

Harriet was torn, full of foreboding, but she said no more. She took up her own lantern and turned back to go to Alex, worrying that George might be too quick and have to face Atwell's knife alone. At the cavern door, Billy Sandford was clutching a dripping hand. She did her best to bind it hastily with his handkerchief, while Crowley and Pollitt pushed past and away in pursuit of George. Major Farnsworth brought up the rear, mopping the wound on his forehead where he had fallen and struck the floor. He paused dizzily at the door and sank to the ground muttering, 'Can't keep up, can't find the bloody gun either.'

Harriet paused a moment to see that he was resting as well as he could with his back propped against the wall, telling Sandford to look after him. She hurried over to Alexandra. She wished she had water to give her, seeing that blood was still soaking out of the wound. She set about binding it with wads of cloth and strips from her own petticoats. There was nothing else to be done. She sat holding her cold hand, trying not to look at the dead body of Albert Burroughs and the blood which had gushed down his contorted features.

When George found Minerva Atwell, she had put down the lantern snatched up at the door and was holding the rope and grapple, as if deciding what to do with it. He could see that there had been a narrow bridge laid across the abyss of Erecura. This was where George had stopped the first time he came here, coming to a dead end on the other side, led there by the lady with the bandaged feet who wanted to lead him to the cave beyond it. Now, now that he had opened his eyes again, he could see endless layered repetitions of scenes of sacrifice to the underworld: numberless fragments of life-endings, death-moments, energy flares. Minerva Atwell could not see any of it, of course. Nor even could Albert Burroughs, who was standing exactly next to her.

She heard George arrive and glanced backwards. 'Don't even try,' she hissed breathlessly. 'I'll stab you, shove you in the pit. Just keep back.'

George said nothing but stood in the darkness by her lantern, silently putting his own on the ground too and watching as she spent precious seconds trying to wrestle the end of the rope from where it had snagged between the beams. Angrily, she cast off the impediment of the ceremonial robe she had been wearing over her dress and it slid in a shimmering heap to the floor. Albert Burroughs moved in so close to her that even she sensed him. She paused and shook her head impatiently as if to flick away a blowfly. As she did so, the rock floor began to crack. George stepped back a little. He wondered whether she had noticed it or not, whether he should tell her; and just as he thought that, the crack widened. A slice of rock gaped wider and jolted down six inches. The planking on which she had stepped sloped suddenly and she gave an abrupt cry of fear.

'Help me!' She threw the end of the rope towards George, the grappling hook in her hand. 'Catch it, hold it!'

George did catch it and he did hold it. He could do very little but double it round a knobble of rock and watch it tighten as the planks and the woman and the rock in front of him slid and rattled into the white steam. For a little while, he could hear Minerva gasping hoarsely and he understood that she was hanging onto the hook for dear life, saving her breath for the effort; but he knew that the rocks falling from above would soon break her grip. After a second or two, just as Aleister Crowley came up beside him, the rope was suddenly slack. She had fallen without a sound. But it was acceptable.

George knelt on the rock, observed silently by Crowley and Pollitt. He picked up the empty robe, held it up, opening his arms wide to the mist and the darkness of the Great Land and chanted slowly in his own sweet mother tongue,

'*After she had crouched down and had her clothes removed, they were carried away. Then she made her sister Erec-ki-gala rise from her throne, and instead she sat on her throne. The seven judges, rendered their decision against her. They looked at her -- it was the look of death. They spoke to her -- it was the speech of anger. They shouted at her -- it was the shout of heavy guilt. The afflicted woman was turned into a corpse. And the corpse was hung on a hook.'*

CHAPTER THIRTY-SIX

'It is unfortunate that we can't help him sort out his legal mess,' said Pollitt, lighting a cigarette (one of Aleister's black and gold ones) and blowing a long stream of smoke into the sunshine.

'I don't see what we can possibly do, except get him out of the country,' said Crowley, quickly retrieving his cigarette case before Pollitt stowed it in his pocket.

'We'll all have to carry on lying and lying and lying until the end of time,' said Pollitt. 'At least he's safe with Arthur.'

'How can we not tell the truth eventually?' asked Alexandra wearily. 'His presence is an essential part of it.' She was feeling at a disadvantage in the conversation because she was sitting in a bathchair with her sore and bandaged foot raised. When she had been carefully helped into it by Harriet, she had wondered if it was the very same chair in which she herself had wheeled Mrs Halliwell about. Now it just made her feel vulnerable and old.

They were all seated on the hotel's southern terrace, tucked out of the way of the gusty wind. But the afternoon sun had a warmth to it, drawing new green blades out of the earth. White clouds were scudding across the sky.

'I think it's very fortunate that you used such an outlandish name for him when you spoke to the police,' said Harriet, patting her hand. 'A little creative storytelling is very healthy.'

'It wasn't story telling – it was truth, as far as I understood it at the time. I had to give a full account of everything that happened, I was forced to, but I think they hardly believed me. Thought I was hysterical. I think I was: and so I kept calling him the Asu-shu-Namir.'

'That's what I mean. But of course, *we* did not know what you were going to say – you were confined to your bed with the nurse and sleeping draughts, recovering from the loss of your poor little toe - and we all agreed to leave all mention of George out of it. It was our plan, I'm afraid, Alex, to contradict you and let the police assume that you were suffering the after effects of loss of blood and shock.'

'And I was, of course,' said Alexandra.

'The other thing is that the hotel nurses think my "brother-in-law" died and yet there is no record of it,' said Harriet.

'It occurs to me that there is every likelihood that as the

investigation gets underway, the police will look into all deaths recorded at the hotel,' put in Crowley; 'and they will come across records pertaining to an Edward Day – and perhaps wonder where or who he is. At that point – and let's hope it's far in the future – Edward Day will have gone abroad and since there *was* no death, there will only be strange tales from the nurses to contradict.'

'Billy Sandford didn't even recognise George in the excitement,' said Jerome knowledgeably. 'I asked him.'

'George was wearing those ridiculous robes, remember,' agreed Harriet, 'and once we got back to the hotel, I took him straight to my room and hid him under the bed.'

'Billy talks exclusively of his heroic moment and the sound of the blade as it sliced through his skin,' said Pollitt. 'He has a terrible wound at least a sixteenth of an inch deep and two and a half inches long. It is already almost healed. Apart from that, he recalls little of the scene in the cavern. He does remember us finding our way back to the hotel and coming out through the false wall of the anchoress's cell.'

'Yes, that was an unexpected development,' said Harriet. 'I never would have guessed that the old wall was a dummy. It absolutely looked convincing. Very old indeed.'

'Yes, because it was very old indeed. A very old dummy wall,' said Crowley. 'The abbey here had been cashing in on what must have been a ready supply of pilgrims to see the anchoress since about the year 1200. Of course, they also had their hidden supply tunnel – that old bridge must have served to cross the chasm and bring necessities in to her cell.'

'She was reputed to have lived to an immense age,' said Harriet. 'Two hundred and twenty-six, the legend says.'

'A series of them, of course. After all, they had the big cavern, the tunnel, access to the river. Rather a congenial set up, if you ask me,' said Crowley.

'It makes me feel horribly cynical,' said Pollitt, drawing his gaze away from the shadows sliding over the valley. 'Billy agrees. It is quite disillusioning.'

'I thought you were horribly cynical already?' said Crowley. 'Fortunately, Major Farnsworth seems to understand very little of what happened either. He is very proud of his leadership role and I have thanked him profusely for demonstrating such courage. He's not even sure of how many were in our party on the way to the rescue, let alone after he had cracked his head on the floor and we led him back. He's still regretting the loss of his service revolver and planning an expedition and thorough search for it. I hope he finds it. But he is unlikely to pass on details of the presence of Edward Day to the investigating officers – and certainly not a George Arden. Let's just be thankful for that: now George can be permanently disappeared. And I shall have pleasure in taking that duty upon myself. I think I shall take him with me in my luggage when I next climb some mountains.'

'Actually *in* your luggage, Mr Crowley?' said Harriet, whom nothing Crowley did could surprise.

'No? Is that not a good idea? Oh well, he will have to pretend to be my valet. And that is mutually beneficial because there are many, many things he can teach me.'

'Not another magical mentor, Crowley?' said Pollitt.

Just then a hotel page came wandering out on the terrace bearing a silver tray, looking vaguely in their direction. It was a letter for Pollitt with a French postage stamp. He opened it and begged their indulgence while he read its contents.

Crowley continued quietly as the boy walked away. 'Nobody shall know of his existence. He shall have a completely new name – a series of names, and no rivalries and squabbles shall distract him. He shall be well looked after and we shall discuss … all kinds of fascinating things. I plan to get to Egypt – perhaps I can set him up there.'

'He'd like that,' said Harriet. 'I think he comes from somewhere out that way.'

'I fear his mind is permanently damaged,' said Alexandra sadly. 'He is deeply scarred by the experience. Minerva Atwell made him believe a thousand mad things while he was drugged, and he seems to believe them still.'

'Oh? You mean his delusion about coming from the remote past and being untouched by Time?' said Crowley. 'Don't worry about that little *idée fixe* of his. I'll look after him. I understand him, you see. I am the very best person to help him.'

Everyone looked at Crowley doubtfully but he affected not to notice.

'In fact, *I* will be the first to leave the country,' announced Pollitt, looking grave, 'because I must visit dear Aubrey very soon. This letter is from Menton and things look bleak. Listen to what he says: *My dear Friend, So pleased to get a letter from you. Have had a vile attack of congestion of the lungs and spent three weeks in bed. It has left me an utter wreck and quite incapable of work. I am simply in an agony of mind over it. Heaven only knows when I shall be able to work again. Pray breathe not a word of this to anyone* …Oh. I shouldn't have read that aloud. That was unforgivable of me. Well, none of you are going to go and tell old Smithers about it, are you? Poor darling. So you see, I need to get on and see him. And under the circumstances, Aleister, I believe it is more appropriate for *me* to get George out. And it will be like this: he will be my sister, Georgiana, and you see how perfect it is? I shall take him – or her – with me to Menton on the Riviera and he shall have *un petit gîte qui donne sur la plage…* and perhaps the very sight of him will infuse life into poor Aubrey. He may even be inspired to draw him.'

'But I need him for *my* research, it is of the utmost significance. You simply want to dress him up in one of your frocks …'

Harriet turned to Alexandra, leaving the two to bicker in the background. 'How's the foot, love?'

'Better. I feel better for being outside. The year is turning back to springtime already. That's best of all. And now those awful pills have worn off …'

Harriet looked at her friend, not sure what to say. For Alexandra's face, perhaps as result of stress and illness or perhaps as a result of the withdrawal of the Supplement, had subsided in the space of a week into that of a haggard woman ten years older than her real age. But it did not matter to Harriet and she smiled. 'It's good. You're on the mend. I'll wheel you round the rose garden a few times, although there aren't any roses yet. You'll have to imagine them. Leave the boys to fight over George. They always seem to.' She stood up.

Crowley raised his hand to stop her. 'Mrs Day, later on, this evening at about sunset, may I request your assistance?'

'Well, certainly you may request my assistance,' said Harriet in surprise. 'And may I ask why?'

'The stone heads,' said Crowley. 'I wish to return them to the well. Perhaps you would like to witness it?'

She nodded and answered, 'Perfect.'

Harriet and Alexandra spent many hours tête-à-tête during Alex's slow recovery, talking over the events of the past few weeks. It was important for Alexandra to get to grips with exactly how and why Minerva Atwell had been so easily able to get into her confidence and exploit her trust. Harriet privately thought that it would take a while for her to regain her self-belief and subtly encouraged her to take up her pencil and make some sketches of the other guests. Mr Slindon was her first victim but none was more willing than Camilla Ives. It took some persuading to get her to let someone else sit. It helped Alex to find a little of her peace of mind and also led to a new commission: young Frederic Goldilocks needed a large portrait.

There was a great deal of police activity and interviews to be endured, of course. They could not retrieve the body of Minerva from the abyss, which they calculated to exceed Gaping Ghyll in its depth. The death of Albert Burroughs was at first a matter of considerable speculation in the local newspapers, as a result of the actions of Mr Slindon, who turned out to be a journalist. He seemed to think that Burroughs, as the victim, deserved his story to be told. He was unable to gather the full details, but for some weeks he sold speculative tales to the local press about secret tunnels and a smuggling gang operating in the Abbey of Death. Journalists began turning up at the hotel and Alexandra found it all exceedingly uncomfortable. She remained as much as possible in her own room, answering no questions and speaking only to Harriet.

There were inquests held on both the deaths. She gave statements upon the role she had played in the set up and execution of Minerva's strange plan; and was reprimanded for her folly in being duped by 'the Atwell trick', as the coroner called the Supplement. But on the whole, she was pitied and thought to have suffered a temporary derangement due to the drugs Minerva had tricked her into taking, Consequently, she was able to avoid being charged as an accessory to murder. It was decided that Burroughs had been murdered by Minerva Atwell, who then took her own life by leaping into a chasm. Nobody mentioned George and Harriet was able to account for her presence at the hotel as being to visit her friend Alexandra Roberts, about whom she was worried. The ends tied up neatly enough, if nobody looked too closely.

Harriet did write a long letter to Dr Watson, detailing everything that she knew, but asked him not to send a reply back to the hotel.

She did not want any correspondence to go astray, particularly as Billy Sandford had become something of a local hero, had begun embroidering the story of his Wound somewhat and was the one who handled the mail. Anyway, she hoped to be home soon. Throughout it all, oddly enough, the Adsullata Spa Hotel continued to receive guests. It seemed the bank actually owned the concern and was anxious to take advantage of a flood of curious and ghoulish visitors.

Meanwhile, at the earliest opportunity, George had been placed in the care of Arthur Radwell, the rusticated friend of Pollitt's, whose parents lived in Bath. There had been some debate about getting him there. Crowley had wanted to hike with him over the pathless foothills of the Mendips, leaving silently through a back window before dawn and taking only the clothes he stood up in. Jerome, upon hearing this, decided to take matters into his own hands. He announced to Billy that he wanted to go shopping and ordered the coach to pick him up at noon. He then simply breezed out of the hotel arm-in-arm with a slender young lady in a demure bonnet; and nobody noticed - or if they did, they said no word.

Arthur was told to keep a careful eye on George, not to take him into society or to ask too many questions. He concluded that Pollitt's young friend was an indiscretion best kept out of the public view; and was kind and mature enough to keep him safely at home. He could not refrain from trying to psychoanalyse him though, and took copious notes on the occasion. It led eventually to Radwell becoming a celebrated 'alienist'. His later case study on George, *Mr X.: Fausse Reconnaisance, Traumatic Neuroses and Endo-Psychic Conflict* was ritually burnt on publication by Aleister Crowley in 1922 at the Abbey of Thelema in Cefalú. George lit the bonfire.

*

'So, you see, my dear Holmes,' concluded Dr Watson, laying down his notes, 'the story comes to its terrible end. Burroughs was murdered by his own erstwhile wife in a scene of unprecedented horror.'

'Yes,' said Sherlock Holmes, 'and what of the May Dutton case?'

'Unsolved, of course. The murderer was himself murdered before justice could be done, although Poetic Justice, of a sort, was served. Burroughs never made a confession.'

'That is most unsatisfactory, Watson, and I am surprised that you consider this case worthy of publication. One assumes that at least the fraud investigation will uncover the wrongdoing of those two reprobates. But what of Bateman? He too was done away with. Surely there is something that could have been deduced from the corpse and the method of despatch?'

'Well, if the *ears* had been missing, Holmes, that would have been a convenient clue. But as you know, the fellow was pushed off a bridge onto a train track. Or we believe he was pushed, but there were no witnesses.'

'H'mm. And this matter of George Arden. Where is he?'

'That, I am afraid, is a mystery.'

'Tut! There is no such thing as a mystery, Watson, and I am surprised you allow such loose ideas to take root in your mind. I see that the lack of my company has permitted you somewhat too much romantic latitude in your ideas.'

'It was by no means straightforward, Holmes,' said Watson defensively. 'We found it impossible to establish that Burroughs was lying in the matter of the death of Valentine Cabot, for example.'

'Tut!' said Holmes again. 'You had a full account from a witness of the disposal of the broken glass beneath the body. It needed but a little force of character to compel these aspects of the case upon the attention of Inspector Miller. With this evidence it should surely be possible to clear Arden's name.'

'Well, I did my best. But we failed to make sufficient connection between the ears in the box and the grave robbing. May Dutton's earrings – well, much as Browning and I were convinced that they were proof of guilt, Inspector Miller was intransigent. A most unworthy member of the force, I am afraid.'

'And this Detective Browning, he did well, you say? A promising young fellow to keep an eye on. You and he worked alongside each other on all these investigations?'

'Well, now you come to ask, Holmes, there was another chap involved. I thought it better to leave him out of it. Too complicating for the readers, you know – another character to understand, another point of view …'

'Who was this other "chap", Watson?' asked Holmes with a slightly grim smile. 'Not Mrs Harriet Day by any chance?'

'I confess, she was of great assistance. But there was another, I might as well tell you. A strange young fellow who attached himself to me, I hardly know why. But he was arrogant, impulsive, quite unsuitable for detective work – smoked far too much, used stimulants and narcotics ...' Watson trailed off as Holmes deliberately reached for the Persian slipper containing his tobacco. 'Yes, anyway, tended to lie about in a silk dressing gown, decadent ennui, that sort of thing. Brilliant but too fond of making astounding assertions for the sake of éclat.'

'You are not by any chance trying to make a point, in your clumsy fashion, about my own habits?'

'Not at all, my dear fellow. This chap was fond of demons and necromancy. Nothing of your kind of work. All nonsense, really.'

'So if he was more of a hindrance than a help, why did you permit him to tag along with you?'

'Well, he did in fact notice a few of the salient features in the case. Anyway, he's no doubt gone back to his undergraduate poetry, perusing the Yellow Book, keeping company with theatricals and so on.' Watson studied his notes so as not to meet Holmes's eye.

Sherlock Holmes looked long and hard at his friend.

Watson cleared his throat. 'Anyway, what do you think of this one? Look, I've written a scene of it already. I thought we could call it *The Hound of the Baskervilles.*'

In theory there is no limit to the power of magic. A magician is like a mathematician; he has complete control of the symbols as long as he keeps to the rules.

I have prepared the elixir of life, that magical draught which gives eternal youth. Like the touch of Midas, it is not an unmixed blessing.

'Black Magic is Not a Myth'
by Aleister Crowley

"The Worst Man in the World"
The London Sunday Dispatch,

2nd July 1933

AFTERWORD

For the student of the period, there will be several little rubbing points in the timeline of this story. I want therefore to apologise to those for whom, like me, it matters that Crowley did not meet his climbing mentor, Oscar Eckenstein, until the Easter of 1898; and especially to those who will be anxious to point out that it was months after this story takes place that Crowley was inducted into the Order of the Golden Dawn (on the 18th November, to be precise), Allan Bennett became his magical mentor and he took up residence (under the pseudonym of Count Vladimir Svareff – but that seemed far too unlikely for fiction) in Chancery Lane (along with the famous skeleton). All this did occur in 1898, but it was after Jerome Pollitt had left Crowley's life. Indeed, it may have been partly because of his absence. There are several other inaccuracies like that. This conflating and rejigging of events became necessary for the flow of the story and believe me, although many other errors may have occurred inadvertently, they are not through disrespect for my subjects. Aleister Crowley and Jerome Pollitt were nurtured in the 1890s: that is to say they - and particularly Pollitt - lived to the full the life of the Decadent. Needless to say, Conan Doyle's fictional Sherlock Holmes, with his anti-social temperament, drug addiction and 'neurasthenic' ennui is just as surely part and parcel of this fin-de-siècle atmosphere. I hope it isn't too far fetched to imagine them co-existing in the London of 1898.

BIOGRAPHICAL NOTES

Aleister Crowley 1875-1947

I have tried hard to forget the extremely colourful life that unfolded for Crowley after the year 1898. As he appears at this point in history, he is just a young man who has recently come into a massive fortune: intense, challenging and self-confident. He will leave Cambridge without taking his degree later this year (a common choice at the time for those with no financial compulsion to take up a profession). But he is already a competition-standard chess player, a daring and unconventional mountaineer, a competent chemist and mathematician, a writer and a poet. The product of an upbringing in an extreme religious sect, by 1898 Crowley has vehemently rejected Christianity – particularly his mother's version of it. Years of deep unhappiness at home and school have led him to fight back and rebel: to choose 'to get in personal communication with the devil.'

Although Crowley's later life is not the subject of this story, some future developments are hinted at and many of his own words are incorporated. In the Twentieth Century, Crowley will become a prolific writer, a spy, a prophet, a visionary, the founder of the religion of Thelema and, for the Daily Mail et al, 'the wickedest man in the world'. And he will twice attempt to make the Elixir of Life. He will attract and exploit his many acolytes – and make many enemies - with the showmanship of a Donald Trump and the hypnotic skill of a Derren Brown, attesting to how unstoppable a combination is absolute self-belief and a brilliant mind. But at the time of our story, Crowley is just on the very cusp of his researches, far from becoming '666, The Great Beast'.[1] His interest in ceremonial magic, however, is serious and becoming all-consuming: the songbirds and cups of blood are fact. Indeed, I have hardly touched upon the full extent of his experimentation.[2] Here's an example of what Dr Watson might really have found going on at Chancery Lane if he had visited a few months later:

As we went out, we noticed semi-solid shadows on the stairs; the whole atmosphere was vibrating with the forces which we had been using. (We were trying to condense them into sensible images.) When we came back, nothing had been disturbed in the flat; but the temple door was wide open, the furniture disarranged and some of the symbols flung about in the room. We restored order and then observed that semi-materialized beings were marching around the main room in almost unending procession. (Confessions)

In 1898, Crowley is also very much in love with Jerome Pollitt. He later described their relationship (in Victorian code) as 'the ideal intimacy which the Greeks considered the glory of manhood'; and to elucidate what exactly that meant, wrote a note in his own copy of his autobiography, saying, 'I lived with Pollitt as his wife for some six months and he made a poet out of me.' It was Crowley's obsessive Occult studies and Pollitt's indifference to them which forced the lovers apart: 'He showed an instinctive distrust of my religious aspirations, because he realized that sooner or later they would take me out of his reach.' (*Confessions*)

Crowley describes his decision to devote himself to his spiritual path as 'jagged and envenomed', 'for he [Pollitt] was the only person with whom I had ever enjoyed truly spiritual intercourse ... He fought most desperately against my increasing preoccupation in which he recognised the executioner of our friendship.'

They broke up in the wake of bitter arguments. Crowley almost immediately regretted his decision and wrote to Pollitt - but the letter miscarried. Shortly afterwards, when they passed each other on Bond Street, Crowley realised too late that Pollitt must have thought he had deliberately 'cut' him. All contact came to an end.[3]

Crowley developed the conviction that he had sacrificed his true love in order to pursue his spiritual path: may even have felt the sacrifice was one required of him. Despite numerous lovers of both sexes, he seems never to have got over the loss. His later writings are scattered with references to Pollitt, including a *ritual to destroy the shell, i.e. to exorcise my Qliphoth [negative emotions] about P__ [Pollitt] and so either to cure or kill, as alive or dead respectively.* Crowley's records of experimentations in astral travel also detail a vision of all those he had 'caused to sin': among them he saw Pollitt's face. His feelings inevitably swung between grief and anger. It must be in this period that two harsh sonnets addressed 'To the author of the phrase: "I am not a Gentleman and I have no friends"' were written, in which he seems to address Pollitt's spiritual despair:

Self-damned, without a friend, thy eternal place
Sweats through the painting of thy harlot's face.

It was dangerous to be a practising homosexual – Crowley, in any case, was avidly bisexual – and he was forced to conceal his passion. He expressed his desires in privately-printed erotic poems and novels, quite unsuitable for public consumption at the time; and it is in these that Pollitt appears. *In The Scented Garden of Abdullah the Satirist of Shiraz*, written twelve years after they broke up, he writes in *The Riddle:*

> *Habib hath heard; let all Iran*
> *Who spelt aright from A to Z*
> *Exalt thy fame and understand*
> *With whom I made a marriage bed.*

The 'riddle' is easily read: the acrostic verses spell out the names Herbert Charles Jerome Pollitt and his own. [4]

In 1914, sixteen years after the break-up, Crowley wrote in his diary that he wished he could find a companion like Pollitt. Crowley's *Not the Life and Adventures of Sir Roger Bloxam, a Novellism* contains the story of the love of the character Sir Roger for Hippolytus. A full nineteen years after the relationship with Pollitt had ended, we once again come across an idealised description of him: *He was a man with golden hair so fine and pale, yet, glowing, that one thought of sun-rays incarnate in gossamer; and his face was like the harvest moon... Will god not give me a name for him? Some name of angel strength and sweetness? Surely Porphyria yearned for him as Phaedra for Hippolytus – Let that, then, serve!* ('Porphyria Poppoea' is Crowley's comedic name for Sir Roger's anus – needless to say, he wrote very frankly about sex).

Thirty years later, Crowley wrote in his *Confessions* (partially published 1929) that 'the fragrance of that friendship still lingers in the sanctuary of my soul.' It seems to have been a true love match which Crowley idealised all the more once it became unattainable.

> *In my deep heart thy name is writ alone,*
> *Men shall decipher - when they split the stone.*

From an 'untitled' poem, unpublished small red poetry notebook. Approximately 1898. Gerald Yorke Collection

Herbert Charles 'Jerome' Pollitt (1871-1942)

Pollitt was 26 years old when Crowley first met him. He had adopted the name Jerome sometime in 1897 (just as Crowley had become 'Aleister' around about the same time) and had taken his degree in 1892. Brought up in Westmorland (now Cumbria), he attended Heversham Grammar School. A bright boy, at Prize Day 1889 it was noted that 'Pollitt, H.C. is considerably first' and he went on to study medicine at Cambridge. Local newspaper listings of the time hint at a leisured upper class existence, detailing attendance at Mayoral banquets, rural festivals and such like, as well as performing at musical events. Wealthy, intelligent and charming, he became a flamboyant, sexually ambiguous and influential personality in 1890s Cambridge. As a leading member of the Footlights Dramatic Club, (he was elected President twice: 1896 and '97), he was noted for his talent. For example, his 1892 performance as 'Première Beddeuse' in the play *Alma Mater* was distinguished by the Cambridge Chronicle for 'very special mention' as he 'danced very gracefully; in fact he made quite an ideal woman'.

With Footlights cast members being all male in those days – indeed education at all levels being sexually segregated – female parts were inevitably taken by males. Pollitt, however, took it a little further; and it was while he was revisiting Cambridge (his family home was in Kendal)[5] to give a performance as his female alter ego, 'Diane de Rougy'[6] that Crowley first saw him. His graceful 'skirt dance', based on 'The Serpentine' of Loie Fuller, would presumably, like hers, have consisted of eurhythmic movements forming rippling shapes of silk, lit up by spectacular changing colours.[7] L.J.Kooistra speculates that Beardsley's 'The Stomach Dance' draws on his own idea of Pollitt's performance (Beardsley presumably never saw Pollitt dance, unless privately).

Pollitt's wealth, personality and talent earned him a place among the elite artistic society of the Decadents. He sat for Whistler and collected his works. He was a correspondent of Oscar Wilde's, sending photos of himself to the writer in exile, including one in a transparent robe (*Wilde, Letters, 777*). Most important of all, he was a collector, patron and personal friend of the artist, Aubrey Beardsley.

A useful source for the conversational 'feel' and behaviour of rich young undergraduates of the time – if not a great novel in itself - is E. F. Benson's *The Babe, B. A.* (pub. 1897). Pollitt is the main model for its gently-comical hero, 'the Babe' himself. Benson introduces him thus:

His particular forte was dinner parties for six, skirt dancing and acting, and the performance of the duties of a half-back at Rugby football. His dinner parties were selected with the utmost carelessness, his usual plan being to ask the first five people he met, provided he did not know them intimately. With a wig of fair hair, hardly any rouge, and an ingénue dress, he was the image of Vesta Collins* and that graceful young lady might have practised before him, as before a mirror.

*Possibly a combination of the Music Hall artistes Vesta Tilley and Lottie Collins. Vesta Tilley was a celebrated male impersonator.

Benson states in his flippant Foreword to the book that his depiction of the Babe is at fault as 'he ought never to have played Rugby for his University as savouring too much of the hero' – in other words, 'manly sport' was not really Pollitt's thing; but here Benson was not just injecting some hetero-normative masculinity into his account. The original of the fictional character is not solely Jerome but also his lover at the time, whose nickname was indeed Babe and who was a sportsman. It was Jerome who favoured embroidery (do we see in this the original of the much later 'Georgie Pillson' in the Mapp and Lucia series?). Benson is believed to have met Pollitt through his brother, Arthur Benson, who was a master at Trinity College, Cambridge and ten years Pollitt's senior. Henry James may have been a connecting acquaintance along with the philosopher Santayana, a relative of Pollitt's.[8] It seems likely that Oscar Browning would also have been a mutual acquaintance.

Benson gives us a review of the Babe's performance as Clytemnestra which, if a tribute to Pollitt's theatrical powers, hints at something impressive: *... his performance was the more remarkable in that he did not repeat himself slavishly: acting was an instinct with him, and each night he acted as his mood prompted him... In a word, he made it clear, that Aeschylus was a most excellent dramatist, and that he was a most excellent actor.*

371

We also get a reference to Pollitt's effect as a female impersonator (in which role, Crowley said, he became 'one of Rossetti's women brought to life') : *A shaggy student from Heidelberg who represented his university, thought she [the Babe in the role of Clytemnestra] was a woman, and, heedless of Agamemnon's doom, fell in love with her on the spot, and was disposed to take it as a personal insult that the Babe was of the sex that Nature made him.*

Benson mentions that the Babe, like Pollitt, decorated his rooms with 'several of Mr Aubrey Beardsley's illustrations from The Yellow Book ... and in his bookcase several numbers of The Yellow Book, which the Babe declared bitterly had turned grey in a single night since the former artist had ceased to draw for it'. Beardsley himself 'was delighted with the references and their testament to the endurance of his fame'.[9]

Pollitt's photograph (in drag as Loie Fuller) had been exhibited next to a photograph of Beardsley in the summer of 1894, which may have emboldened Pollitt to write to the artist, then at the very height of his notoriety. He became a personal friend, visiting him, commissioning and purchasing work from him (such as the erotic drawings of *Bathylle*); and advancing the frequently cash-strapped artist large sums of money when creditors threatened. *You are the great enchanter who has dispersed Bailiffs with a stroke of your pen,* wrote Beardsley on 26th March 1897, thanking Pollitt for the much-needed sum of twenty sovereigns; (in context: twenty sovereigns was about half a year's wages for an agricultural worker at that time). Perhaps not surprisingly, Beardsley's surviving letters to him show real warmth. He breaks from the conventional greeting of 'My dearest -' to address him playfully as 'My dear pretty Pollitt', 'Dear wonderful person' or even 'My Dear Politiano'. One letter reads: *A thousand thanks for your thrice kind telegram and letter. It would be delightful beyond Archangels' dreams to have you down here. Do come. How charming to see you the livelong day, my sympathique and amusing collector* [11 Dec 1897].

There has been scholarly speculation about the nature of Beardsley's interest in Pollitt. L.J.Kooistra in *Sartorial Obsessions: Beardsley and Masquerade*[10], feels that Pollitt's attractiveness for Beardsley had more dimensions than merely that of financial backer: 'the precise nature of Beardsley's relationship with the man he addressed as "My best good Friend" and for whom he signed himself

"Yours entirely, pen and pencil" (*Letters* 286) may never be known, but it seems likely that the two shared an interest not only in erotica and theatre but also in transvestitism.' Malcolm Easton speculates that Beardsley's apparently tortured sexuality was due to a repressed transgender nature.[11] If that were so, perhaps it found expression by proxy through Pollitt's crossdressing.

The noble art of female and male impersonation was – and remains - by no means unusual in British theatre, performers often becoming immensely popular. It should be emphasised that for the Victorians, this centuries old tradition did not imply transgressive sexual activity: the June 1907 edition of the respectable magazine The Sketch features a montage of bewigged beauties, entitled 'The Wig Maketh The Woman: Cambridge Undergraduates as Girls'. Two of Pollitt's portraits feature among them.

It is in Beardsley's letter of 11th December 1897 that we get a little glimpse of Pollitt with Crowley. He says, *Your Cambridge Bard must indeed be decorated and issued from the Arcade. I will protect him in the finest covers.* It is fair to assume that the 'Cambridge Bard' is the young poet Crowley, while 'the Arcade' is a reference to the premises in Burlington Arcade of the publishing house run by Leonard Smithers (who had quite a by-line in pornography and published *Aceldama* and *White Stains* in limited editions in Amsterdam). The reference to being 'decorated' and 'the finest covers' is surely an expression of willingness on the part of Beardsley to provide illustrations for the book, no doubt as a favour to Pollitt. It is more than likely that the process of getting Crowley's work published was much facilitated by Pollitt's connections among the 'Decadents'. Crowley certainly inscribed a copy of *Aceldama* to Beardsley but there is no evidence that it was presented to him. In any case, Beardsley was far too ill to make a start on any drawings, struggling as he was to complete outstanding commissions at this time and barely able to work more than three hours a day. His health was declining steadily. He died in March 1898, aged 25. He mentioned Pollitt in a letter written to his publisher on his deathbed, requesting that 'all bad drawings' be destroyed. Pollitt, like the publisher, refused to destroy the artist's 'obscene' work and preserved his collection.[12]

Jerome Pollitt's biography deserves to be written – his later life is sadly obscure. We know he continued to collect art and exhibited works by Beardsley and Whistler in his own home in 1910. He served in the Medical Corps in the First World War. His death is recorded in Hemel Hempstead in September 1942.

It would be fascinating to know what he thought of Crowley's increasingly hostile press coverage, apparently mad behaviour and disastrous public image throughout the 1920s and '30s; whether he ever regretted the ending of their relationship; ever read the words written about him in Crowley's autobiography or ever wished he had responded to the 'messages' sent 'now and again' by 'To Mega Therion', The Great Beast 666.

FOOTNOTES

[1] He told a judge in 1934, 'The Beast 666 only means Sunlight. You can call me "Little Sunshine".'
http://www.tomegatherion.co.uk/news.htm#1954

[2] 'I had by this time become fairly expert in clairvoyance, clairaudience and clairsentience.' *Confessions of Aleister Crowley*

[3] *Yet in the Gare de Lyon she [Porphyria Poppoea] bade him write "Did I say `Always'?" thinking that Hippolytus would understand that she still loved him, and - may be - follow her. Did he ever get the letter? Did he interpret it amiss? False friends had crept into their intimacy - and also fear. I do not know how it was; but Porphyria Poppoea never renewed those hours - that love - that infinite passion of Hippolytus. Sir Roger Bloxam learned later that he, musing deeply as was his wont when walking, had passed Hippolytus in Bond Street, and that Hippolytus thought that he had cut him purposely. Also, Porphyria Poppoea, fearful of a repulse, never followed up on her letter from the Gare de Lyon. Seven times the Father of all Light whirled Earth about him through the Zodiac -- and she knew surely that he was her true lover for all time and all eternity. So, weeping, she caused a great monument to be set up, with an inscription in the Persian language* [q.v. The Scented Garden]. *And now and again she sent him messages; but his great heart was broken - even as hers. Many a lover has possessed her since Hippolytus; but she has scorned them even while she abandons herself to their caresses. She loves Hippolytus. Hippolytus!*
https://invisiblehouse.org/ref/roger_bloxan.pdf (sic)
from 'Not the life and Adventures of Roger Bloxam, a Novellism', Ch. 29. The chapter heading is: 'SIR ROGER BLOXAM AT CAMBRIDGE, AMSTERDAM, AND BIRMINGHAM. AN ADVENTURE OF PORPHYRIA POPPOEA.. THIS TIME WE MEAN BUSINESS. (CHAPTER CCCXXXIII)'. N.B. Crowley's chapter numeration is deliberately jumbled up in this work, and here he

has assigned it the same Roman numerals as Liber CCCXXXIII 'The Book of Lies' pub. 1912 or 1913.

[4] In 'The Scented Garden of Abdullah the Satirist of Shiraz' or 'The Bagh-i Muattar', 1910, the 'Reverend P D Carey' [Crowley] also writes about the beloved's blond hair in an exact parallel of his description of Jerome in his *Confessions* and in the quote from *Roger Bloxam*. Perhaps therefore we can assume that Crowley had Pollitt in mind when he wrote the following, imagining a meeting after death: *Shall I find you, sweet acolyte of Salmacis or of Terpsichore ... Will it be you with your fine golden hair like spiders' webs in the sun, changed to an aureole, and your seductive face still as ever the incarnation of one single never-ending scarlet kiss? ...Oh come to me there, darling! Lean upon the golden rampart, and watch for me to come! Be first to meet me, Sweetheart! Forgive me for all the wrong I did you here. I will try and be a good wife to you, darling, if you will give me one more chance to hold your love. I had heaven in your kisses, and I went to seek it in the cloister....I loved you always; it was but a boy's folly; forgive me! I may never cling to you on earth again: pray God that Heaven may be one long, long life of such bliss as we had of one another long ago...* https://www.100thmonkeypress.com/biblio/acrowley/books/scented_garden_1910/scented_garden_text.pdf

[5] The envelope of a letter from the artist James McNeill Whistler, now in the Smithsonian, shows his address to have been 'H.C.Pollitt, Thorny Hills, Kendal'. https://www.si.edu/sisearch/collection-images?edan_q=whistler%2Bletter

[6] His stage name was an homage to the notorious bisexual demi-mondaine courtesan and cabaret artiste, Liane de Pougy (1869-1950). 'Liane', whose birth name was Anne Marie Chassaigne, died Sister Anne-Marie, having turned to religion in later life, after a scorchingly daring career.

7 There is an album of Pollitt's theatrical photographs currently in the archives at Harvard's Houghton Library, so far unpublished. https://strangeflowers.wordpress.com/2013/10/11/dress-down-friday-diane-de-rougy/ (but his various glamorous appearances in The Sketch can be viewed online via the British Library and Genes Reunited).

[8] Information kindly provided by Mr Keith Cavers of the E.F.Benson Society

[9] *Aubrey Beardsley, A Biography* by Matthew Sturgis (Harper Collins).

[10] *Essays in Haunted Texts: Studies in Pre-Raphaelitism in Honour of*

William E. Fredeman ed. David Latham (Univ. of Toronto Press).

[11] *Aubrey and the Dying Lady: a Beardsley Riddle* by Malcolm Easton (Secker and Warburg, 1972).

[12] I have of course used poetic licence in imagining that Pollitt would visit Beardsley in Menton – there is no evidence to suggest that he did; just as it isn't clear whether he turned up in Dieppe in August 1897 (although Beardsley's letters certainly imply that he was expecting him). His letters do however sometimes give us little insights into Pollitt's activities: 'I have just found your letter in an unexpected pocket, it reminds me that you were hopping between the ancestral mansion and the goods station on the lookout for your belongings. I hope all your treasures are housed now.' (3rd November 1897).

BIBLIOGRAPHY

There are many works written about **Aleister Crowley**, often of mixed usefulness. As Lon Milo DuQuette says, 'Crowley's adventures and achievements – more than any dozen men of ambition and genius could realistically hope to garner in a lifetime – seem almost to be distractions when weighed against his monumental exploits of self-discovery. His visionary writings and his efforts to synthesize and integrate the esoteric spiritual systems of East and West make him one of the most fascinating cultural and religious figures of the twentieth century'.

He's also one of the most vilified, inspiring a firestorm of prurient outrage in his lifetime: and to this day. Innumerable conspiracy theories attach to his legend (the best one I read recently was that David Bowie, born in the year Crowley died, was his Moonchild – to which I can only quote Crowley himself: 'I get fairly frantic when I contemplate the idiocy of these louts'). It must be added that many of these wild stories stem from his own impish humour combined with deliberate obfuscation of his work. He set up fearsome gargoyles to discourage idle curiosity. I would strongly recommend therefore that a reader begin with a neutral attitude and read Crowley's own words first.

For his magickal theories, *Magick Without Tears* is very enjoyable. Follow this with *Confessions*. After that, you'll be forearmed with a taste of his own acerbic wit, towering arrogance and razor-like intellect should you choose to tackle one of the many biographies.

I wouldn't recommend launching into his esoteric writings without a thorough grounding in more general works. Highly recommended: Lon Milo DuQuette's *Understanding Aleister Crowley's Thoth Tarot* (Weiser Books) and also, for a humorous overview of Qabalistic teachings, *The Chicken Qabalah of Rabbi Lamed Ben Clifford* (Red Wheel/Weiser).

Online resources such as the podcasts at livingthelema.com by Dr David Shoemaker give an excellent insight into contemporary Crowley-based spiritual practices. There are also some great blogs out there. Thanks to all of these and sorry if I've missed yours:

http://ghostblooms-van-asten.blogspot.co.uk/2011/11/how-sweet-passion.html

https://www.lashtal.com/

http://www.tomegatherion.co.uk/home.htm

Crowley's works online:

https://archive.org/details/CollectedPdfsByAleisterCrowley

https://hermeticlibrary.com.

For **Aubrey Beardsley,** Matthew Sturgis's biography is well-written and sensibly steers clear of scandal: *Aubrey Beardsley: A Biography.* Beardsley's *Collected Letters* are of course the source for his attitudes to 'dear pretty Pollitt'.

For **Inanna,** I have imagined that Minerva Atwell came across an even earlier version of this http://etcsl.orinst.ox.ac.uk/section1/tr141.htm. In the mid-1870s, cuneiform writing had not long been understood. I therefore deliberately avoided reading too much other than late nineteenth century interpretations in order to get closer to what Minerva might have understood from such a text. I drew instead on my general reading, not to mention the many lunchbreaks spent in the galleries, when long ago I worked at the British Museum, marvelling at the Burney Relief, the Silver Lyre of Ur and the Ram in the Thicket.

None of them were there when Alexandra and Minerva visited this magical place, but I think if George ever wanders through these days, he'll recognise them for sure.

ABOUT THE AUTHOR

Charlie Raven lives in England. In the Seventies, she was inspired by Tolkien, T.E.Lawrence and Bowie. In the Eighties, she got involved in LGBTQ rights. By the Nineties, she was raising an unconventional family. In the Noughties, she went through a painful learning curve. In the Twenty-Tens, she very gratefully and humbly returned to sanity. As an INFJ type, it takes her a long time to think up a witty riposte to insults. She has three children who often say she is 'weird in a good way'; and she goes away and thinks about this.

I'm so glad you got all the way to the back end of this book. If you've enjoyed this story, please consider giving it an online review.